D1124737

# THE
# FRANCHISER

*Books by Stanley Elkin*

# THE
# FRANCHISER

## STANLEY ELKIN

*Foreword by William Gass*

NONPAREIL BOOKS · BOSTON

This is a NONPAREIL BOOK published in 1980 by

David R. Godine, Publisher, Inc.
306 Dartmouth Street
Boston, Massachusetts 02116

First published in 1976 by Farrar, Straus & Giroux, Inc., New York.

*Library of Congress Cataloging in Publication Data*

Elkin, Stanley, 1930-
  The franchiser.

  Reprint of the ed. published by Farrar, Straus,
Giroux, New York.
  I. Title.
[PZ4.E44Fr 1980]    [PS3555.L47]    813'.54
ISBN 0-87923-323-0                    79-92109

Sections of this book appeared, in slightly different form, in *Fiction* and *Iowa Review*.

MANUFACTURED IN THE UNITED STATES OF AMERICA

FOR JOAN

*Photograph by George Bacso*

# FOREWORD

## *by William Gass*

You do not write a foreword to the novel of a friend, and the man, among men, you admire and love most, with an easy conscience or a restful mind. To place any words ahead of a work like this is the act of an upstart, an interloper, an interventionist; so I shall say briefly what moves me most when Stanley Elkin's prose becomes my consciousness, and simply hope that others will be drawn to it, and find, if not my pleasures, others equally important and enduring.

Stanley Elkin puts his imagination to work by placing it like a seed within the soil of some vocation. *Vocation:* that is no trade-school word for him. What is your name? where are you from? what do you do? Among those who survey the habits of Americans, there are many who find these questions, which are likely to be among the first answering holes we fill in on forms, and the first we put to strangers, indicative of our indifference to the essential self. Should men and women, after all, be defined in any important way by their work? The answer, of course, is yes, otherwise the activities that largely support our lives and consume our time would be unfriendly, foreign, and irrelevant to us. Our occupation should not be something we visit like the seashore in summer or a prisoner in a prison, despite the fact that the work may be unpleasant and dangerous and hard, like that in a mill or a foundry or a mine. Even if it is like speaking a foreign language we haven't learned, that incapacity itself is totally defining.

In *Boswell*, Elkin's first novel, the occupation was that of a celebrity seeker, but it may be a merchant's, as it is in *A Bad Man*, or a bailbondsman's, as it is in the brilliant story of that name. Again, a gloomy grocer may be his concern, or a debt collector, the disc jockey of *The Dick Gibson Show,* or a franchiser like Ben Flesh—jobs that are often seedy or suspect in some way. Elkin does not wonder what it would be like if he were a professional bully, or an elderly ragman, though new to the nation, a peddler trundling a cart down the street and crying "Regs, all cloze." He does not say, What if I were running my own radio show?—and then write. His fictions are not daydreams; there is no idleness in them, no reveries. They are not acts of ordinary empathy, either, in which the novelist listens in on some way of life and then plays what he hears on his Linotype. Instead, Elkin allows the activity itself to create his central characters, to find its being in some gainly or ungainly body, and then he encourages that body to verbalize a voice.

*Voice:* for Elkin, that's no choir boys' word. Just as in Beckett, the *logos* is life. There is not a line in *The Franchiser* that doesn't issue from one. And what is this occupation it speaks for, but acts and their names, agents and their frailties, the textures of their environments? . . . things, words, sensations, signs—all one. And the mouth must work while reading him, must taste the intricate interlace of sound; wallow, as I now am, in the wine of the word. With the whole book to follow, one is still compelled to quote:

> He loved the shop, the smells of the naphthas and benzenes, the ammonias, all the alkalis and fats, all the solvents and gritty lavas, the silken detergents and ultimate soaps, like the smells, he decided, of flesh itself, of release, the disparate chemistries of pore and sweat—a sweat shop—the strange woolly-smelling acids that collected in armpits and atmosphered pubic hair, the flameless combustion of urine and gabardine mixing together to create all the body's petty suggestive alimentary toxins. The sexuality of it. The men's garments one kind, the women's another, confused, deflected, masked by residual powders, by the oily invisible resins of deodorant and perfume, by the concocted flower and the imagined fruit—by all fabricated flavor. And hanging in the air, too—where would they go?—dirt, the thin, exiguous human clays, divots, ash and soils, dust devils of being.
> "Irving, add water, we'll make a man."

And this is precisely how Elkin makes a man—out of the elements he lives in, the body he is confined to, the world he works in, the language he knows.

From time to time the voice halts, fills its trunk, and sprays us with speech. How long has it been, how far back must we go, to encounter such speeches, such rich wild oratory? If I were to hazard a guess, I would say we should find it again in *The Alchemist*, in *Volpone*, in *Every Man in His Humour*, and if that seems an extreme claim, simply compare Jonson's characteristic rodomontade (as wonderful as the word that is supposed to condemn it) with the piece you will shortly encounter, the speech that begins: "How crowded is the universe. . . . How stuffed to bursting with its cargo of crap." And goes on: "A button you could be, a pocket in pants, a figure on print." And on: "I am talking of the long shot of existence, the odds no gambler in the world would take, that you would ever come to life as a person, a boy called Ben Flesh." And on: "You weren't aborted, you didn't end up in a scum bag. You survived the infant mortality stuff. You made it past measles, polio, mumps. You outwitted whooping cough, typhoid, VD. God bless you, boy, you're a testament to the impossible!" And on, page after page: "Ben, everything there *is* is against your being here! Think of get-togethers, family stuff, golden anniversaries in rented halls, fire regulations celebrated more in the breach than the observance, the baked Alaska up in flames, everybody wiped out—all the cousins in from the coast. Wiped out." Until it ends:

> "So! Still! Against all the odds in the universe you made happy landings! What do you think? Ain't that delightful? Wait, there's more. You have not only your existence but your edge, your advantage and privilege. You do, Ben, you do. *No?* Everybody does. They give congressmen the frank. Golden-agers go cheap to the movies. You work on the railroads they give you a pass. You clerk in a store it's the 20 percent discount. You're a dentist your kid's home free with the orthodontics. Benny, Benny, we got so much edge we could cut diamonds!"

Central to the theme and movement of the book, this harangue is one of fiction's finest moments.

*The Franchiser* is engaged, then, in the naming of names, the names of places and people, of course, but above all the names of things: commercial enterprises of all kinds, name brands, house brands, brandless brands, labels, logos, zits. Elkin composes a song from the clutter of the country, a chant out of that "cargo of crap" that comprises our culture, the signs, poles, boxes, wires, the stores along the roads and highways, our motorcars. He writes with the stock in trade and with the salesman's slang. About the tissues, rags, and wipers that are appropriate to every fixture and furnishing—bowl, screen, or clockface, asshole or cheery cheek—he knows, and taps out the call sign, grasping the peculiar argot of every agency, the specific slant of every occupation, the angle, the outlook—the edge.

There is, in Elkin, only the "rich topsoil of city asphalt"; there are no lisping winds or drooling streams. He dances to a wholly urban oo-la-la. He cannot see the forest for the picnic tables, the cookout pits, the trash containers with their loose heaps of bottles, Dixie cups, and paper plates; and on those plates he spots the catsup smears, the mustard marks, the crumbs from cookies and potato chips, and he understands at once whether they were reconstituted, ruffled, extra-hearty, or Mexicanized. Nature is a Kodacolor picture wall in one of Ben Flesh's Travel Inns. It is where you go to get wool for fine suits, wood for boardwalks, food for fast foods, electric warmth for blankets, power for power tools. There is one moment —you will reach it—when Ben Flesh finds himself in Nature (ominously in, as though she really were the Mother of us All).

> In nature. His scent in the thin air like a signal to the bears, to the cougars. Out of his element, the franchiser disenfranchised. Miles from the culture, from the trademark and trade routes of his own long Marco Polo life.

Elkin is not concerned with High Culture, either. He knows it not. The city, itself, is his Smithsonian, and there is real lust in his love for it, not merely the usual honor and respect. He has been happily captured by this vast dump of dreck the city has become, and the country has become as it has become a city. He adores this spill of drink and splat of spittle, this rind of flesh, dry ash, and peel of paint, this loud honk the city is, and all its elements; even if it is a steel shaving, this mother of muggers and vulva of vulgarity, this hospice for rape and every kind of wretchedness—the city; although it is only a loud shout, a long hurt, and place of enlarging hate—he loves it, its objects, its stone scapes, lit ways, and glowing windows, this shag of hair and shard of glass the city is; the bag, can, weed, and bitter litter it makes; the cold smoke, the poisoned air it holds; this dog leaving that the city is: Elkin has an embracing passion for it. He celebrates it as no one has done or has been able to do (if we except only Augie March), and although he knows motels, as habitable space, are like the shaven cunt of a packaged whore, still he hums his hymns; although he knows how many streets are ugly, foul-smelling, and dangerous, as full of *E. coli* as a lower intestine, he warbles away; even though he knows money is society's perfumed, silver-plattered shit, he goes on loving the prime rate; he knows fame is a faded billboard now for rent, and yet he goes on touching the famous as if they were kings who could cure; he knows, and yet he goes on loving the menace and the waste, the tacky, cheap, lovelorn, gimcracky life our modern lot has all too often come to; he loves it exactly as the saint loves the leper—*despite* and *because* —not in blindness or through any failure of taste, but because it is all so deeply and dearly human to him; because, as Rilke put it, it is good just to be here—*Siehe, ich lebe!*—since existence itself is outrageously chancy and strange and stable and ordinary (it is like that flameless combustion of gabardine and pee); and all of it—our whole cornpone commercial culture—becomes so transformed by Elkin's attention, his love and his writing, so changed, altered beyond any emblem, that even an enemy of crud such as I esteem myself to be —grim, bitter, and unforgiving—is won over, and I walk through the dime store in a daze of delight.

Here then we have no namby-pamby style. The roll call rolls on: wristwatches and lamps, you name it and Elkin will name it; the rhetoric rises like a threatening wind, and the effect is like that of a storm on those who like them: exhilarating, and a little scary.

It was a hotel, dark except for the light from an open elevator and a floor lamp by one couch. The Oriental carpets, the furniture, the registration desk and shut shops—all seemed a mysterious, almost extinguished red in the enormous empty lobby. Even the elevator— one of four; he supposed the others weren't functioning—seemed set on low. He looked around for Mopiani but the man had remained at his post. He pressed the button and sensed himself sucked up through darkness, imagining, though it was day, the darkened mezzanine and black ballrooms, the dark lamps and dark flowers in their dark vases on the dark halved tables pressed against the dark walls of each dark floor, the dark silky stripes on the benches outside the elevators, the dark cigarette butts in the dark sand.

There is no fear of excess here, either, because Elkin oversubscribes to everything. Centers will not hold him in spite of his academic training, his professorial position. He goes to extremes simply to have his picture taken standing at an edge. His language carries him away (there is a pile-up of images at every corner, like a crash of cars); his characters get carried away; his words first explore, then explode the world.

He is not content with nice precise observations, in which, for instance, a policeman's long holster looks like a weapon, "its pistol some bent brute at a waterhole, the trigger like a visible genital" (wonderful and radical enough), but the uniform itself becomes a weapon, and then parts of this new mechanism are beautifully described: "the metal blades of Mopiani's badge, the big key ring with its brass claws, a tunnel of handcuffs doubled on his backside, the weighted, tapered cosh, the sergelike grainy blue hide, the stout black brogans, and the patent-leather bill of his cap like wet ink."

He is not satisfied with the simply sensuous (Ben Flesh standing in his tux, "his formal pants and jacket glowing like a black comb, his patent-leather shoes vaulted smooth and tensionless as perfect architecture," as though he "might be standing in the skin of a ripe bright black apple"). It does not matter that apples are every other color, or that eggplants come close to patent black in their most bruised moods; just try *eggplant* instead of *apple* and feel the effect of the change.

Not satisfied, never content, Elkin presses beyond his mountains of apparently realistic detail, with their dangerous slides of wit; he passes safely through the misleading forests of simple fun, the satiric gibes, the sirenlike lists; he pushes on into the nuclei of his various vocations (the dance studio, for instance, one of Ben Flesh's failing franchises), pushes, presses, until they are more than metaphors, more than merely the nice idea that "work for rent" has been set up on signs. He searches inside of whatever one of them possesses his

imagination at the moment to find the form—the spreading itch—
of the image itself: its finality, its limits, its outer edge; for then that
occupation, because it is the wholehearted consequence of a thought
that has put on a pair of pants and found a passion that they conceal
like an excited penis; this work, with all its learning and its lingo,
dreams itself back over the whole world of the fiction like a cloud,
settles over us all like a communal hallucination; whereupon we
realize that Elkin is a visionary writer; he is Brueghel or he is Bosch;
he pictures people at picnics, at weddings; Icarus falls suddenly
through the white sky; in the middle of a figure eight a skater dies,
a sodden sleeper floats out of the nervous corners of our eyes; and
the exuberance with which Ben Flesh has traveled the cloverleafs,
generously giving hitching thumbs a ride; his and our relish for
existence, for the least as well as the large, for the sweet names of
things, turns to dumb drunkenness, to petty meanness, to slobby
gluttony; vice emerges like a green haze from virtue's smiling mouth;
the dance of life becomes the dance of death, but—-more than that
—the dance of death is no better off: the bones play like tickled
ivories some sugary welcome to the spring or some soft September
song.

The dance develops, step by step, as Ben Flesh decides to honor
his losses with a gala, and trays of slivered turkey and skin-thin beef
are bought with a Diner's Club card and taken to the studio. People
are lured in off the street by bribes, and the Wurlitzer is applauded
to get in practice for the time when there will be a real band. "Night
and Day" is played, and "Happy Days Are Here Again." A bottle
of catsup falls from a shopping bag and spills its blood on the floor,
where it soon shows Flesh the paths of the dancers, its "beautiful
red evidence" making the music visible. It isn't long before this mess
is mixed with bits of pork and rice, assorted hors d'oeuvres, soft
crusts, and chunks of chicken that explode "like delicious gut under
the dancer's weight." It is a nightmare made out of reality by adding
more: do people tend to put out butts on the ballroom floor? then let
fall a thousand cigs like flaming stars; do guests incline to crumb
their canapes, spill their drinks? let litter float down upon the party
like the ash that preserved Pompeii; do old folks like to love the old
songs? then let them be set upon by "On the Road to Mandalay."

Elkin plays the real world *loud;* and by turning up the volume he has already rendered the hellish glow many a heaven casts before he gets around, in *The Living End*, to depicting our conventional ones— depictions, however, that rival, recall, revive Brueghel, Bosch.

The machine plays "The Night Was Made for Love." It plays "I'm Sitting on Top of the World." The dancers continue to turn through their own slop, and Flesh makes a great and crazy speech presumably about convenience (complete convenience, not just that of convenience foods), the total ease of chemical creams, the relief afforded by flowered sheets and pretty pillow cases, the comfort control he calls the real measure of mankind. It is an astonishing replay of the earlier "oration" I mentioned, and there will be others, later, even more amazing. "Nobody, nobody, nobody even had it so good. Take heed. A franchiser tells you." Liquor continues to leak from the plastic cups. "Smile, you fuckers, laugh, you shitlings. I come from Fred Astaire, *everybody dance!*"

Flesh, in effect, foams at the mouth; he represents America at its best; he is the word become Ben; he utters pure pop; he speaks Lite beer; his verbs are coated with a secret recipe, Vic Tanny keeps his prepositions slim, though his nouns are all frozen custards and spun milk; yet what his long rant is really about is the movement, the form, the true table-turning of this incredible novel.

*Vision,* I said. For Elkin, it is no visionary's word, no politician's promise, preacher's ploy. It is the unerring instinct of the verbal eye.

Ben's name knows the worst: the flesh fails, and Ben is stricken with a scribbler's sickness; he is MS'd up, to put it as poorly as possible; nevertheless (our author notes), though as illnesses go, M.S. is truly big-league—while one is sitting down (as authors do) it is an invisible disease. In-visible. Our language, in Elkin's hands, opens like a paper flower. The symptoms of this sickness are drawn inside out with an unfailing artistry of line. Once again, they circumscribe a vision. It involves the unity of hell and heaven—this vision—even a nervous interplay; it is a vision of value, to complete the *v*s, of how life is nurtured by decay; it is a victory for the material, for the carnal spirit, because even as Ben weakens, as both his flesh and his Fotomat fold, and the hyper-real world of the novel completes its business and makes its final sale, its hero is having an ecstasy attack; and because love is finally Ben Flesh's forte, he retains his edge to the end.

To turn to account . . . to disable disabilities by finding their use . . . to celebrate circumstance . . . to turn on a light in the heart of darkness . . . well, all flesh is grass, as the prophet said, but the word of the Elkin shall franchise it forever.

The author wishes to thank Washington University for its generous support, and to thank, too, Leanna Boysko, for her invaluable assistance in the preparation of the manuscript.

# THE
# FRANCHISER

# I

Past the orange roof and turquoise tower, past the immense sunburst of the green and yellow sign, past the golden arches, beyond the low buff building, beside the discrete hut, the dark top hat on the studio window shade, beneath the red and white longitudes of the enormous bucket, coming up to the thick shaft of the yellow arrow piercing the royal-blue field, he feels he is home. Is it Nashville? Elmira, New York? St. Louis County? A Florida key? The Illinois arrowhead? Indiana like a holster, Ohio like a badge? Is he North? St. Paul, Minn.? Northeast? Boston, Mass.? The other side of America? Salt Lake? Los Angeles? At the bottom of the country? The Texas udder? Where? In Colorado's frame? Wyoming like a postage stamp? Michigan like a mitten? The chipped, eroding bays of the Northwest? Seattle? Bellingham, Washington?

Somewhere in the packed masonry of states.

He guides the pale-blue Cadillac up the perfectly banked ramp, around one loop of the creamy cloverleaf, positioned, in the large, long automobile, centripetally as a slot car—lovely. And down, shooting the smooth rapids of traffic, into the wide cement of American delta. Like a water skier brought, still on his feet, to shore. He waits at the lights, in some darker medium now, a rich topsoil of city asphalt, waving to the man next to him, miming petition, throwing thanks like a blown kiss, and on green edges forward, to his left. Coming into the service station. (There is cash in his pocket. Credit cards. A checkbook. Licenses. His name and address a block braille on a dozen plastic cards.) And stops. Out of the way of the pumps. And seeing the attendant, his politeness on him like a mood, good behavior premeditated as a sentence in a foreign language, as a question from the floor, gets out of the car, goes to him, the attendant, a young man who barely glances at him. Waits. Walks with the fellow as he goes behind the Chevy Impala at the Regular pump to copy down the number of the plate onto the clamped carbons, accompanying him to the driver, smiling at the silent transaction of proffered charge slip and returned signature, waves to the lady in the Impala as she moves off, turns cheerfully to the attendant, and addresses him in chipper, palsy-walsy American.

"Say, buddy, can I bother you a minute?"

"Sir?"

"I was wondering. Can you tell me—can you tell me just where the hell I am?"

And knows that whatever Jack—he reads the name stitched in red on his coveralls—tells him, it will be welcome news, for he already likes this town, likes the feel of it. He has seen from the highway the low modern buildings of new industrial parks, their parking lots comfortably settled with late-model cars, a bright convoy of good machinery in the wide sealanes of parallel parking.

"Why, this is Boyle Avenue," Jack says.

"Boyle Avenue," he repeats, smiling. Yes, he likes the sound of it. "But what city, please?"

"What *city?* Why, Birmingham."

"Michigan? Alabama?"

"Birmingham, Alabama."

"Ahh."

Jack moves away, going toward a Pontiac Grand Prix which has just pulled up to one of the pumps. "Birmingham, Alabama," he calls after him. "That's wonderful. I thank you, sir. I thank you kindly."

He turns back to the Cadillac, suddenly remembers something, and pauses. "Golly, what's the matter with me? If my head weren't on my neck I wouldn't know where to put my hat. Here, son. Here, Jack." He tries to give Jack ten dollars. "For your trouble. And thanks again. You're a life saver."

"Hey," Jack says, "you don't have to—"

"No no. You're entirely welcome. My pleasure." He gets into his car. Birmingham, Alabama. I'll be. It's a beautiful day in the United States of America.

# II

I took Nate's hand.

"Hey," Lace said.

"Hay is for horses."

"Come on, let go. Let *go.*"

"Spare me your colorful crap, Nate. Save it for the hicks. I'm glad to see you, so I shake your hand. I know all about your handshake."

"Nothing's settled."

"Right. You can have it back when I'm finished. I'm finished. How are you?"

"Nothing's settled. My handshake's my contract. I ain't no greeter."

"No? This isn't Las Vegas?"

He had gotten to Harrisburg in the afternoon. He spotted Mopiani from the Caddy as he drove up, the man pneumatic in the cop's criss-crossed leather that bound Mopiani's tunic, the thick straps and ammunition loops potted with bullets, the long holster like a weapon, its pistol some bent brute at a waterhole, the trigger like a visible genital, the uniform itself a weapon, the metal blades of Mopiani's badge, the big key ring with its brass claws, a tunnel of handcuffs doubled on his backside, the weighted, tapered cosh, the sergelike grainy blue hide, the stout black brogans, and the patent-leather bill of his cap like wet ink. He leaned against the blond boards that covered the entrance to the building and smoked a cigarette. In his other hand he held a walkie-talkie.

Flesh lowered the electric window.

"Mopiani."

"Who's that?"

"How you doing? How's private property?"

"Who's that?"

"It's Ben Flesh. I've come to give myself up. Where's Nate?"

"I don't know you."

"You don't know shit. What's the walkie-talkie for, Mopiani? The Big Bands?"

"Get away. The building's closed. Don't look for trouble. Move along. Go on. Break it up."

"What am I, a crowd?"

"Just move along. The building's shut."

"You're impregnable, Mopiani. Look at me."

"The building's shut down, I said."

"That a real walkie-talkie?"

"What's it look like?"

"Give it here a minute." He reached out. "Come on, I'll give it right back." Mopiani let it go. Flesh pressed a button on the side of the machine. "Nate? You on the other end of this thing? Nate? It's Ben Flesh." He released the button.

Nate Lace's voice came back immediately. "Ben."

"Tell the police force I'm all right."

He gave the instrument back to Mopiani. The man turned his back to him and leaned his ear into the machine, though Flesh could hear everything Nate said. Mopiani nodded.

"Mr. Lace says it's all right. I'm sorry I hassled you. I didn't recognize you." Ben followed him to a sort of doorway in the wide wall of boards. He waited while Mopiani unlocked the padlock. He took the key not from the ring but from his pocket. Flesh had to bend to go through.

"Where am I going?"

"1572. It's the Presidential suite."

It was a hotel, dark except for the light from an open elevator and a floor lamp by one couch. The Oriental carpets, the furniture, the registration desk and shut shops—all seemed a mysterious, almost extinguished red in the enormous empty lobby. Even the elevator—one of four; he supposed the others weren't functioning—seemed set on low. He looked around for Mopiani but the man had remained at his post. He pressed the button and sensed himself sucked up through darkness, imagining, though it was day, the darkened mezzanine and black ballrooms, the dark lamps and dark flowers in their dark vases on the dark halved tables pressed against the dark walls of each dark floor, the dark silky stripes on the benches outside the elevators, the dark cigarette butts in the dark sand.

He'd stayed here on business once. The Nittney-Lyon. He'd met Lace in strange places before, but this was the strangest. Imagine their names thrown fifteen floors by Mopiani's walkie-talkie. "Nate?" "Ben." Quicker than prayer.

Nate's floor was lighter than the lobby. He glanced at the ceiling of the long corridor. Here two bulbs burned in their fixtures; there, three were out. There was no pattern. Probably Nate had unscrewed them.

The door to the suite was open, Nate at a desk watching him, his walkie-talkie next to the phone. He grabbed Nate's hand. "Hail to the Chief," Flesh said.

"Hey come on, let go. What the hell's the matter with you?"

"I'm glad to see you, so I shake your hand."

"Nothing's settled."

"Yeah. Right. You can have it back when I'm finished. So how are you?"

"I ain't no greeter."

"No? Ain't this Las Vegas? Didn't you used to be Joe Louis?"

"What are you doing here? We didn't have no appointment."

"This place is spooky. Come have a drink with me."

"I've eaten. You still driving? I see the Cadillac out front. What is it, you afraid to fly? Do you think you'll fall on the ground? More people are killed on highways each year than in the airplanes. You should know that. What are you doing here anyway? We don't have no appointment. Why don't you fly? It's more convenient."

"I'm loyal to the highway."

"It's crazy. Loyal to the highway. It's crazy. How'd you know I was here?"

"I read about the distress sale."

"You see? If you flew you'd have been here first maybe. Now maybe whatever you wanted I already sold it."

"I knew Bensinger's troubles weeks ago. I called him about the the TV's, but he thought the Sheraton chain would bail him out."

"Me. *I* bailed him out."

"You're Geronimo, Nate."

"What's that supposed to mean? How do you like my new store? Hey? This is really some store I got. TV's?"

"How much?"

"Sealed bids."

"What sealed bids? I need a few color TV's. I'm opening a Travel Inn."

"I'm sorry. It's the only way I do business. Sealed bids."

"What is it with you, you like to get mail? I'll pay you cash and send it in a letter."

"I can't do it, Ben. Listen, I'll go this far for you. You need TV's. I'll give you a price on some black and whites."

"Black and whites? From the Nittney-Lyon? Eight years ago I stayed in this hotel. They were old *then*. The *white* was fading. Even if they were still in their boxes with the silicon pouches I couldn't use them. I already told you, I need color. It's in my contract."

"How big's your Travel?"

"A hundred fifty."

"I ain't got 150 color."

"The Nittney-Lyon has 360 rooms."

"Right. Three hundred color's what I got. All in good condition."

"Bullshit on your good condition. I figure it'll cost me a hundred a set over the purchase price to get them in shape."

"Never. Why do you say a thing like that?"

"It's cable TV. The guests flip the channels like they're winding their watches."

"They're in good condition."

"What time is it?"

"Three. I don't know. Around three. Why?"

"We'll watch Merv Griffin. If his suntan works for me I'll give you a hundred twenty-five a set."

"I have to be truthful, it's not a bad price. But you'd have to take two hundred."

"Businessman! All right. I need a hundred and a half. I'll take two hundred. I'll use the extra for spare parts."

Nate smiled. "You're a tonic, Ben," he said. "I figure seven weeks I got to be in Harrisburg. With no one to talk to but Mopiani. You know what that Cossack does when he's not on duty? Army-Navy stores. He window shops Army-Navy stores, checks out all the Army-Navy stores to see if there's something new he can strap to his belt." He sighed. "I don't know. I bought a great hotel. A beautiful store. I think I'm in over my head this time. A million one it cost me. Two weeks going day and night to do an inventory. What am I going to do with this stuff?"

"You know."

"I don't. I really don't. I don't know."

"Come on, Nate, you know what to do with the little soaps, the paper shoeshine cloths, the switchboard, the telephones, the dance floor and bandstand. A million one. You're here two months you'll clear five hundred thousand. Four Otis elevators you got like Apollo space capsules. When you've picked the bones dry, you pay your taxes and sit on the thing till the city condemns. They pay to knock the hotel down and you parcel the property into small lots and sell it off for more than you put up in the first place."

"Hangers. You need hangers?"

"Richmond sells me hangers."

"And not television? Richmond don't make you take their televisions?"

"I'm not a sharecropper, Nathan. It ain't a company store."

"The shipping is your responsibility."

"I haven't bought anything yet. I haven't seen the color."

"Turn it on, turn it on."

"What? Here? In the Presidential suite, sky-high, where the reception's like a page from *National Geographic*, the test pattern like an engraving? No. We'll go to—309. We'll watch with interference. I want to see the ghosts, the squiggle Mopiani's walkie-talkie makes on the screen—the Number 12 bus going by, rush hour, all the city's tricky electric shit. I want you to take your worst shot. Then, *then* the shipping's my responsibility."

We went to 309. Nate had to get Mopiani to hunt up a key, to scrounge around in the hotel's cellar for an hour looking for a way to turn the juice on in that part of the building. He had to fetch five more sets from rooms I selected at random and fix plugs he'd taken from lamps to the wires he'd cut behind the TV sets that ran through the walls to the master antenna. The whole thing must have taken four hours. Then we shoved plugs into every socket, stuffing them full, caulking, tuck-pointing the electric slots tight. Putting on different channels, spinning a roulette of network and U.H.F. Channel 6's closed circuit, the camera panning from a barometer to a dial that showed the speed and direction of the wind, to a clock that told time, to another that gave the temperature, to ads on signs. I guess the Nittney-Lyon was still paid up for the service. It was in black and white but almost the only thing I watched with any interest. On other sets grave Cronkite spilled the beans, Chancellor's glasses reflected light, Howard K. Smith and Harry Reasoner sat connected at the shoulder like Siamese twins. After a while Nate left and took his palace guard with him, and I watched the wind speed and direction, the barometer and temperature, keeping my eye peeled for the slightest change.

Nate returned in an hour. "Satisfied?"

I nodded. He put out his hand and I took it. "At last," I said, "the Nate Lace Special."

"Listen, I never once went back on a handshake."

"I know that, Nate."

"That's why I jerked my hand back from you before. It wasn't nothing personal."

"I know that."

"I got a handshake it stands up in court."

"Yes."

"Your feelings shouldn't be hurt."

"My feelings feel fine."

"Just so you know."

"You're colorful, Nate."

"Well—"

"No. You are. You're colorful. You got more color than all the TV's. Me too."

"I never thought of you as colorful."

"No, I didn't used to be. Now I'm colorful too. Partner. Idiosyncratic, Technicolor partner."

"What the hell's that supposed to mean?"

"Our vaudeville styles, pal. Our personalities like hard acts to follow."

He was looking at me. "The twenty-five thousand. We'll arrange an arrangement."

"Right. I have to organize the sets and figure a way to get them fixed and work it out for a truck to take them to my Travel Inn. Is it all right if I stay here tonight?"

"Yeah, sure. The place is empty. With you I figure I've already doubled the occupancy rate."

"Hey, Nate?"

"What?"

"Do me a favor. I'll give Mopiani the keys. Get on the walkie-talkie and ask him to put my Cadillac in the garage."

"You and your cars. If you flew you wouldn't have to worry about parking."

# 2

*Forbes* would not have heard of him, *Fortune* wouldn't. There would be no color photographs of him, sharp as holograph, in high-backed executive leathers, his hand a fist on wide mahogany plateaus of desk, his collar white as an admiral's against his dark, timeless suits. There would be no tall columns of beautifully justified print apposite full-page ads for spanking new business machines with their queer space-age vintages, their coded analogues to the minting of postage, say, or money—the TermiNet 1200, the Reliant 700, Canon's L1610, the NCR 399—numbers like license plates on federal limousines or the markings on aircraft.

Though he actually used some of this stuff. G.E. had an answer for his costly data volume traffic; Kodak had found a practical alternative to his paper filing. He had discussed his microform housing needs with Ring King Visibles. He had come into the clean, bright world of Kalvar. A special card turned even a telephone booth into a WATS line. Still, *Fortune* would do no profile. *Signature*, the Diners Club magazine, had never shown an interest; T.W.A.'s *Ambassador* hadn't. There was no color portrait of him next even to the mail-order double knits and shoes.

Yet, he couldn't deny it, he'd have enjoyed reading about himself. It would shake them up—all those gray sideburned gents of razor resolution. He could not divorce his memory of their sharply resolved photographs and fine tuned f-stop pusses in the magazines from their fuzzier, more edgeless presences in real life. (He had met some of them in real life, but it was always their pictures in *Fortune* he carried in his head.) And their biographies—all the high echelon raided, that cadre of the corporate kidnapped swooped down upon like God-marked Greeks; feisty, prodigy tigers, up-shirt-sleeved and magnate tough; and the others: the white-haired wooed, and your pluggers, too, your up-from-the-ground-floor loyalists, and Chairmen of the Board Emeriti who still carried menial memories in their skulls. And the familied inheritors. (Though these you seldom saw: class, *class*.) Or, even rarer, the holders of the original patents who chaired their own board. What would such men make of him?

What would they make of his having entered the Wharton School of Business on the G.I. Bill in 1946 under the impression that he would learn to type, take shorthand, master the procedures of bookkeeping, of proper business letters—he'd set his sights on an office job, the idea of 9-to-5 as romantic to him and even mystical (the notion of yoga rhythm and routine) as it was antithetical to those who wanted more, who, having learned to kill, could never return to an only ordinary life—to discover instead that economics was a science, money an art form? Or of the remarkable telegram he'd received in his junior year at Wharton, the only telegram he'd ever gotten that wasn't sung? He knew as he ripped it open that it could not be bad news, his parents having died in an automobile accident while he was still in the army. (Not even a telegram *then*. Basic training in Fort Chaffee, Arkansas. Not even, when it came down to it, informed. His sister out of town when it happened, when he called—routinely—that weekend and there had been no answer. And no answer the next weekend either, or the next. And, returning on furlough to Chicago before being sent overseas, no answer at the door. And his key didn't even fit it anymore, as though basic training had given not only *him* a different shape but by God *everything* a different shape, his clothes, even his keys. "Hey, what's going on?" he'd asked a neighbor. "God, didn't you know? Didn't they tell you?" "Tell me what?" "They were killed. Dead a month. Didn't the Red Cross get in touch with you?" And angered—for the first time in his life really pissed, roaring into the long-distance telephone to his commanding officer: "What the hell *is* it with you people? I want my compassionate leave or I'll go A.W.O. fucking L. It isn't the time off. It's the *principle!*" Answer-

ing his neighbor's questions from across the hall, making his answers his argument: "I didn't fucking know. You didn't goddamnit
tell me. The Red no damn good Cross didn't get in touch with
me." Wanting, see, his books balanced even then, not looking for
something for nothing, only for justice, the principle of the thing.
And still no more notion of what he was about than a babe. They
gave him the leave. Leave piled on leave while Truman brooded
and made his decision to drop the atomic bomb and the war ended,
and then getting the government to approve his matriculation at the
Wharton School of Business, arguing that if the army had not
given him compassionate leave he might have seen active duty,
might have been wounded. Unwounded, undisabled, they were
getting off cheap.)

He would never forget the telegram, had an image to this day of
the uneven lengths of yellow strips of capital letters pasted on the
yellow Western Union blank, like a message from kidnappers:

WOULD LIKE SEE YOU BEFORE I DIE. WOULD LIKE DISCUSS
AMENDS. REPARATIONS. HAVE BECOME RELIGIOUS IN OLD
AGE. WISH TO DO RIGHT BY GOD BY DOING RIGHT BY YOU.
HAVE CERTAIN THINGS SPEAK YOU ABOUT. DONT THINK I
UNAWARE YOUR EXCELLENT PROGRESS AT WHARTON. BEEN
GETTING WONDERFUL REPORTS FROM PROFESSORS. MUCH
ENCOURAGED WHAT I HEAR ABOUT YOU SINCE STOPPED
PESTERING ADVISER ABOUT SHORTHAND AND TYPEWRITER
INSTRUCTION. PLEASE VISIT ME HARKNESS PAVILION SUITE
1407. FARE POCKET MONEY FOLLOW. YOUR GODFATHER
JULIUS FINSBERG.

Fare followed, pocket money followed, and he had an impression
of sequence, of something suddenly organizing his life, as if somewhere someone had tripped a switch to trigger a mechanism that
gave a fillip to events, like a parade, say, at its headwaters, its side
street or suburban sources, the horses sorted, the bands and floats
and marchers suddenly geometrized by some arbitrary imposition
of order, a signal, a whistle.

He recognized Julius Finsberg's name, knew him to be his godfather, though he could not recall ever having seen the man, and knew that till then, till the time of the telegram, the office had been ceremonial only, a sinecure from the days when Finsberg and his father had been partners in a small theatrical costume business in New York, a business just large enough to support one family but not two. It was when Ben was a small boy that the partnership dissolved, amicably as it happened, Julius buying out Al, though it could just as easily have been the other way around. They had, Ben remembered his father telling him, cut cards, the low man having to pay the high. At the time—this was the Depression—his father had considered that he'd won, the three thousand dollars being more than enough to give him a new lease on life in Chicago, though it was not long afterward that he'd begun to brood.

"Who'd have thought," he'd said, so often that Ben had the speech by heart, "that Cole Porter would come up with all those hit tunes, that Gershwin and Gus Kahn and Irving Berlin and Hammerstein and that other guy, what's his name, Rodgersenhart, had it in them, that they'd set America's toes to tapping, that Ethel Merman and Astaire would catch on like that, or that Helen Morgan would sing her way into America's heartstrings? The Golden Age of Costumes and I sold out my share in what today is the biggest costume business in the country for a mess of pottage! I don't blame Julius. *He* didn't know. I'm not holding him responsible for my bad timing. To tell you the truth, it was only after he gave me the three thousand that I made him your godfather—you were already six. I felt guilty sticking him with the business. Well, what's done is done. After all we're not starving. I've got a nice shop, but when I think what might have been . . ." From then on his father ate his heart out whenever he heard—he would permit no radio in the house, no phonograph—someone whistling a popular show tune.

When he was called to New York in the spring of 1950 Ben was twenty-three years old. He went directly from Penn Station to the Harkness Pavilion. It was still early morning. He politely inquired of the head nurse on the fourteenth floor whether Mr. Finsberg was receiving visitors.

"No. Mr. Finsberg is very ill. His condition is grave."

"Oh," Ben said.

"Are you a member of the family?"

"Not the immediate family. Mr. Finsberg is my godfather."

"You're *Ben?*"

"You know my name?"

"Go in. It's 1407. Well, you'd know that from the telegram, wouldn't you?"

"You know about the telegram?"

"Did you get your pocket money?"

"It's in my pocket. You know about my pocket money?"

"We shouldn't delay, Ben. Your godfather is a very sick man."

They entered the room, Ben feeling a little guilty. Here was someone about to change his life perhaps. If the man had been behindhand in his attentions, Ben had been equally remiss. Their mutual indifference to each other made him feel, if the relationship existed, a sort of godson out-of-wedlock.

The old man lay diminished beneath a giant cellophane wrap, the oxygen tent. Ben could hear the frightful crinkle of his respiration. He sounded as if he were on fire.

"He's sleeping," the nurse whispered.

"I can come back."

"No, no. There might not be time."

"What does he have?" Ben whispered.

"Everything," the nurse said.

"I'll come back later," he whispered.

"I won't hear of it," she whispered back. She went to an enormous cylinder of oxygen and turned some handles. Immediately his godfather began to gasp for breath.

"Uugh—kagh—" his godfather skirled. The tent collapsed.

"What are you doing?" Ben demanded.

"Mr. Finsberg," the nurse said, "your godson's arrived."

"Uugh—Ben? Uurgh. *Ben's* here? Arghh. Uughh. Okk." She turned the oxygen back on and Ben watched the bubble reconstitute itself. "Ben. Is that you, godson?"

"Yes, sir."

And then the executives would really hear something, poring over *Fortune*'s profile in their Lear jets or in their all but empty first-class cabins as they sipped captain's compliments. Would learn—as he'd learned—that there were more ways to the woods than one, that inheritance or self-creation were not the only alternatives in the busy world of finance, that there were all sorts of success stories, qualitative distinctions, that the world was a fairyland still. That he, Ben Flesh, the owner of franchises from one end of the country to the other, was where he was today because—

"Sit down, please, Ben. What I have to say will take some time. As I am old, as I am dying—"

"Oh no, sir, you're—"

"As I am *dying*, I have to conserve my energies. Seeing you stand is a drain on those energies; watching you tire tires me. Please, godson. Please sit down."

He looked around for a chair. Only then did it strike him how curious a place it was. Except for Julius Finsberg's hospital bed and the oxygen and two hat racks of the medical on either side of his bed, they might have been in a first-class apartment. It was not like a hospital room at all. From his position he could see something of the other rooms in the suite, none of them having the least thing to do with the practice of medicine. There was a living room with a sofa and easy chairs. There were coffee tables and lamps. At the far end of the billiard room was a gaming table with slots for poker chips at each corner. There were oil paintings on the walls and he could see, off the hall, two guest bedrooms, an open bathroom with decanters of bath salts and oils on a ledge beneath the vanity. He could see a kitchen with an automatic dishwasher, a refrigerator with a tap for ice water.

His godfather lay in the dining room. Near his bed a table was set for eight, the crystal and silver and china beautiful against the thick white tablecloth. Napkins were folded like tiny crowns beside each place setting. He removed one of the chairs from the dining-room table and drew it beside his godfather's bed. He sat at the man's right beside a stanchion that supported an I.V. upside down in its collar, trying to ignore the clear tubing that led from the bottle of dextrose and was attached by a sort of needle, not unlike those used to pump up basketballs, to his godfather's wrist. The hand, like a loaf on a breadboard, was taped to a wide brown splint. His other arm, he saw, was receiving plasma, and a catheter ran from beneath the bedclothes to a spittoon. This he noticed only after he had sat down. The spittoon was between his shoes and every once in a while he heard a tiny splash.

"I am privileged," his godfather began, "as most men are." It was difficult to hear him, the voice muffled as it was by the great tent and working against the hiss and boil of the oxygen. (Nor was it easy, really, to see him, his face a smear behind the clouded plastic, like features masked by exploded bubble gum.) "You can hardly live in the world and not come under the influence of *some* advantage. Like golfers, all of us have our little handicap, however measly. So thank your lucky stars, Ben. It itches." He paused and lifted his dextrose hand, bringing the board up parallel with his nose and rubbing it. "Ouch. Son of a bitch. I think I've got a splinter. Nurse. Nurse!" he called. A middle-aged woman in a tweed suit came from the hall.

"My godfather wants the nurse," Ben said.

"I'm the nurse," the woman said and went up to the old man. "Just hold on while I sterilize this sewing needle with this match."

She turned off the oxygen and his godfather gasped. Terrified, Ben watched the old man thrash about, rolling first on one needle, then the other.

"Uugh—ach—hurry—*hurry!*"

The nurse burned the needle till it glowed red, wiped the carbon off with Kleenex. She turned the oxygen back on and stuck her head in under the tent with his godfather.

"Gracious," she said as she tried to get at his godfather's splinter, "there's hardly light to see. I shall have to speak to the window washer again. I asked him just yesterday to wash off your tent. You heard me, Mr. Finsberg. You heard me, didn't you? There, that's got it."

She came out from beneath the tent.

"Do you?" his godfather said. Some blood was coming from the side of his nose.

"Do I what?" Ben asked.

"Thank your lucky stars?"

"Well no, sir, not literally."

"I'm not speaking literally. I was in the theatrical costume business, I'm speaking figuratively."

"Here," the nurse said, "will you look at that? You could pick your teeth with it." She held up the splinter. "Should I keep this to show Mrs. Finsberg?"

"No," his godfather said. "Give it to the boy."

The nurse handed Ben the splinter. He took it and slipped it into his wallet with his pocket money and return ticket.

"How crowded is the universe," his godfather said and moved the plasma arm vaguely. "How stuffed to bursting with its cargo of crap. Consider, Ben. You could have been a pencil or the metal band that holds the eraser to the wood, the wire of lead that runs through it. The black *N* in 'Number 2' stamped along one of its six sides. Or one of its six sides. Or the thin paint on another. You might have been a vowel on a typewriter or a number on a telephone dial or a consonant in books. There are thousands of languages, millions of typewriters, billions of books. You might have been the oxygen I breathe or the air stirred by this sentence. It is a miracle that one is not one of these things, a miracle that one is not a thing at all, that one is animal rather than mineral or vegetable, and a higher animal rather than a lower. You could have been a dot on a die in a child's Monopoly set. There are twenty-one dots on each die, forty-two in a pair. Good God, Ben, think of all the dice in the world. End to end they'd stretch to the sun. Then there are the rich, the blooded with their red heritage like a thoroughbred's silks. You might have been a stitch in those silks, a stitch in any of the trillions of vestments, pennants, gloves, blankets, and flags that have existed till now. Let me ask you something. How many people live? Consider the size of their wardrobe over the years. A button you could be, a pocket in pants, a figure on print.

"—I was discussing the rich. There are many wealthy. More than you think. I'm not just talking beneficiaries either, next of kin, in-laws, distant cousins, the King's *mishpocheh*, the Emperor's. But the rich man himself, the wage earner, the *founder*. Fly in an airplane in a straight line across one state. You couldn't *count* the mansions or limousines, you couldn't *count* the swimming pools. So many, Ben. You're not one of them, and not one of the family, and *still* you exist. I am talking the long shot of existence, the odds no gambler in the world would take, that you would ever come to life as a person, a boy called Ben Flesh."

He was very excited. He raised himself on the boards taped to his arms and leaned toward me, speaking so close to the oxygen tent that with each word he seemed about to take some of it into his mouth.

"Think of the last of their lines. How many do you suppose have been the last of their lines? Queers, say, or the imperfectly pelvic'd or ball-torn or so wondrously ugly they could never make out and didn't have the courage or the will to rape? Whatever the reason the last of their lines, end of the road, everybody out. How many? Forty million? Fifty? I don't have the statistics. —I'm reminded of those rich men again; you could have been the paper for a stock or a bond; you could have been change in somebody's pocket or a lost dollar nobody found. —But at *least* fifty million. So great a number, yet you managed to be born, you made it anyway, you wormed your way. And if you happen to be white, that's a miracle squared. Are you following my argument? White people are a minority, you know. As land is to sea, white is to black, to yellow and mongrel Pak. So we keep compounding the miracle like the interest rate on money never touched.

"It's incredible really. Amazing. Who could believe it? You weren't aborted, you didn't end up in a scum bag. You survived the infant mortality stuff. You made it past measles, polio, mumps. You outwitted whooping cough, typhoid, VD. God bless you, boy, you're a testament to the impossible! And not just that, but you aren't broken or damaged, there are no birth defects; you've your full complement of fingers, your fair share of toes. Your brains are present and accounted for. You're literate, you do sums. The Dean's list at Wharton. I know, I know. And even without parents you've got clothes, shelter, sex, what to eat—you know, the drives, the hydramatics of being, four on the floor and more where that came from. Yes, and you get the point of jokes and have a favorite movie and maybe even the room where you stay is done up in your best color. My God, lad, you're a fucking celebration!

"And over and beyond everything, your inventory of good fortune like leaves on trees, there's still some advantage left over. Nurse, *Nurse!*"

The woman ran back into the room.

"What is it, Mr. Finsberg? Is something the matter?"

"Nothing. Nothing. I wanted you to see this phenomenon." He poked his plasma board at the tent and pointed me out.

"You'll tear the tent, sir."

He leaned back and closed his eyes. I thought he had passed out. But in a moment he began to speak again.

"The wars," he said breathlessly, his eyes still shut. "You were drafted. But you lived to tell the tale. In my own lifetime, just in my own country, there's been the Spanish-American, the First War and Second, plus a little showing the flag here and a little more there. And maneuvers going on all the time. Even as we talk, maneuvers going on, war games, and if plenty buy it in the line of duty, a lot more buy it and it's only an accident. In car wrecks on highways, your own parents, for example—and may I belatedly say how sorry I am? Al was my partner and Rose my friend, and I miss them dearly, the both. And the houses burned down that you weren't in—all the chance crap, all the hazard, actuarial rough stuff."

He opened his eyes. "Am I on the right track?" he asked softly. "Will you leave here singing? Humming the tune?

"What I'm looking for is the argument priests used to give, maybe still do, about how long a time eternity takes. Like if a birdie were to carry one grain of sand in its beak from a beach and fly across the ocean with it and then go back for another grain and shlep *it* overseas and lay it down by the first and then go back for a third and so on and so forth, and have to do that on all the beaches in the world, one grain at a time, and the same with deserts and all the sand traps in all the golf courses on earth, including miniature, and all the hourglasses and kids' sandboxes and throw in, too, every grotty piece of sand in tennis shoes from picnics at the beach and the gritty leftovers in all the crotches of jockstraps and bathing suits from all the summer vacations in history and all the winters in Miami and other resorts—and when the birdie did all that, that would be only a fraction of a fraction of just the first second of what's left of eternity! All right, *listen:* And say that the heat in Hell at the time our feathered friend makes his first trip is already the boiling point of water, and that it gets one degree hotter every time not just that the goddamn bird completes a trip but *every time he flaps his fucking wings,* and the pain and hotness of that heat at the end of all those trips would be to ultimate pain only what putting a pair of mittens on the coldest day in the coldest winter in the world would be to the ultimate comfort of your hands. *And you could have been any one of those grains of sand, or any one of those seconds of eternity, or any one of those B.T.U.'s!*

"Ben, everything there *is* is against your being here! Think of get-togethers, family stuff, golden anniversaries in rented halls, fire regulations celebrated more in the breach than the observance, the baked Alaska up in flames, everybody wiped out—all the cousins in from the coast. Wiped out. Rare, yes—who says not?—certainly rare, but it *could* happen, *has* happened. And once is enough if *you've* been invited. All the people picked off by plagues and folks eaten by the earthquakes and drowned in the tidal waves, all the people already dead that you might have been or who might have begat the girl who married the guy who fathered the fellow who might have been your ancestor—all the showers of sperm that dried on his Kleenex or spilled on his sheets or fell on the ground or dirtied his hands when he jerked off or came in his p.j.'s or no, maybe he was actually screwing and the spermatozoon had your number written on it and it was lost at sea because that's what happens, you see—there's low motility and torn tails—that's what happens to all but a handful out of all the googols and gallons of come, more sperm finally than even the grains of sand I was talking about, more even than the degrees. Well—am I making the picture for you? Am I connecting the dots? *Ben, Ben,* Nick the Greek wouldn't lay a fart against a trillion bucks that you'd ever make it to this planet!

"So! Still! Against all the odds in the universe you made happy landings! What do you think? Ain't that delightful? Wait, there's more. You have not only your existence but your edge, your advantage and privilege. You do, Ben, you do. *No?* Everybody does. They give congressmen the frank. Golden-agers go cheap to the

movies. You work on the railroads they give you a pass. You clerk
in a store it's the 20 percent discount. You're a dentist your kid's
home free with the orthodontics. Benny, Benny, we got so much
edge we could cut diamonds!"

"I have none of these things, Godfather."

"Oh, listen to him. Everybody gets *some*thing wholesale. *Everybody.*"

The nurse came and gave his godfather some pills.

"I have the G.I. Bill," Ben said thoughtfully. "They pay my tu-
ition at Wharton."

"There you go," his godfather said, smiling, swallowing.

Ben nodded.

He was, of course, a little disappointed. Had it been his godfather's intention to bring him from Philadelphia just to demonstrate
how fortunate he was to be alive? The telegram had spoken of
amends, reparations. Having seen the hospital apartment in which
the man was to die, he had begun to grasp how much money his
godfather had. The taxi had brought him up Broadway. He passed
the enormous hoardings, wide as storefronts, read the huge advertisements for plays, musicals, the logos for each familiar, though he
rarely went to the theater. (He had seen, he supposed, the emblems and clever trademarks, individual as flags, in magazine ads or
above the passengers' heads on buses in Philadelphia.) But seeing
the bright spectacular posters for the plays like a special issue of
stamps stuck across Broadway's complicated packages as he viewed
them from his deep, wide seat in the back of the cab, had been
very exciting. Why, the musicals alone, he thought now, and tried
to recall as many as he could. *Arms and the Girl, The Consul, Gentlemen Prefer Blondes, Great to Be Alive,* and *Lost in the Stars. Miss Lib-
erty, Kiss Me, Kate, South Pacific, Texas, Li'l Darlin', Where's Charley?*
They played songs from all these on the radio; he'd whistled them.
Nanette Fabray was in one of the shows. Pearl Bailey was. Bambi
Lynn, Vivienne Segal. Pinza and Mary Martin. Ray Bolger and
Byron Palmer and Doretta Morrow. Kenny Delmar. And how
many of these stars wore costumes his godfather had supplied?
And that was just the musicals. The circus was in town. Could the
man have dressed circus performers? Why not? And the Ice

Show—*Howdy, Mr. Ice of 1950.* And there was a Gilbert and Sullivan festival on and the ballet. Even if he supplied just a tenth of the costumes . . . God, he thought, if you added them all up and threw in the dramas and all that was going on in Greenwich Village, there were enough people in Manhattan alone wearing costumes—and think of the costume changes!—to dress a small city. That was the kind of action his godfather had. Gee!

"Uugh, agh! Uuch. Awgrh."

"The tent, Godfather?"

"The bedpan! Get help. Hurry, boy. Where are you going? That's the guest bedroom. No, that's the linen closet. Not in there, for God's sake, that's the bar! There, that's right."

He grabbed a resident—the man wore a stethoscope over his turtleneck—and rushed with him and a nurse back to his godfather's suite. He remained outside.

The nurse and resident came out in a few minutes. Ben looked at them.

"You didn't tell me you were Ben," the resident said.

"How's the weather in Philly?" the nurse asked.

He could hear his godfather calling his name. "I'd better go in," Ben said.

The man was sitting, his pillows fluffed up behind him.

"You seem more comfortable," Ben said.

"Never mind about that," he said irritably. "I'm a goner. There's something we have to straighten out."

"Yes, sir," I said.

"Here's the long and short of it," my godfather said. "I palmed a deuce."

"Sir?"

"I palmed a deuce. You don't spend the whole of your working life in the theatrical costume business without picking *some*thing up. You know how many magicians' costumes I've turned out over the years? Let me count the ways. Sure, and the magician needing his costume immediately, five minutes after the phone call from his agent. Having to be in Chicago, the Catskills, Pittsburgh, St. Louis. It was always rush rush rush with magicians, and they hang over your shoulder while you work. Magicians! Well, it *has* to be that way, I suppose. Magicians have special requirements. They have to be there to tell the tailor everything. Well, wouldn't they?"

"I guess so. I never thought about it."

"Wake *up*, for God's sake!"

"Yes, sir."

"So, well, anyway, there was this magician and one time I, you know, he was hanging around waiting for his costume to be ready and I, I asked him to teach me to palm a deuce."

"I don't understand," I said.

"Do I have to draw a picture for you? When we cut, your father and I, to see who'd buy out who and low man had to pay the other guy the three thousand bucks— You see, I *wanted* the business. If your old man had cut a queen or a jack or even a ten I wouldn't feel so bad, because probably I could have beat him without the palm. But he cut a *four*. *A fair four*. I *had* to cheat. Son of a bitch. It's been on my conscience for years. Then, your father, he had to go and make me your godfather because he felt he'd stuck me with the business. What a sap. Well, who was the sap? Because I didn't have any kids of my own then, see? I wasn't even married. So it meant a lot to me, being your godfather. But I couldn't face you. What I'd done to you, you know? It was as if I'd taken the bread out of your mouth, my own godson and I'd taken the bread out of his mouth. You've got a sister. You don't see *her* here, do you?"

"No, sir."

"Because she was never my goddaughter and I don't give a shit what happens to her. You follow?"

"I think."

"Because I was a sport in those days. What the hell, I wasn't married, *I* had no responsibilities." He lowered his voice. "I used to go backstage with some of our customers. You follow?"

"I think—"

"So naturally I fell in with this show-biz crowd. Hoofers, singers. And spent less and less time in the shop. I'd tell your dad I was making contacts for us, for our business, and in a way I was. Do you understand what I'm saying to you?"

"Well, I—"

"That's when they took me to Tin Pan Alley."

"Tin Pan Alley?"

"And there was this kid in Tin Pan Alley. He was always hanging around."

"I see."

"And whistling. You follow?"

"I don't—"

"And everywhere I'd go in Tin Pan Alley there'd be this whistling kid, whistling tunes, Ben, the most beautiful tunes you ever heard. My *God*, what a whistler he was!"

"I follow."

"What?"

"I see."

"That whistler's name was Jerome Kern!"

"My God!"

"He had a friend. A hummer. And, Ben, if it was possible, the hummer hummed even more beautiful than the whistler whistled."

"He was—?"

"Richard Rodgers."

"Wow!'

"And through Kern and Rodgers I got to know another character in Tin Pan Alley. A piano player. I'd listen to him play these incredible songs on his piano and I swear to you I had to catch my breath. It was like I was a sailor boy listening to the sirens."

"Cole Porter," Ben said.

"You better believe it."

"Jesus."

"So you see? I knew. I had my ear to the ground of Tin Pan Alley and I knew there was going to be a—what do you call it?—a renaissance in the American musical theater. And I saw new beautiful costumes in my sleep and I knew that the theatrical costume business was going to be the talk of the town. That's when I asked the magician to teach me to palm the deuce. That's it, that's the story."

"Gee."

"Your father never knew."

"I'm glad. He would have eaten his heart out."

"He would have eaten his heart out."

Ben nodded.

"So," his godfather said after a while, "we've got business. I'm dying and I want to put things right."

"You don't owe me—"

"Never mind. This is something I'm doing for myself. You ain't got nothing to do with it. Never mind what I don't owe you."

I sat in my dining-room chair with my feet by the spittoon of pee and waited for him to go on.

"I'm a very wealthy man. Well, look around, you can see I'm going out first class."

"Please, Godfather."

"Facts are facts, Ben."

"All right."

"I said 'That's the story,' but I left something out. After your father and I dissolved the partnership I married a girl from Tin Pan Alley."

"Yes?"

"She was a hoofer, but really a trained ballet dancer. She had this incredible pelvis, Ben. Well, you can imagine what twenty years of plié would do to a girl with a fantastic pelvis to begin with. To make a long story short, Ben, Estelle turned out to be very fecund."

"Oh?"

"Ben, that woman had babies like a mosquito lays eggs. There are eighteen, Ben."

"Eigh*teen?*"

"Four sets of triplets, three sets of twins."

I could have been one of the triplets, he thought. I could have been one of the twins.

"I'm rich, Ben, but blood is thicker than water."

"Oh."

"I'm rich, yes, but after estate taxes, and— My wife gets about a million outright; the rest is left in trust for my children."

"I see."

"What do you see?"

"That this was a deathbed confession. That now you feel better."

"Is that what you think? No, boy. You're provided for. I *had* to provide for my godson. What they're getting is money, but it won't come to even a quarter million apiece. I'm leaving you something more valuable."

He went to the Wharton School of Business. What, he wondered—he multiplied by eighteen, he added a million—was more valuable than five and a half million dollars?

"Don't you want to know?"

"Well, yes, I—"

"I'm leaving you the prime interest rate."

"The what?"

"You go to Wharton. The prime rate. The rate of interest a bank charges its best customers. I've made out my will. It's all there. Loans from my bank at the prime rate, whatever it is on the day of my death, and no matter how high it climbs afterward, the loan or loans outstanding never at any time to exceed the value of the money left to any one of my surviving children, the principal and interest to be guaranteed by them on a pro-rated basis up to and until your first bankruptcy. The only restrictive stipulation I'm putting on you is that whatever monies you borrow have to be invested in businesses. No shows. I've seen too many angels bust their wings backing the wrong shows. The kids know all about it and they agree. Ben, Godson, *that's* your edge. There's your advantage. The world is all before you, kid. Not money but the use of money! I know you can't take it all in right now, but let me tell you, it's the best thing I could have done for you."

As a matter of fact he *did* take it all in. It was like a letter of credit. This was the postwar world. Opportunity flourished everywhere. He went to Wharton. He would graduate in a year. Academically at least he would know the ropes. A foundation was being laid here. His eyes were wet with grief for his godfather and with a sense of the significance the man's gesture meant for himself. Slowly he raised himself from the chair in which he was sitting and slowly gathered pieces of the plastic tent in his hand and bent down and leaned in, pulling it over his head as he would a sweater. He kissed his godfather, Julius Finsberg. The old man's eyes were wet. Ben felt a draft. It was the oxygen.

"Listen, you son of a bitch," his godfather said, "you study hard at Wharton. You're just godblood. I don't want you sticking my kids with a bankruptcy from some half-assed investment. Study hard. Promise me."

"I promise," he said.

Then his godfather said something Ben had difficulty understanding.

"What's that, Godfather?" he asked gently.

"I said," his godfather said, "that in that case you have a friend at Chase Manhattan." And then he died. The prime rate was 1.45 percent on commercial paper on four-to-six-month loans.

Let *Forbes* and *Fortune* put that in their pipes and smoke it!

So much, he thought, for those who think I was never innocent, who believe I drive hard bargains, force others to the wall with my bruiser's gift for what is only business. So much for those who think I always looked older than my age and attribute my tastes to an instinct in me for more and more again and then something extra for the house and afterward a little left over that I must scrounge and have. Who think there was never a time when people had to take my knots out. My father wormed *my* hooks, too. Listen, what do you think? I razzed Sis and touched her things in the hamper. Mom and Pop died together on a highway I have changed the look of forever. A partnership was dissolved by intrigue, and fate worked like a robin in the intriguer's head to build a conscience there like a little nest. What bloodlines! I was adopted posthumously and made the one whole number in a family of fractions, of thirds and halves.

Why do they say me when they mean Nate? How easily I gave in to him on the extra televisions. He's the liquidator, I'm the one who builds and builds. I practically founded this country, for God's sake. Show a little respect, please.

He imagined Nate in his suite, protected by a sleeping Mopiani in the vast deserted lobby.

It was almost dawn. He had to make arrangements in the morning about the TV's. He would be out of Harrisburg by lunchtime, catch a bite at a plaza on the turnpike with the comers and the goers. Damn shame he hadn't slept. It was a going period for him. (He was not unlike Mopiani, actually. He had his rounds, too, his stations.) It was better than two hundred miles to Youngstown. He wouldn't be there till six-thirty, six at the inside. It would be better not to rush, do his business leisurely and stay over in Harrisburg another night, get a fresh start the day after.

# 3

Mornings, seven o'clock, seven-thirty, were different. Something alien in mornings, foreign. There were cities—Harrisburg, Syracuse, Peoria, Memphis—which seemed, if you saw them only on spring or summer mornings, as if they were located in distant lands. It had to do with the light, the dewy texture of wide and empty streets, the long caravan of store windows, his view of the mannequins unobstructed, their stolid stances and postures, their frozen forms like royalty asleep a hundred years in fairy tales, struck where they stood motionless in their spelled styles like figures on medals, the disjunctions all the more striking for the clothes they wore from seasons yet to be. That was foreign. Though he'd never been out of the country, not even to Canada.

Or the long narrow galaxy of traffic lights, a stately green aisle of procession, Ben passive in the open-windowed Cadillac behind the wheel, drawn at thirty miles an hour, pulled up the main street like a man on a float, music from the stereo all around his head like water splashing a bobber for apples.

He loved his country—it was America again—at such times, would take up arms to defend it, defend the lifeless, vulnerable models in the windows of the department stores, their smiling paradigm condition. Loved the blonde, tall, wide-eyed smashers and their men, vapid, handsome, white-trousered and superior, goyish, gayish, delicious, their painted smiling lips like ledges for pipes.

"Some of my best friends are mannequins," he said. "Fellas, girls, it was up to me I'd give you the vote and take it away from real people. Send you to Congress to make good rules. Aiee, aiee," he said, "I'm a happy man to see such health, such attention paid to grooming."

He stopped for a hitchhiker and bought the kid breakfast at a plaza. The boy was about nineteen, Levi'd, his denim work shirt covered by a denim vest of a brand called Fresh Produce. He'd seen an ad on Nate's color TV in Harrisburg.

"That was an odd place to hitch a ride," he told the kid when they were back on the turnpike.

"No, I look for out-of-state plates. That time of day salesmen come by to get back on the highway."

"Clever," Ben said approvingly. "I like to know such things. Other people's tricks of the trade, the shortcuts and gimmicks they live by, that's always interesting to me. Cops wear clip-on neckties so they won't be strangled in fights. Did you know that?"

"No."

"That's an interesting thing, isn't it?"

"Cops aren't my bag."

"You're not into cops."

"No."

"There's where you make your mistake. A boy your age. You should be into everything."

"I got time."

"Sure. I'm in franchises. I have about a dozen now. But I've had more and I've had less. I'm like a producer with several shows running on Broadway at the same time. My businesses take me from place to place. My home is these United States."

"You've got Idaho plates."

"I buy my machines in Boise. I get a new one every year. You think we need the air conditioning?"

"I don't know."

"I'll set the thermostat for seventy." Ben thought the boy was laughing. "What's funny?"

"Nothing. I was thinking. A drifter in swell threads and a late-model car."

"What about you?"

"I don't have the threads and I ain't got the car."

"Otherwise we're the same," Ben said.

"I haven't got a dozen businesses."

"I'll give you a job. I'll make you the manager of my Baskin-Robbins in Kansas City."

"Sure you will."

"Sure I will."

"My mom said never take ice cream from strangers," the kid said. He tried to pass it off as a joke but I could see he was uneasy. Probably he thought I was a fairy. I understand. An aging guy in a Cadillac, a breakfast buyer. Only the knowledge that he could take me kept him from telling me to stop and let him out. He made moves in his mind. He was thinking he could push in the cigar lighter and burn me if I tried something. He was thinking karate chop, the advantage of surprise. Break my arm with the armrest, he was thinking. Get me with his backpack that he held in his lap, that when he wore it in the city where I picked him up it made him look like an astronaut. Actually a kid like this, probably on spring vacation, going to see his girlfriend in South Bend, Indiana, or toying with the idea of dropping out maybe, what good to me was he? Every day I try to be ordinary, routine as the next guy. I drop my diction like an accompanist. Sing, sing your key, I'll pick you up. But the kid? His assumptions soured the air and I turned on the radio.

"You're not Baskin-Robbins material," I told him and could almost smell his relief as I ignored him. And I did what I always do when I'm with healthy good-looking people. I saw myself from his viewpoint, saw my gnashing jaws, a thing I do when I drive and which dentists have pointed out to me, saw my ugly Indian-nickel features, my long coarse sideburns, my pot which seems larger than it is because I have no ass. I felt his physical smugness and could have shot holes in his Frisbee.

"What's with you? You into meditation?" Ben asked.

"Meditation?"

"It's twenty-five miles since we spoke."

"I was listening to the music."

I turned the radio off and pulled onto the shoulder of the road. "I've got to pee," I said and pulled the keys from the ignition. That was to make him think I was afraid of him and set him at his ease. Even so he could have misinterpreted me, thought the pee a stratagem to get him to pee and thus expose himself to me. I went deeper into the woods than necessary, almost hiding. When I got back he was gone. I drove off. He was hitching about two hundred yards up the road. He spotted me and made to go off into the woods. That made me mad and I stopped. I opened the door and signaled him closer. He looked miserable, shamefaced, but he stood his ground.

"Hey, you," I said.

"I ain't riding with you."

"Never mind you ain't riding with me. You haven't thanked me for the ride you already rode with me."

"Thank you."

"Let's hear it for the breakfast."

"For the breakfast. Thank you."

"And the lessons I taught you about life."

"What were those?"

"What, you forgot?"

"You didn't say much."

"You weren't paying attention. What about those twenty-five miles? They were the first lesson. The second was that opportunity strikes once. I want you to know something. Never forget this. You blew it, you fucked up. I was prepared, such was my mood, to make you the manager of my Baskin-Robbins franchise in the Country Club Plaza in Kansas City. If you knew shit about locations you'd know that that's the flagship of the chain in Kansas City, the crème de la crème, we're making it a flavor. I want you to know I trusted you. I would have given you ice-cream lessons. And here's the part I hope eats your heart out. I *still* trust you. I am an equal-opportunity employer, your putzship, and all there was to it was for you to say the word. Not saying the word cost you about $30,000 a year. In the neighborhood of. I want you to know that the word was yes. I want you to know that the word is always 'yes.' "

"I don't believe you."

"You don't believe what? What don't you believe?"

"That you'd give a job like that to a stranger."

"Of course I wouldn't give a job like that to a stranger. Who mentioned strangers? It was what you said about salesmen having to come up that street. I figured you for a kid with a head on his shoulders."

He came a little closer.

"No," I said. "Stay where you are. You're all washed up in the ice-cream business. You won't ever understand this next part, but it's the truth, real as my Cadillac. I'm a benefactee. A benefactee benefacts. That's the tradition. That's fitting. I went to Wharton. Books must balance. You could have gotten me off the hook but you blew it. You want a ride? You are no longer in the running upward-mobilitywise, but it's starting to rain and if you want a ride I'll give you one."

"Yes, sir," he said.

"In the back seat," Ben told him. "I don't care for your dirty aspersions. You're too suspicious to hitchhike."

When they were on their way Ben told him about his cousins. He knew what the young man didn't, that the boy was entitled to the story. Since he had disinherited him, obligations had been created. Legally the kid was entitled to nothing, but Ben felt bad about this. The boy, a guest in his Cadillac, was already out $30,000. Ben owed him something.

"This is the true story," he began, "of Julius and Estelle Finsberg's children, my godcousins, or 'How I Got to Play the Palace.'

"Julius Finsberg was a bachelor almost all his life. He didn't marry until he was past fifty. He was, at that age, settled, a man of habits deep as grain. As I reconstruct it, nothing ever happened to him. He was that rare being in our go-getting country, a man whose life had never been touched by our public events, whose convictions had never been nudged, shoved neither north by northwest by war nor south by southeast by peace. He would already have been thirty-eight in the First War, too old by a whisker for conscription. And forty-nine in 1929, the prime of life for a man in a small sedentary theatrical costume business, a business almost impossible to wipe out in a Depression, for everyone knows there's no business like show business and the show must go on. He was a paradigm for a man. I mean, he might have served as a model for the uncontingent life, a man who would probably have got by in any century. And that's significant, too. Born in one century, he died in another. We think of such men as respectable, responsible. They are the average from whom we get our notions of tone, our ideas of stability. Consider, for example, the year of Finsberg's birth—1880. By the time he came to awareness photography was an established fact, trains, electric light, the telephone, automobiles. Even radio and aviation were in the air. He lived, that is, in conjunction with the incipiency of things, taking for granted all those objects and ideas that developed as he developed, in neck-and-neck relation to the world, so that he moved, or seemed to, as it moved, creating in him alphas of stability and settlement and an imagination which could take anything the world could dish out. He died in 1950 at threescore and ten, as if God Himself were an actuary.

"I said nothing ever happened to him, but that isn't the same as saying he took no initiatives. He did. Falling in love in his fifties was an initiative. It must have seemed the oddest event in his life. Yet even then he lived with the incipiency of things. The love songs whistled and hummed and played on the pianos of Tin Pan Alley came into existence even as he overheard them, so living still in his Johnny-on-the-spot connection to the world, to the lyrics and melodies of songs not yet even copyrighted. And this is the point. Such a man, a man for whom there have been no surprises, when such a man is surprised, the surprise has got to be devastating. It gives him the tidal wave and sets him apart from himself, defying all his Geneva conventions. He'd been my father's partner. My father spoke well of him. When Julius fell in love my father could not understand that Julius's old loyalties and habits and routines were sabotaged, and never detected Julius Finsberg's scorched-earth policy against the character and personality of Julius Finsberg. Julius's love—a girl much younger, a hoofer—giving him ambitions, big ambitions, big ideas. So he cheated my father and went into business for himself. And this was part of his stability and honor, too, your man of fifty being no fool, understanding as well as any detached gossip that he could make no dowry of a body already almost used up, knowing he would have to offer such a girl door prizes of wealth, loss leaders of power and connection.

"Only there *are* no smooth revolutions. The habits and orthodoxies of a lifetime are not overturned in a minute. It was all very well to will my father harm, but another thing altogether to alter his flesh's bone structure, its overbite and fingerprint and timbre.

"This is what happened. When he married his hoofer—it took him three years; he was fifty-three—he married self-consciously and slowly. Not only did he intend to take a wife, but to take a mother, to have sons, daughters, earnests to what I have called his orthodoxy, pawns to his respectability, and so I imagine that he fucked to conceive, willing his sperm home, body English on the tip of his prick, bobbing, weaving, dancing his gism up the hoofer's alley like a bowler. She had triplets—daughters. But Julius wanted a son—a man wants a son; it was Julius who designed the costume for the male lead in *Carousel*, who, working from Hammerstein's 'My Boy Bill' lyric, invented the big leather belt worn over the loops of the trousers like a rope, the woodsman's checked shirt and cowboy's bandanna, inventing all that tender denim swagger, symbols not of masculinity but of responsible tenor fatherhood—and again he fucked to conceive, his concentration in orgasm complete, all encompassing. He had twin boys and now had sons as well as daughters, but triplets, twins, embarrassments finally to a man his age. Where was the single son or individual daughter he had yearned for to make his normal life normal again? So again he took his hoofer to bed and again fucked only to conceive. Triplets. By this time he should have suspected, accepted. But he had been a bachelor for fifty-three years. He was set in his ways. He was passionate to father not crowds but an individual.

"Every time in the first seven years of his marriage he took the hoofer to bed he impregnated her, and every time she yielded triplets or twins. Triplets alternating with twins in the hoofer's seven fat years. And I don't think he had voluntarily surrendered his right to an individual son or individual daughter even then. But he was sixty now. It was his body that abandoned Julius Finsberg, not Julius Finsberg his body.

"My father had named him my godfather, yet it wasn't until he knew he was dying that I heard from him. Nobody gives nothing for nothing. I was to be the individual son he had wanted all his life, so that when he died his eleventh-hour sponsorship of me became his last bid to recover the ordinary. In a way I was more godson to him—I the benefactor, you see, he the beneficiary—than he godfather to me.

"I went to his funeral. It was end of term and I had to ask my professors' permission to put off my exams. I said my godfather had died. I told the truth. I admitted he was a man I barely knew. They would not recognize the connection. I told them I was in his will. I explained how he had left me the prime interest rate. This was the Wharton School of Business. This they could understand. They comforted me and told me I could take my exams whenever I felt sufficiently recovered.

"I went to the chapel where my godfather was laid out and approached the mourners' bench. I introduced myself and offered my condolences. This was the first time I had even seen the mother, the hoofer, the first time I had ever seen—what's the term I'm looking for?—the children? The triplets and twins? My godcousins? Godbrothers and godsisters? The siblings? No, this was a sib*ship*. A Sixth Fleet of family. I think I backed off when I saw them. I *know* I rubbed my eyes. There were eighteen of them. Eighteen. Yes. Only seven years separated the oldest from the youngest. There were eighteen, nine boys and nine girls. Identical triplets, identical twins. But not just discretely identical, the part in each set identical to the other part or parts of the set, but identical to each other set, too, somehow equal to and collateral with the whole. Each girl slightly favoring the father and each boy the mother, so that even their sexual differences seemed to cancel out the very notion of difference, and they looked, the boys and the girls, like one person. Exactly like, because of the subtle distinctions in their sizes and ages—sixteen years old to ten—a single person caught between two opposing mirrors, each subsequent reflection a shade smaller in perspective.

"It was astonishing. Though I didn't understand this at the time, I have come to realize that my godfather had indeed been set in his ways, so stubborn in them in fact, so much the immutable bachelor at fifty-three and four and five, and so on, that his very sperm, his very *genes* had become like a single minting of dimes, say. Granted strength he could have fucked from now till doomsday and not produced a child unlike the eighteen he had already produced.

"As I came to know them, I saw that their gestures were the same, their mannerisms and tics, their voices. When they spoke together the prayers for the dead, it was like the Mormon Tabernacle Choir.

"They knew about me. They knew who I was. They loved their father and they loved me. Indeed, they had been told by the old man to look upon me as a sort of stepbrother, and because I was as different from them as they were like each other, they seized upon me, for all the difference in our ages, as small children might attach themselves to an *au pair*.

" 'Look at his brown hair,' they said. Their own was black. 'Look how fair his complexion.' Theirs was dark. 'See how straight he stands.' They had a tendency to slouch. Their mother I had not much to do with, but the Finsberg children would not let me out of their sight."

He was the brother these brothers and sisters had never had. He had a sense even then that they loved him, and when they knew each other better he understood that Julius had talked him up at dinnertime, the godbrother in Chicago they had never seen, had kept them informed of bits of gossip learned about himself in rare letters exchanged with his own father, Julius's ex-partner. They'd known, for example, that he'd been drafted, knew where he took his basic training, were quite up to date in fact with his comings and goings, even things about his studies at Wharton.

"How could you know stuff like that?" he asked Patty, LaVerne, and Maxene. "My father was already dead when I entered college."

"Your sister," Cole said.

"That's right," said Oscar. "Father corresponded with your sister after your parents were killed in the auto wreck."

"I don't understand," Ben said. "What *about* my sister? I mean, I know how he wanted a son or a daughter. Why didn't he take an interest in my sister?"

"That's easy," Ethel said, "Dad wasn't your sister's godfather."

"It wasn't the same," Lorenz said. "Do you think it was the same, Jerome?"

"No," said Jerome.

"Neither do we," said Irving and Noël.

"He used to tell us," Ethel said, "he didn't give a shit about your sister."

"Didn't you resent me?"

"Not for a minute," Gertrude said.

"I know *I* didn't," Kitty told him. "When I learned you'd been a serviceman, I hung up a little blue star for you in my bedroom window. This was after you'd already been discharged."

"There was a Wharton Business School pennant above my dresser," Lorenz said.

"We wanted what Father wanted," said Helen.

"A change," said Sigmund-Rudolf.

"That's it," said Mary.

"A different face like," Moss said.

"You're one of us now," Gus-Ira said.

"All for one and one for all," said Lotte.

They took him up.

The Finsbergs were a close-knit family, and since no car ever built could possibly have held them all, after the war Julius had purchased one of the first new city buses that came off the assembly line. On one side of the bus was a picture of a redbud and, on the other, sprigs of mistletoe. On the rear there was an immense scissor-tailed flycatcher, the representations painted against a background of blue, white, olive, green, wine, and a sort of reddish mud. These were the official emblems and colors of the state of Oklahoma, the show Julius liked to think had paid for it. They kept the bus in the driveway of their large house in Riverdale. Julius had never learned to drive and none of the children was old enough. Only the hoofer—Estelle—could drive it, but now that Julius was dead she no longer had the heart.

One day during the week of mourning Estelle came up to Ben. "After this is over," she said, "the children would like to go on a trip. They thought you might take them in the bus."

"I don't think I can drive a bus."

"Why not? It's the same principle as the deuce and a half. You were in the motor pool."

"You know about the motor pool?"

Ben took them to Jersey.

"Isn't it beautiful?" Ethel said.

"Mother never took us *this* far," Cole said.

"We never left the Bronx," said LaVerne.

"Oh, Ben," said Lotte, "it's really marvelous. It's like a picnic. Let's have a picnic. Wouldn't that be fun?"

"I'd like some ice cream," said Oscar. "Ben, may we stop for ice cream? Please, let's."

"Yes, Ben, yes," said the others happily. "Oh, Ben, please," they said.

"Ice cream would be just the thing," Lorenz said seriously. "We could buy our cones and eat them in the bus."

For all that he knew how they liked him, he was not really sure where he stood with them. Though they told him they looked on him as one of the family—wasn't he in Daddy's will?—the fact was that he had become a sort of factotum to the Finsbergs. He had gone with Estelle to help pick out the casket and had ended up making nearly all the decisions and arrangements for the funeral. (He soon discovered that except for the enormous *immediate* family Julius had propagated, there was no other, no surviving brother or sister, no cousin or uncle or aunt. Estelle herself was as bereft of relations as Julius.) Now he had become the children's chauffeur. He felt in camp-counselor nexus to them and the truth was they frightened him a little. Being left the prime interest rate was very complicated and he was unsure of what his guarantors would and would not stand for.

So he took what had been their request for ice cream as a kind of polite command.

"Ice cream, ice cream," they chanted.

"All right," Ben said.

He drove west on Route 4 and within five minutes he spotted the bright-orange roof of a Howard Johnson's. He stopped the bus and the twins and triplets jumped out excitedly. "Oh, isn't this grand?" they said when they were inside and ordering their cones. They had never seen so many flavors.

"Look, Ben," Mary said, "it says they have twenty-eight flavors." The triplets all ordered triple scoops and the twins double. They ordered all the flavors and each had a lick of every flavor. They bought Ben a single scoop of vanilla.

"Oh, look," said little ten-year-old Sigmund-Rudolf, pointing to the logo on the wide mirror behind the counter, "see the funny man. That's Simple Simon."

"Yes," said Kitty, who was eleven, "and the man in the chef's hat, he must be the pieman. Is he, Ben? *Is* he?"

People were staring at the strange group.

"Yes," Ben said. "Come on, kids, why don't we finish our cones in the bus like Lorenz said we should?"

They got back into the bus and Ben drove on. They turned off Route 4 and onto Route 17.

"Gosh, Ben," Oscar said, "look. There's that same ice-cream parlor. We must be going in circles. Are we lost?" he asked worriedly.

"Are we, Ben?" Patty said.

"No," Ben said, "that's just another Howard Johnson's."

On the Hamburg Turnpike Gertrude spotted a third and outside Paterson Jerome saw a fourth.

After that they decided that the first one to see the next orange roof and little turquoise tower of a Howard Johnson's would be the winner and would get a wish. Ben zigzagged through the New Jersey countryside. It was getting late and he started to look for signs to the George Washington Bridge.

He followed Saddle River Road, left it, and came to Route 23. Just after they passed "Two Guys," Lotte, who was sitting right behind the driver's seat, jumped up. "*I* see one, *I* see one!" she shrieked.

"Where?" screamed Noël.

"Where, where?" Irving shouted.

Ben almost lost control of the bus.

"There. Right there," Lotte yelled.

"She's right," the kids agreed.

"Oh, Ben," she called in his ear, "I get a wish, I get a wish."

"Gosh," they all said as they passed by Howard Johnson's. "Will you just *look* at that?" "Golly," said some of the twins. "Boy," chorused Patty, LaVerne, and Maxene.

"I get my wish," Lotte said. "I wish—"

"Don't tell your wish or it won't come true," Ben said.

"But, Ben, I have to. Otherwise it *can't* come true."

"I don't figure that," Ben said.

"Well, remember how you told us that Howard Johnson's was a—what did you say?—a *chain?*"

"Yes."

"Well, I wish that you would use your prime interest rate to buy one."

"But why?" Ben said. "Why are you all so excited about a restaurant? You can have ice cream whenever you want."

"It isn't the ice cream," Jerome said.

"Of course not," said Noël.

"It isn't the ice cream, silly," Helen said.

"No," said Cole and Ethel.

"Well, what is it then?"

"Don't you see?" Irving asked. "Don't you under*stand?*"

"What? Don't I see what? *What* don't I understand?"

"That those places," Lorenz said,

"they're—" said Jerome and Mary,

"—all the SAME," said Sigmund-Rudolf and Gertrude and Moss.

"Just—" Gus-Ira said

"—like *us!*" said they all.

"And that, Buster, is the true story of how I got into the franchise business," Ben told the hitchhiker.

"What?" He'd been sleeping.

"I was telling you how the pig got its curly tail. Oh, these origins, my *pupick* pasts and golden bough beginnings. Sleep, kid, sleep. I was only muttering my mythics and metamythics, god-fairies spitting in my cradle, spraying spell, hacking their juicy oysters of fate in my puss."

He had said "chain." He had assumed that a man named Howard Johnson made ice creams, an ice-cream scientist, someone with a visionary sweet tooth, a chemist of fruits and candies, a larky alchemist who reduced the tangerine and the mango, the maple and marzipan to their essences, who could, if he wished, divide the flavor of the tomato and the sweet potato from themselves, a tinkerer in nature who might reproduce the savor of gold, the taste of cigarette smoke. He knew there was a Ford, thought there was probably a Buick and a Studebaker. He believed in the existence of a Mr. Westinghouse. Remington, Maytag, Amana, and the Smith brothers were real to him as film stars or the leaders of his country. He could believe, that is, in the existence of millionaires, men with a good thing going, who knew their way around a patent and held on like hell. Indeed, this was one of the things that had determined him to study shorthand and typing and bookkeeping at the Wharton School. He had no good thing of his own and had believed that the best thing for him would be to place himself in the service of those who had. One of the things he could not imagine once he came to understand the inevitability of death—this would have been at around two and a half—was how he would be able to support himself when his father died. He had no skill with the pencil or the needle, and though he tried—summer vacations, Christmas holidays—to apprentice himself to the designer and even the cutter and tailor in his dad's costume business in Chicago, smaller than even the partnership in New York before its dissolution—they made tutus, leotards for ballet academies, costumes for high-school musicals, and had a tiny share of the public-school graduation-gown market—he was, boss's son or no boss's son, always rebuffed, reduced to running errands, delivering merchandise. They had no patience with him. Schmerler, his father's tailor, thought he was a pain in the ass. *"Gay avec,"* he'd tell him, "you're an American. What do you want? Look at my eyeglasses, thick as a slice of bread. Lift them, they weigh a pound. They break pieces off my nose and tear my ears. This is something an American boy should want? Unheard of. Go to the cutter. Ask him to shake hands. Count his fingers." And one time when he'd been after Schmerler to show him how to use the Singer—he thought there was a Singer—the man had turned on him angrily. "Did you ever? What's the matter, you got your eye on your own little place in Latvia? Go away, leave me alone, study bubble-gum cards, learn what the different cars look like, do their dances, eat hot dogs at the ball park, drink Coca-Cola, and make a taste in your mouth for beer." And, when he insisted, Schmerler had handed him a sewing needle. "Stick me," he said. He held up the forefinger of his left hand.

"What?"

"Stick me here."

"What for? No."

"Baby. Pants pisher." He grabbed the needle from the boy and plunged it into his finger. He drew no blood. "You see? Nothing's there. The blood's all gone. My blood knows I'm a tailor. It left for other parts. The finger's cold, the hand. There's no more circulation. I wear fur gloves in the summer on the Sixty-third Street beach." Then he drew the boy to him. "You know what, Benny? I only wish my kids loved me a tenth what you love Dad."

But it wasn't what Schmerler thought, and though he loved his father well enough, it was something else entirely which drove him to seek information about the business. It was his knowledge that his father would die. It wasn't to his father that Ben went, but always to Schmerler or to Kraft, the cutter, or to Mrs. Lenzla, the designer. In the shop he avoided his father as much as possible for fear that he might blurt out why it was so important for him to learn the business, accusing the man of his death, slapping his face with it. And this lonely fear persisted. He simply could not imagine how he would support himself. Even in high school, where he did well, working hard in the hope that something would come up, some talent he had not known about might emerge, articulating itself like a print in the photographer's bath—the fear of his future persisted. He made good grades, was often on the Honor Roll. He went out for the drama club, won a good part in the school play, was accepted in the chorus, made the football team, worked for the paper, was given a by-line, each success frightful to him, taking no encouragement from any of them because all it meant was that he was equally good in all things, that he had no one calling, and then, realizing this, going the other way, not working hard at all, actually hoping to fail, but still discouraged because though his grades went down they went down uniformly and he was benched the same day that his by-line was taken away and his column assigned to someone else, and within a week to the day that the choral director, Mr. Sansoni, shifted him from the tenor section to the baritone, where his voice might be swallowed up in the greater number.

So he knew he had no calling, no one thing among his talents that he did better than any other one thing, and nothing at all that he did better than others. And worrying constantly about his father's health, though the man was in good health, had no complaints. To the point where, if Ben got sick, even if it was just a cold, he withdrew to his room, locked it, used bedpans rather than risk encountering his dad in the apartment for fear of giving the man his cold, avoiding as well his mother and sister in case he should pass it on to them, who might pass it on to his father. Waiting until they had left the apartment and only then going to the kitchen, taking his food from cans, which he could then dispose of, from boxes of crackers and cookies—holding the box, he would spill however many he wanted onto the floor and then pick them up—his liquids from paper cups.

"Ben," his father would say, outside his son's locked bedroom, "it's only a cold. Don't be such a hypochondriac. What are you frightened of?"

Pretending sleep, he wouldn't answer.

And no reason at Wharton to suppose that the household names of ordinary American life were not living, breathing people, actual as himself, only luckier, better off. There had been classes where when the professor called the roll it was like hearing the listings on the New York Stock Exchange.

"Bendix."

"Present."

"Boeing."

"Here, sir."

"Braniff."

"Here."

"Burroughs."

"Yo."

Carling. Crane. Culligan. Disney. Dow. Du Pont. Elgin. Fedders.

"Flesh."

Firestone nudged him.

"What? What is it?"

"He called your name."

"What? Oh. Yes. Here, sir. Yes, sir. Present."

So there was no lack of contact. Yet—this was before his godfather's telegram, before, in fact, he came to accept that he would not pick up shorthand—he never actually thought of them as contacts, not in the sense that others used the term. He could not get over the idea that certain men had certain things going for them, that it was in their nature, even in the nature of duty itself, perhaps, to perpetuate it through brothers, sons, some primogenitary circle of the inner that closed upon itself and made a wall. If he had any expectations they were not great so much as marginal. Perhaps Goodrich might write a letter for him someday, open a door—if he could prove himself—to a branch manager or personnel director of one of the more remote plants. All he wanted was what he never believed he could have. All he wanted was a job. Enough money to pay his rent, purchase his food, buy his clothes, to save against the day when he might have enough to make a down payment on an automobile.

So of course he believed in a man named Howard Johnson, and what the twins and triplets had suggested seemed as naïve to him as anything he'd ever heard.

It was Lotte, the girl who made the wish, who had looked into it, who found out that for $40,000—this was 1951—he could purchase a Howard Johnson franchise from the headquarters in Boston.

"What? He sells his name? His *name?*"

"Oh, there are rules, Ben. You have to buy everything direct from the company."

"The eggs?"

"No, I don't guess you have to buy the eggs, but the fried clams, the ice cream, the syrups and cones. And you can't serve after midnight unless you're on the turnpike or something. There are all kinds of procedures you have to follow."

"He sells his *name?*"

"Ben, you graduated from the top business school in the country. Didn't you learn anything?"

"I made Dean's list seven times. They didn't give Shorthand, they didn't give Franchises."

"Oh, Ben."

Lotte was seventeen. They were standing in the driveway of the house in Riverdale beside the bus.

"He sells his *name*" was all Ben' could say. "His *name*. Do other people do this, do you know?"

"Oh yes, Ben, lots. Lots do."

He was excited because he knew that he had something going for him now. He would discover which men's names were for sale and he would buy them and have that going for him. He would have them at the rate banks gave their favored customers and he would have *that* going for him, too. He was very excited. He had never been so excited. They stood in the driveway on the left-hand side of the bus and Ben took Lotte in his arms and kissed her beside the sprigs of mistletoe, the painted, official flower of the state of Oklahoma.

# 4

It was something like the beginning of his fiscal year. His dealings with Nate, his brief stay in Youngstown, his drive with the kid he'd dropped in Chicago, all that was outside of time.

He'd gone to Youngstown to discuss the purchase of the Westinghouse affiliate there. He dealt with Strip and Girded, Cramer's lawyers. He'd known them for years.

He'd misunderstood. It was a television station.

Not radio?

No, TV.

I'll be damned, television. Well, how much?

Two and a half million was the asking price.

He'd thought it was radio.

Television.

How could he have gotten something like that mixed up?

Strip didn't know. Girded asked why he hadn't called first or written a letter. These things had to be cleared with the FCC. It could take years.

He'd thought it was radio. Well, it was good to see them again anyway. They were his lawyers, too. Did they remember when they'd handled the 7–11 deal for him?

Oh yes.

Well.

He really should have called.

"It's all right. I'm on my way to Chicago anyway."

"Chicago!"

His Fred Astaire Dance Studio.

"Oh yes." How was he feeling? Strip wanted to know.

"Fine."

That was good, Girded said.

"What are you looking down? Your shoes match. Fine means fine. F-I-N-E."

Well, that was good.

"Remission." If he could think radio, they could think remission.

"Really?"

"Knock wood, yes."

Well, that really *was* good.

TV. Jesus, he could have sworn radio. Two and a half million for television. "What's the market?"

"A quarter million."

Ten bucks a head?

Something like that, yes.

Gee, he'd thought radio.

They took him to lunch and shook hands and he went back to his hotel.

Well, not his *fiscal* year, his geophysical one, his minute rounds. He patrolled America. In a way Nate was right. He *should* fly more. He recalled how astonished he had always been watching through the oval windows of airplanes the gradual dissolving of the clouds, America appearing like an image in a crystal ball, and he could look down and see the land, the straight furrows in the plowed ground like justified print, the hard-edged Euclidian geometry of survey and civilization. From his Cadillac he could get just the barest sense of this, a ground-level geophysician.

Mr. Flesh stands tux'd, his formal pants and jacket glowing like a black comb, his patent-leather shoes vaulted smooth and tensionless as perfect architecture. He might be standing in the skin of a ripe bright black apple. He feels, in the inky clothes, showered, springy, bouncy, knows in remissioned tactility around his shins, his clean twin sheathing of tall silk hose, can almost feel the condition of his soles, their shade like Negroes' palms. He is accessoried.

In his old-fashioned white dress shirt his delicious burgundy studs are as latent with color as the warning lights on a dashboard. Onyx links, round and flat as elevator buttons, seal his cuffs, and dark suspenders lie on him with an increment of weight that suggests the thin holsters of G-men, and indeed there *is* something governmental in his dress, something maritime, chief-of-staff. The golden fasteners beneath his jacket could be captain's bars. A black bow tie lies across his throat like a propeller.

The studio is in the Great Northern Building on Randolph Street, in a loft. (Or this is how it seems. He knows there are floors above this one.) He remembers the days when the seventh-floor corridor had been flanked with the branch offices of costume jewelry and watchband firms, a barber shop, lawyers' offices, his father's theatrical costume business. Now, except for the barber shop, there is only the studio ballroom and the rooms for private instruction made over from the old lawyers' suites. A sort of stage is at one end of the large room. He knows it is only his father's long old cutting tables shoved close together—nailed and covered over with Armstrong vinyl asbestos Chem-tile. He knows that the waterfall of velvet that flows over the lip of the "stage" conceals only the carpenter's reinforcing scaffold, scaffold like a wine rack; that the flats, flies, tormentors, teasers, and borders that ornament the stage with perspective are only a plywood contact paper studded with a kind of gritty sheen like the surface of a ping-pong paddle.

He knows it is a losing proposition. Yet feels good anyway. Reassured by Randolph Street invisible at his back behind the opaque drapes, by the restaurant, a Henrici's he can almost feel, the Woods Theater, the Oriental, the novelty jokes and tricks shop he remembers from his youth across the street, the out-of-town-paper stand on the corner, the proliferating porno bookstores he finds so appealing, as all muted lust is appealing to him, bringing out qualities of shyness and the awkward, the peremptory imposition of respected distances, boundaries, the territorial waters of self. Like his students. Wallflowers who bought their courage with their lessons, who came out—as if it were an accredited finishing school—at the parties and balls and galas they threw themselves every few weeks at the end of one session or the getting-to-know-you beginning of the next. Getting to know again and again—the turnover never as great as the recidivism—those they knew from before. He had seen them, expansive as the fathers of brides at the punch table, or stopping the hors d'oeuvres tray as it went past carried by an instructor, demanding that their guests, themselves hosts, eat, drink, at last forcing the instructors themselves into accepting a hospitality that was by its very nature communal, and disguising this by a boisterous, reflexive generosity. Ballroom dancing? They had taught themselves to solo.

Clara was with a private student. She had said that she would turn the student over to Jenny or Hope, but Flesh insisted that she finish the hour. He had left the Office of Admissions and come into the ballroom. He sat down in a straight-back chair—a chair like a chair at a dinner table—near one of the staggered, tall, smoked mirrors that offered the room the illusion of several entrances.

He had not looked at the books but had a pretty good notion of how things were. He could tell from the music—or lack of it—that business was bad. In the old days he could stand in the Office of Admissions and hear fox-trot, bossa nova, cha-cha, waltz, polka, rhumba, and tango rhythms coming from record players in the private instruction studios. It had been like being in a bazaar where many tongues were spoken. Now only the "Carousel Waltz" wafted through the thin wallboard of one of the private instruction studios. After sitting a moment he got up and went back into the Office of Admissions.

"For God's sake," he told Luis, his Latin rhythms instructor, who was working the switchboard, "it's like a morgue in there. Why isn't there any music in the ballroom?"

"Overhead."

"Suppose the phone rings? If there were music the caller would hear it in the background. He might think something's happening here."

"I got that FM you brung last time. It's tuned to this all-music station, just like you said. If the phone rings I turn it on."

"Yeah, well, it wasn't a good idea. Suppose there's a commercial? I think we should go back to the old system."

"Sure, Mr. Flesh. What do you want to hear?"

"What is it, you do requests? I don't care. It's too quiet. Turn on the stereo. Where's Clara?"

"Clara's still back there with the waltzer."

"And Hope and Jenny? Where's Al?" Al was his other male instructor.

"Jenny and Hope are around somewhere. I think they're doing each other's hair for the gala. You want me to get them?"

"No, the phone might ring. How many do we expect at the gala tonight?"

"Gee, Mr. Flesh, I can't say. There's the Fishers, they'll be here. Runley said he was coming. Johnson and—"

"You can name them? My God, you can *name* them? It's bad as that? That's terrible."

Luis nodded.

"Where's Al?"

"Al went to get cookies for the gala."

"Cookies."

"It's pretty quiet, Mr. Flesh. The old people stay in their condominiums. Those buildings got social directors who teach them the steps. A lot are afraid to come downtown. It's different times, Mr. Flesh."

Flesh nodded. "Here," he said. He took his Diners Club card out of his wallet. "Run down to Fritzel's. Have them make up a tray of sliced turkey. Get roast beef, too. Rare. Tell them rare. Make it so we can serve at least fifty people."

"There won't be no fifty people, Mr. Flesh," Luis said.

"They can take what's left over in fucking doggy bags!" Flesh roared. "I'm feeding fifty people! The gala's at nine, right?"

"Nine, yes, sir. Nine."

"It's not yet eight. All right, give the guy ten bucks. Let him bring the stuff over and set it up for us. When you're through at Fritzel's, cross over to Don the Beachcomber and have them do us some hot hors d'oeuvres. They deliver?"

"No, sir, and Don the Beachcomber ain't no take-out joint either, Mr. Flesh."

"Luis," Flesh said, "I got five people working for me—you,

Clara, Al, Jenny, and Hope. One is off somewhere buying cookies and two are having their hair done. Now if a busy guy like me with a hot commercial property like the Fred Astaire Dance Studio can let his personnel crap around on company time, Mr. Beachcomber can send someone in a rickshaw with the hors d'oeuvres. Here, give him twenty bucks. I want the stuff at nine-thirty. Liquor, what about liquor?"

"We ain't licensed, Mr. Flesh."

"I ain't selling, Trini, I'm giving it away. Martinis. Scotch. Bourbon. And plenty of ice. I don't want to run out of ice."

"Jesus," Luis said. "Holy shit."

"Goddamn," said Flesh, "that's brilliant, Babaloo. Can you lay your hands on some pot?"

"*Pot?*"

"Pot, yes, some nice good grass. For me. And *good* stuff. Go into a head shop and have them roll it. Custom. Stitches were taken here once. They followed each other like teeth in zippers."

"Yeah, well, but like those cats don't take Diners Club."

Ben peeled off about a hundred dollars and shoved it into Luis's hand. He had not been this excited in a long while. "Here, take this. If anything else looks good to you. We're going first class."

"First class?"

"All right, I won't mince words. We're going *down* first class. Go now, Desi. Run, boy. Fetch the goose. If you see Al, send him up with the cookies. If they're stale I'll have him grind them up on the stage for a sand dance. Is that in our curriculum, Pancho? Can you tell me that, Niña, Pinta, and Santa Maria? Wait, before you go—the sound system. Turn on the bubble machine. Hit the lights, please, Cisco."

Luis went into the ballroom and turned on their big Wurlitzer equipment. Music poured from the ballroom like an element. Flesh rubbed his hands and went to the small room where Clara was giving her student private instruction in the waltz. He rapped on the door. "Five minutes, Miss Clara," he said softly, and opened the door. "The Blue Danube" was playing on the portable phonograph. A black man only a little younger than himself held Clara in his arms. One hand was up her behind.

"Hoy," Flesh said.

"Who the dude?"

"Oh, Jesus," Clara said.

"Who the dude?"

Flesh pointed his finger at the man. "I am your preceptor. Fred Astaire sent me. I give the Waltz Exam." He lifted the tone arm off the record and set it down at the beginning. "Ready, begin—da *da* da da *da*, da *da!*"

"What's this shit going down?"

"Waltz!" Flesh commanded.

"Hey, fuck, you crazy?"

"You, Bojangles, *waltz!*"

"Please, Mr. Flesh," Clara said.

"I want to see turns and rolls," Flesh said. "I want to see three-quarter time with a strong accent on the first beat."

"Beat? I'll beat your ass, cocksuck."

"I'm telling Fred."

"Mr. Flesh."

"No, Clara, Fred has to know these things." He turned off the record player. "Listen, boy," he said to the black man, "I understand. Miss Clara tried to bring you along too fast. These things take time. She had you dancing above your station. Miss Clara, dear, get Tom the tom-tom."

"I'll kill this honky turd," the man said quietly.

Flesh turned to Clara. "What is it here, a massage parlor?"

"You don't understand, Mr. Flesh."

"I understand, *I* understand. They've taken up shuffleboard, nine-hole golf. My dancers sit on seats like catchers' mitts on big tricycles in St. Petersburg, Florida. They swim laps and play bridge in the clubhouse. They're into macramé and decoupage and they fold paper to make yellow-bellied sapsuckers and even the ladies have fishing licenses. *I* understand. Where are *you* going?" He had turned to the Negro.

"I want my money back."

Flesh nodded and moved toward Clara. He reached his hand down into her brassiere and plucked out two five-dollar bills. He handed the man the cash. "She cheated you," he said. "You'll stay for the gala."

"Suck my comb, honky."

"Doesn't he know about the gala?"

"It's a party," Clara said. "It's for the students enrolled in the public session."

"I don't need no funky party."

"It's on the house. Five dollars a tit? Good God, man, are you nuts?" Ben shook his head.

"They white tits," the man said.

"Like hell," Flesh said, "they're black and blue."

Clara was crying. Flesh put his arm around her. "The gala," he said softly. "Get yourself ready. If I'm not back by nine, start without me."

He stood by the Oriental when the show broke. He spoke softly to people as they came out of the theater, careful not to frighten them. He wrote the time and address down for them on slips of paper and folded the slips gently into their hands. He made it sound as reasonable as he could, hinting, though not stating outright, that it was a business proposition. If people thought it would cost them a dollar or two, they were more likely to trust you. He was very careful about whom he approached. Some he asked to go on ahead and others he asked to wait with him, telling them he would be fifteen more minutes at most.

They came into the lobby of the Great Northern. They held their shopping bags from Stop and Shop and their green parcels from Marshall Field's.

"You let in the ones with the slips, didn't you, Henry?" he asked the night man.

"Yes, sir," Henry said.

"Good," Flesh said. "I'll be responsible for these folks," he told the man. He turned to his group. "Ladies and gentlemen," he said, "I think we're going to have to use all three elevators tonight. Henry, would you unlock the other two, please?"

Henry did as he was asked and Ben carefully directed people to specific elevators. "I'll ride up," he said to those he had not assigned an elevator, "with you people." He was the last one in. "That's all right," he said, "smoke if you got 'em."

The people from the other elevators were waiting for him on the seventh floor. "Good," he said, greeting them. "Can you hear it? It's just as I said." He cocked his head down the corridor in the direction of the ballroom. "Please," he said, "follow me." They went in single file toward the music. "Already," he said, calling back to them over his shoulder as they passed the barber shop, "we're a sort of conga line. That's the spirit." He kicked back with his right leg. He held the ballroom doors open for them.

The spherical chandelier with its adhesive strips of seamed mirrors spun slow as a device in a planetarium, throwing its romantic galaxies against the walls and ceiling and on the seven or eight pairs of dancers on the big dance floor—focusing purples, greens, yellows, blues, and reds, sliding across shoes, jackets, gowns, and arms, and dilating to wider, indescribable colors. Revolving discs of light around the room lasered the chandelier. Clara danced with a serviceman, Al, Hope, and Jenny with regulars Flesh remembered from his last visit. Three older couples moved expertly to "The Night Was Made for Love." They were like the surprisingly graceful, aged ice skaters one sees on public rinks. He wondered if they had learned their stuff here. Several people sat along the walls in chairs near the high columns of smoked mirrors. Luis and the Fritzel's and Don the Beachcomber men were fussing over the meats and hors d'oeuvres at a long linen-covered table. A man Flesh could not account for tended bar.

The song ended and Clara turned toward the stage, where the sound system was, and led the applause. "Very good," she said over the applause. "It may seem ridiculous to applaud a recording, but I want you all to get into the habit of clapping for the band, so that when we go on our outings to Pewaukee or the Café of Tomorrow and a real band is playing, you'll just do it automatically. It's very important actually. Musicians are human and if they know you appreciate what they're doing, they'll put that much more liveliness and effort into their playing. Remember, people, a dancer is only as good as his accompaniment. You people on the chairs," she said, "now even though you sat out the last dance I want to hear *you* applaud also."

"Why's that?" one of the seated women asked.

"That's a very good question, Mrs. Gringer," Clara said. "Do any of you students know the answer to that? Mr. Clone?"

"To show you're polite?"

"Well," Clara said, "it shows that, too, of course, but there's an even more important reason— Mrs. Lamboso?"

"Well, if you're sitting down while everyone else is dancing, they might think you're a wallflower or too shy when maybe all it is is that nobody has asked you. This way, if you applaud, prospective partners will see that you take an interest and maybe you'll get asked to dance."

"Very good," Clara said.

"It *is* very good," Flesh said, "but I thought Mr. Clone had a good point."

"Oh, Mr. Flesh; ladies and gentlemen, this gentleman is our host for tonight's very special gala—Mr. Ben Flesh."

They applauded and Ben nodded. "Thank you," he said. "I've brought some guests to join us tonight." He turned to his group. "The food and drink is over there. Why don't you all put your parcels on the stage where they'll be safe. Then you can join the festivities."

"Maestro," Clara said. Jenny left her partner, came to the stage, and put on more records. She played "Night and Day," "I Hadn't Anyone Till You," "September Song," "Two Sleepy People," "Falling in Love with Love," "Get Out of Town," "My Heart Belongs to Daddy," "Blue Moon," "Let's Take a Walk Around the Block," "Love Thy Neighbor," "Moonglow," "What Is This Thing Called Love?" and "You Brought a New Kind of Love to Me."

Flesh smoked the joint Luis had brought him and listened to the beautiful music. The last tingling left his hand. He was suddenly caught up in a complex and true and magnificent idea. He would have to tell them, but could not bear to break into the music or the gorgeous motions of the dancers. One of the people he had brought with him—a woman in her mid-fifties—was dancing with a golden-ager. Her left hand lay gently on his right shoulder. Flesh was touched by the shopping bag she still carried. In her dreamy mood she held the bag by only one beautiful handle and a bottle of ketchup dropped from it, making a lovely splash on the floor.

Their shoes looked so vulnerable as the dancers guided each other through the sticky stuff that Ben wanted to cry. Lai-op, lai-op, lai-op. They smeared the ballroom floor with a jelly of ketchup. It was beautiful, the pasty, tomato-y brushstrokes like single-hued rainbows. The high heels of the women smashed explosively against the broken glass adding to the percussive effect of the music. Everything was rhythm. He climbed on the stage and gulped when he looked down and saw the splendid red evidence of the dance. Studying the floor, he perceived from the various footprints, the rough male rectangles and female exclamation points, where each couple had been, their progress, where they had occupied space others had occupied before them, the intensity of color recapturing the actual measure, the music made visible. From these and other signals he felt he understood why what they did was called the "conversation step." It was a conversation of spatial displacement, the ebb and flow of presence, invasions, and polite withdrawals as each couple moved in to take the place other couples had abandoned. A minuet of hitherings and yonnings, the lovely close-order drill of ordinary life. So civilized. So gentle were men. He explained this to them over the loudspeaker, explained how it was possible to re-create from the ordinary shmutz of a broken ketchup bottle, not just where the dancers had stood, but where they had stood in *time*, that movement was nothing more than multiple exposure. Perhaps, were he musical—he *felt* musical, as musical as Terpsichore; wasn't she the Goddess of Dance? who would be the Muse of Song? muse, music, ah yes, music; there were no accidents, idiom was fundamental as gravity; who would be the Goddess of Song? it was on the tip of his tongue; oh yes, it had to be . . . it had to be—*Orchestra!*—he could, by reading their glide, even have told them the *song* that had been playing at the time. There was more. As he studied the dancers he realized that not only—if you knew how to read the signs—did movement remain, a testimony lingering like scent that men had been by, but that it was impossible to teach what all already knew. Everyone could dance. Every motion snuggled to every rhythm, to *any* rhythm. It had something to do, he explained, with the tides, with the universal alphas, with pulse itself. And he tied in menstruation and the throbs and ripples of orgasm. It was beautiful, but they weren't listening.

He fumbled with the amplifier and found the button that cut off the power, and he stood on his father's old cutting tables and spoke to them from his heart.

"My dearest ladies," he said, "my most charming gentlemen. Please, this is very important. What's sacred is important. You don't know this, you'll not be able to follow it all. Try not to blame yourselves. There's no blame here. We are all swell people. Do you know what's happening here? (Don't sidetrack me, God; let me stick to the point, oh, Lord.) Everyone concentrate. I am going to link the world for you. I am going to have it make sense, but you must concentrate. Same here.

"All right. What am I talking about? How, if I'm to link the world, *can* I get sidetracked? Not possible. It's all relevant. Be patient. Everything will come clear. Then— Who has water? I'm very dry. Luis, pleeth. Jenny, any?

"I stand on my father's long old cutting tables. Bolts of graduation cloth unwound here like spools of film, the texture of the trim like oil slicks. Costumes were made for ballerinas. We are in a room with a musical *tradition*. Yes, and what made this possible, this room, this night, our gala, were the selfsame songs you danced to earlier, written by pals of my godfather, who was able to leave me the prime rate of interest because of those songs. You *see*? We dance to the prime rate of interest itself. We compound it. Nothing is lost. Follow? That's one circle. Earlier I spoke of the rhythms, motion. Ah, God, we thank Thee for Thy do-si-dos, our hithers and yons, the wondrous cake walk and hopfrog of reality. We thank Thee for dressage and our Lippizaner life. Clara, you understand, don't you?"

"No," Clara said.

"I does," the black man said.

"Yes, but that's not my point. Do you know how good the world is? Listen, it's better than you think and better even than it has to be. I go with Clone. Politeness, gratuitous as flowers, counts. It structures life like scaffolding. Under this stage *is* scaffolding, the carpenter's hundred wooden $X$'s. Would a man do that for money?

The *care*, the nails like a driving rain. For *money?* Good Christ, friends, the man built to hold us all, to let us jump." He jumped. "I believe the amazing world of Kreskin is amazing, and who could invent a card trick or make up a good joke? The lady who dropped the ketchup—"

"That was an accident," she said.

"No, no, there are no accidents. The lady who dropped the ketchup— I saw into her shopping bag. There are Hefties there, liners for garbage cans. How civilized! Maybe all that distinguishes man from the beasts is that man had the consideration to invent garbage can liners. What a convenience! We die, yes, but are compensated by a million conveniences. Hefties are just the beginning. We perfect ourselves, we reach toward grace— I foresee a time when there will be flowered sheets and pillowcases in motel rooms. This is a deflection to convenience and the magnitude of the human spirit, the leap to comfort. The chemical creams," he said excitedly, "the chemical creams. You know, the little sacks of powder you put in your coffee. I foresee a day—someone may be working on this right now—when non-dairy creamers shall be mixed with saccharine in the same packet! There you go: convenience! And do you think for one minute that the man now waiting for this great idea's time to come will have thought it up for mere money? *No.* Unthinkable. It will hit him on an airliner like an inspiration, for the grace of the thing, only that, for the convenience it would make, and if he profits by his idea, why the money will be only *another* convenience. Someday a visionary shall come among us. He will lobby Congress to legalize pot on the principle that it would be a terrific boon to the snack-food industry! Oh, friends, the quality of all our lives shall rise like yeast. I love this world, this comfortable, convenient world, its pillow condition." He was breathless. But he had more to tell them. Mystery was on the tip of his tongue. He studied them, watched them watching him.

"I come," he said, "from Fred Astaire! I bring Ginger Rogers' spicy 'Hi.' Fred says tell them. He says make them understand. He says when you see Miss Clara, Miss Jenny, and Miss Hope, when you see Mr. Luis and Mr. Al, when you get to Chicago and stand on the cutting tables on the evening of the Nineteenth Annual Fiscal Year Gala, when you hang suspended from your suspenders in the convenient clothes of romance, your uniform of cruise and ceremony, suspended in them, your feet barely touching your hose, your hose your shoes, your shoes your pop's cutting tables, your pop's cutting tables your planet, let them know that our work, the work we do, is important, that to walk is good but to dance is better, that what we do here is the ultimate leap; to go behind gravity's back and spit in the face of the heavy. Hah? Heh?

"Listen, Fred didn't say about this part, this part's mine—Fred ain't in it—but I want to give you some notion of the world we live in. I drive the road. I go up and down it. I stay in motels and watch the local eyewitness news at ten. Murders are done, town councils don't know what to do about porno flicks, everywhere the cops have blue flu, farmers nose-dive from threshers, supply and demand don't work the way they used to, and even our President's at a loss and his advisers divided. The left hand don't know what the right is doing and only the weather report touches us all. The time and the temperature. What we have for community. Only that. The barometer adjusted to sea level, the heat wave, the drought, the cold front stalled over Wisconsin, today's low and if it's the record. And the *fuss* that's made! My God, the fuss that's made and only because it's what the local eyewitness news thinks holds us together. Some view of us it has, pals. As if we lived in the wind under the same umbrella. I see this. City after city and state after state. And, oh yes, something else, the good will and chatter, the hard-news guy lying down with the sports one, the jigaboo weatherman with the lady reporter. We should take over the stations and put out the real news. For everyone murdered a million unscathed, for every fallen farmer so many upright. We would put it out. Bulletin: Prisoners use sugar in their coffee! Do you see the sweet significance? We argue the death penalty and even convicts eat dessert. The cooks do the best they can. They have their eye out for the good fruit and the green vegetables. Oh, the astonishing manifestations of love! Rainbows wouldn't melt in our mouths! The state's bark always worse than its bite, brothers, and goodness living in the pores of the System, and Convenience, thank you, God, the measure of mankind. Nobody, nobody, nobody ever had it so good. Take heed. A franchiser tells you.

"Smile, you fuckers, laugh, you shitlings. I come from Fred Astaire, *everybody dance!*"

He jerked a record from its sleeve and slapped it on the machine. He turned the volume up and shrieked into the microphone. "Business is bad but we do a big volume." He turned the sound down some. They had gathered beneath him at the foot of his tiny stage to watch him and listen. He swayed above them. He might have been a band singer in the forties. The music was "Dance, Ballerina, Dance."

"*Do* it," he commanded. "Dance, dance." He made spiraling gestures with his fingers. Some of the people he had brought with him began to shuffle aimlessly. A few eyed each other, seeking partners. "That's right, mother," he told an old woman who held her arms out to Luis. He climbed down from the stage and began to move people around like a chess master playing several games at once. He pulled them to him in pairs, holding them by their wrists as if he would force them to shake, like a peacemaker, he thought, like love's policeman.

"Fred Astaire sent me," he whispered. "I'm this social traffic cop." He moved among them and started them dancing like a spinner of plates on sticks in nightclubs. "Good," he said, "good, good."

He scrambled back up on the stage, powdering his tuxedo trousers with paw prints of dust. He loosened his tie. "Caveat emptor," he crooned. "This is only the fabulous introductory offer. It's going to cost you. What, you think it's cheap to throw the sheets over modern times while the owners are away? You think illusion is free, buddies? This shipboard ideal we make here, this *Queen Mary* ambience? I got a shine on my shoes it cost me two dollars. You want to see real stars, go to the country, look up, get a stiff neck. Ours have six points and you can reach out and touch them on the walls—convenience, convenience—like the astronomy decor in airplanes. Come, come, we'll lie together in the time machine. When 1933 comes we'll Carioca down Main Street, everybody do the Varsity Drag. We'll Beer-Barrel Polka in the high-rent district and nobody leaves till he does the Continental!"

He explained the rates to them. The music was "Fascinating Rhythm." He told them it would cost them thirty dollars an hour and that they had to sign up for a minimum of twenty-five hours. Calmly he explained that it was cheaper than psychoanalysis. They were dancing now. The song was "But Beautiful," then "Dancing in the Dark." If they thought the thirty an hour was stiff, he said, they should understand that a lot of the fee went into outings and galas like this one and that, if they chose, they could take up to ten of their hours with a private instructor, with Luis or Al, with Miss Jenny, Miss Hope, or Miss Clara.

"These aren't bimbos," he said while the stereo played "Dream." "These are accredited people. Most of my people trained with Alex Moore's International Society of Dance Instructors. Al and Miss Clara are two-time winners of the New York *Daily News* Harvest Moon Ball, the third jewel in dancing's triple crown."

The song was "Flat Foot Floogie" and several dropped out. They chewed his sandwiches and he made them a solemn promise. It was a tradition in ballroom instruction that an hour was only fifty minutes. Fred had authorized him to throw back the missing ten minutes into each hour. Did they have any idea, he wondered, how much of a leg up—he laughed delicately at his joke—that would give them on the Arthur Murray people? That was four hours and ten minutes of additional instruction. If they applied themselves they would run the Arthur Murray people off the floor. It was better than a hundred-and-twenty-dollar rebate. He didn't understand how Fred could do it, but there it was. They danced to "Happy Days Are Here Again" and ate egg rolls from Don the Beachcomber. They moved over fallen hors d'oeuvres, stepping on the soft crusts and squashing them like bugs. Bits of pork and rice, of shrimp, chunks of chicken exploded like delicious gut under their weight. Dark sauces thick as blood stained the dance floor. He told them about "Recreation, companionship, instruction, and therapy." That was their motto, he said. He told them they must understand that there was nothing authoritarian in the word "instruction." If others he could name didn't, the Fred Astaire people believed in freedom of individual expression. He saw, he said, in the movements of his black friend, a potential for the strong, masculine rhythms of Chassidic dancing. If that's where the man's talents lay he knew a rabbi in Skokie— They were dancing now with their drinks in their hands. The song was "I'm Sitting on Top of the World," and as the men dipped the ladies, liquor spilled from their plastic glasses onto the dance floor. He tried to explain how the dance field was like karate in a way. Oh, it wasn't combative, of course, the reverse if anything, a karate of the inside out. He meant that just as there were degrees, levels of competence in karate, white belts, brown, green, he thought, and black, there were the same sorts of measurements in dance. There had to be. One had to know where one stood. Someone had placed a plastic glass on the floor with a cigarette in it that was still burning. Ben watched the hole, outlined like a filament in a light bulb as it grew wider and wider. The song was "I Can Dream, Can't I?" What was he saying? Oh yes, karate. In ballroom dancing it worked differently. They didn't get belts. Medals. There were bronze, silver, and gold medals. One could earn these, though of course there was no guarantee. You had to know where you stood, but there had to be standards. Some people made silver at the end of the twenty-five-hour course, but he'd be frank, this was the exception. Usually it didn't happen until forty hours and often, he *had* to be frank, he wanted them to know what they were getting into, seventy-five, sometimes not then. Gold medalists were rare. *He* had a feeling they were born. Independent judges were brought in. Incorruptible men who couldn't be bought. If you got a medal you knew you'd earned it.

"Like the Olympics," he said. "Swing, waltz, fox trot, cha-cha, and tango. All the high stepper's catchy pentathlon."

Were they necking? *Necking?*

"Is everybody happy?" he asked softly. "I come from Fred Astaire. He looks forty-eight. All old movie stars look forty-eight." For some reason he was on the verge of tears. "Why," he wondered aloud, "were there never any black streakers?" The song was "I'll See You in My Dreams." He was winding down. Who was he, fucking Cinderella? Would he cry in front of them? Snap out of it.

"Hey," he said, "they found tuna fish on Mercury!"

It was "I Hadn't Anyone Till You."

"All right," he said, "I'll give it to you straight. I saw Fred Astaire one time at a franchise convention. He seemed embarrassed.

You want to know the truth? I don't dance, don't ask me, and the outings I was talking about, you know where we take you? To places where they rewrite the lyrics and do special material. You know? Like at summer camp. *That's* the gala. The band plays these show tunes and Al changes the lyrics to whatever's topical or institutional. The bronze medalists get their name in a song and we boost the outfit and ain't that something? Jesus.

"Listen," he said, "I have this Cadillac. I'm a dancer. I go north in it and west. I do all the directions and turn corners and stay in my lane and trace the cloverleaf and cross the bridges. Good God, am I a dancer! America's my ballroom. It's my eats, *listen* to me! Something's happening. I'll tell you a secret. This dancing. I think it may be evil. As comedy is evil. I don't think salvation has either a sense of humor or a sense of rhythm. Life is the conversion of the individual. God's piecework. A custom-tailor God, every attention paid to details, the slant of the pocket and come back Tuesday. I think I may be doing evil with my franchises."

"Hey, Mr. Flesh," Luis said.

"There may be something genuinely evil in the idea of an N.F.L. Maybe the Miami Dolphins is an evil concept, the Houston Astros, Burger King, the American League. Franchises like some screwy version of Manifest Destiny."

"Mr. Flesh."

He heard his name called and made Hope out in the queerly lighted room, Band-Aids of blue and purple, of yellow and red sliding across her face and bare arms as the revolving mirrored ball punched out refracted messages of spectrum. She was shaking her head.

"Yes, Hope," Flesh said. "I come from Fred Astaire. Everybody dance."

He turned from the microphone and placed another recording on the turntable, setting the volume high as he could.

*"The free dance lesson!"* he announced, roaring into the microphone and clapping his hands—the right hand had begun to tingle again—in time to the music. "Left foot *for*ward, right foot *back*. Basic left turn, right box *turn*. *Butter*fly, *ser*pentine, advance right *turn*. Lilt left fleckerl, quarter turn right. Left rock, right rock, chassé swing

step, three step cross. Pony trot and pony circle, Cinderella grapevine, fallaway grapevine, arch turn, breakaway, loop turn, she go,
he go, right spot *turn*. *Tuck*-in, *arch* turn, change of place with
right-hand *lead*. Right-hand loop, right-hand loop and change of
hands. *Push* spin, rhumb square, promenade, pivot; Cuban walk
and backward *rock*. Walk across basic, hinge and tuck-in, golf step,
airplane, promenade *twist*. Side basic, swivel basic, shoulder to
shoulder, and *tap* and point. Outside now and fan and corte, open
left turn with outside finish, gauche turn, corkscrew, strike and
samba. *Choo choo, choo choo, boto fogos*. Paddle turn, right turn,
merengue chassé. Wheel. Arch. Step time, mark time, march time;
promenade twist and wheel and cape. Right turn, left turn, left
change, right change—everybody *hold!*"

They were staring at him.

"Well," he said. "It's three o'clock in the morning," he said. He
was out of breath. "Good night, ladies, g'night, ladies, it's ti' t'say
g'night. Gala's over. Fred thanks you. Out. Beat it."

His guests moved off.

"Excuse me," a woman said.

"What?"

"Excuse me."

"What do you want?"

"You're standing on my shopping bag." Ben moved his foot. She
gathered her parcels and left.

Al and Jenny, Luis and Hope had disappeared.

Flesh sat on the edge of the stage, "Some stage," he said. "I can
touch the floor with my feet."

"I never heard anything like it. What the hell was that all
about?" It was Clara's voice. She must have been sitting in one of
the wallflower chairs. The room was lighted by the small colored
spots.

"It's like living in a jukebox," Flesh said. "A pinball machine. I
can't see a thing. Turn that crap off. Let's have some light." He
heard the rustle of Clara's gown, her hand flick a switch. They
were momentarily in complete darkness.

"That better?"

"Turn the lights on. Let's see the damage." The lights came on.

"Jesus," Flesh said. "After the ball is over. Oh boy. Look at my floor. It's like a giant pizza." There were crushed egg rolls, butterfly shrimp with their wings torn off, here and there barbecued ribs like tiny picket fences. Slabs of white turkey like the wood beneath bark. Rounds of roast beef floated in puddles of spilled Scotch, spilled bourbon.

"Al'll get it in the morning."

"Yeah. How'd we do?"

"Nobody signed up."

Flesh nodded. "Good."

"Good?"

"We can't accept any new applicants."

"Why?"

"Why. They're cutting down on federal aid to education. I don't want to lower our high standards."

"You shutting us down, Mr. Flesh?"

"Yeah, we're closing out of town. We ain't taking it to Broadway."

"Then what was that pitch all about?"

"In the morning I want you to call Nate Lace. He's at the Nittney-Lyon Hotel in Harrisburg, Pennsylvania."

"Who's Nate Lace?"

"No one. A liquidator. An old pal. When's the session over? When's graduation?"

"Chibka has two more private lessons. The group session goes another three weeks."

"Three weeks, yeah. Get Lace. I want him for Commencement speaker."

"Mr. Flesh?"

"Look at me in this suit. You ever see anything so ridiculous?"

"What's going to happen to us?"

"Yeah. Well, to tell you the truth, I think I can find a spot in the Follies for Luis, but you don't fit into the big picture. If you really love him, let the lug go."

"What are we going to do, Mr. Flesh?"

"We're going to liquidate. Fire sale. Everything must go. We're closing down the Carioca." She would be forty in maybe three years. Her figure was nice. He liked the long line of her legs, her flat chest and tough prettiness. "Listen," he said, "you know how lonely it's supposed to be at the top? Let me tell you, it's lots lonelier at the bottom. I don't know what you're going to do, Clara. I don't know what's going to happen to Al or to Jenny or to Hope or Luis. Is that *really* his name? Shit, sister, there are shopping centers in Niles, in Buffalo Grove, La Grange, Glencoe. Bring your taps. Teach ballet to six-year-old Jewish kids." She was crying. "Come on," he said. "Clara, don't. What are you doing? Hey. Stop." He moved closer to her, and not knowing what would happen he held his arms open to her. She came toward the middle-aged man. He held her unsteadily. "I come from Fred Astaire," he said softly, "everybody dance."

He tried to lead, and when he slipped from time to time on the puddings of scattered food or in the liquor, she caught him and held him up. He made a low hum in his throat as they danced. He liked the sound. He sang to her from his guttural hum. "I'm taking off my top hat, I'm taking off my topcoat, I'm taking off my tails."

"What was that stuff?" she asked. "That speech you made?"

"Who knows? My father's spirit's in this room. I feel it."

"Your father?"

"Yes. He'd be, what, seventy-five years old now. Hey, Daddy, you see how things change? This here's Clara."

"Hi, Mr. Flesh," Clara said.

"Did you see how they spilled things? Boy, I tell you," he said, "the *public*. Hey, Papa. You know something? I broke the law. I'm a possessor. I could be put in jail. Almost fifty fucking years old and I could be put in jail. I bet you never broke a law." He let Clara go. "I'm sorry, Papa." He was crying, shaken so hard by his sobs it was difficult for him to breathe. "I'm sorry you died in a crash," he sobbed, "I'm sorry to have taken Fred Astaire's name in vain, sorry my dancers live in a time when no one wants to learn the steps, sorry to God for a freedom which I helped shape by accepting all the credit cards—the Diners Club and Master Charge and BankAmericard and Carte Blanche and all the oil company things. Sorry for my rotten health of body and heart. Ah shit, Papa, it's a hell of a way to start a fiscal year."

"Are you all right?" Clara asked.

"No," he cried, "no. No. I'm not." He wiped his eyes and began again to dance with her. When he let her go he put his hand into the pocket of his tuxedo jacket. "Here," he said.

"What?"

"Your money. The two fives I took from you earlier."

"You gave that back to him."

"I did? Then what's this I'm holding?"

"What's what you're holding? Where?"

# III

W here has he seen these men? Their sport coats are the nubby textures and patterns of upholstery from credit furniture supplements in Sunday newspapers. They are crosshatched, double knits, drapery, checks like optical illusions, designs like aerial photographs of Kansas wheat fields, Pennsylvania pastureland, or the russets of erosion in western national parks. The pockets of their blazers are slashed, angled as bannister. Change would fall out of them, he thinks. The flaps are mock, shaped like the lower halves of badges. Their notched, pointed collars ride their shoulders like the conferral of wide, mysterious honors, the mantles of secret orders—and Flesh supposes they belong to these. He has never seen such shoes. Many are glossy white loafers, the color and sheen of wet teeth in ads. Gratuitous, useless buckles vault the white piping that rises from their shoes like welts. The jewelry and fixtures in the center of their false straps could be I.D. tags, or metal tablets, or slender sunken scutcheons. He sees no belts in the tight cuneiform-print trousers, in the plaids like colored grids, like cage, windowpanes, that climb their legs like ladders. The pants hold themselves up, self-supportive, a flap of fabric buttoned to a rim of itself like flesh sealed to flesh in operations. He marvels at their bump-toe shoes, their thick fillets of composition heels like shiny mignon or rosy cross sections of pressed geology. At their shirts like Christmas ties.

Where has he seen such men? Sitting beside him when he had ridden on airplanes, with their slim gun-metal attaché cases open on their laps like adult pencil boxes. (He has no attaché case, travels even lighter than they.) Huddling with maître d's behind the velvet ropes in restaurants. In convention at Miami Beach and San Diego in low season. With widows in the public rooms, restaurants, and oyster bars of good commercial hotels. With unmarried women a dozen years younger than themselves who chew gum. Yes. Yes. And always together, always in pairs or pairs of pairs, their flings a cooperation and conspiracy, their style a fever. (Though it wasn't "fling." They would have entire wardrobes of such clothes, their closets actually hazardous, flammable, with Fortrels, Dacrons, low-banked acetates, back-burnered polyesters, double knits.) And made brave, it could be, by the very resiliency of their clothing, the flexible permanent press that snapped back into place like rubber bands, that would not hold a wrinkle or keep a clue, as though they wore, these loud and husky men, garments blessed by gods, an invulnerability they perhaps took seriously, a vouchsafement of safety that made them louder, easily tripping their anger as galosh-shod boys might stomp in puddles. Not so he, Flesh, in his wools and silks and cottons, his earthy, dry-clean-only fibers, his easily trampled crops of clothes. Nor Lace the Liquidator, that creased and rumpled, raveled man.

Oh why, why, why do I mourn them? Why do they touch me so, wrapped in their crazy laundry? These Necchi men and Falstaff distributors, this pride of Pontiac dealers and Armstrong linoleum licensees? Am I not one of them? And if my kindling point is higher, what doth it avail a man to keep his cool if his eyes boil, for the truth is, I cannot look at them without something profound in my throat forcing the maudlin hydraulics of the heart. Maudlin and sober still. These are my Elks, my Vets of Foreign Wars, my Shriners and Knights of Columbus and Pythias, my Moose mobs and Masons of all degrees. Oh. Oh. Variety Club is the spice of life. They do good work: tool the cripple, and patiently teach the retarded their names, bus the underprivileged to the park and usually it doesn't rain. God's blessing on them. Mine. All praise to the raising of their hospitals, to their raffle good will. Just, damn it, make them careful where they drop their ashes or swing their cigarettes! One live ash on a single pant leg and we could all go up. It would be the Chicago fire in Columbus, Indy, Wichita—all the landlocked campuses and home offices. (Home offices, yes, those legislative capitals of our trades where we, patriots to machines, to goods and services, pilgrims to the refresher course, all those wee congresses of American style, where last year's figures and this one's plans and promos hang out, where we honor the founders and applaud the record beaters, inspired and instructed, seminar'd, on-the-job-trained in Hamburgerology, the new models, sign placement, the architecture of the access road, lapping it up, taking it in, community relations, how the Civil Rights Act of '68 has opened the way to the black dollar, which credit cards to honor, and all the rest. Business and Sociology, the first on our block to key the restroom, guard the fountain, cage the clerk. Inspired by their inspiration, enthused by their enthusiasm, standing when others stood and humming the bouncy anthems of our firms, tears in *my* eyes in the face of all this blessed, sacred, smarmy hope even if I know, as I do know, what I know. And loving it all anyway, my cellophane-window nameplate, the long capitals of my name and place of business.)

There was a Ford LTD mounted on a platform in the lobby, turning, stately and slow as a second hand, pristine, mint, and looking on its pedestal and under the cunning lights as no automobile ever looked in the streets. A museum piece, a first prize.

He went to the desk and registered. A Chase-Park Plaza bellman carried his bag and room key past the conventioneers still waiting to sign in.

He didn't go much any more, sending his proxies more often than not, those he hired to run his franchises for him.

It was spring and the prime interest rate was 2.93 percent. Though they were already into April, the sky was the color of nickels, loose change, and the temperature never higher than that of a mild winter in a plains state. Flesh still wore his long dark cashmere coat, a fedora pulled low, tight on his head, a scarf. That was why he had spotted him—he was not so famous then—sore thumb, high profile, visible in his white suit as a man falling from a building. It was not white *really*, not the stark white of letterhead, but richer, the white of faintly yellow piano keys, of imperfect teeth, old texts.

It was—this occurred to him—the "in person" white of presence, like limelight burning on a magician on a stage. He had never seen anyone so bright. And it *was*, once he recognized him, as if the man were on fire, his white hatless hair like whipped smoke.

He saw him from the back, knew him from the back. Ben rose from his bench in the park and followed him to a little play area where the statues of characters from *Alice in Wonderland* were grouped. He stood beside the statue of Alice and the Mad Hatter, and when a few who recognized the man approached him with their cameras, Ben politely deflected them. The man, unconscious of his bodyguard, gazed at the frigid figures, and Flesh, everywhere at once, held up a strategic hand, extended a black cashmered arm, waved his dark scarf, swung his fedora, ruining their shots.

"Isn't that—?"

"Shhh. Yes. Please," Flesh urged, "he's not to be disturbed."

"I'm not disturbing him. I just wanted—"

"I'm sorry," Flesh said, "I know. All you want is to take his picture but the man's superstitious. He believes you steal his substance when you photograph him."

"That's crazy," he said, "his pictures on all those—"

"Portraits. Oil paintings. You want to get your oils and brushes, okay, but no photographs."

"I never heard anything like—"

Then getting a little rough, shooing, pushing, shoving.

"Hey, this is a park. It's a free country. Who you shoving?"

"The camera," Flesh demanded.

"No."

"Go on, beat it. I tried to be nice." He put his hand in his overcoat. The man backed off.

"I'll be damned," he said, "if I ever buy another bucket—"

"Yeah, we've lost you to Steak 'n Shake. These things happen."

"But he's so pleasant on television."

"Look, fella," Ben said kindly, "he has a lot on his mind. Leave him be, why don't you?"

"I just wanted—"

"Sure," Flesh said. He patted the fellow on his back and sent him off, then walked around the circumference of the statue in order to study the man from the front. The face was benign as an angel's, with his mouth closed the white goatee and mustache like a kempt fat mushroom, the dangling strings of his black tie like a wishbone or a character in an Oriental alphabet. Flesh was surprised to see that the white suit coat was double-breasted, like a chef's. The eyes behind the horn-rimmed specs twinkled with vision. Flesh came up beside him. "Howdy," Ben said. The man glowered at him. "Howdy." Flesh moved closer. They were almost touching.

"Lord, the man hours that gun into that," the fellow said, nervously acknowledging him. "Look that Mad Hatter."

"Look that Alice," Flesh said. The man moved to another grouping. Flesh followed silently. "Look that Queen," he offered.

"Look that Mock Turtle," the white-suited man said wearily.

"Look that Cheshire Cat."

"Look that pigeon shit."

"Ben Flesh," Ben Flesh said, extending his hand.

"Colonel Sanders," the man said grudgingly.

Ben pushed his hand out farther. The man took it finally and Flesh grasped the chicken king's hand in both his own and pulled it toward his face. Before Colonel Sanders knew what was happening Flesh opened his jaws wide as he could and shoved as much of the man's hand inside his mouth as possible. He sucked the startled man's knuckles, ran his tongue along his lifeline, chewed his nails, the heel of his hand, tasted his pinky. The Colonel made a fist and fought for his hand, which Ben still held to his mouth.

"Lemme be. What's wrong with you?"

And Ben could not have told him, couldn't have said that he'd pulled his first stunt, an engram of character and aggression. He stood before the Colonel with the man's hand still at his lips. He was blushing. "Finger-lickin' good," Flesh said. "It's true. What they say. About Dixie," he added lamely.

The Colonel shook his hand about, drying it. He looked down at his suit, changed his mind. Flesh whipped out a handkerchief and waved it across the top of Colonel Sanders's hand like a shoeshine cloth. He whistled, snapping the handkerchief smartly one last time, and returned it to his pocket.

"I'll be damned," Colonel Sanders said. "You're a fool."

"Listen," Ben said, "I'm sorry. I don't know what made me . . ."

The Colonel looked at me curiously. Then seemed suddenly to relent. He was taller than I would have expected—six foot one, better. Taller than myself.

"My height?" the Colonel said.

"Sir?"

"My height. People like their avunculars stubbly little Santas. Eb Scrooge's old boss—what's his name—he was a shorty. All of 'em, squatty, florid little fellers. Only your father figure is supposed to be tall. Well, you know what my real significance is, Jack? It ain't the finger-lickin'-good routine. I mean to go down as the first avuncular in U.S. history to break the height barrier, bust six two. One day I'm comin' out the closet altogether entire, speak the King's English, iambic pentameter. That's what I'm *really* after. Oh, I ain't fixin' to put out the twinkle in my eye or extinguish the roses in my cheeks—just very manly, very deliberate and *distingué*. Stand up straight, unhunch my shoulders, give my backbone its head, let America see what's been hid from it too long—that a man can be lovable, turn out a good product, and *tall* all at the same time."

"I never realized," Ben told him, "what an idealist you are."

"Shucks," said the Colonel. "Schucks, pshaw, and . . ." He drew Ben toward him conspiratorially, looked both ways when they were nose to nose.

"—and?"

"—and pshit!"

They went to lunch at La Caravelle. "Unless you prefer Clos Normand," the Colonel had said.

"I've never been to either."

"*I* know. Le Perigord." Then changed his mind. "No, that's all the way east." Decisively. "Caravelle."

It was the largest of intimate rooms, and there was, for Flesh, the sense that, remove the tables and cloak room—he thought like this, the franchiser vision, his blueprint imagination—lift the rugs and install the proper equipment, and one would have a gentlemen's barber shop of the sort found in the basements of immense commercial travelers' hotels.

Ben Flesh examined the table linen while Colonel Sanders looked over the wine list and bantered with the *sommelier* in French. He lifted the bread basket—it was cunningly made bread, baked to look like slabs of wicker—and tore into the most delicious roll he had ever eaten. He offered the Colonel one but the man shook his head.

"Flours the palate," he said. "Tarts up the old wine cellar. Well, Ben," he said, "it's Ben, right?"

"Yes, sir."

"What you up to, Ben? Why you bothering me?"

"We're in the same line of work."

"We are, are we? Well, you sure don't dress for it. You dress like a lawyer or a cardiologist. You a lawyer or a cardiologist, Ben?"

"No, sir, I'm a franchiser."

"Franchiser, eh? What sort franchises you sell? What's your product?"

"I buy franchises."

Colonel Sanders looked at him suspiciously. "You're a damn liar, son. If you bought franchises you'd see the contract calls you the 'franchisee.' "

"That's always sounded like a cross between a Frenchman and Chinaman. I call myself a franchiser."

"An' you want to talk to me 'bout a Colonel Sanders— Well, that'll have to wait. I don't believe in business lunches. Here's the wine. They do a wonderful half liter of Château Pomme hereabouts. That all right with you? It's a '53 white. The red's better, of course, but it stains my beard."

The *sommelier* poured an inch of wine in the Colonel's glass. The chicken king rinsed, nodded judiciously, and the *sommelier* filled Ben's glass.

Sanders ordered for them both. Ben was to have *cassoulet*, the Colonel a cold *bouillabaisse* and some cold asparagus.

"How's your *cassoulet?*" he asked.

"It's wonderful. I never knew beans—these *are* beans?—could be so good."

The Colonel took a fork and poked around in the stewy mound on Flesh's plate. "Yes, sir, beans, pork sausage, and—son of a bitch!" he roared, "that's *duck!* Son, don't eat that. Where's that son bitch *garçon?* You see where that peckerhead got off to?" He shouted for the waiter.

Ben winced.

"Who you shamed for, skippy?" the Colonel demanded. "That's *duck* they give you. You squeamish for these people? Publishers, bud. Publishers, agents, editors, and starving writers. Expense accounts. Credit cards. Why, we the onliest folks in this restaurant showing them cash. Waiter!"

"Sir?"

The Colonel harpooned a piece of tanned flesh from Ben's plate. "*C'est le canard! Ce n'est pas l'oie! Cochon! Merde!*"

"It's delicious," Ben said.

"It's fuckin' *duck!*" Sanders roared. "It's s'posed to be *goose!*"

The waiter tried to take Ben's plate, but Ben held on. "I like duck actually," he said.

"Fah! Leave it be then. He *likes* duck. Let 'em eat duck. Boy," he said, when the waiter had gone, "you are surely a disappointment to me. Okay. Now we've had our scene, let's aid digestion with some good conversation. What's your pet peeve?"

He was still a young man, still in his early thirties. I was still innocent, my character, which is not shaped, as psychologists would have it, in the formative first five or six years or we are back to Calvinism, infant damnation, the loss of the will, but, as I truly believe, in the thirties and forties, still unformed but just beginning to happen, thicken, as chocolate pudding thickens, begins its first resisting circle in the stirrer's slowed spoon. So I was still a young man, not yet me, not yet myself.

"My pet peeve? I don't know. Deliberate cruelty, I guess."

" 'Deliberate cruelty,' " he said. "Forget the duck. My mistake. You bring your goose with you. You are goose *e*quipped. Deliberate cruelty. Your pet peeve is deliberate cruelty? Ben, if you're tellin' the truth you'd better do yourself some more window shopping or you've bought yourself an ulcer for sure. Deliberate cruelty, hell. What other kind is there? No, lad. No, son. Get something refreshing you don't have to rub shoulders with it in the street every day, it ain't there like wallpaper, the last thing you see when you turn the light off at night, the first thing you see in the morning. Now *I* got a pet peeve a man can be proud of. You say, 'What's that?' "

"What's that?"

"Well, it so happens I like baseball. Always have. Now we don't have no franchise in the South, not yet, even though some our best ballplayers come from down there. Oh, Louisville, where I live, we got us a good minor-league club, but you can't get very excited about a minor-league team you know there's a *major*-league team about. You follow me?"

"Minor-league baseball is your pet peeve."

"Shit. That ain't no pet peeve, that'd be a petty peeve. Hell no."

"That there are no major-league clubs in the Southland."

" 'The *Southland.*' Kid, you ain't even trying."

"I'm sorry."

"Well hell, what kind of half-ass pet peeve would it be if any Tom, Dick, or Harry could get it first off? It's okay. I'll tell you. In my line I travel a lot, get to places where the TV and radio pull in the big games. I mean the Yankees and Red Sox, the Cubs, Cincinnati, *Dee*troit and Philly, the Senators, Cards. Well, I mean now I've made a study and ever' one them broadcast busters they go crazy somebody fouls one off into the stands." He began to mimic the announcer. " 'Oh. There's a scramble among the fans. A kid's chasing. Hey, he's got it! Sign that youngster up. Well, there's a young lad who's going home with a souvenir he'll never forget.' If they'd just get through *one* game without they say something like that. That's *my* pet peeve. Who you envy?"

"Envy?"

"With me it's song writers. All their experiences. Whoosh. Good Lord, those fellers are always sittin' on top of the world or they down in the dumps below sea level. Sailors with girls in every port got the same opportunities. And the same apparatus. More maybe, but they cain't even hum, let along sing the poetry part. Dumb-ass tars."

"I hadn't thought of that."

Yes, lyricists and composers figured in his life, in his godblood.

"You want dessert? They do a lovely flan."

"I'm stuffed. I just want coffee."

The Colonel took a Bull Durham pouch from a pocket inside his jacket and, opening it, pulled out two Russian cigarettes and offered one to Ben. "Light the holler."

"They're strong."

"Shh," Colonel Sanders said. "Quieten down. Let's just set."

Over their coffee, through the thin smoke of their Sobranies, Flesh studied the man.

"Can't get over it, can you?"

"Get over—?"

"Me. My cheeks are thinner in person. The cartoon features? Air-brushed. My flush? Pancake powder. A character actor would spot it in a minute. 'Number five,' he'd say. Yes and you know my best feature, kid? My lap. We built everything up from that foundation. Oh, my footlight being, my proscenium presence. You shocked, sonny? No no, kid. Roosevelt never stood and Lenin and Trotsky turned a mustache and a beard into history. French barbers made the Commie revolution. Image. You got about as much image as a shoe salesman. You could buy up all the franchises in the world, but you ain't got the face for a billboard. Jesus, son, you haven't the face for nothing your own. You're growing dim. You're fading on me. Get into the disappearing-ink trade, that's *my* advice. What you up to? Why'd you come for me?"

"I was drawn," he said. "I am hypnotized by a trademark."

They stopped at the Colonel's suite in the Pierre. Flesh waited in the living room while Sanders changed.

"There, that's better," the chicken prince said coming out of his dressing room. "Had to get out of that damn suit. 'Nother ten minutes inside that thing I'd feel like a great big damn sideline, like I was rolled in lime." He had changed to a light-brown pin-stripe and there was a Windsor knot in his tie. "How you like that? How I look?"

"Fine," Ben said.

"Yeah. Want to walk up to the Frick, or we could do the Metropolitan? It's two years since I've seen the Rembrandts."

"I thought we might go up to Riverdale."

"That a sanatorium?" The Colonel laughed. "That's some sanatorium and you got kin there. Old folks with long bony fingers. You powerful attracted to the aged, a lad your years."

"No no," Ben said. "It's this residential section in the Bronx. You'll like it."

The twins and triplets were there. It was variously their Easter break, spring vacation, or Spring Clean-Up Week. Whether by accident or design, things had so worked out for the Finsberg stock that though they attended prep schools, colleges, universities, and graduate schools in different parts of the country, their vacations not only overlapped but actually meshed. It was as if Fieldston School, where all of them had attended high school and where Kitty and Sigmund-Rudolf were now seniors, was the Greenwich Mean Time of the academic year, its openings and ends of term and all holidays in between somehow a determinant chronometric pulse that radiated out to the two small liberal-arts colleges, three large state universities, and one important graduate school where the other twins and triplets were enrolled.

They looked more alike than ever. Audrey Hepburn's boyish cut in *Roman Holiday*, though now two or three years past its universal modishness, was still popular with and suitable to the girls, and something in the genes of the boys—men now, some of them—had permanently waved their fine black hair so that it lay on their heads like loose bathing caps or visible turbulence. And, relaxed in sneakers and jeans on their holidays, in their white shirts loose over their trousers, the tall, rather powerfully built though flat-chested girls and young women were strikingly like their slim, somewhat stunted brothers. Also, they were of an age, seventeen the youngest, twenty-three the oldest, where all had reached their full height—five foot, ten inches. The girls' low rich voices were identical in pitch to the slightly highish timbre of the young men's.

"I'd like you to meet my godcousins," Ben said to the Colonel. "Lotte, Ethel, and Mary; Patty, LaVerne, and Maxene; Gertrude,

Kitty, and Helen, say hello. This is Cole, Oscar, Sigmund-Rudolf, Jerome, Lorenz, Noël, Irving, Gus-Ira, and Moss."

"Jesus," Colonel Sanders said.

"Gosh, Ben," said Gus-Ira, "except for the suit, he looks just like Colonel Sanders."

"He *is* Colonel Sanders," Ben said.

"Is this a show?" the Colonel asked. "What are they?"

"They're my guarantors, Colonel. They help with my businesses."

"Are we going to have chicken from the Colonel, Ben?" young Sigmund-Rudolf asked.

"Are we, Ben?" chimed in Ethel, Cole, Noël, and LaVerne.

Sanders was a little nervous. "Hey," he said, "hold up. You ain't spuk to my people. You just don't go up to the Colonel his own self and get you a franchise. There's channels. How I know Riverdale is zoned for chicken?"

"Jeepers," said Jerome, "were you thinking of putting it up in *Riverdale*, Ben? That's a *swell* idea. The closest carry-out place is Fordham Road."

"And that's just chinks," Patty said.

"They're cold before you get them home," Irving said angrily.

"Cold chinks. Yech," Kitty said.

"Yech," they all said, for they had identical tastebuds.

"Hold on," Colonel Sanders objected.

"You know what I'm wondering?" Helen said.

"What's that, Helen?" Ben asked. He knew them all, had never since he'd first met them and learned their names at their father's funeral years before confused them. Not even Estelle, now a troubled woman of close to fifty, could keep them straight, but Ben knew, had always known, because he went instinctively beyond externals, penetrating even the subtle externals of twin and triplet character to something marked in them, as certain of their differences as a geologist of landscape, of fault, strata, and where the ice age stopped, hunching the mineral deposits, informed-guessing at the ores and oil fields, water-witching what was—forget age, forget sex, forget names even—the single distinctions, one from another, that they bore—their infirmities, their mortalities, distinct to him and strident as the graffiti of factions.

Each had told him—and he'd never forgotten; something perhaps in the pitch of the confession—his, her peculiar symptom. The Finsbergs, for all their money and education and charm, for all the chic victory of their urban good looks, for all their style and chipper well-heeled spirits, their flush wardrobes and Parisian French, their skill on skis, and their slope bright wools sharp as flares, for all their American blessings, were freaks, and carried in their bloodstreams and pee, in their saliva and fundament and the tracings of their flesh, all the freak's ruined genetics, his terrible telegony and dark diathetics. It was Julius, set in his ways, throwing himself like an ocean into Estelle's coves and kyles, till all that was left of his genes and chromosomes was the sheath, the thread of self like disappearing cheshire garments resolved at last to their stitching. Obsessive, worn-out, he had made hemophiliacs of the self-contained and self-centered. Julius's progeny—that queer wall of solidarity and appearance, that franchise of flesh—were husks, the chalices in which poisoners chucked their drops and powders.

"Pick me up," little Gertrude had said to him when she was only eleven, "try to lift me."

"Why? What for?"

"I bet you can't," she said.

"Of course I can."

"Then prove it. Try to pick me up."

He moved behind her, put his arms around her slender waist, and strained backward. He couldn't budge her. Gertrude laughed. "Come on, it's a trick," he said. "What is it?"

"It isn't a trick. Go on, you get another turn."

"It's a trick. Well . . . Okay." He stood in front of her, bent down suddenly, and wrapped his arms tightly just under her buttocks and clasped her to him. Using all his strength, he managed to raise her one inch above the floor. He held her up for no more than two seconds and then dropped her. She dragged him down with her as she fell.

"It's a trick. What is it?" He was short of breath.

"I haven't any bone marrow," Gertrude said. "My bones are all filled with this like iron."

"What are you talking about?"

"I can't be X-rayed," she said. "My bones show up as dark tools, like carpenters' things and plumbers'."

And LaVerne's organs lined the side of her body, her liver and lungs and kidneys outside her rib cage. Ethel's heart was in her right breast. Cole had a tendency to suffer from the same disorders as plants and had a premonition that he would be killed by Dutch elm blight. Mary could not menstruate and Gus-Ira was a nail biter allergic to his own parings. When he bit them he broke out in a terrible brocade of rash. Lorenz's temperature was a constant 102.5, and Patty, who had perfect pitch, could not hear loud noises. Kitty would still be a bed wetter at thirty and Lotte, the one he'd kissed years before beside the bus, enjoyed perfect health until her twenties, when she began to come down with all the childhood diseases—measles, whooping cough, chicken pox, adenoids, and colic. Noël had cradle cap. Helen was a mean drunk.

"I'm racially prejudiced," Irving, one of the sweetest of the family, told him.

"You, Irving? Racially prejudiced? You're one of the most reasonable people I know."

"I'm racially prejudiced. It's like a disease."

"All of us have a little prejudice. I guess we fear what we don't understand. We roll our windows up when we drive through Harlem. We lock our doors."

"I'm racially prejudiced," Irving said calmly. "I hate the niggers. I hate the way they smell. I can't stand the moons on their fingernails. I want to gag when I see their woolly hair. Their purple blubber-lips make my skin crawl. They're lazy and drunk and want our women. The bucks have dicks as big as the Ritz and the women swell our welfare rolls. I'm racially prejudiced. I wish genocide were legal. I think we should drop A-bombs on their storefront churches and fire their barbecue stands. I'm racially prejudiced. It's a disease."

And Maxene's hair had begun to thin when she reached puberty—she wore wigs cunningly woven from her brothers' clippings and trims—and Moss's beautiful eyes could not see certain kinds of metal. And one of the boys, Oscar, had things wrong with him in the gray social areas of illness. He was at once an alcoholic and a compulsive speeder.

Jerome was chronically constipated.

"I don't move my bowels more than twice a month. Two dozen times a year."

"What does the doctor say?"

"The doctors don't understand. They give me enemas. I'm not compacted. The stools are normal. My breath is sweet. The tongue's a good color. They think it's something to do with metabolism, that my body doesn't create as much fecal matter as other people's do. It's something to do with the metabolism."

It was something to do with the metabolism with all of them, some queer short circuit in the glands and blood, the odd death duties of the freak. Human lemons, Detroit could recall them. Like, he thought, giants' and giantesses' niggardly life spans, fat men's, as if there were a strange democracy of displacement in nature, that if you took up more room than others you could have it less long. And though he never mistook one twin for another, never confused a triplet, had perfect pitch for their shell-game life, knowing at all times which pea was under what shell, he never forgot that they were freaks. They were almost all the family he had, as he, in an odd way, was almost all the family *they* had, and though he loved them they frightened him, troubled him with their niggered woodpiled chemistry.

"What I'm wondering," Helen said, "is . . ."

"I know," Lorenz said.

"We do too," said Cole and Kitty.

"Whether we get to find out the secret recipe," Gus-Ira said quietly.

The Colonel stared at them. "I don't know what this is," he said, "but it's fishy. Now if they's one thing a fried-chicken guy like me can't stand it's something fishy. I 'us studying on the scupture in the Central Park and this feller"—he pointed to Ben—"come up and started fussin' me. I thought I'd be nice, do like we do down home. Next I know we in some taxi car driving thoo all New York

City, people everwhere, tall buildins, projects, folks in skull caps, over bridges and past the whole rickety racket of this Lord forlorn squashed-together mess. Then we turn a corner and—whoosh—we in the open, we in country. Green lawns, trees, gret big ol' houses, and I think to myself, Why it's like—what do you call it—*Brigadoon*, as if . . ."

Patty, LaVerne, and Maxene started to sniffle. Instantly the others took it up. The Colonel looked at Ben, but he was as confused as Colonel Sanders. The sound was alarming. It was as if they stood together in the flu ward of a hospital. Then the sniffles became sobs, wails, a declension of grief.

"Hey," Colonel Sanders said, "what's wrong with you fellers? What's that caterwauling? You boys fairies?"

"Tell him, Ben," Ethel blubbered.

"Ben doesn't know," Noël grieved.

"He doesn't, he doesn't," the rest moaned. They wrung their hands.

"What is it?" Ben asked.

"It's fishy," Colonel Sanders said.

Gradually the crying subsided. Oscar pulled himself together. "He reminded us."

"Reminded you?"

"Mother gave birth one last time," Lotte said.

"In '47," said Helen.

"March it was," Sigmund-Rudolf said.

"Opening night."

*"Brigadoon."*

"Mother was *so* excited."

"We all were," Kitty said. "Sigmund-Rudolf and I couldn't have been more than six or seven at the time, but we all were."

"We were," said Moss, Gertrude, and Jerome.

"We were backstage."

"Mom was in her seventh month."

"She went into labor."

"It was the excitement."

"Father told her to be careful."

"It was only her seventh month."

"He didn't want to take any chances."

"But a *musical!*"

"You couldn't keep Mother away from a *musical.*"

"She'd been a dancer."

"There was hoofer in her blood."

"She said it was certain there'd be a doctor in the house."

"Something's fishy."

"We got swaddling cloths from Wardrobe."

"Plaid."

" 'Make sure there's plenty,' Father told the wardrobe mistress, 'it's sure to be triplets.' "

"We all thought so."

"She'd never been bigger."

"It was a boy."

"Just one."

"He passed during 'Almost Like Being in Love.' "

Gus-Ira recited the lyrics. " '. . . For I'm all aglow and alive,' " he finished melancholically.

"The *i*rony," said Cole softly.

"It stopped the show," Mary said.

"And baby brother," said Gertrude and Kitty.

"Fritz–Alan Jay," Lotte said.

The twins and triplets sighed.

"That's when Pop first started to take an interest in you."

Ben Flesh shuddered. He recalled the moment he had taken the Colonel's hand in his mouth. It was strange. He didn't understand it, but he knew he had just changed in some obscure, important way. He hadn't known about Fritz–Alan Jay, hadn't realized till they'd just now casually mentioned it the nature of his surrogacy, its true measure. Why, I'm not their godcousin at all. Despite the difference in our ages, that I've turned thirty and almost half of them are still in their teens, I have been their baby godbrother, dead in infancy, alive for those few minutes only between the solo that stopped the show and the hawking of the orange drink in the outer lobby. The idea altered him. He felt emboldened. He turned from the kids and addressed the Colonel. "*Is* there?"

"What's that?"

"*Is* there a secret recipe?"

"The secret recipe's a secret," the Colonel bristled. "I see what you-all up to now. You taken me out here to divulge my ingredients. Never, sir. Never."

"I'll have a bucket analyzed."

"Haw."

"I can do that. I don't even need a bucket. A breast will do. I'll have the white meat analyzed and the dark will come right along with it."

"It's patented. You'd have to own one my franchises to sell my chicken. I'd sue your wings off you you sold chicken to go to come to taste within a country mile like mine. I'd enjoin your gizzard and injunct your drumsticks."

"Haw!"

"Don't argue, Ben," Mary said. "If you want the franchise we'll get it for you. Won't we, brothers, won't we, sisters?"

"Aye," they said.

"Haw!" Ben said. He roared it at them, at gravid Gertrude, rooted by weight; at Kitty the bed-wetter; at xenophobic Irving, whose hatred boiled his spittle; at LaVerne, who stepped absentmindedly into her lungs, putting on her organs like a drunk getting into a girdle in a routine; at Gus-Ira, who broke out when he bit off a hangnail; and Ethel, who wore her heart in her brassiere, and at all the rest of that wormy diked, Maginot geneticized, clay-foot crew—their father's theatrical costumes made flesh, a wardrobe of beings, appearance shining on *them* like spotlight.

"What's wrong, Ben? Are you upset?"

"Haw!"

"We'll co-sign."

"Don't fret, Ben."

"*Haw!*"

"We'll be responsible."

"When *I* say," Ben said.

"What, Ben?"

"When *I* say. When *I* say the prime rate is prime, when *I* say the interest is interesting, when *I* say."

"Haw," their guest said. "Haw."

Ben looked at him. The man had removed his glasses. He touched a corner of his mustache like a villain in melodrama and, as they all watched, began to peel it back from his face like a Band-Aid of hair.

"What?" Ben said. "What's this?"

"I ain't him," the man said. "Haw! Haw and hee hee!"

"But—"

"I ain't him. I'm not he. I'm Roger Foster of Cedar Rapids, Iowa, and I own airport limousine services in three states."

"You're not the chicken prince?"

"I'm Roger Foster of Cedar Rapids, Iowa," Roger Foster said.

"Then what— But why— You look—"

"Certainly. I *look*. There's a basic resemblance. I enhance it. I'm a Doppelgänger. Just like these guys." He indicated the twins and triplets.

"Does this mean you can't get the franchise, Ben?" Gus-Ira said.

"When I say," Ben said weakly.

"The mustache was too much trouble to trim," Mr. Foster said. "Frankly, I don't see how *he* does it. The goatee is real. The basic resemblance was there. All I had to do was get the eyeglasses, grow the beard, and work something out with the mustache. The rest—I told you in the restaurant. 'A character actor would spot it in a minute.'"

"But why?"

"But why. Are you any different? Are you any different with your borrowed businesses? So I put the Kentucky Fried Chicken suit on once in a while. What the hell? It's fun. Mistaken identity is a barrel of laughs, kid. *You* saw. The folks in the park. The tourists wanted to take my picture. I was a sight for sore eyes. As all celebrity is. I enhance the resemblance. I enhance my life. I enhance everybody's life. Where's the harm in a Doppelgänger just so long as he's a nice man?" Roger Foster asked.

"A Doppelgänger," Ben said.

"Sho. Sure. But you— You're something else. You're a Doppel*gäng*ster. You're a Doppel*gäng*ster with your franchises and your big Doppelgängster Ring in Riverdale."

"No," Ben said. "What I do—"

"What *you* do. It's a U.S.A. nightclub performance. You do John Wayne and Ed Sullivan. You do Cagney and Bogart. Liberace you do. Sinatra, Vaughn Monroe. Tell me something. Which is the *real* Howard Johnson's? Which is the *real* Holiday Inn or Chicken from the Colonel?"

It was the late summer of 1960. The prime rate on four-to-six-month paper was 3.85 percent.

He stood looking down on the crowd below from the big revolving bucket reared back from true like a chariot overturning or spinning like a ride in an amusement park. From his vantage point—from theirs, only his shoulders, neck, and head visible, he must have seemed a gravedigger, a man immobilized in a torture barrel, someone locked in quicksand, a living bust of a man, something, to judge from their hoots and catcalls, that evoked reprisal, scorn, some Salem quality of the publicly shamed—he could see out over the shopping center to the welted lines of parked cars in the big lot like the hashmarks of giant fishbones. He saw the low flat roofs of shoestores, jewelers, men's shops, dress shops, bakeries, a Western Auto, a cafeteria, a Woolworth's, record shops and greeting card, a pharmacy, a Kroger's, an optometrist's, the immense decks of discount stores, each tar or asphalt roof pocked with vents and utility hatches, studded as domino. He called for his manager to turn off the sign, but the angle was difficult, leaving him, when it stopped, uphill of his audience.

"Hey, Sigmund-Rudolf," he called, "swing me around. Another 180 degrees should do it."

Sigmund-Rudolf was to manage the place during his summer vacation. He had practiced stopping the sign on a dime. His error was deliberate, just high spirits. (Ben didn't mind, was glad Sigmund-Rudolf found it in his heart to be playful, for Sigmund-Rudolf's disease, his bad seed, was perhaps the most humiliating. He had been saddled not with homosexuality—at nineteen he was one of the more virile boys and had as hearty a heterosexual appetite as any Finsberg—but with the *symptoms* of effeminacy; its starchless wrists and mincing tiptoe, its Cockney lisps, and something in the muscles of his face which widened his eyes and rolled them up to mock rue and exaggerated his frowns and put lemons in his lips—all the citrics of plangent faggotry, his lack of physical control programmed: the sissy coordinates of his every gesture, his muscles hamstrung with epicenity, girlishness, like a cripple of vaudevillized femininity or an unevenly strung marionette.)

The boy swung the sign around to where Ben wanted it. Now he was canted toward the crowd like a man about to be spilled from a cannon. He grasped the rim of the bucket for support—he would look like Kilroy, he thought—and began his address.

"My fellow New Yorkers," he said. "There was once a countryman who had a place back in the hills with his wife and small babe. One day a neighbor who lived miles off where the trail from the county road left off at the beginning of the big woods came to him with a letter addressed to the countryman in care of the neighbor that the neighbor said had been left with him the day before. There was a notation on the envelope that read 'Please Forward,' but it was the neighbor's impression that the postmaster had written both the 'in care of' and the notation to forward as well as the neighbor's name, for if the countryman looked he would see that his name, the countryman's, and *his* name, the neighbor's, had been written in two different hands, and that it was a known fact that the postmaster was a shirker. Then he explained that his, the neighbor's, wife had been poorly and could not be left alone and so he, the neighbor, had had to wait until a day when his young 'uns would be home from school before he could bring the letter that had been left in his charge. This was a Saturday and he had left as early as he could.

" 'I'm sorry your wife is poorly,' the countryman said, 'and I thank you for the trouble you took to bring me my message, for I know that the spot where the trail from the county road leaves off at the start of the big woods is a long way to my place back in the hills where I live with my wife and small babe.'

" 'You we'come,' the neighbor said and the countryman invited the neighbor to set a spell while his woman made some lemonade for the neighbor to drink after his hot and dusty trip. 'Thank you kindly,' his neighbor said, 'for the truth is, I am sorely parched.'

" 'You we'come,' the countryman said and told his wife to bring the lemonade. Then they both, the countryman and the neighbor, sat down on the porch swing. The neighbor could see that the countryman was a mite uneasy, though he tried to hide it by carefully matching his push on the swing with his own, the neighbor's, push.

" 'Excuse me,' the neighbor said, 'I misremembered myself and have plumb forgot to give you the letter.'

" 'Oh, that's all right,' the countryman said, but from the relief on his, the countryman's, face, he, the neighbor, could see that it, the letter, had in fact been on his, the countryman's, mind.

"The neighbor excused himself and asked if he could go on back to the outhouse as he had 'business.'

" 'Surely you may,' the countryman said.

" 'Thank you kindly.'

" 'You we'come.'

"Now the neighbor had no 'business,' having done it, his business, in the big woods after starting out with the letter for his, the neighbor's, neighbor, the countryman. All he wanted was to give the countryman time to read it, the letter, and when he figured that he had had enough, time, to read the letter, it, he, the neighbor, came back outside and returned to where he had left him, the countryman, sitting, on the porch, the porch.

"Now when he returned, what was his surprise to see that there were tears in his eyes. He didn't want to ask him about it and he knew it so he told him.

" 'From my brother.'

" 'Oh?'

" 'He says Paw is dying. I must be off. Enjoy your lemonade.' He kissed his wife and small babe and solemnly shook his neighbor's hand, but the neighbor, feeling he had badly served his neighbor the countryman by delaying the twenty-four hours before he brought the letter, and fearing, too, that it might already be too late and wishing to make amends, rose and offered to go back with him and take him to the city where he knew the countryman's father lived and was now dying or already dead.

" 'Take me? How you fixin' to do that?'

" 'In my pickup.'

" 'You got a pickup?'

" 'I live where the trail from the start of the big woods leaves off at the start of the county road. I do.'

" 'Thank you.'

" 'You we'come.'

"And he was good as his word, that he had a pickup and that he would drive them, himself, the neighbor, and the countryman, to the city, where his, the countryman's, Paw was dying or already dead.

"They drove all day and all night and the morning of the next day and the miles flew by and they were already close to the city where his, etc., etc., was dying or already dead, when the pickup sputtered and steamed and gave out.

"The countryman was heartbroken. 'I am sure sorely sorry,' he said. 'I would not have had that to happen for anything. Why to think,' he, the countryman, said, 'and all you wanted was to he'p a neighbor, me, a countryman, up to his eyes in it, shit, trouble, and your pickup is all busted and won't never to run again and lick up the miles like they 'us on'y just steps. I am sorely sorry and when this is all over I will save and save till I get enough, money, to buy you another one, a pickup. And now I must be on my way to my Paw's sick side. Thank you.' And he was already out his side of the pickup before he, the neighbor, could properly say, 'You we'come.'

" 'Ho'd up,' he called, 'ho'd up.'

"The countryman looked back and, seeing it was his neighbor calling, stopped in his tracks in the road.

" 'What?'

" 'It ain't busted,' he said.

" 'It ain't?'

" 'I to'd you.'

" 'Why don't it to go then?'

" ' 'Cause we worked her too hard. The radiator boiled over. All we need is to get us some water and pour it in the radiator and she'll go again good as new.'

"There was a stream close by the road and the neighbor, who kept a five-gallon gas can in the back of his pickup for just such emergencies, took the can and filled it at the stream and carried it back and poured its contents into the radiator and, after waiting a few more minutes for the engine to cool, started the pickup smooth as anything and they were on their, the neighbor's and the countryman's, way again as if nothing, the pickup sputtering and steaming and giving out, had ever happened. But the neighbor noticed that there was an odd expression on the countryman's face. It was a troubled expression, but not the same sort of troubled expression he had seen when he had first returned from the outhouse where he had gone to pretend to do a business he had already done in the big woods on the way to his, the countryman's, place back in the hills, in order to give him time to read the letter he, the neighbor of the countryman, had brought him, the neighbor of the neighbor. A naturally polite man, he did not want to trouble this already troubled man with his curiosity but he must have seen this because he too was a polite man and knew that that was on his mind and he decided finally to introduce the subject as much for his satisfaction as for his.

" 'If,' he said, 'a wheel was to bust, what would to happen then?'

" 'If a wheel was to bust? Why, I'd just get a new wheel and stick 'er on.'

"The countryman nodded.

" 'What about if that thing you poured that 'ere water in from that stream was to crack and couldn't to hold no water—what then?'

" 'The radiator?'

" 'That what you call 'er?'

" 'The radiator, yes, sir.'

" 'What would to happen?'

" 'Well then, I guess I'd have to have them solder the crack or have them to put in a new radiator.'

" 'Them?'

" 'The mechanics.'

" 'I see. Thank you.'

" 'You we'come.'

" 'Suppose the engine itself?'

" 'Same thing.'

" 'The mechanics?'

" 'Yep.'

"The countryman nodded.

" 'And the same,' the neighbor said, 'if it was pistons or rods or a transmission or a carburetor or if the battery was to die.'

" 'The mechanics.'

" 'Sho.'

"The countryman paused for a moment, then turned in his seat to face the neighbor. 'Where,' he asked, 'do them mechanics get all that 'ere machinery?'

" 'Spar parts,' the neighbor said.

" 'Spar parts?'

" 'Sho. You got you a intricate, complicated thing like a pickup, you got to be sure you can get your spar parts if somethin' should to go wrong and she should need replacin'. They's whole entire catalogues of spar parts. Not just for this pickup but for ever entire one we done passed or done passed us on the way to the city here, and not just for pickups but for sedans and coupes, too, and for convertibles and delivery trucks and the big rigs highballin' it down the turnpikes and byways. For motorcycles and bicycles and everthin' that moves.'

" 'I'll be,' the countryman said, 'I'll be.'

" 'Sho,' his neighbor said.

"Well, they continued on into the city, and when they came to where the countryman's brother lived and were told by his wife, the countryman's sister-in-law, which hospital her father-in-law, her husband's and brother-in-law's Paw, was at, they went there at once.

" 'You go on in,' the neighbor said. 'I'll find me a spot in the lot.'

" 'The lot?'

" 'The parking lot. They's plenty sick folks in yonder hospital and they all have kin want to visit with 'em and cheer 'em up or'—and here he looked down, averting his eyes from the countryman—'if it's too late for that—to say goodbye.' The neighbor looked up to see how the countryman had taken this last part, but instead of the sorrow he had expected to see on the guy's puss, what was his, the neighbor's, surprise to see not sorrow but a curiosity so sharply defined it might have been language.

" 'Go on,' the countryman said, 'about the parking lot.'

" 'Well,' the neighbor said, 'they's nothing to go on *about*. The hospital knows that sick folks' kin want to come visit and have to have a place to park so they put up parking lots. That's all they is to it.'

" 'They charge money?'

" 'They do.'

" 'The mechanics with the spar parts, they charge money, too?'

" 'Course they charge money. Sho they do. You born yesterday, or what?' he asked with some impatience.

" 'Seems like,' the countryman said. 'Seems like an' that's a fac'.' The neighbor looked at the countryman, who now seemed preoccupied. 'Well,' the countryman said abruptly, bringing himself back from wherever it was he had been woolgathering. 'You go on and park in the parking lot while I straightway attend to my bidness.' The neighbor let the countryman out of the pickup and drove off. When he returned, what was his surprise to see the countryman still standing where he had left him. If it were not for the fact that he now held a small white paper bag that he had not had before, he would have sworn that the countryman had not moved a muscle.

" 'It's 'leven fifty-two,' the countryman said.

" 'No,' the neighbor said, 'cain't be. I heard the noon lunch whistle when we was still back in the pickup waitin' on the engine to cool.'

" 'No,' the countryman said, 'not *that* 'leven fifty-two. Where Paw's at.'

" 'Oh.'

" 'When you druv off to the parking lot I got to studyin' on how we 'us gone to find my Paw in a gret big ol' hospital like this 'un. I seen the winders. Take a full *day* to hunt in ever room, and s'pose he already dead an' they fixin' to bury 'im an' there I 'us stumblin' roun' huntin' 'im down in his room like some ol' coon with a bad cold. What I do then, his ol'es' boy an' not even on time for his buryin'. And even if he still alive, ther I be bargin' in 'mongst all them sick folks, goin' roun' to wher they sleepin', all scrunched down in they beds, the sheets up over they heads an' shiv'rin' from they chills an' fevers an' me aksin', "You my paw, mister? It's me, you Paw?" '

" 'Well, that's not the—'

" 'That's not the way they do it,' the countryman said. 'I remembered all you to'd me 'bout the spar parts and the parking lots and all them kin drops by to tell goodbye to all them sick folks an' I thunk, Why they mus' be some place right chere on the fust floor right wher you fust come in wher they keep the names and rooms wher them sick folks is. And I'll be swacked if it weren't jus' the way I s'posed. I go in and right way ther's this nice lady in a uniform settin' at a table an' she aks me whut do I want.

" 'How much you charge to tell me wher my paw is dying?' I aks and I start to give her my name an' stop, thinkin', *No*, that's not the way they do it, they'd use his name 'cause he's the one dyin' an' I give her my paw's name an' she smiles an' looks him up in what she to'd me later was a d'rectory an' ther it is—'leven fifty-two.'

" 'How much she charge?' the neighbor asked.

" 'Well, that's the bes' part. She don't charge nothin'. That part's free.'

" 'I be,' he, the neighbor, said.

" 'Aks me 'bout this chere paper bag I'm ho'din'.'

" 'I 'us goin' to.'

" 'It's little chocolates. For Paw. Paw likes chocolates.'

" 'Chocolates.'

" 'I got to studyin' whut you said 'bout all them kinfolks—'

" 'You to'd me that part.'

" 'I to'd you the part 'bout you sayin' how they come to tell they sick folks goodbye. I ain't to'd you nothin' 'bout how I remembered the part where you said they come to cheer 'em up.'

" 'Oh.'

" 'And I studied on *that* part and I got the idea that they mus' be some place right close by that they'd call it somethin' all cheery like the Wishing Well wher kin could get some baubles fur their sick folks, an' I aks the lady an' she points it right out an' it ain't but thutty foot from wher I'm standin' an' she says, "Oh, that would be the Wishing Well," an' I went to it and they had everthin' you could want—toys and little ol' lacy nighties an' comical books an' chewin' gum an' the very same chocolates that my paw so dearly loves. Hershey Kisses they call 'em.'

"And with that the countryman tells the neighbor that it was time he went up to see his father and asks him, the neighbor, to come along, he's come this far. The neighbor agrees and starts toward the stairway, but the countryman calls him back, telling him that if it's a building where they put sick folks, then it would have to have an elevator or how would folks sick as his paw get up eleven stories and they would ride where the sick folks ride and it would have to be close by and if there was a charge why he, the countryman, would pay for them both since he, the neighbor, had been so nice already.

"They found the elevator and rode to the eleventh floor and the countryman asked the colored girl who ran the elevator what it would cost them and she said it was free and he, the countryman and his friend, the neighbor, got off without a word, their faces solemn as they could make them. When the elevator doors closed behind them, the countryman hooted in wild laughter and the neighbor, seeing the joke at once, joined in.

" 'Fool nigger,' the countryman said, laughing so hard his nose began to run, 'she thinks you're *sick*.'

" 'She thinks *you* sick, you mean. You the one aks her how much she charge.'

" ' 'Cause I 'us makin' out you too sick to talk for your own self.'

"Well, they giggled on this for a while and at last a nurse came up to them and asked if she could help them.

" 'We's Paw's kinfolks,' the countryman said, recovering himself, 'come to see sick folks in 'leven and fifty-two.'

" 'This way, please,' the nurse said, and she led them to the room where his, the countryman's, father lay, not dying as it, the letter, had said, but sitting up in bed watching afternoon game shows on TV and laughing every time folks in New York or out on the coast answered the question wrong and lost their money.

" 'Dumb Eastern and Coastern fucks,' the old man roared and laughed fit to bust. 'Look that Eastern fuck, give the Captain the wrong answer and he just lost his car.'

" 'I brung chocolates, Paw,' the countryman said.

" 'Thanks, son, they's my favorites. Don't never be like them Eastern and Coastern fucks, don't never gamble.'

" 'I won't, Paw,' the countryman said.

" 'Saw a man this mornin', Coastern fuck he was, dumber 'n dog shit, an' he lost his dream house 'cause he didn't know which curtain it 'us standin' behind. His own house, an' thet dumb Coastern fuck couldn't remembers its *address!* Got all confused an' all he could remember was where he'd left his pig. Don't never gamble, son. You neither, neighbor. Special when you don't stand to gain nothin' by it. Have a chocolate.'

" 'Thanks, Paw. The letter said you 'us dyin'. You don't seem like you dyin'.'

" '*Ain't* dyin',' his father said.

" 'You ain't?'

" 'Naw. They run some tests. Figured what I got.'

" 'Yes?'

" 'Well, once they could name its name, there was a medicine for it that could fix it.'

" 'Can I aks you sumfin'?' his boy, the countryman, said after a while.

" 'Sho,' his father said. 'Shoot.'

" 'This here medicine—they charge money for it?'

" 'Fool! Course they do.'

" 'That's jus' what I thought,' his visitor's neighbor's neighbor, his son, the countryman, said."

Ben Flesh paused. They were staring up at him.

"*Because*," he said, "distance demands its road, the bowel its vessel, the disease its medicament. It is the lesson learned by the countryman the day he thought his paw would die. I have not mentioned it, but even after he saw his father on the mend, this *too* went through his mind: 'He's got a body. If it dies it will have to be boxed, have to be buried. *They ain't through with us even after we quit of them.* And it was as if he, a countryman, a farmer, a dealer in earth all his working life, thought about it—earth—for the first time. It was as if, my friends, he had discovered the uses of real estate. He had learned the secret of being—*that existence has its spare parts, that the successful life is only a proper knowledge of accessory!*

"I am Benny in the Bucket, the spirit of Bernie Baruch upon me. *Baruch. Atoh. Adonai.* Bless this enterprise, oh, Lord. *Bahless* it.

Give us a *bahreak!* Whet appetites left and right, visit cravings on the pregnant for carry-out chicken, impress upon Mums giving birthday parties the advantages of convenience foods and inscribe everywhere upon the universal palate a taste for the Colonel's white meat and dark, hanging it there like wallpaper or a fixed idea; tangle its aromatics with the hairs of the nose and make consumers to go in the streets with fried skin chewy as gum in their mouths and licking on bones as on all-day suckers. Doggy my Americans, Pop, foxify them for me and the Colonel." And looked up.

"Well, folks, I felt I couldn't ask my manager, Sigmund-Rudolf Finsberg there, to open our doors for business without first making a few remarks appropriate to the occasion. Now I know you're getting hungry, I know you're anxious to get in there and find out for yourselves what all the fuss is about, why I and my colleagues have gone to such pains to bring Kentucky Fried Chicken to Yonkers— 'Meals the Whole Family Will Enjoy at Prices Every Family Can Afford.' And in a few moments I'll be giving Mr. Finsberg a high sign worked out between us just the other day. You'll find special grand-opening specials that will have you picking chicken out of your teeth for a week, but first—uh—first—first . . ."

He wondered what he was up to. Even as he'd told them his story, he'd wondered. What was he doing? What was being done to him? It was nothing like stage fright, no amateur's last-minute wish to be elsewhere, anywhere. He wondered something else. Not only why he was doing this, but what prevented him from stopping. He could not let them go. He couldn't stop talking. He hadn't prepared, he'd meant only to get their attention, Benny in the Bucket a simple stunt of welcome. But why this logorrhea? He suspected his character, a vessel thrust forward by resentment, his stalled personality waiting on anger like a player of a board game waiting on a pair of thrown fours, say, to advance his counter. And why *resentment?* He remembered when he had shouted over the long-distance telephone at his commanding officer. He grew in fits and starts, lived in phases and stages like a classic kid in Spock or Gesell. Why couldn't he stop? What did he resent? And if he was angry, then why was he so happy?

*"Anyone want a ride in the bucket?"*

"Then I think it's time we—"

"Know what? This is hallowed ground. It is. I was here last weekend checking our equipment. There was this fantastic crowd. In the parking lot, the mall. I couldn't figure it out. Then there were these—these sirens. I thought, Jesus, what is it, is it burning down? The shopping center? *Is Macy's burning?* I got a ladder and climbed up the bucket to see. There was a motorcade, limos. What the hell? That's what I thought—what the hell? Nixon stepped out and was helped up on the roof of a big black Lincoln. I wondered if he could see me in the bucket. What about the Secret Service guys? What did *they* make of me? ASSASSIN POPS CANDIDATE FROM FRIED CHICKEN AERIE! Hallowed ground. Jack Kennedy a few days after. The media. Dave Brinkley up close, Cronkite standing. The truth squads of both parties, shadow cabinets. Paul Newman's been by, Bob Montgomery. This is hallowed American ground of the twentieth century. A shopping center in a white suburb with good schools. One day it will be remembered like an old-time battlefield—some, some Gettysburg of the rhetorical. You heard 'em here first, all the campaigners to whose thumbs we entrust our red buttons and our black boxes. It's the Lyceum here, the new stump! What merely civil acts could follow such performance and presence? What quotidian acts of the market basket and shopping cart? What out-on-a-limb toe balances and triples? How can I top *them?* My God, *friends*, it's Colonel Sanders who should be here today! The Colonel himself in his blinding whites. Standing where I stand and tossing chicken parts like lollies from the float. Not Ben Flesh in the flesh but *him*. No surrogate—not after Nixon, not after Kennedy. *Him! His* State of the Union! But you know?" He beat his breast with his fists. *"You know? When you come right down to it, this—this is the State of the Union!* BEN IN THE BUCKET! BENNY IN THE BARREL!

"Open up! I'm the truth squad! The secret ingredients of Colonel Sanders' Fried Chicken from far-off Kentucky are, well, chicken of course, sage, onion, salt and pepper, flour, cornmeal, eggs, and shortening—And plenty of ACCENT!

"Open the doors, it's opening day. Go on, go in. We ask only that you take a number!"

He pulled himself up to the lip of the bucket and threw his arms over its sides. He hung there suspended. He would appear to them, he thought, exactly like a man lying facedown on a diving board would appear to swimmers directly beneath him.

"They asked me," Flesh said, "they asked me, 'Ben, why chicken?' 'Everybody has to eat,' I told them. 'Each must eat, all must bite the calorie and chew the carbohydrate. We must be nourished. This is a need. The play goes to the man who makes necessity delicious.'

"Mrs.," he called down to a woman in white shoes, "people have feet. There'll always be a demand for shoes." He saw a young man. "They have bodies which have to be clothed. The Washington clothing lobbies are among the most powerful in the country." And another man: "They've got to live somewhere—houses, apartments. A landlord prospers." He spotted an old lady: "Human feeling, the sense of family—*there's* a bond. Greeting cards. The long distance. Cemetery plots. Real estate is real." And a girl: "They have to be distracted. Books, records, trips to Nassau on the Youth Fare." And a teenage boy: "Pornography is a growth industry!" He had his eye on a husband and wife, the man's arm around the woman's shoulder: "The course of true love never runs smooth. There are lovers' quarrels. People fight. They kiss and make up. Say it with flowers. Sweets to the sweet." There was a boy with glasses: "They have eyes that wear out with all there is to look at. You couldn't go wrong in optometry!"

And just then he went blind in his left eye.

He was not with the Wine and Spirits Association of America people, not with the Toyota Dealers, not with the Midwest Modern Language Association. He paid top dollar for his room and walked the corridor of restaurants and expensive boutiques, tiny, some of them, as roomettes on trains, that linked the lobbies of the Chase and Park Plaza Hotels. He smiled at everyone. Without a name tag, in his sober suit of natural fibers he must have looked like one of the managers of the hotel, or like Koplar himself perhaps, or even a well-turned-out house detective. Except that there were no more house detectives. They were security personnel now, and some he knew in the better hotels spoke with cultured European accents. Whatever happened to the house detective, whatever happened to the house physician? The hotel dicks were all from Interpol and the docs were revolving pool personnel, family doctors on retainer. Less romantic than the old days of Dr. Wolfe. Oh yes.

He went into one of the shops and bought a purse of softest calf's leather, paid for it with an American Express card which the girl checked against the February 1974 list of closely printed American Express numbers, American Express Deadbeats of February 1974. It was like a musical comedy. ("Do you take Diners? Master Charge? Carte Blanche? American Express? BankAmericard?" "Yes, sir, oh yes." He could have paid for it—an $85 purse—with his driver's license or Blue Cross card. He carried his credit cards in his inside jacket in a Bicycle Playing Cards packet.) He gave the woman Kitty's address—she was Mrs. Roger Sayad now—and asked that it be sent.

"Will there be a card?"

"Yes. A card." She handed him a small white envelope and a card. He wrote Kitty's name on the envelope, tore up the blank she had given him, and enclosed his Sunoco credit card.

"It's sentimental. This used to be honored at Best Western motels."

The saleswoman looked at him.

"Among so many conventioneers—I represent only myself this trip—I am seized by the spirit. I am taken with a frenzy for the old days, you follow? My heart leaps up. You follow my heart leaping up?"

She smiled weakly and he wanted to tell her that he wasn't drunk. And he wasn't.

But he could tell no one anything anymore. His tears embarrassed them. The kid hitchhiker a few days ago was something else. That story had been one from old times. He went up to his room.

What reminded him, what started the whole damn thing, was the sight of all those businessmen. In Miami Beach—that would have been just four years ago, the prime rate had been 7½ percent—he'd attended two conventions at once, K-O-A and One Hour Martinizing.

Dr. Wolfe.

A pallid wafery man with thinning hair that seemed to grow out from a tuft of widow's peak and stretch back over his head, growing uphill but somehow the dark individual strands like the ribs of a fan that covered almost all his scalp. A head of hair like a magic trick. Flesh with more was balder. A quiet man who spoke in a low monotonous voice. Dr. Wolfe. In order to hear him Ben found himself leaning into Wolfe's speech, as if shouldering a stiff wind, heavy weather. With his head bent toward his host's conversation, there was an odd nautical quality to his step. Flesh felt like a sailor rolling along beside him. They might have been walking upwind on a deck. The faint praise was faint. Dr. Wolfe. "Have lunch with me." It was more command than invitation. The man was a bore. Ben could not rebuff bores, regarded their conversation as down payment on his own.

"Those K-O-A'ers needed to hear that."

"Well—"

"It was interesting. But I'm not sure you were correct."

"I'm new in the business. It was simply an outsider's first impression."

"No no, it was stimulating. But what would the presence of motorcycle packs do to our family trade?"

"I didn't really say anything about motorcycle packs. I wasn't thinking of opening up the campsites to Hell's Angels."

"Once the word got around they'd come, though. They could come singly, or in pairs. They might not *seem* motorcycle packs, but then, when they were all together, you'd see what you had."

He didn't care to argue the point. It was just something that had occurred to him during the open meeting and that he'd offered in the packed Fontainebleau Hospitality Suite during "Give and Take Hour." "I thought you said you liked the idea."

"I said it was interesting. It needs to be discussed."

Ben didn't care to discuss it.

"We'll go outside the hotel. I've been eating in that pharmacy up Collins Avenue. The prices they charge here are ridiculous."

"Listen, I'm a little rushed. I'm supposed to be with One Hour Martinizing in an hour."

"Yes?"

"I'm giving a talk on the subject 'Come Back Thursday.' " Wolfe didn't smile.

"It's just up Collins Avenue. By the time we got seats in the coffee shop we'd have to gobble our sandwiches."

"Yeah, okay."

"K-O-A's a family trade," Wolfe said when they were seated at the counter in the drugstore eating their egg-salad sandwiches. (Wolfe had ordered for them both.)

"What about hostelers?"

"Hostelers are people's children. They're decent."

"Oh." Flesh had begun to hate the man.

"It's all very well," Wolfe said, "for you absentee landlords, but I have to live at the campsite. We're in Boca Raton. If your proposal went through, if it got in our bylaws, *I'd* be the one to suffer, I'd be the one subjected to the terror."

"I didn't put it as a proposal."

"There'd be dope, fights. We'd be kept up half the night. My wife can't take that."

"It would be up to the individual, wouldn't it?"

"Yes? It would be the Public Accommodations Act all over again. Civil rights. If I wasn't in compliance, I'd lose my license."

"Well, I didn't put it as a proposal."

"It was warmly received. And that other. What was it—serve beer on the premises?"

"All I said was that if K-O-A had a small retail food and beverage outlet—"

"That'd be beer. You'd have a problem with the hostelers. A lot of those kids are under age. There'd be false I.D.'s. I see nothing but trouble. For a few shekels. Is that all that matters to you, shekels?"

"Look, Mr. Wolfe—"

"I don't say I couldn't use the money. Lord knows I could. But I got enough grief as it is."

"Well, you don't have to worry about me. They asked for ideas. It was all off the top of my head."

"My wife's bedfast."

"I'm sorry?"

"Sixteen years. She's bedfast. She's incontinent. She wears a diaper."

"Oh, I'm sorry," Ben said.

"And all those steroids. Her bones are so soft I can't use nothing but down. Down pillows, a down mattress I gave seven hundred shekels for. Doctor wants her to sit up some each day. Had to get her a down chair. Swan's down. Special made. My wife sits down on down," he muttered. "She isn't old enough yet for Medicare. I have to pay for those steroids out of my own pocket. They keep changing her medications but it's all steroids. This is the first convention I've been to since she come down bedfast. Only reason I could get away is it's in Florida and my sister-in-law said she'd take care of my wife. She lives in Miami. I use her apartment. Don't even get to stay in the hotel."

Flesh nodded. "I was on steroids once," he said. He offered the information as a way of reaching some accord with the man, but he was astonished at Wolfe's reaction.

"*You? You* were? Yes? Tell me."

"Well, it wasn't a big deal really. I don't think I could have been on them more than two weeks, but at the time it scared hell out of me."

"Yes? Yes? What?"

"I went blind in my left eye."

"Oh yes," Wolfe said. He was grinning.

"I say 'blind,' but it was, I don't know, white. As if I had my eye open in a glass of milk."

"Hah," Wolfe said.

"It didn't last long. At first I thought I had a tumor. That's what scared me. I went to an ophthalmologist and he referred me to a neurologist and the neurologist put me in the hospital for observation."

"Yes?"

"Well, it wasn't a tumor."

"No."

"And the doctor put me on steroids and the blindness cleared up in, I don't know, it was almost ten years ago, three, maybe four days."

"A retrobulbar optic neuritis."

"That's right," Flesh said. "How would you know that?"

Wolfe laughed. "It's how it starts. Ten years ago, eh? What were you—thirty, thirty-two?"

"I don't know. About thirty-two. It's how *what* starts? What are you talking about?"

"It's the nation's leading crippler of young adults, sonny. You've got multiple sclerosis, same as my sixteen-year-bedfast wife."

"What are you talking about? I don't have multiple sclerosis. It was retrobulbar optic neuritis."

"That's right. That's it. That's how it starts."

"It was ten years ago."

"Sure. You're in remission."

"I don't have multiple sclerosis."

"No? Wait one or two years. You're in remission, that's all. I know more about the nation's leading crippler of young adults than any neurologist in the country. I read all the literature. It was the British proved that anybody gets optic neuritis winds up with M.S. Didn't your doctor tell you that?"

"No," Flesh said.

"Course not. It's a stress disease. You could be in remission another five years, but you've got it, neighbor. It's progressive and it's degenerative and it eats your nerves like moths in the closet. Lay in down and don't be so sure you want the hippies and them kids with their choppers and drugs. You need rest."

"Fuck you," Flesh said.

"That's all right, I'll get the check. My treat."

Ben moved off. "Lay in down," Wolfe called. "Get insurance. Lay in down, foam rubber, creams and unguents for the bedroom, for your abrasive big-shot ways." He could hear Wolfe's laughter behind him as the man trailed him back to the hotel.

Dr. Wolfe.

He had been blind. He had been a blind man. And once he'd had a heart attack. Later, he tried to explain it to Gertrude.

"You were only half blind, you could see white. Me, I've got bones like monkey wrenches and the Guess-Your-Age-and-Weight man at the fair doesn't know what to make of me."

Just as he didn't know what to make—before he knew what the blindness meant, before Dr. Wolfe told him—of himself.

"In the old days, yes," he'd told Mary, "in the days when I was between twenty-one and thirty-eight and coming down with my character like a disease. Before I got to be whatever it is I've turned out to be. When I was turning out to be it. I didn't know what to make of me. Except it seemed significant that I'd been in World War II. I didn't ever see action, but that was part of the pattern, can you understand this? I was in the world war but I didn't see action, I was blind but only in one eye and just for a few days, and even your sister reminded me that I could see light, that the visible somehow translated itself in my brain to pure energy—to white, to light. And, oh yes, that I was an orphan, but late-blooming, orphaned only after I'd turned twenty. Already a man. Which didn't make me Oliver Twist. And I had a godfather. More cushion. *And* an inheritance. And even that mitigated. We're not talking about lump sums—not even as much as my piddling severance pay when I left the army of MacArthur and Eisenhower, just this mitigated, administered inheritance, not money but the interest on money, the privilege of borrowing dough. And a college graduate, but even that, my education, off center somehow, me not knowing what I was getting into at Wharton, odd man out in that scioned, silver-spooned set, maybe the only person there not preparing to step into someone else's shoes, not in training for a life laid out like clean clothes on the *bedgevant*. And a heart-attack victim, too, don't forget, when I was thirty-eight. But not a victim. I didn't die, didn't see *that* action either. Just let off the hook with what the doctor called a 'warning.' He meant I should change my life. But how can I change what I don't understand? The blindness that was not real blindness and the orphan lad who was no lad. A soldier in the biggest war in history who never got close to combat. And the heart attack that went away. All this pulled-punch catastrophe that has been my life. The phony inheritance and mixed blessing. I don't understand this stuff."

"What about me?" LaVerne asked when he attempted to speak to her about it. "What about me with my askew architecture, my organs with their faulty wiring, my insides like left-hand drive? As if I were a bridge built by racketeers."

"That's not what I'm talking about. You're unique."

"Unique. Terrific. Unique. Death's Special Introductory Offer."

"What, am I discounting your risk? Is that what you think? No no. Who am I to cut anyone's losses? That isn't the point. All these things—they've got me programmed for an Everyman. A little of this, a little of that. My smorgasbord life."

"You'll dance on our graves."

"That ain't it."

She turned away from him in bed. Her nightgown had ridden up her backside. "It ain't? That's it."

He called Irving.

"Yes," he said, "in St. Louis . . . Oh, I don't know, about an hour ago . . . No, at the Chase-Park . . . Because I don't like to impose . . . All right, come on, Irving, what 'offended,' what 'hurt'? You know my habits. The truth is, I hate making beds. Sometimes I shoot right in the sheets. Why should Frances lean over my laundry? . . . No, certainly not. Your sister *isn't* with me . . . No. No . . . Call the desk. See if I'm registered with anyone. Come over, search the room. As a matter of fact, that's a good idea. Bring Fran. I'll take you both to dinner at the Tenderloin Room. You'll cut up my meat for me . . . Yeah. Hah hah, yourself . . . No, Chicago. I'm going on to Kansas City . . . Yeah, right, Irving, it's a surprise audit on the One Hour Martinizing. I got word you been skimming the first six minutes on me . . . So tell me, Irving, how's business? . . . What? The niggers again? . . . All the way out to Overland? Irving, I already closed up the Delmar location. You wanted west county, I gave you west county. What is it, you Daniel Boone, you got a manifest destiny? Irving, darling, the niggers are going to push you into the sea . . . Into the Pacific, yes. What good is a dry-cleaning service in the ocean? Saltwater's bad for the material . . . No, I'm not making jokes at your expense . . . I appreciate it's a sickness with you . . . Really, have dinner with me. Yeah, I understand. Right. Sure . . . Certainly I understand. You don't like to come into the inner city . . . Irving, give Frances a kiss, I'll see you both at the plant in the morning. Bring the books."

# 2

He loved the shop, the smells of the naphthas and benzenes, the ammonias, all the alkalis and fats, all the solvents and gritty lavas, the silken detergents and ultimate soaps, like the smells, he decided, of flesh itself, of release, the disparate chemistries of pore and sweat—a sweat shop—the strange woolly-smelling acids that collected in armpits and atmosphered pubic hair, the flameless combustion of urine and gabardine mixing together to create all the body's petty suggestive alimentary toxins. The sexuality of it. The men's garments one kind, the women's another, confused, deflected, masked by residual powders, by the oily invisible resins of deodorant and perfume, by the concocted flower and the imagined fruit—by all fabricated flavor. And hanging in the air, too—where would they go?—dirt, the thin, exiguous human clays, divots, ash and soils, dust devils of being.

"Irving, add water, we'll make a man."

His godcousin looked up from the presser. "What color?"

"Hello, Ben," Frances said. She was her husband's countergirl.

"Frances, how are you?" Ben leaned across the counter and kissed her. "Did you bring the books?" he asked Irving.

"Please, Ben," Irving said, "not in front of the *shvartzeh.*"

"Irving, she's your *wife.*"

"I know, I know," he said, "it's a sickness."

Frances was black. Marrying her had been a sort of experiment in social vaccination. He had reasoned that if polio, measles, and smallpox could be defrayed by actually contracting them, then perhaps he might be able to cure his racial prejudice by marrying a black woman. The blacks he knew in New York—Irving, still living in Riverdale, had attended Columbia University, where he majored in anthropology, and commuted to and from the campus in rolled-window, locked-door cabs—were, except for their color, indistinguishable from most of the whites he knew. They spoke with New York accents, something the anthropologist could never really get over. It was his idea to leave the city to seek a bride. Afraid to go South, where, at the time of his contemplated courtship, the prohibitions against miscegenation were either still on the books or, if technically legal, enforced by the vaudevilles of Klansmen, he chose St. Louis, neutral territory, a place where blacks still sounded like blacks, where, though their civil liberties were underwritten by law and municipal ordinance, they still lived in ghettos and did the dirty work when they could find it.

In the days when his tortured godcousin, then an M.A. candidate in anthropology—a subject he studied for the same reason he would choose a bride—had first hit upon the idea for his cure, Ben had again and again been subjected to Irving's rhetoric, speeches that might, with certain alterations, have been memorized from *Guess Who's Coming to Dinner*.

"I know what I'm doing, Ben, I'm not going into this thing with my eyes closed. I know what people will think. Oh, my friends will be very 'polite' of course. They'll come to the wedding and bring gifts. They'll drink our health and say, 'It's marvelous what Irving's done. What courage! What courage on *both* their parts!' But they'll never get used to it. They'll never adapt. There'll be unintended snubs, invitations not sent, embarrassing silences when me and the jigaboo run into them on the street, pregnant pauses, or, even worse, circumlocutions. They won't really know how to handle it. We'll make them uncomfortable. And some of my 'good' friends—oh, they'll mean well, I suppose—will try to warn me of the dangers and consequences. 'All right,' they'll say, 'so you want to run off and be an idealist. Terrific. Wonderful. Hurrah for Martin Luther Finsberg, but aren't you forgetting something? What about the children? What will they have to pay for your idealism?' They'll reason that if I want to marry dark meat that's my business, that I'm free, white, and twenty-one, but it's unfair to our little nignogs."

Flesh had given him his job, had made him manager of the franchise in St. Louis. He was the only one of the Finsbergs still connected with any of the franchises.

Ben moved behind the counter and plunged in and out of the ranks of garments suspended from the conveyor in their polyethylene bags like FBI silhouettes, police-force torso targets. "Out of my way, Hart, Schaffner and Marx. Watch it, you Brooks brothers. I'm coming through, Kuppenheimer. Straighten up, chest out, tummy in, Hickey. How many times do I have to tell you? Lookin' good there, Freeman. Ah, madam. Itchy-kitchy Gucci, Pucci."

The girls at the creaser and topper machines laughed. Flesh walked up to the Suzy, an adjustable dress form on which men's and ladies' garments could be hung for special attention—spot cleaning, alterations. Nothing was hanging on it at the moment. "Shameless," Flesh said and gave it a feel. The shirt folder rocked with laughter. She was a huge black woman in a short skirt and, because of the heat, a man's ribbed undershirt. Ben looked at the woman and pointed to her chest. "Hey, that's cute, sweetheart. You got some tits on you, momma."

"Christ, Ben," Irving whispered, "don't talk like that. These girls carry switchblades and razors."

"She don't mind," Flesh said, not bothering to lower his voice. "You mind—what's your name?"

"Gloria."

"You mind, Gloria?"

"Naw," she said.

"See? Gloria doesn't mind."

"Yeah, you're right," Irving whispered, "they have no morals."

"Irving," Ben said.

"I know, I know," Irving said softly.

"The books," Ben said.

"I want you to see them, Ben, but there's something I'd like to discuss with you first."

"Something wrong with the books? I'll catch you out in a minute. I went to Wharton. I speed-read double-entrywise."

"No, of course not. The books are perfect. This is something else. I was going to write you."

"Because if there was something funny about the books I wouldn't laugh, Irving."

"The books are fine. Look, can we go over by the sign?" Irving moved toward the front of the store. Ben followed. "Listen," Irving said, "there's something I have to . . . What are you doing?"

"This poster." He held up a large cardboard poster. Men and women were smiling in their dry cleaning. He rubbed his hand across the front of the advertisement. "Jesus, Irving, it's a dry-cleaning plant. Look at the dust. The damn *ads* are *schmutzick!*"

"They're filthy in their habits," Irving said, "they're not a clean people."

"Look here," Ben said, taking a display from the front window and holding it for Irving to see, "look at the lapels on this suit. Look at the guy's tie. These fashions are from 1955. Look at the dress the broad's wearing. Look at their fucking hairstyles. What is it, the nostalgia craze? Can't you get new displays?"

"Ben, I would, but they steal them. You know how they are. They rob them to hang up on their walls for paintings."

"Come on, Irving."

"It's a sickness, Ben."

"Get well soon, you're running a business here. Look at the One Hour Martinizing sign." He pointed to the neon tubing—an enormous green '1' framing successively smaller green and red 1's, 1's within 1's within 1's like hashmarks. He touched the sign. "My finger isn't even warm. The tubing's insulated by dust. It hums and crackles like shortwave. Look at the dark spots where the neon ain't flowing. The fucker's got hardening of the arteries, blood clots, neon myocardial infarction. Does it even shine in the dark, Irving?"

"That's what I wanted to talk to you about. The equipment. It's old, Ben. They have Valclene now. It's odorless and it does a terrific job. With Valclene we wouldn't need a steam tunnel, we wouldn't need a stretcher."

"We've got a steam tunnel, we've got a stretcher."

"You're missing the point, Ben. We could get rid of at least one girl. It would practically pay for itself. We'd save money."

"What's Valclene? How much is it?"

"It's an entirely new process, Ben, odorless. I don't know the exact cost. Maybe $17,000, $20,000 tops."

"Yeah? How many years would that girl you'd get rid of have to work to earn that much money? Three? Four?"

"That's not the point. That's not the only advantage. All right. These people work cheap, but—"

"Irving, listen to me. You know what the dry-cleaning business is worth today? How many pair of slacks did you do this week?"

"I don't know, I'd have to—"

"A dozen? A half dozen? You haven't noticed the wash-and-wear fabrics are knocking us on the head? They put suits in the washing machines now. Suits. Sport coats!"

"Not winter suits, Ben."

"No, not winter suits. So suddenly it's a seasonal business."

"Ben, with the new equipment—"

"With the new equipment, what? What with the new equipment? Forget the new equipment. And I don't have to look at the books. I don't even *want* to see them. I can guess what they say. I know all about the books. Best sellers they ain't. So what's this shit about new equipment? Irving, you forgot your anthropology so quick? You don't know that the do-it-yourself coin-op places are changing the dry-cleaning culture in this country? That they're kicking our brains off? That this new outfit—what's its name?—American Cleaners, yeah, American Cleaners, will take any garment and do you a job on it for 69 cents? A suit 69 cents, a sport coat. A dress. What do we get for a dress, a buck ninety-five?"

"They don't do the kind of job we do, Ben. They don't turn out a product like ours. Not for 69 cents. How can you compare?"

"Irving, I'm delighted by your pride. I really am. I am. That's good. That's beautiful. Really." He lowered his voice. "Irving, you've got white pride. But let's not talk about machines, all right? Unless maybe you want to take the stuff in and run it over to American Cleaners. We could use their machines. The coin-ops. We'd clean up, yes?"

"Why are you making fun of me?"

"I'm not making fun of you."

"I work like a nigger in this place. Damnit, Ben, my brothers and sisters and I guaranteed your loan. $14,000. My father made you our responsibility in his will. Why do you treat me like this? Why do you mock our relationship?"

"I don't mock our relationship. I cast it in bronze. Ping ping. I chip it in marble. Tap. Tap tap. I baste, tack, braid, plait, stitch, sew, and crochet it in fabric. In *fabric*, Irving, *fabric*. Fabric is the fabric of our relationship! Skin of my skin, cloth of my cloth. Don't you know anything? Anthropologist! What's the matter, don't you recognize these digs? It's the Finsberg Memorial Library here, my allegiance to costume, my tribute to Godpop. Fitting. Hah! Fitting's fitting. Needles and pins, Irving, pins and needles. Needles, pins, and thread warped us and woofed us. Yay for yarn. Rah for ribbon. Whoopee for wool. Lest we forget, Irving, manager, godcousin, kid, this is for Julius, this is for him, the yellow tape around his shoulders like a *tallith*, around his neck like an Old Boy's tie, pins in his red lips like a cushion tomato. Lest we forget! We owe everything—you, me, Estelle, the sibs, all of us—to dress, garb, caparison, wardrobe. We are what they wore. Millinery made us. Raiment did, weeds. Vestments, trousseau, togs, layettes. Traps, Irv, habits, duds, and mufti. Regimentals, jungle green and field gray. Redcoats. Canonicals and academicals. Sari, himation, pallium, peplum. Tunic, blazer, leotard, gym suit. Cassock, soutane, toga, chiton. Trews, breeks, chaps, and jeans. Jodhpurs, galligaskins, yashmaks, burnoose. Breechclouts and sou'westers. Spatterdashes. Greaves and ruffs. Unmentionables and Sunday-go-to-meeting. Irving, Irving, call the pelisse!"

"We don't do much greaves, we send the yashmaks out."

"Well I'm very pleased with what I see," Ben Flesh said. "The place is in good hands."

"We're dying on the vine, Ben. Smell it in here. Feel how hot it is. All right, they're niggers—I couldn't ask white people to work in a place like this—but even the jungle bunnies have to have their Coca-Cola. Christ, Ben, you know what I pay for *salt* tablets? No dry-cleaning plant's like this today. They're modern, cool as drugstores, with no more odor to them than lobbies in airports. Ben, we're in violation of the health codes. It's a good thing the spades ain't union or we'd really be in trouble. As it is, I think the inspector wants to be paid off."

"Pay him."

"But why not convert? Why not meet the new specs? It doesn't make sense, Ben."

"Pay him. Raise the girls' wages."

"I used to smoke. Two packs a day. I can't touch cigarettes anymore. They taste like this, like chemicals."

"The Surgeon General has determined that cigarette smoking is dangerous to your health."

"What's this? *Good* for my health? It's poison. Look, I have my inheritance. I'll put the stuff in myself."

"You're my manager. I own the place. The manager doesn't put in a gum-ball machine without my approval. He doesn't put in a can for charity. I like everything just as it is. I *like* the smells. I like the way they make my eyes sting and contract my nostrils like toxic snuff. This is for Julius and for my father, who was once his partner. This is what they would have known. I like it the way it is."

"You like? You run it."

"You're quitting?"

"Yeah. Why not? What am I doing managing a dry-cleaning joint? I'm worth almost half a million dollars, you know that? I'm educated. I have advanced degrees. Yeah, why not?"

"And Frances, your house nigger, you're worth a half million, you're educated, you're quitting Frances, too?"

"What's Frances got to do with it?"

"Nothing. Except she's part of your cure, that was your idea. And this place, this is part of your cure, too. You were exactly the right man for the job. That's right. *You.* Because your genes crackle like static electricity in the presence of schmutz, cleaning syrups, and your indoor heat waves. Your fate is to scrub, scour, mop, wring out, to run the world through the mangle. You dip, rinse, sluice, and douche. You don't hate niggers, you're in love with the cleaning lady! For Christ's sake, look around you, you've put together a harem in here. When you die laundresses will stick you in a tub and lower you in fuller's earth."

"It's a sickness."

"Yeah yeah."

"Yes."

"You kinky dummy! Earth turns you on. Look at your finger-nails. You look like you've been on your hands and knees in the garden."

"Why do you talk to me like this? Aren't we friends?"

*"Friends?"*

"Aren't we?"

Ben took Irving's face in his hands.

"The same nose, eyes, lips, teeth, ears. The same hair. The same give to the flesh, the same resistance. I close my eyes and I feel your tan. The same tan."

"The same?"

"As your sisters'."

"Are you on about that again?"

"Ah no, lad, of course not. Slip on something from a polyethy-lene bag. We'll kiss. You'll drive in drag to Kansas City with me. We'll stop at rest areas on the Interstates and neck. We'll put two straws in our Coke. We'll sip and giggle."

"Jesus, Ben. *I'm* kinky? What are you?"

"A family man." He raised his voice. "A family man. The whole damn Finsberg family. A family man!"

"Listen," Irving said, "I'll stay on until you can get someone else."

"Yeah, sure."

"Or *I'll* look. I'll find somebody trustworthy."

"Okay. All right. Whatever." He was waving his right hand as if it had cramped, shaking it back and forth at chest level, clenching and unclenching his fist.

"What is it? What's wrong?"

"Paresthesia." Ben started to laugh.

"What? What is it?"

"Poetic justice, symbolism. Irony and fate. Life's rhyming cou-
plets, its punch lines. The goblins that get you when you don't
watch out."

"What are you talking about?"

"Needles and pins. What form does, what made us what we are
today. Cloth of our cloth, etc. *Me. I'm* the Finsberg Memorial
Library! They stitched it in my body and used my nerves for
thread. I'm a fucking pin cushion!"

From Wolfe's mouth to God's ears.

He'd been driving for hours, on his way from his St. Cloud,
Minnesota, Dairy Queen to his Mister Softee in Rapid City, South
Dakota—his milk run, as he liked to call it. His right hand had
fallen asleep and there was a sharp pain high up in the groin and
thigh of his right side.

Mornings he'd been getting up with it. A numbness in his hand
and hip, bad circulation, he thought, which left these damned cold
zones, warm enough to the touch when he felt them with the freely
circulating blood in the fingers of his left hand or lifted his right
hand to his face, but, untouched, like icy patches deep in his skin.
Perhaps his sleeping habits had changed. Almost unconsciously
now he found the right side of the bed. In the night, sleeping
alone, even without a twin or triplet beside him, the double bed to
himself, some love-altered principle of accommodation or tropism
in his body taking him from an absent configuration of flesh to a
perimeter of the bed, a yielding without its necessity or reason, a
submission and giving way to—to what? (And even in his sleep,
without naming them, he could tell them apart.) To ride out the
night sidesaddle on his own body. (No godfather Julius he, not set
in *his* ways, unless this were some new mold into which he was
pouring himself.) Pressing his head—heavy as Gertrude's marrowless bones—like a nighttime tourniquet against the flesh of his
arm, drawing a knee as high up as a diver's against his belly and
chest, to wake in the morning cut off, the lines down and trailing
live wires from the heavy storm of his own body. Usually, as the
day wore on, the sensation wore off, but never completely, some
sandy sensitivity laterally vestigial across the tips of his fingers, the

sharp pain in the region of his thigh blunted, like a suction cup on the tip of a toy arrow. Bad circulation. Bad.

Unless. Unless— Unless from Wolfe's mouth to God's ears.

He checked into the Hotel Rushmore in Rapid City and asked the clerk for a twin-bedded room. And then, seeing the width of the single bed, requested a rollaway be brought, narrower still. This an experiment. In the narrow bed no place to go, his body occupying both perimeters at once, returned as it had been in the days before he'd shared beds, the pillow beneath his head almost the width of the bed itself, tethered by a perfect displacement, lying, it could be, on his own shadow. But in the morning the sensation still there, if anything worse, not to be shaken off. (Never to be shaken off.)

And a new discovery. At Mister Softee handling the tan cardboard carton of popsicles, as cold to the touch of his right hand as dry ice. He thought his blood had thickened and frozen. Something was wrong.

He got the name of a doctor from his Mister Softee manager, saw Dr. Gibberd that afternoon, and was oddly moved when the doctor told him that he would like him to go into Rapid City General for observation.

A black woman took him in a wheelchair to his bed.

It was very strange. Having voluntarily admitted himself to the hospital, having driven there under his own steam—his 1971 Caddy was parked in the Visitors' lot—and answered all the questions put to him by the woman at the Admissions Desk, showing them his Blue Cross and Blue Shield cards, his yellow Major Medical, he had become an instant invalid, something seductively agreeable to him as he sat back in the old wheelchair and allowed himself to be shoved up ramps and maneuvered backward—his head and shoulders almost on a level with his knees—across the slight gap between the lobby carpet and the hard floor of an elevator and pushed through what he supposed was the basement, past the kitchens and laundry rooms, past the nurses' cafeteria and the vending machines and the heating plant, lassitude and the valetudinarian on him like climate, though he had almost forgotten his symptoms.

"Where are we going? Is it much farther?"

"No. We almost there." She shoved the brass rod on a set of blue fire doors and they moved across a connector through a second set of fire doors and past a nurses' station, and entered a long, cinderblock, barracks-like ward in which there were perhaps fifteen widely spaced beds down each side of a broad center aisle. Except for what might be behind a folding screen at the far end of the ward, the beds were all empty, the mattresses doubled over on themselves.

"This is the boondocks," Ben said. "Is it a new wing?"

"You got to ask your doctor is it a new wing," she said and left him.

A young nurse came and placed a hospital gown across the back of the wheelchair. She asked Ben if he needed help. He said no but had difficulty with his shirt buttons. Unless he actually saw his fingers on them, he could not be sure he was holding them.

"Here," she said, "let me." She stooped before him and undid the buttons. She unfastened his belt. "Can you get your zipper?"

"Oh sure." But touching the metal was like sticking his hand into an electric socket. The nurse made up the bed. He sat back down in the chair and, watching the fingers on his right hand, carefully attempted to interlace them with the fingers on his left.

"Modest?"

Ben nodded. It was not true. In sickness he understood what he never had in health, that his body, anyone's, everyone's, was something for the public record, something accountable like books for audit, like deeds on file in county courthouses. If he was ashamed it was because he couldn't work his fingers. He stood to take off his pants and shorts. Then he smiled.

"Yes?"

"I was just thinking," he said.

"Yes?"

"I'm Mister Softee." She turned away and completed the last hospital corner. "No," Ben said, "I am. I have the local Mister Softee franchise. It's ice cream." She folded the sheets back. "It's true. Anytime you want a Mister Softee, just go down and ask Zifkovic. Zifkovic's my manager."

"Please put your gown on."

"Tell him Ben Flesh sent you," he said and burst into tears.

"What is it? What's wrong?"

"I don't know," Ben said, "I don't know what's happening to me."

"That's why you're here," she said, "so we can find out." She helped him out of the chair gently, unfolded and held open the gown for him. "Just step into it," she said, "just put your arms through the sleeves." He had to make a fist with his right hand so his fingers wouldn't touch the rough fabric. She came toward him with the gown. His penis moved against her uniform. "Can you turn around?" she said. "I'll tie you up the back."

"I can turn around." He was crying again.

"Please," she said, "please don't do that. You mustn't be afraid. You're going to be fine."

"I can turn around. See?" he sobbed. "Is it smeared? My ass? What there is of it. All belly, no ass. Is it smeared? Is it smeared with shit? Sometimes, I don't know, I try, I try to wipe myself. Sometimes I'm careless."

"You're fine," she said. "You're just fine. Please," she said, "if you shake like that, I won't be able to tie your gown for you."

"No? You won't?" He couldn't stop sobbing. He was grateful they were alone. "So I'd have to be naked. How would that be? This—this body na-naked. Wouldn't that be something—thing? No ass, just two fl-flabby gray pouches and this wi-wide tor-tors-*torso*. They say if you can squeeze a half inch of flab between your forefinger and thumb you're—you're too fat. What's this? Three in-*in-inch-ches*? What does that make *me*? I never looked like you're supposed to look on the—on the beach. I've got this terrible body. Well, I'm not the franchise man for nothing. It's—it's like any middle-age man's. I'm so *white*."

"Stop," she demanded. "You just control yourself."

"Yeah? What's that? Shock therapy? Thanks, I needed that? Well, why not? Sure. Thanks, I needed that." He turned to face her. He raised his gown. *"Flesh the flasher!"* He was laughing. "See? I've got this tiny weewee, this undescended cock."

"If you can't control yourself," she said.

"What? You'll call for help? Lady, you just saw for yourself. You don't *need* help. *You* could take me." He sat on the side of the bed, his legs spread wide, his elbows on his thighs, and his head in his palms. But he was calm. "I just never took care of the god-damned thing, my body. I just never took care of it. And the only thing that counts in life is life. You jog?" he asked suddenly.

"What's that?"

"Do you jog?"

"Yes."

"I knew. I knew you did. You smoke?"

"No."

"Right. That's right. Ship-fucking shape."

"I think one of the interns . . ."

"No," he said calmly, "I'm okay now. No more opera. But you know? I hate joggers. People who breathe properly swimming, who flutter kick. Greedy. Maybe flab is a sign of character and shapelessness is grace. Sure. The good die young, right?"

"Why do you loathe your body so?"

"What'd it ever do for me?"

"Will you be all right now?"

"I told you. Yes. Yeah." He got into bed. When he pulled the covers up his hand tingled. The nurse turned to go. "Listen," he said.

"Yes?"

"Tell Gibberd he can skip the preliminaries, all the observation shit. Tell him to get out his Nation's Leading Crippler of Young Adults kit. The kid's got M.S."

"You don't know what you have."

"Yes. Wolfe the specialist told me. He gave me egg salad and set me straight."

The nurse left him. He tried to feel his pulse with the fingers of his right hand and couldn't. He did five-finger exercises, reaching for the pulse in his throat, his hand doing rescue work, sent down the carefully chiseled tunnels of disaster in a mine shaft, say, to discover signs of life. He brought the fingers away from his neck and waved to the widows. He placed three fingers of his good hand along a finger of his right and, closing his eyes, tried to determine the points where they touched. He couldn't, felt only a suffused, generalized warmth in the deadened finger. He took some change the nurse had put with his watch and wallet in the nightstand by his bed and distributed it on his blanket around his chest and stomach. Still with his eyes closed, he tried to feel for the change and pick it up. He couldn't. He opened his eyes, scooped up a nickel, a dime, and a quarter with his left hand and put them in the palm of his right hand. Closing his eyes again, he very carefully spilled two of the coins onto the blanket—he could determine this by the sound—and made a fist about the coin still in his hand. Concentrating as hard as he had ever concentrated on anything in his life, and trapping the coin under his thumb, he rubbed it up his forefinger, trying to determine the denomination of the remaining coin. It's the dime, he decided. He was positive. Yes. It's the dime. The inside of his thumb still had some sensitivity. (Though he couldn't be sure, he thought he had felt a trace of pulse under his thumb when he had held the dead necklace of his right hand against his throat.) Definitely the dime. He opened his eyes. His hand was empty. He shoved the change back in the nightstand and closed the drawer.

"I say, are you *really* Mister Softee?" The voice was British and came from behind the screen at the far end of the ward.

"Who's that? Who's there?"

"Are you?"

"Yes."

"Jolly good. They're rather splendid."

"Thanks."

"Mister Softee." The name was drawn out, contemplated, pronounced as if it were being read from a marquee. "Apropos too, yes?"

"Why's that?"

"*Well*, after your performance just now for Sister, I should have thought that would be obvious, wouldn't it?"

"I'm sick."

"Not to worry," the invisible Englishman said cheerfully. "We're all sick here." Ben looked around the empty ward. "Sister was right, you know. You *are* going to be fine. You're in the best tropical medicine ward in either Dakota."

"This is a tropical medicine ward?"

"Oh yes. Indeed. One of the finest in the Dakotas."

"Jesus," Ben said, "a tropical medicine ward."

"Top drawer. Up there with the chief in Rapid City."

"What do you have?" Ben asked.

"One saw you through the crack where the panels of my screen are joined. One saw everything. One saw your bum. It *is* smeared, rather. What do *I* have? Lassa fever, old thing. Came down with a touch of it last year. Year it was discovered actually. In Nigeria. Odd that. Well, *I* wasn't in Nigeria. I was in Belize, Brit Honduras, with RAF. What I meant was, Lassa *fever* was discovered in Nigeria. Trouble with a clipped rather precise way of talking, articles left out, references left dangling, pronouns understood, is that it's often imprecise actually, rather."

"What was odd?"

"Beg pardon?"

"You said, 'Odd that.' What was odd?"

"Oh. Sorry. Well. That a disease could be said to be *discovered*. Of course all that's usually meant is that they've isolated a particular virus. But I mean, if you *think* about it the virus must have been there all along, mustn't it? And I should have thought that people, well, you know, *natives*, had been coming down with the bloody thing since *ages*. I mean, when Leif Erikson, or whoever, was discovering your States, some poor devil must have had all the symptoms of Lassa fever, even dying from it, too, very probably, without ever knowing that that's what was killing him because the disease had never been *named*, you see. Now it has. Officially, I'm only the ninth case—oh yes, I'm in the literature—but I'll bet populations have died of it."

"I don't think I understand what—"

"Well, only that I know where I stand, don't I? Just as you, if you were right about yourself, know where *you* stand. Is that an *advan*tage? I wonder. Quite honestly I don't know. Yes, and that's strange, too, isn't it, that I know things but don't know what to make of them? Incubation period one week. Very well. Weakness? Check. Myositis? Check. And the fever of course. And ulcerative pharyngitis with oral lesions. Yellow centers and erythemystositic halos. Rather like one of your lovely Mister Softee concoctions rather. Myocarditis, check. Pneumonitis, pleuritis, encephalophitathy, hemorrhagic diathesis? Check. Well, check some, most. What the hell? Check them *all*. Sooner or later they'll come. I mean I *expect* they will. Gibberd's been very straight with me. I think it pleases him how classic my case has been. Yet one can't tell, can one? I mean, what about the sleeplessness? *I* sleep like a top. I was sleeping when you were brought in, wasn't I? It was only your *rack*et woke me. Well, what *about* the sleeplessness? Or the slurred speech? One has some things but not others. There was the headache and leg rash and even the swollen face, but where was the leg *pain?* And this is the point, I think: What I have is incurable and generally fatal. Generally fatal? *Generally? Fatal?* Will this classic condition kill me or not? Incurable. *Al*ways incurable. But only generally fatal. Oh, what a hopeful world it is! Even in hospital. So no more racket, you understand? No more whimpering and whining. Be *hard*, Mister Softee!"

"All right," Ben said.

"Yes, well," his roommate said. "Are you ambulatory? I couldn't really tell. I saw you stand. But I saw Sister help. *Are* you? *Ambu*latory?"

"Yes."

"Oh, good. I wonder if I could trouble you to come back of the screen. One is rather in need of help."

"You want me to come back there?"

"If you would. If it isn't too much bother. Oh, I see. The contagion. Well. There's nothing to fear. Lassa can't be contracted from anyone who's had the disease for more than thirty-two days. One's had it a year and a half."

One could call the nurse, Ben thought. I have been orphaned and I have been blinded. I am Mister Softee here and Chicken from the Colonel there. Godfathers have called me to their deathbeds to change my life and all this has been grist for my character. I am in one of the go-ahead tropical medicine wards in Rapid City, South Dakota, and a Lassa fever pioneer needs my help. Oh well, he thought, and left his bed and proceeded down the long empty ward toward the screen at its rear. He stood by the screened-in sick man.

"Yes?" Ben said.

"What, here so soon? Well, you *are* ambulatory. Good *show*, Mister Softee! I'm Flight Lieutenant Tanner incidentally. Well then, could you come back of the screen, please just?"

"Come back of it."

"Yes. Would you just?"

Flesh went behind the screen. The Englishman was seated beside his bed in a steel wheelchair. Heavy leather straps circled his weakened chest and wrapped his flaccid legs to hold him upright in it. Flesh looked down meekly at the mandala of spokes, then at the Englishman's bare arms along the chair's wide rests. They were smeared with a perspiration of blood. Tiny droplets of blood freckled the man's forehead, discrete reddish bubbles mitigated by sweat and barely deeper in color than blown bubble gum. A sort of bloodfall trickled like tears from the hollow beneath his left eye and out over the cheekbone and down his face.

"Leukopenia, check," the Englishman said.

"My God, you're bleeding all over."

"No. Not actually *bleeding*, old fellow. It's a sort of capillary action. It's complicated rather, but the blood is forced out the pores. It's all explained in the literature. Gibberd told me I might expect it. It was jolly good luck *your* happening to be by. There's a box of Kleenex in that nightstand there. Would you mind? If you'll just tamp at the bloody stuff. Oh, I say, forgive that last, would you just? I should have thought to think that would do me rather nicely."

"Maybe I'd better call the nurse."

"She's *rather* busy, I should expect. There are people who really need help, for whom help is of some help, as it were. As I don't seem to be one of them—incurable, generally *fatal*, I'm taking the darker view just now, old boy— I should think you would have thought we might work this out between ourselves."

"Yeah, between ourselves," Ben said. "Pip." He took the Kleenex and began to dab at the man's skin.

"There's a good fellow. That's got the arm, I think," the Englishman said.

"This never happened before?"

"No no. Absolutely without precedent. I say, do you *real*ize?"

"What?"

"That if this disease really *was* discovered in 1970—well, it was, of course, but I mean if it didn't *exist* before 1970—why, then I'm only the ninth person to have experienced this particular symptom. We're breaking freshish ground here, you and I."

Ben, working on the bloodfall at its headwaters just under the Englishman's left eye, started to gag. He brought the bloodied Kleenex up to his lips.

"Be firm, Mister Softee." Ben swallowed and looked at him.

"I think that's it, rather," Ben said quietly.

"Yes, well, it would be, wouldn't it, except that the insides of my thighs seem a bit sticky."

"No no. I mean that's *it*. *Generally* fatal. I'm taking the lighter view. I'm calling the nurse."

"Mister Softee."

"What?"

"We've the same doctor."

The same spring that Ben Flesh lay in the tropical medicine ward of Rapid City General—the prime interest rate was 6¾ percent—a record heat wave hit the northern tier of the central plains states. Extraordinary demands on the energy supplies caused breakdowns and brownouts all over. The hospital had its own auxiliary generator, but the power situation was so precarious that the use of electricity, even there, was severely cut back, if not curtailed entirely. There was no electricity to run the patients' television sets, none for air conditioning in any but the most crowded wards, or in those rooms where the heat posed a threat to the lives of the patients. It was forbidden to burn reading lights, or to play radios that did not run on batteries. All available electricity was directed toward keeping the lights and equipment in good order in the operating theaters, maintaining the kitchens with their washers and driers, their toasters and refrigeration units (even at that Flesh suspected that much of what he ate was tainted or turning), to chilling those medications that required it, to operating the laundry services (though the sheets were changed now every third or fourth day instead of daily), and to keeping the power-hungry instruments going that analyzed blood and urine samples and evaluated the more complicated chemistries and tests. The X-ray machines, which required massive doses of electricity, were now used only for emergencies and only the dialysis machine and iron lung, top priorities, were unaffected by the brownout. Even electroshock therapy was suspended for all but the most violent cases, and Flesh was kept awake nights by the shrieks and howls of the nearby mad, people so far gone in their terror and delusion that even powerful tranquilizers like Thorazine were helpless to calm them.

"It isn't the heat," the Englishman said, as they both lay awake one night while the screams of crazed patients in an adjacent ward came through their open windows. (The windows had to be opened, of course, to catch whatever breeze might suddenly stir.) "It's the humidity drives them bonkers."

"They were already bonkers," Flesh said irritably.

"That exacerbated it then," the Englishman said just as irritably.

"Shit."

"You know," the Englishman said, "I don't remember heat like this even in Brit Honduras."

"Brit Honduras, Brit Honduras. Why can't you say British Honduras like everybody else?"

"Everyone in RAF called it Brit Honduras."

"And that's another thing—Raf. Can't you say R.A.F. like any normal human being?"

"I'll say what I bloody well please."

"Then be consistent. Say 'Craf.' " (The Englishman had been on detached duty with the Canadians at their air base in Brandon, Manitoba, when the first symptoms of his Lassa fever had begun to manifest themselves.)

"Why should one say 'Craf' when it's the Royal *Canadian* Air Force? I should have thought you would have heard of the Royal Canadian Air Force *exer*cises. I'd have to say 'RCAF,' wouldn't I? The whole point of an acronym is to save time. One could, I suppose, say '*R*-caf.' That might be all right, I should think. Yes. '*R*-caf.' That's not bad. It has a ring, just. One *could* say that."

"Don't say anything."

"I say. Are you saying, don't say anything?"

"Don't say bloody anything. Shut bloody up. Go to sleep just. Close your eyes and count your symptoms, check."

"Well, we *are* in a temper. You're bloody cheeky, Yank."

" '*Yank*.' Jesus. Where'd you train, on the playing fields of the back lot? Why don't they run my tests? I know what I have anyway. Why don't they read the lumbar puncture thing?"

"Well, they've their priorities, haven't they? The lumbar puncture. *That* was manly. You screaming like a banshee. Louder than our lunatic friends."

"That needle was big as a pencil."

" 'Please stop. *Please!* Oh goddamn it. Oh Jesus. Oh shit. Oh fuck.' Oh me. Oh my. Oh dear. Be adamant, Mister Softee. Be infrangible. Be *stiff*, Mister Softee. Be obdurate, be corn, be kibe!"

Flesh shut his eyes against Tanner's taunts and took the darker view. "I'm taking the darker view," he said quietly. "I'm taking the darker view because I'm going to kill him."

In the morning the nurse came for Ben with a wheelchair. It was more than a hundred degrees in the ward.

"Is it my tests? Are my tests back?"

"You have a phone call. You can take it at the nurses' station."

"A phone call? Gibberd?"

"No."

"I can't think who it could be. No one knows I'm here. Is it a woman?"

"A man."

She wheeled Ben to the phone and put the receiver in his left hand.

"Mr. Flesh?"

"Yes?"

"Zifkovic."

He'd forgotten about his manager. "Yes, Zifkovic, what is it?"

"How you feeling, sir?"

"The same. I'm waiting for my test results. Is anything wrong?"

"The stuff's all turned, sir. It's rancid glop. There must be a ton of it. The Mister Softee's all melted and running. We were working with ice for a time but I can't get no more. It's a high tide of ruined vanilla. The fruit flavors are staining everything in sight. I got the girls working on it with pails and mops but they can't keep up. A truck come down from Fargo with a new shipment today. I told him that with this heat wave we couldn't accept, but he just dumped it anyway. It's outside now. A whole lake of the shit. What should I do, Mr. Flesh? Mr. Flesh?"

"It's a plague," Flesh said. "It's a smoting."

"What? Mr. Flesh? What do you want me to do? You wouldn't believe what this stuff smells like."

"I'd believe it."

"You got any suggestions, Mr. Flesh? I didn't want to trouble you. I know you got your own problems, but I don't know what to do. You got any ideas?"

"Be hard, Mister Softee."

"What? I can hardly hear you."

"Nothing. I have no suggestions." He handed the phone back to the nurse. "It's the plague," Flesh said. "A fiery lake of Mister Softee, check."

"There you are, Mr. Flesh," another of the nurses said, coming up to him. "Dr. Gibberd has your test results. He's waiting for you."

Flesh nodded, allowed himself to be returned to the ward.

Gibberd, standing at the Englishman's bedside, waved to him. He indicated to the nurse that she set a screen up around Flesh's bed. He was carrying a manila folder with the results of Ben Flesh's tests. They were all positive. It was M.S. all right, Gibberd told him, but of a sensory rather than a motor strain. The chances of its becoming motor were remote. The fact that he'd been in remission all these years was in his favor. He really wasn't in such bad shape. For the time being there would be no treatment. Later, should it shift to a motor M.S., they could give him Ritalin, give him steroids. How would he know? Well, he'd be falling down in the streets, wouldn't he? There'd be speech impairment, wouldn't there? There'd be weakness and he wouldn't be able to tie his shoes, would he? There'd be nystagmus, don't you know? Nystagmus? A sort of rotation of the eyeballs. Anyway, there was no real reason to keep him in the hospital. They needed the beds. Flesh looked around the empty ward.

"As a matter of fact," Gibberd said, "I wish I were going with you. Where you off to now? Someplace cool?"

"I can drive?"

"Of course you can drive. I've told you, there's no strength loss, no motor impairment at all. It's just sensory. A little discomfort in your hand. So what?"

"But it's America's number-one crippler of young adults."

"M.S. is a basket term. You'll be fine. These symptoms should go away in two to three months. Boy, this heat."

"The heat, check."

"Well. Get dressed, why don't you? I'll write up your discharge papers. Be sure to stop by the cashier on the way out. Really. Don't worry about the M.S."

"Sensory discomfort, check."

"I guess you'll be wanting to get back to your Mister Softee stand before you leave. This *heat*. I could use a Mister Softee myself right now."

"The Mister Softees are all melted. The Lord has beaten the Mister Softees back into yogurt cultures."

"What's that?"

"Plague."

"What's all this about plague?"

"The plague is general throughout Dakota. We're being visited and smited."

"Well. Good luck, Mr. Flesh."

"Doctor?"

"Yes?"

"What about him?" Flesh jerked his thumb in the direction of Tanner's screen. The doctor shook his head.

"He'll be shipped off to Guernsey eventually. The R.A.F. maintains a hospital there for incurables."

The doctor extended his hand. A shiver of electric plague ran up

Flesh's hand and arm when Gibberd touched him. He felt he could start the hospital's engines just by touching them, that the energy was in his hands now, in the ruined, demyelinating nerves sputtering like live wires in his fingertips.

Gibberd left and Flesh dressed. He was about his business, heading toward the cashier and the Cadillac. (Probably it wouldn't start; the battery dead, check. Check the oil.) Then suddenly Ben turned back. He stood for a moment in the center aisle, staring in the direction of Tanner's screen. "Tanner," he said, "I don't want you to say a thing. Don't interrupt me. Just listen just.

"Gibberd has given me my walking papers. He has given me my dirty bill of health. It's interesting rather. Here we are, two guys from opposite sides of the world. Yank and Limey. Strangers. Do-be-do-be-doo. Flight Lieutenant Tanner of Eng and Brit Honduras with Nigerian virus in his gut, and me, Ben Flesh, American—don't interrupt, please just—Ben Flesh, American, ranger in Cadillac of Highway this and Interstate that. Yet somehow the both of us ill met in this hotshot trop med ward in Rap Cit S-dak. You know what? Don't, don't answer. You know what? Never mind what, I'll get to what later.

"Well. Strangers. Sickmates on the edge of the Badlands. Both incurable and generally fatal. Oh, I know a lot about *my* disease, too. When Dr. Wolfe first diagnosed my case—you remember, I told you about Dr. Wolfe—I boned up on it in the literature, in *What to Do till the Doctor Comes*. It's progressive, a neurological disorder of the central nervous system, characterized by muscular dysfunction and the formation of sclerotic, or hardening—be hard, Mister Softee—hardening patches in the brain. One's myelin—that's the soft, white fatty substance that encases the axis cylinders of certain nerve fibers: what a piece of work is a man—one's myelin sheath is unraveling like wool. It snags, you see? Like a run in a stocking. I am panty hose, Lieutenant. Vulnerable as.

"Incurable. Generally fatal. Usually slow and often, in its last stages, characterized by an odd euphoria. I was blind once, I tell you that? No family to speak of. I have heart disease and many businesses. Is this clear? No, don't answer. The point is, the lines of the drama of my life are beginning to come together, make a pattern. I mean, for God's sake, Tanner, just consider what I've been through, I've told you enough about myself. Look what stands behind me. Theatrical costumes! Songs! My history given pizzazz and order and the quality of second- and third-act curtains, coordinated color schemes for the dance numbers, the solos and showstoppers, what shows up good in the orchestra and the back of the house, and shines like the full moon in the cheap seats. I got rhythm, dig? Pacing, timing, and convention have gone into making me. Oh, Tanner, the prime rate climbs like fever and we ain't seen nothing yet. Gibberd dooms me. You should have heard him. He makes it official. He dooms me, but very soft sell so I can't even be angry with him. It's getting on, the taxis are gathering, the limos, the cops are up on their horses in the street, and I don't even know my lines—though they're coming together—or begin to understand the character.

"What do you think? Shh, that was rhetorical. What do you think? You think I should kick my preoccupations? The stuff about my godfather and my godcousins? All the Wandering Jew shit in my late-model Caddy, going farther than the truckers go, hauling my ass like cargo? Aach.

"Me and my trademarks. I'm the guy they build the access roads for, whose signs rise like stiffened peters—Keep America Beautiful—beyond the hundred-yard limit of the Interstates. A finger in every logotype. Ho-Jo's orange roof and the red star of Texaco. D.Q.'s crimson pout and the Colonel's bucket spinning, spinning. You name it, I'm in it.

"So. Doomed. Why? Shh. Because I am built to recognize it: a lip reader of big print and the scare headline. Because I'm one of those birds who ain't satisfied unless he has a destiny, even though he knows that destiny sucks. How did I get this way? I used to be a kid who ate fruit.

"Anyway. As I was saying. You know what? You know what I think? Shh. Hush. I think you're dead. Don't bother to correct me if you're not. That's what I think. I think you're dead there behind your screen, that you'll never see Guernsey. The dramatic lines demand it. Theatricality's gravitational pull. Who are you to go against something like that? You're too weak. You have to be strapped to your chair, for God's sake. So. It's nice how you can let your hair down with strangers. We were strangers, right? Have we ever met, sir? Do you know me; has there been communication between us in any way, shape, or form; have we gotten together before the show; have promises been made to you? *Thank you very much, sir. Thank you very much, ladies and gentlemen.*

"So it's agreed. We're strangers, locked each into his own symptoms, you into Lassa fever and me into my sensory problems. And somehow, as strangers will, somehow we got to talking, and gradually understood each other. I wiped your blood up. You saw my asshole with its spoor of shit. Well, strangers get close in such situations. Now I have my dirty bill of health and I'm told to move on and Dr. Gibberd tells me you're for Guernsey when your orders come through. And here's where I'm supposed to go behind them screens and shake hands. Well, I won't! I won't do it. That ain't going to happen. Because you're dead! Slumped in that queer way death has of disarraying things. So that's it. The destiny man thinks you've been put here on earth to satisfy one more cliché, to be discovered stone cold dead in a Rapid City General wheelchair. For what? So one day I'll be able to say in my impaired speech— 'There wash thish time in Shouf Dakota, and I wash on the shame woward wi-with thish young chap from the R.A.F. (He called it "Raf.") —And we got pretty close. The two of us. There was a terrible heat wave and neither of us could sleep. We were kept up half the night by the screams of mental patients who couldn't be quieted because the power was out, and even though the hospital had its own auxiliary generator, there wasn't enough power for electric-shock treatments, so we told each other the story of our life, as fellows will in hospital, and got pretty close to each other, and finally I was discharged and I went over to young Tanner's screen to say goodbye and found him dead.'

"Well, fuck *that*, Lieutenant! I like you too much to use you around fireplaces. We'll just skip it because I ain't going behind no screen to make certain, because if you *are* dead, by Christ, I don't think I could take it. I would grab a scissors and cut the lines of my drama. On the other hand, please don't disabuse me of my sense of the fitness of things. Keep still just. So long, dead guy."

He turned and started to the exit, but just as he got there he heard a loud, ripping, and unruly fart. Well, how do you like that? he thought. What was it, the critique of pure reason? Or only the guy's sphincter relaxing in death? Flesh shoved hard against the handle on the fire doors.

He was like a refugee now. A survivor, the last alive perhaps, the heat a plague and waiting for him in his late-model Cadillac baking in the hospital's open parking lot. He unlocked its doors and opened them wide but did not step in. Whatever was plastic in the car, on the dash, the steering wheel, the push-button knobs on the radio, along the sides of the doors, the wide ledge beneath the rear window, had begun to bubble, boil, the glue melting and the car's great load of padding rising yeast-like, separating, creating seams he'd been unaware of before, like the perforations on Saltines.

What has happened to my car?

It was as if an earthquake had jostled its landscape. Things were not aligned.

He feared for his right, hypersensitive hand, its stripped nerves like peeled electrical wire. If he touched anything metal in the automobile, if he so much as pressed the electric window control, it would ignite. He waited perhaps ten minutes, stuck his head inside to see if the car had cooled off. Imperceptible. Leaving the doors open, he walked back inside the hospital and went up to a fourteen- or fifteen-year-old boy who was sitting in one of the chairs in the waiting room.

"Kid," he said, "I'll give you five dollars if you start my car for me and turn the air conditioning on."

The boy looked at him nervously.

"It's all right. Look. Here." He held the money out to the boy. (It was difficult—his fingers had no discrimination left in them—to separate the bill from the others and remove it from his wallet.) "It's right there on the lot. You can see it from the window. The Cadillac with the doors open. I've just been discharged from the hospital. I'm not supposed to get overheated. Please," he said and started to leave, turning to see if the boy was following. He had not left his chair. "Well?" Flesh said. "Won't you do it? I'm not supposed to get overheated. Doctor's orders. Look, if you're afraid, I'll stay here. Here, here are my car keys. Go by yourself. Take the money with you."

"I don't drive."

"What? You don't drive? Don't they have driver's training in your high school? That's very important."

"I go to parochial school."

"Oh. Oh, I see. Parochial school. The nuns. If I came with you I could tell you what to do. I could stand outside and tell you just what to do. It's easy. They make it look like a cockpit but it's easy. All I want is for you to start it and turn the air conditioning on High. It's urgent that I get out of the heat. I've been in the hospital and the car has been standing. It's like a blast furnace. If five dollars isn't enough—"

"All right," the boy said uncertainly.

Flesh accompanied him to the car, keeping up a nutty chatter. "Parochial school," he said, "sure. Notre Dame. The Fighting Irish. Tradition. What are you so afraid? Parochial school. Broken-field running. You could be off like a shot if you wanted. What could *I* do? I'm sick. You could dodge. Fake me out. You'd go between the parked cars. What could a sick guy like me do? I couldn't catch you in the Cadillac. Relax please. Who's sick? Maybe I know him?"

"What do you mean?"

"I found you in the waiting room. You're visiting somebody. Who?"

"My dad."

"Oh, your dad. What's his name? We're fellow patients. Maybe I know him."

"Richard Mullen? He had a heart attack."

"Dick Mullen's your pop? *Dick* Mullen?"

"Yes, sir."

"Oh, he'll be fine. I heard the docs talking. He's out of the woods."

"You really heard that?"

"Oh, absolutely. Out of the woods. On the mend. His last two cardiograms have been very exciting. They've definitely stabilized.

· 138 ·

He mustn't let you see you're worried. I mean, you mustn't let him see you're worried. Who's your patron saint? Pray to your patron saint for a cheerful countenance. Pop's going to be terrific."

The kid began to cry.

"What's this? What's this? What kind of a patron saint are we talking about here? Some deafo?" Flesh looked into the sky. "That's *cheer*ful countenance, not *tear*ful!" He smiled and the boy laughed. They were at the car, Ben standing behind the boy at the driver's side, feeling the terrific heat.

"Get in," he said. The boy hesitated. "What, you think I'm the witch in Hansel and Gretel? You think I could fake *you* out? A broken-field runner from parochial school? Get in, get in." He handed the boy the keys and told him what to do and, once the engine had started, how to work the air conditioning. He had the boy close all the doors. "Let me know when it's cool," he said. "Rap on the window with your knuckles." In a few minutes the boy came out of the car. They changed places. Ben lowered the window and tried to give him the five dollars, but the boy shook his head. "Take it, go on, don't be crazy. Take it, you saved my life."

"Really," the boy said, "it's all right."

"The laborer is worth his hire. Take the money. Buy yourself some Mister Softees."

"No. Please. Really. I don't want the money."

"What, listen, is this a religious thing? Is this something to do with parochial school?"

"What you told me about my father," the boy said. "What you heard from the doctors about his improvement. That's all the payment I, you know, need. Thank you."

Flesh was thinking about his health, the prognosis, the things he'd read since Wolfe had first explained the meaning of his blindness. He was thinking of what one day he could expect to feel in his face, flies walking lightly in place of his cheeks, the heavy sensation of sand between his toes and in his socks even when he was barefoot, of weakness in his limbs, of hunks of deadened flesh along his thighs and torso like queer grafted absences against which the inside of his arms would brush as they might brush against rubber or wood, sensations he could not imagine now, feelings under his thumbnails, the ridges of his cock, things in his pores, stuff in his lip, thinking of the infinite symptoms of the multiple sclerotic.

"Yeah," he said. "I understand. You're a good boy. Tell Mother. She probably needs cheering up, too." And he put the car in gear and drove against the fantastic record heat wave, looking for a hole in it as pioneers traveling west might once have looked for passes through the mountains, as explorers had paddled and portaged to seek a northwest passage. He used side roads and Interstates, paved and unpaved secondary state roads and county, bypasses and alternates, limited-access divided highways and principal thruways, feeling chased by brownouts and power-failed space, civilization's demyelination, slipping safely into temporary zones of remission and waiting in these in motels until the symptoms of the heat wave caught up with him again and the electricity sputtered and was snuffed out like a candle and the air conditioning died.

He gassed up wherever he could. The pumps would not work where the electricity failed, and whenever he came to one of those zones of remission—the heat, constant everywhere, did not in itself insure a brownout; rather the land and towns, invisibly networked with mad zigzag jigsaw power grids, grids like a crossword, secret-coded with electrical messages he couldn't break (in a single block the power might be off in five adjacent buildings but on in the sixth and seventh and off again in an eighth and ninth), had been mysteriously parceled; agreements had been made, contingency plans had gone into effect, Peter robbed here to pay Paul, there permitted to hold his own, a queer but absolute and even visible (the lights, the lights) negotiation and exchange like the complicated maneuvers of foreign currency, the towns seeming to have grown wills, a capacity to conspire, to give and to take; he had an impression of thrown switches, jammed buttons, broken locks—he first sought out service stations, accepting Regular if there was no Premium, refreshing his oil even if it was down by less than a cup, filling everything: his radiator, his battery, even the container that held the water that sprayed his windshield, to the brim, the brim. Only then did he seek a motel. And, registered, walked to a hardware store, not wanting to use any of his precious gasoline in the wasteful stop-and-start of town driving. In the hardware store he would purchase five-gallon cans and carry them back empty to the gas station closest to his motel to have them filled. These he would store in his trunk, moving his grips and garment bags onto the backseat of his car. (At one time he had as much as sixty gallons in gas cans.) And flashlights, too. And batteries. Bandoliers of batteries, quivers of them, an ordnance of Eveready. And in bookstores atlases, guidebooks of the region to supplement the service-station maps, the Texaco and Shell and Mobil and Phillips 66 South Dakotas and Nebraskas and Kansases and Colorados he already had. Finally to return to the motel, not yet undressing even, pulling a chair up to the television and switching from channel to channel— these were hick towns, the sticks, on cable TV, near the eastern edges of mountain time, the western edges of central—to catch the weather reports. (He bought a portable radio which he took with him into the motels to listen to the forecasts on the local radio station.) Becoming in that frantic week and a fraction since he had left Rapid City behind him, the stench of his spoiled, dissolved flavors in his nostrils—he'd stopped to see Zifkovic first, with him investigated the extent of the damage, the high-water mark of the melted Mister Softees, the smashed artificial strawberry and broken chocolate, the ruined crushed banana and pineapple and decomposed orange, the filmy vanilla and the serums of lime and lemon, all the scum of melted fruit, oils now, wet paint—a savant of conditions, an anchorman of drought and heat, a seer almost, second-guessing the brownouts, seeing them coming, a quick study of the peak hours, and not wanting to be caught in the motel room when the town stalled, dreading that, forgetting even his symptoms in his incredible concentration and prophecy. Hitting at last on tricks, calling the local power stations and electric companies, on ruses getting through to the executives themselves, calling long distance to Omaha even, misrepresenting himself. (The Mister Softee experience in South Dakota had taught him what to say: "Mr. Rains, Herb Castiglia here. I'm Innkeeper at the Scotts Bluff Ramada and I've got this problem, sir. I've got an opportunity to buy a ton of ice. Now the son of a bitch who's pushing it wants forty cents a pound for the stuff. That's a cockeyed price and for my dough the guy's no better than a looter. He won't sell less than a ton, and at forty cents a pound that comes to eight hundred bucks. I'm over a barrel, Mr. Rains, but I've got two or three thousand dollars tied up in my meats for my restaurant. What I need to know is if there's going to be a brownout, and, if so, how long you expect it to last. If she blows I'm okay for six to eight hours, but in this heat any longer than that and the stuff will turn into silage. What do I do, Mr. Rains? I got to cover myself. Can you give me a definitive no or a definite yes?") And striking responsive chords in Mr. Rains, in Mr. DeVilbiss, in Mr. Schopf, small businessman to big, getting at last the inside information he could not get on the half dozen or so channels available to him on the cable TV, or the local country-music and farm-report radio stations. And acting on these advices, skipping town, hitting the road. Driving after dark on the hotter days, the hundred-plus scorchers—to cut down on the air conditioning, to keep it on Low instead of High as he'd have to do in the daytime, conserving his gas, four days and he hadn't had to tap the reserves in his trunk—and looking over the broad plains for the lights of a town, any town, a prospector of the electric.

But his body—he'd been sick, he'd been in hospital, M.S. was a stress disease—couldn't adjust to the new hours and he had to return to the old pattern of traveling the highways during the day, thinking to change directions when the radio told him of the brownouts in western Nebraska—he'd been heading for Wyoming, for the high country, mountains, as if electricity followed the laws of gravity, pushing his Cadillac uphill (but that wasted gas, too, didn't it?) toward the headwaters of force—and drop toward Kansas. He couldn't decide. Then, on Interstate 80, he saw detour signs spring up sudden as targets in skeet, the metal diamonds of early warning. He slammed his brakes, slowed to fifty, forty, twenty-five, ten, as the road turned to gravel and dirt at the barricades and the traffic merged two ways. A tall girl in an orange hard hat stood lazily in the road holding up a heavy sign that said SLOW. Her bare arms, more heavily muscled than his own, rubbed death in his face. He yearned for her, her job, her indifference, her strength, her health. He stopped the car and got out. "Tell me," he said, "are you from west of here or east?"

"What? Get back in your car, you're tying up traffic."

"Where do you live? West, east?"

"Get back in that car or I'll drive it off into a field for you."

"Look," he said, "all I want . . ." She raised her arms, lifting her sign high and plunging its metal shaft into the earth, where it quivered for a moment and then stayed, stuck there like an act of state.

"You want to try me?" she threatened.

"I want to know if they've still got power west of here."

"Power's all out west of here. Get back in your car." He lowered his eyes and returned to his car and, going forward slowly and slowly back, made a U-turn in the dirt and gravel narrows.

"Hey," the tall girl shouted. "What the hell—"

On the sixth day, on Interstate 70, between Russell and Hays—the radio was silent—he looked out the window and was cheered to see oil rigs—he remembered what they were called: "donkey pumps"—pumping up oil from the farmers' fields, the ranchers'. The pumps drove powerful and slow as giant pistons, turning like the fat metal gear on locomotives just starting up. Ridiculous things in the open field, spaced in apparent random, some almost at the very edge of the highway, that dipped down toward the ground and up again like novelty birds into glasses of water. Abandoned, churning everywhere unsupervised and unattended for as far as he could see, they gave him an impression of tremendous reservoirs of power, indifferent opulence, like cars left standing unlocked and keys in the ignition. There was no brownout here. (Of course, he thought, *priorities*: oil for the lamps of Asia, for the tanks and planes of political commitment and intervention. Flesh was apolitical but nothing so drove home to him the sense of his nation's real interests as the sight of these untended donkey pumps in these obscure Kansas fields. Wichita had been without electricity for two days while the thirsty monsters of vacant west central Kansas used up enough to sustain a city of millions.) He pulled off the Interstate at Hays and went up the exit ramp, heading for the Texaco station, the sign for which, high as a three-story building, he had seen a mile off, a great red star standing in the daylight.

It wasn't open.

He crossed the road and drove to the entrance of a Best Western

and returned to his car. Somehow he forgot what he was about and continued by mistake for perhaps three miles on the dirt road. The sheer comfort of the ride on the dry, packed dirt—it was like riding on velvet, the smoothest journey he had ever taken—lulled him, so that finally it was his comfort itself that warned him of his danger, that taught him he was lost. Oh, oh, he mourned when he discovered what had happened. A pretty pass, a pretty pass when well-being has been so long absent from me that when I feel it it comes as an alarm, *it* a symptom. He looked for some place he could turn the car around and came at last to a turnoff for a farm. Dogs howled when he pulled into the driveway. He saw their grim and angry faces in his headlamps and feared for both them and himself when they disappeared from sight—moving as slowly as I am, they will be at my tires now—dreading the thump that would signal he had killed one. But he managed to turn back up the dirt road he had come down—it no longer seemed so comfortable a ride—and regained State Route 15, turning north toward Schuyler.

As he had feared, Schuyler—allowed only the faintest print on the map, and not on the Shell map at all—was nothing but a crossroads, a gas station, a tavern, a couple of grocery stores, an International Harvester Agency, and three or four other buildings, a grange, a picture show, a drugstore, some other things he could not identify in the dark, homes perhaps, or a lawyer's or a doctor's office. He stopped the car to consult his map again.

It would have to be Columbus, eighteen miles west. The 1970 census put the population at 15,471. A good-sized town, a small city, in fact. Sure. Very respectable. He had high hopes for Columbus and turned on the radio. He could not pull in Columbus but he was not discouraged. It was past 2 a.m. after all. Good-sized town or not, these were solid working people. They would have no need or use for an all-night radio station. He started the engine again and swung left onto U.S. 30. (U.S. 30, yes! A good road, a respectable road, a first-class road. It went east all the way to Aurora, Illinois, where it spilled into the Interstates and big-time toll roads that slip into Chicago. It paralleled Interstate 80 and even merged with it at last and leaped along with it across 90 percent of Wyoming, touching down at all the big towns, Cheyenne and

Laramie and Rawlins and Rock Springs, before striking off north on its own toward Boise and Pocatello and west to Portland in Oregon. He was satisfied with U.S. 30. U.S. 30 was just the thing. It would absolutely lead him out of the wilderness. He was feeling good.) And when he swung west onto 30 and got a better view of the Schuyler gas station, he saw the pump in the sway of his headlights. *The pump!*

Good God, what a jerk he'd been! Of course. Oh, this night had taught him a lesson all right! That he need never fear the lack of gas again. All he had to do when the gauge got low was to head for the hick towns with their odd old-fashioned gas pumps that didn't give a shit for brownouts or power failures, that worked by—what?—hydraulics, principles of physics that never let you down, capillary action, osmosis, all that sort of thing. He was absolutely cheerful as he tooled along toward Columbus. He was tired and grotty, but he knew that as soon as he hit Columbus things would work themselves out. He would get the best damn motel room in town. If they had a suite—sure, a town like that, better than fifteen thousand, certainly they would have suites—he'd take that. He would sleep, if he wished, with the lights on all night. There was electricity to burn—ha ha—in Columbus. He felt it in his bones.

And sure enough. In fifteen minutes his brights picked up the light-reflecting city-limits sign of Columbus, Nebraska—population 15,471, just like the map said—touched the glass inset sign and seemed to turn it on as you would turn on an electric light. And just past it, somewhere off to his left—and this must still be the *out*skirts—two great shining lights. Probably a party. Two-thirty and probably a party. Oh, what a live-wire town Columbus! He would have to build a franchise here. Tomorrow he'd scout it and decide what kind. Meanwhile, on a whim, tired as he was, he turned left on the street where the two great lights were burning and drove toward them.

He seemed to be driving down an incline in a sort of park. Probably it wasn't a party as he'd first suspected. Probably it was the Columbus, Nebraska, Tourist Information Center. But open at night? Jesus, what a *town!* What a *live wire*, go-to-hell-god-damn-it *town!*

Then he was perhaps a hundred or so feet from the lights and in a kind of circular parking lot. He parked and took his flashlight and walked toward the lights.

It was not until he was almost upon them that he saw that they were not electric lights at all, that he saw that they were flickering, that he saw that they were flames, that he saw that they bloomed like two bright flowers from twin pots sunk into the ground, that he saw that they were set beside a brass plaque, that he saw the inscription on the plaque and read that these twin combustions were eternal flames in memory of the dead and missing Columbus Nebraskans of World Wars I and II, Korea, and Vietnam.

"Oh," he groaned aloud, "oh God, oh my God, oh my, my God, oh, oh." And he wept, and his weeping was almost as much for those Columbus Nebraskans as it was for himself. His cheerfulness before, his elevated mood, was it the euphoria? Was it? No, it couldn't have been. It was too soon. Maybe it was only his hope. He hoped it was his hope. Maybe that's all it was and not the euphoria. Feel, feel his tears. He was not euphoric now. His disappointment? No, no, disappointment could not disappoint euphoria. No. He was sad and depressed, so he was still well. Hear him moan, feel his tears, how wet. Taste them, how salty. He remembered, as he was admonished by the inscription on the plaque, the dead soldiers and sailors and marines and coast guardsmen of Columbus who had died in the wars to preserve his freedom. He remembered good old Tanner, dead himself perhaps in Rapid City General, and the father of the kid—though he'd only heard about him—who started his car for him, the man with the heart attack. He prayed that the lie he'd told was true, that the boy's father's cardiograms had stabilized. (He was sorry he'd lied to the boy. See? He was sorry. He felt bad. How's *that* euphoric?) He recalled the boy himself, the broken-field runner.

"Oh, Christ," he said, "I, *I* am the broken-field runner. I, Flesh, am the broken broken-field runner and tomorrow I will look at the map and see where I must go to stop this nonsense and wait out this spell of crazy weather."

Except for the eternal flames, Columbus was black till the sun rose.

So it was not the first time he was fooled. Nor the last.

The last—he stayed on three days in Hays, Kansas, because in the morning the power came back on; he was very tired, exhausted; he needed the rest—was the evening of the day he decided to leave Hays. At five o'clock the power failed again. Rested—he felt he could drive at night once more—he climbed back into the Cadillac and returned to Interstate 70. His gas cans—screw the hick pumps, he'd decided, and had accumulated the twelve cans by then and had had them filled—were in the trunk, his grips and garment bags again on the backseat. He'd eaten at the motel and was ready for the long drive west. (He'd decided to go to Colorado Springs.)

After the layover in Hays it was pleasant to be back on the highway again, pleasant to be driving in the dark, pleasant to be showered, to wear fresh linen, to be insulated from the heat wave in the crisp, sealed environment of the air-conditioned car, to read the soft illuminated figures on the dash, the glowing rounds and ovals like electric fruit.

He leaned forward and turned on the radio, fiddled with the dial that brought up the rear speakers, and blended the sound with those in front. His push buttons, locked in on New York and Chicago stations, yielded nothing but a mellow—he'd adjusted the treble, subordinating it to the bass—static, not finally unpleasant, reassuring him of the distant presence of energies, of storms, far off perhaps but hinting relief. He listened for a while to the sky and then turned the manual dial, surgical—and painful, too; this was his right hand—as a ham, fine tuning, hoping to hone a melody or a human voice from the smear of sound. It was not yet nine o'clock but there was nothing—only more sky.

But of course. I'm on FM, he realized when he had twice swung the dial across its keyboard of wavelength. He switched to AM and moved the dial even more slowly. Suddenly, somewhere in the soprano, a voice broke in commandingly, overriding the static and silence. Flesh turned up the treble. It was a talk show, the signal so firm that Ben assumed—he had left Kansas and crossed the Colorado line—it was Denver.

"The Dick Gibson Show. Go ahead, please, you're on the air."

"Hello?"

"Hello. Go ahead, please."

"Am I on the air? I hear this guy."

"Sir, turn your radio down."

"I can hear this guy talking. Hello? Hello?"

"Turn your radio down or I'll have to go to another caller."

"Hello?"

"We'll go to a commercial."

There was a pause. Then this announcement:

"Tired of your present job? Do you find the routine boring and unchallenging? Are you underpaid or given only the most menial tasks? Then a job with the Monsanto Company may be just what you're looking for. Monsanto Chemical has exciting openings with open-ended opportunities for men and women who have had two years' experience in the field of Sensory Physiology or at least one year of advanced laboratory work in research neurophysiology. Preferential treatment will be given to qualified candidates with a background in ethnobotany and experimental cell biology, and we are particularly interested in specialists holding advanced degrees in such areas as the determination of crystal structures by X-ray analysis, kinetics and mechanism, or who have published widely in the fields of magnetic resonance, molecular orbital theory, quantum chemistry, and the nuclear synthesis of organic compounds. Applicants will be expected to have a high degree of competence in structure and spectra and advanced statistical mechanics. Monsanto is an equal-opportunity employer."

"The Dick Gibson Show. You're on the air, go ahead, please."

"Dick?"

"Yes, sir."

"Dick, I've had this fabulous experience and I want to share it with your audience. I mean it's a believe-it-or-not situation, a one-in-a-million thing. It's practically a miracle. Can I share this with your audience, Dick?"

"Sure, go ahead."

"Yes. Thank you. Well, to begin at the beginning, I'm a brother."

"A brother."

"Yeah. But you see my parents split up when I was still a little kid and then my mom died and my father was too sick to take care of us, so my brother and me were farmed out to different relatives. What I mean is, I went with my mother's sister, my aunt, but she couldn't take care of the both of us so my brother went with an older cousin. I was six and my brother he must have been around eight at the time. Well, my aunt married a soldier and they adopted me legally and he was transferred and we pulled up our roots and we moved with him, and I was, you know, what do they call it, an army brat, going from post to post with my aunt and my new father, the corporal. He was a thirty-year man and we like traveled all over, pulling up our roots every three years or so, and when I was old enough to leave the nest I got a job with this company, and as time went on I met a girl and we dated for a while and finally we decided to get married. Now we have children of our own, a boy seven and a cute little girl four.

"Well, sir, I'm with the J. C. Penney store, and I made a good record and Penney's opened up a new store in the suburbs and about a year ago my department head asked me if I'd consider moving to the new store with the idea in mind that I could train the new kitchen-appliance salesmen and be the head of the department and run my own ship. Well, of course when an opportunity like that opens up, you jump at it. Opportunity knocks but once, if you know what I mean."

"I know what you mean," Dick Gibson said. "What are you getting at, please?"

"You mean the miracle?"

"Yes, sir."

"That's what I was getting at. Yesterday a guy comes in for a present for his wife's birthday. He was thinking in terms of a toaster, but he didn't know exactly what model he had in mind, so I asked him if he had kids and he said yeah, he had two kids, twin boys, ten years old. 'Well,' I said, 'in that case you probably want the four-slice toaster.' That's our Ezy-Clean pop-up job with an adjustable thermostat control and a crumb tray that opens for easy cleaning in a handsome chrome-plated steel exterior. I have the same toaster in my kitchen."

"Yes?"

"Oh yeah. So he asked to see it and I showed it to him and I told him that he could compare it to any model on the market at the price and it couldn't be beat and that's the truth. Well, to make a long story short, he went for it. I mean, it was just what he had in mind without knowing it and I asked, as I always do, if it would be cash or charge. He said charge. I asked if he wanted to take it with or have it sent. He said take it with. So he gave me his charge plate, and when I went to my machine to write up the sales slip, I couldn't help but notice when I read his charge plate that he was my brother."

"Really?"

"My long-lost brother."

"That *is* a coincidence."

"Wait. When I went back, I was like shaking all over and he noticed it and he asked what was wrong and I said, 'Are *you* Ronald L. Pipe?' And he says, 'Yes. What about it?' And I tell him, I tell him I'm Lou B. Kramer!"

"Oh?"

"Well, I expected him to fall down in a dead faint, but he doesn't bat an eye. Then I realize, I realize Kramer's my *adopted* name, my stepfather's name, the corporal's."

"The thirty-year man's."

"Right. And it's been, what, twenty-eight years since we laid eyes on each other. He's bald, and I'm prematurely gray and I've put on a little weight from all that toast. Of *course* we don't recognize each other. So I tell him his history—our history—that when he was eight years old his folks split up and his mom passed away and he was raised by an older cousin. 'Can this be?' he asked. 'How do you know this?' And I explain everything, who I am and everything, and that if he'd paid cash or if it hadn't been for my habit of reading my customers' names off their Charge-a-Plates we'd never have found each other to this day."

"Well," Dick Gibson said.

"Wait. That's just the beginning of the coincidence. I punched out early and we had a couple of beers together."

"I see."

"We both drink beer!"

"Gee."

"We're both married and have kids!"

"How do you like that?"

"His wife's birthday is the day after tomorrow!"

"Oh?"

"*My* wife was born in the springtime, too!"

"Hmn."

"We both *bowl!*"

"You both do?"

"I average 130, 135."

"And he averages?"

"About 190."

"Do you have anything else in common?"

"We're both Democrats. Neither of us is a millionaire."

"I see. Well, that's really— I'm going to have to take another—"

"*We both watch Monday-night football!*"

"—another . . ."

"When we go out with our wives—when we go out with our wives—"

"Yes?"

"*We both use babysitters!*"

". . . call."

"*Neither of us has been in prison; we both like thick juicy steaks. Dick, Dick, both of us, both of us drive!*"

"Thank you, sir, for sharing your miracle. The Dick Gibson Show. You're on the air, go ahead, please."

Flesh couldn't stop laughing. Things would work out. He left Interstate 70 and turned off onto U.S. 24 to drive the remaining eighty or so miles to Colorado Springs. At Peyton, Colorado, where his headlights ignited a sign that read COLORADO SPRINGS, 24 MILES, the signal was so powerful that he might have been in Chicago listening, say, to the local station of a major network.

When he was almost there, there was a station break. "This is Dick Gibson," Dick Gibson said, "WMIA, Miami Beach."

Then he panicked. It's not, he thought, because it's so close that it's so clear, *it's because all the other stations have failed!* It's because America has everywhere failed, the power broken down!

And that, *that*, was the last time he was fooled.

Yet the lights were on in Colorado Springs.

Colorado Avenue was a garden of neon. The lights of the massage parlors burned like fires. The sequenced circuitry of the drive-ins and motels and theaters and bars was a contagion of light. A giant Big Boy's statue illuminated by spots like a national monument. The golden Shell signs, an old Mobil Pegasus climbing invisible stairs in the sky. The traffic lights, red as bulbs in darkrooms, amber as lawn furniture, green as turf. The city itself, awash in light, suggested boardwalks, carnivals, steel piers, million-dollar miles, and, far off, private homes like upturned dominos or inverted starry nights. Down Cheyenne Mountain and Pikes Peak niagaras of lights were laid out like track. Don't they know? he wondered. Is it Mardi Gras? Don't they know? And he had a sense of connection, the roads that led to Rome, of nexus, the low kindling point of filament, of globe and tubing, as current poured in from every direction, rushing like electric water seeking its own level to ignite every conductor, conflagrating base metals, glass, the white lines down the centers of the avenues bright as tennis shoes, stone itself, the city a kind of full moon into which he'd come at last from behind its hidden darker side. The city like the exposed chassis of an ancient radio, its embered tubes and color-coded wire.

He drove to the Broadmoor Hotel and checked in. Only a suite was available. That was fine, he would take it. How long would he be staying? Open-ended. A bill would be presented every three days. That was acceptable. They did not honor credit cards. No problem. He would pay by check. He could give them two hundred dollars in cash right then if they liked. And was willing to show them his money. That wasn't necessary. All right then. Could he get a bellboy to help with his bags? He was tired. Then he could go to his rooms at once. The boy would take his car keys and bring his bags up when he had parked Mr. Flesh's car for him. Fine. His suite was in the new building. The new building, was that far? Oh no. Not at all. Another boy would show him the way. That was fine. That was just what he wanted.

He tipped his guide two dollars and sat on a Georgian chair by a white Georgian desk and put a call through to Riverdale.

He shoved the cartridge into the stereo and dedicated it aloud to Irving's wife, Frances. *My Fair Lady* took him past St. Charles to Wentzville, *Candide*, played twice, to the Kingdom City exit, *West Side Story* to Columbia, where he ate lunch. He put his '74 Cadillac through the Kwik Kar Wash. It cost him seventy-five cents and, as far as he could see, did no better job than his Robo-Wash in Washington, D.C., which took no longer and was a quarter cheaper. The difference—though there was no one ahead of him now—would have to be in customer convenience. His lot was shallower, the washbarn closer to the street. His customers, when there was a line, had to wait in the street. That meant a few bucks off the top to the cop every week. This guy's machinery, set off to the side at the rear of his lot, permitted his customers to form a sort of U-shaped line, maybe eleven cars long, no, twelve or thirteen— he hadn't allowed for the cars at the pit of the U—before they backed up into the street. Still, the sharp turn they had to make at the back of the lot to get into the barn must have chipped plenty of fenders. The management had put up a "Not Responsible" notice, but Flesh could guess how much that was worth. The insurance company would hassle him plenty, and why not? The customer couldn't read the disclaimer until he had already committed himself, made or begun his turn into the narrow passageway, and it was too late, particularly if there was a strand of cars behind him, to back out. Sure. Six of one, half dozen of the other. The guy could keep his extra twenty-five cents. Flesh would rather deal with cops than insurance companies any day of the week.

What the hell was he thinking about? He'd dumped his Robo-Wash two years before. A mistake from the first. Strictly a novelty. A place to give kids the illusion—sitting in their cars while foamy water shot at them from all directions—that they were snugly drowning in the sea, and the illusion, as giant brushes like rolls of carpet rose up from the floor and left the wall, that they were being softly crushed. A novelty. A ride. Family entertainment. And never mind the self-creating traffic jams, not that there could have been that many. He'd picked a lousy location. Washington was black. Those people cared for their cars, polished them like flatware, either doing it themselves or, going the other way, springing for two-fifty and three-dollar jobs. He couldn't have had the Robo a year.

He'd gone to Kitty with the proposition, told her the money—what had it cost him? under $12,000 probably—wasn't significant enough to trouble the sibs with, and asked her to co-sign for him personally.

Kitty, the bed wetter, had never married. She did not think it fair to ask her husband to sleep on rubber sheets. Strangely, she never pissed her sheets during an afternoon nap or when she dozed off reading in a chair or watching TV. Only at night did she lose control, at night when the dreams came. The dreams, Flesh thought, the *dreams* she must have!

"This is really something, Kitty," he'd said on their way to the place in Queens where he had first seen the Robo-Wash. "Wait, you'll see."

"Ben, it isn't necessary. You know I trust your judgment. We all do. I don't have to see the car wash. If you say it's good, I believe you."

"No. You have to see it. I want you to know just what you're getting into. After all, I'm asking you to guarantee the loan personally. I want you to get an idea of the potential."

"That's the part I *don't* understand. Why come to me? If it's all that great, my brothers and sisters would go along with it as a matter of course, and you say the money isn't significant."

"Well, that's the point. See, this is what I have in mind, Kitty. Up to now I've hit you kids collectively because the sums more often than not have been considerable, but suppose we do this, suppose I start up a series of small businesses and approach you one by one. We might all make more money." Years before he had begun to cut them in, as co-signers of his loans, for a small share of the profits, though they had never actually had to put up a penny. He'd argued that they were entitled to it. Under the terms of their father's will he was not obliged to do this, but he insisted. The sibs, though well off, were none of them making the fortune their father had made. Some, profligate, had already gone through a good deal of their capital. And that, of course, was the argument he had used to convince them, for they truly had not wanted to change an arrangement which had never actually cost them anything. "Look, Gus-Ira, I know *you* don't need it. You're a doctor, you do very well, but Oscar, the rock band, the bus he paid for and outfitted to travel in, what about him? Until he cuts a hit record he could really *use* the money. What the hell, even if it only pays the gas and oil for one of those trips he makes to the rock festivals, it would come in handy." In this way, addressing the generosity of each, he had finally gotten them to accept the six or seven hundred dollars a year apiece that he gave them.

"Well yes," Kitty said, "but I don't know anything about business. I trust your judgment."

"I just want you to see. I don't want you to trust my judgment. You shouldn't go into things with your eyes closed. Wait, Kitty, it's just a bit farther. We're almost there."

He turned off Queens Boulevard and went out Jamaica Avenue. They had to go more slowly now. There was much traffic. It was a densely commercial street. He honked at the double-parked trucks. They drove along under the elevated tracks, saw the shower of sparks from passing trains burn themselves out like meteors, shooting stars. They proceeded past Laundromats, $5 a pair shoe outlets, gas stations, Chinese restaurants, taverns.

"Where is this place?"

"It's only a few more minutes."

And turned into the Robo-Wash. He maneuvered the Cadillac carefully into place, guiding it gently as he could to the struts and chocks. They were in an odd cinder-block building like a tiny covered bridge, the walls tapestried with machinery, the ceiling veined with pipes that ran overhead like rods for shower curtains. Flesh read the instructions:

1. Make certain front wheels are properly aligned with T-bar. Both tires must be in contact with metal chocks.
2. Turn off ignition.
3. Car must be in neutral.
4. Lower window on driver's side and insert 50¢ in slot. Quarters or half dollars only.
5. Raise all windows! Do *not* touch brakes or steering wheel.

"You've got to watch this, Kitty. You've never seen anything like it."

He slipped seven quarters into the machine.

"But that's $1.75. It says fifty cents."

"This will give us a better opportunity to see what it can do. Raise your window. Is your window up?"

"Yes."

"Here we go then."

They heard a subterranean growl as some sort of metal hook rose below them, engaged and grappled the axle. "She's locking it," Ben said. "It's amazing. It adjusts universally. Like the tone arm on a phonograph that mixes ten- and twelve-inch records."

Then there was a long hiss like the sound of air escaping from a tire.

"Oh, Ben," Kitty said.

And then, as the car began to be pulled forward, sheets of water, panes of it—the extra dollar and a quarter, Ben thought happily—slapped at them from every direction at once, like waves, like a riptide, and so thick that the illusion was they were *indeed* in the sea under water, Kopechne'd. Detergent added now, dropping like snow, foaming the windows, frothing their vision, Kitty grabbed his hand and squeezed.

"Something's wrong," she said, "the extra money you put in, you must have jammed it or something. Oh, Ben."

While the car rocked back and forth—he had not turned off the ignition, had left it in drive; it was being tugged back as it strained against the hooks; Kitty, of course, hadn't noticed—the heavy brushes came out of the walls, closing in on them like the trick rooms of matinee serials. The timing was off, the brushes embracing the car even as the water continued to shoot out of every pore in the pipes, crushing the detergent against the windshield, twirling, lapping at the car like the bristled tongue of some prehistoric beast. Kitty had both arms around his neck. "Please, Ben. Oh God. Please, Ben. When does it stop?"

"I don't know. Something's wrong," Flesh said, pressing the brake and causing them to lurch forward. "Jesus, do you think it'll crush us? I can't see out." It was true. The interior was almost totally dark.

The brushes were all about them now, scraping the long sides of the car, settled on the roof, rolling and bumping as the Cadillac, in drive, threw their timing off still further and Ben pulled at the bottom of the steering wheel with one hand. From his side he lowered his electric window a bit. "I want to see if—" Then lowered Kitty's.

"Ben, let's get out," Kitty said nervously. "It's beginning to come in. We've got to get out."

"We can't," he shouted over the sound of the water and the grunt and grinding of the brushes, "we'd never be able to open the doors. The brushes are up against us. Even if we could get out, the bristles would tear us to pieces."

"Oh, God. Oh, Ben," Kitty screamed. "When does it stop?"

"We've still got to go through Rinse," Ben yelled.

"*What?*"

"*Rinse. It's part of the cycle!*"

And that's—Kitty practically in his lap now, her arms thrown about his neck like a drowner, her legs capturing his as though she meant to shinny up him to safety—when he felt the warm trickle of her pee as it rolled down his thigh and knee and splashed against his shoes and puddled the thick carpet of his Cadillac.

So he knew why he'd approached her. For his priviness to those wild dreams that no man but himself shared, not of the dead, not even of sex, but simply of excitement, Kitty's kiddy spook-house conjurings, her fervid invocation of plight, trap, and wicked pitfall that froze her reason and loosened her urine, to induce in her that high-strung roller coaster, snap-the-whip, loop-the-loop, vertiginous vision he'd somehow recognized in her from the beginning—known would be there—but till now had never seen. He shoved the lever into neutral, shut off the engine.

"It's like this at night, isn't it?"

"Oh, Ben."

"At night. In the dark. This is how it is then, isn't it?"

"Please."

"Isn't it?"

"Yes," she said. She was whimpering.

"It's all right," he told her, "the brushes, they're just cloth, the bristles are smooth as chamois."

"Oh, Ben."

"It's all right," he said, "everything is fine. Look, Kitty dear, they've already gone back into the walls."

"Oh, Ben," she said. "Oh, Ben, oh, you son of a bitch."

She raised no objection when he told her brothers and sisters about his Robo-Wash proposition. But it was a long time before she would speak to him again.

He drove the remaining 120 miles to Kansas City without the tape deck or radio. Oh my oh my but he had the memories.

# 3

Ghiardelli Square in San Francisco. Atlanta's Underground. Yes, and Hartford's Constitution Plaza. Louisville's Belvedere. Minneapolis's Mall and L.A.'s Century City. Denver's Larimer Square and Chicago with its Old Towns and New Towns. The Paramus Mall in New Jersey. Lincoln Road in Miami Beach—a bad example. Pittsburgh's Golden Triangle—a good one. St. Louis with its Laclede's Landing. The new Cincinnati. The new Detroit, Milwaukee. Albany's billion-dollar civic center.

What was not highway was Downtown, the New Jerusalem. America's Malls and Squares and Triangles like figures in geometry. Just the white man fighting back. Regrouping. Floating promises with bond issues. What had been white and then black was now white again. Phoenixy. The old one-two. Real estate's chemotherapy, its surgical demolitions and plastic surgery. Like a cycle in nature or a rotation of crops. Allowing the blighted inner cities to lie fallow, the cores to oxidize—all those Catfish Rows of the doomed. Then Reclamation, Rehabilitation, Conversion, Salvation. Resurrection. The Tokyoization of the United States, the Boweries beaten into Berlin showcases. As if America had lost a war, a lulu, a Churchillian son of a bitch. We shall fight them on the beaches, we shall fight them on the streets, we shall fight them on the slums and on the ghettos. We will never surrender. We will smear them. But as if we hadn't, didn't, and the worst had happened, the bottom dropping out of victory. And were now being reparated, mollified, kissed where it hurt and made better. Given this—what?—Democracy and these—what?—monuments of the mercantile, these new Sphinxes and new Pyramids, these new wonders of the world. And everything's up to date in Kansas City.

The prime interest rate is 11 percent and he stands in the five-story lobby of the Crown Center Hotel, the first jewel in Hall-mark's Triple Crown.

He has seen, from the highway, the twin saddles of the Harry S. Truman Sports Complex, two sloping stadia like counters in shoes, home of the Chiefs, home of the Royals—what, he thinks, what a franchise!—glimpsed the three-million-dollar scoreboard, tall as a high-rise, the glassed-in private boxes and suites along the rim of the stadia like handsome molding. (He has read that some of these rent for $18,000 a year. Eighteen Thousand Dollars.) And has proceeded through Kansas City's squeezed downtown with its decaying warehouses and skyscrapers, some abandoned, nostalgia in the making like a bacteria culture, and out Truman Road and onto Grand Avenue to the Crown Center, passing the hotel with its high cantilevered tower like a machine-gun-emplacement on a prison wall, the windows like stereo speakers or light meters on cameras. Passing the Crown Center Shops on his right, the squares and plazas and fountains and open ice rink on his left, Hall's huge office complex, vaguely—he has seen line drawings, even knows where the apartments will stand—like a locomotive, and turns right into the parking garage, and parks—no room on the Jack of Hearts, no room on the Jack of Diamonds, no room on the Queen of Spades—on the Queen of Clubs level. Of course! Hallmark *cards.* And has pulled his grip out of the trunk, his garment bag. An attendant comes up to him. "Better lock your car, sir." And it is as friendly as—he's Queen of Clubs—an admonishment not to show his hand. He wonders as he walks toward the double set of doors what is above him, a king? Of what suit? Does the parking lot hold a pair of kings? What is above the pair? And is now close enough to read the sign above the double doors: TO WEST VILLAGE AND CROWN CENTER SHOPS. Ah. Aces high for hotel parking. He has been dealt a losing hand, trumped, out cut. He stands pat however and continues on through the doors.

And is in West Village, Chelsea Court, the shops like five-sided open-ended cubes hanging suspended in multileveled space and attached to each other by catwalk, the black-painted iron stairs of fire escape and spiral staircase. And is unsteady on his feet, overcome by a sense of standing among the fallen blocks of giant children. It is a *theater* of merchandise, he is overwhelmed by an impression of having stepped backstage. He looks about him, is momentarily confused, cannot tell audience from actors. Each store is a perfect set. And trade is dialogue. It's like market day in some European town, it's like a fair. He could be in a shop window, he could be in the street, in a crazy, zigzag perpendicular of streets; he could be standing ankle deep in some archaeology of the retail, the palimpsest digs of commerce. Nutty, displaced bourses, bazaars, booths and kiosks, the chic salesmen and saleswomen become mongers, costers, colporteurs, discreet tradesmen, hawkers, cheapjacks, chapmen. Some actually wear aprons over their mod clothing; others, their sleeves rolled above their forearms, posture like artisans, as if they have just this minute put the finishing touches on wares they have made themselves. He listens for and momentarily expects to hear work songs, street cries, folk solos, rags, arias: "Straaaw*berreeez!* Nay-ills and *hat*chets! Tenniss rackettsz, skeee wear *here!*" He sees a credit card change hands and is mildly surprised. Even cash would have surprised him here. He expects barter, solid elemental stuff—silver, gold, pinches of gold dust laid out on scales. There is something claustrophobic in this three-dimensional marketplace. The clever names of the shops oppress him. He reads them but has as much trouble taking them in as he has had when he has tried to read the news moving by in a huge electric typeface along the side of a building. Athlete's Foot (sport shoes); The Candle Power & Light Co. (sculpted wax candles); Sunbrella (sporty sun goggles); The Signal House (model railroading). Some shops are of a sort he has never seen before in his life. There is a place called Wine-Art where one buys the equipment and essences for making wine. There is a place called Bits and Pieces which sells nothing but miniature handcrafted furniture for dollhouses. He looks closely at a grandfather clock no more than two inches high. Its pendulum swings, its minute and hour hands register almost the same time as his wristwatch. (There is a two-minute discrepancy; he is certain it's his watch which is slow.) Another shop, The

Stamp Pad, sells customized rubber hand stamps. He casts about somewhat wildly for an exit, finally spots one, makes his way by means of necessary detours—once he had driven this way, doubled back and forth, taken sudden instinctive, erratic swings south and north, looking for a hole in a heatwave—doglegs, travels a maze, climbs up one level in order to get to another beneath it.

He is out of West Village but still in Crown Center Shops. The stores are more conventional here but still—for him—troubling. Here and there along the corridor there are benches, like benches in museums. Lord Snowden is a men's haberdasher, Habitat a furniture store, Ethnics a gallery of folk art. There are too many specialty shops, a place that sells yarn, another that does soap. There is The Board & Barrel, with its gourmet cookware; The Factory (a hardware store). There are The Bake Shop, The Candy Store, The Cheese Shop, The Flower Shop, The Sausage Shop, The Fish Market, The Meat Market, The Poultry Market, The Produce Market. And these, with their bare, spare generics, are somehow even more coy than the shops that are puns and double entendres. Though he feels that they have missed a bet, that they might have put in a broker and called it The Stock Market.

Yes. It is *precisely* what he had thought. As if America has lost a war with France, say, or England, or with, perhaps, its own past, knuckled under to its history. What's a nice guy like me doing in a place like this? he wonders. A man of franchise, a true democrat who would make Bar Harbor, Maine, look like Chicago, who would quell distinction, obliterate difference, who would common-denominate until Americans recognize that it was America everywhere. The Stamp Pad, indeed. He would show them rubber stamp!

He sees a sign for the Crown Center Hotel and makes for it. No detours. No doglegs. No catwalks. No ups, no downs.

And is standing in the lobby of the hotel. There is, incredibly, along the width of its western wall, a *waterfall*, a tall slender stream of water no wider at its source than the stream that might come from heavy firehose, but opening out as it drops, spreading, diverted to two channels like the twin barrels on a shotgun, hugging, lower down, rocks, slipping over what appear to be mossy boulders, splashing plants, lichen, citrus trees, and spilling finally into a collecting pool, a sort of hemisphere of walled-off bay. The waterfall is reached by escalators, by exposed balconies two stories above him. Guests, tourists, stroll along iron-railed gangways that crisscross the waterfall like bridges in Japanese gardens. They stand at different levels, as if on scaffolding, spread out and up and down like notes on sheet music. And Flesh watches a woman toss change in the pool. Several sit for their photographs. He has guessed the appeal. It is the appeal of surrealism and odd juxtaposition. Something pit-of-the-stomach in the notion of bringing the outdoors in, just as the elevators at the tower end of the lobby, though entered from the lobby itself, climb the outside of the building, riding up gravity like effervescence in club soda. An appeal in inversion. He suffers a sort of vertigo for the people displaced above him in the air on their balconies and catwalks and scaffolds like so many window washers or house painters or construction workers. He has himself just come from the Center's suspended cubes, sick in his stomach and feeling the heavy, off-center nausea of the weight, for example, in loaded dice.

He looks away from these human flies and sees that he stands above an excavation, an upholstered pit, roughly at the center of the immense lobby. It is a sunken barroom, the depth of the shallow end of a swimming pool. Low, handsome furniture—chrome, leather the color of the cork tips on cigarettes—is grouped in a deliberate randomness which gives the illusion of a house made up entirely of living rooms. There is something odd about the bar, though he cannot at first put his finger on it. He still holds his light suitcase, his garment bag rests on his arm like a towel on the sleeve of a waiter. He walks around the perimeter of the bar. The tops of the drinkers' heads are at a level with his knees. The waitresses, carrying their trays, come up to his chest.

Then he realizes what is so strange about the bar. There is no bar. People are served from low consoles about the size of shields. (An impression reinforced by the crown and heraldry emblazoned on their fronts.) But that still isn't it. Not entirely. Now. Now he knows. The consoles are not unlike the rolling carts pushed up and down the aisles of airplanes. The girls might be stewardesses, the young men stewards.

The franchiser understands the place now. With its nature brought indoors and its machinery out, with the lowest point in the lobby giving the sense of flight. The elements have been split, transposed, not just inversion but an environmentalist's hedge against the continuity of the present. He might be, he might be in some zoo of the future. This is what a waterfall was like. Those were called trees. Those smaller things plants. When there was still fuel, people used to fly in heavier-than-air machines to go from one place to another. They were served food and drink on them. If you'll come this way and step into the machine, you can get a good view of the outdoors, the "streets," as they were called in those days. People used to move about in them.

They were way ahead of him, way ahead of the franchiser with his Robo-Washes and convenience-food joints, with his roadside services and dance studios and One Hour Martinizing, with his shopping center movie houses and Firestone appliance stores and Fotomats. Why, he was decadent, a piece of history, the Yesterday Kid himself, Father Time, Ol' Man River—his America, the America of the Interstates, of the sixties and middle seventies, as obsolete and charming and picturesque as an old neighborhood.

(Later that night he would go with other men to a restaurant called The Old Washington Street Station. He would read the legend on the back of the menu: "Surrounded in an atmosphere of early Kansas City history, The Old Washington Street Station invites you on a journey through our historic past. Ninth and Washington was the location of one of Kansas City's first cable railway powerhouses. For your dining pleasure, an authentic reproduction of an early Kansas City streetcar has been provided in our main dining room. We invite you to make yourself at home, enjoy our good food, your friends, and fond memories of Kansas City's rich heritage."

"Is this true?" he would ask the waitress. He had a few drinks in him.

"Is what true?"

"What it says here. Is it true?" He would point to the legend on the back of the menu.

"Oh yes."

"Terrific," he would say, and bring his finger down smartly in the middle of the paragraph. "That's what I want. That's just what I want for my dining pleasure. Wheel it over."

"What?"

"The Kansas City streetcar. And don't tell me you're all out. I can see it from here. Boys," he would say, "I'm very hungry."

And would study the menu like a map, asking, genuinely unsure, "Should we stay here? Look, look what's upstairs. It shows you. We could eat in the jailhouse, we could eat in the courtroom or the barber shop. We could eat in the haberdashery or the penny arcade. We could eat in the orchard. We could eat, we could eat in the library or the parlor or the governor's mansion or on the porch or gazebo and wet our whistles in the Brass Bed Cocktail Lounge."

"Benny's a little loaded."

"Benny's whistle is lubricated."

"Come on, Benny, calm down, son. Let's just stay right here in Grandma's Garden."

"Macintyre," he would say, "you silly bastard. Grandma's Garden. You hear that, Lloyd? You hear that, Frommer? Grandma's Garden. The stupid son of a bitch calls it Grandma's Garden."

"Hey, come on, now," Macintyre would say, "watch your language. I know you've got a few drinks under your belt, but there's a lady present. Now, come on, Ben, just try to behave yourself."

"Watch *my* language? Watch *my* language? I *am* watching my language. Take a look at your own, you fuckhead. You wanted to eat in Kenny's Newsroom, you wanted to go to Harlow. What were some of those other places? Lloyd? Frommer? Wait, wait, don't tell me: Yeah. The Snooty Fox. He wanted to eat in a railroad car, he was willing to try a *warehouse*. Jesus!"

"The Warehouse is supposed to have the best K.C. strip steaks in K.C."

"Yeah," he would say, "and you know why? 'Cause they're so *aged*, you asshole."

"I told you before. I warned you."

"Forget it, P.M., he's had too much to drink."

"Sure, Paul, take it easy, he's three sheets to the wind."

"Oh, my God, 'P.M.,' you lousy afternoon, you dumbass evening, 'three sheets to the wind.' " He would be laughing. There would be tears in his eyes. "And, yeah, wait, wait, somebody said something about The Monastery. And which one of you fatheads wanted to try Ebenezer's? Which one Yesterday's Girl? You want yesterday, you schmucky hickshit? *Yesterday?* They'll give you— they'll give you . . . Listen, you really want picturesque? Let's get out of here. I know this charming Holiday Inn." And would stand up, shouting, his voice carrying through the entire restaurant: "Who here remembers Thursday? Huh? Anybody recall Saturday? How about it? Thursday? Friday? *Saturday?* Those were the days, those were the good gold goddamn candyass days. Huh? *Huh?*"

And would be pulled down, Frommer and Lloyd peacekeepers still, but pulling him by his bad arm, holding on to his paresthetic right hand, Lloyd's metal graduation ring against Flesh's skin like an electric prod, the hands restraining him—how could they feel what he felt?—as alien nervewise and texturewise as moonrock.

"Oh," would scream, "Aiee," would call, "*God!*" would cry.)

He presents his confirmation at the desk, registers, asks if his room is near where the other Radio Shack franchise people will be.

He strolls through the exhibits in the Century Ballroom.

"Hey," says Ned Tubman from Erlanger, Kentucky. "How you doin'?"

"Fine."

"I seen your name tag. Bowling Green, hey?"

"Right."

"Western Kentucky State University?"

"Yes."

"What's shakin'?"

"Oh, you know."

"Foxy. Close to the chest. Well, I'll tell you. —When'd you say you opened up?"

"About three years ago."

"Three years. Well. How long Fort Worth sit on *your* application?"

"I don't know, I don't remember."

"What was it? You slip 'em somethin'?"

"Who?"

"You know—Fort Worth."

"I bought it outright."

"Oh. Outright. Say listen, I didn't mean— But if you bought it *out*right— Me, I had my application in fourteen months. By the time they okay'd me, Lexington was gone, Richmond was took, Berea, Bowling Green—" He pointed to Flesh's badge. "Every last college town in the state. They come up with Fulton."

"Fulton's a pretty good size."

"Yeah, I was gonna take it but then they told me about Erlanger. Said it had an institution of higher learning. I switched."

"And it doesn't?"

"Oh yeah. Oh yeah, it does. It does surely. It got the Seminary of Pius X."

"Oh."

"You ever try selling stereo to them fellows? *Po*lice band? Headsets? Tape decks? Shit. Well— Good luck to you."

"Same to you."

"I'll lay in Gregorian chants, 'Perry Como Sings the Lord's Prayer.' "

"Sounds good."

"Yeah, sure. Meanwhile, you get the real college kids. Marijuana, the Pill— Those are the turn-ons, man. Biggest thing ever to hit the music industry. Know what I heard?"

"What?"

"That R.C.A., Zenith, Sony, and Panasonic gave E. Y. Lilly and Pfizer and the rest them drug companies money to develop the Pill."

"No kidding?"

"The truth. Heard they sponsor the Mafia and the drug traffic."

"I don't see—"

"Why you think a lid of grass so cheap? It goes against every law of supply and demand. That's the record companies, mister. The record companies do that. They give the pot farmers price supports."

"Oh."

"Subsidize poppy fields."

"Really?"

"Pot and poppy parities, yes sir."

"I see."

"Sure."

"I never thought about it."

"I will. Open your eyes."

"God bless."

The displays are compelling. Each screened booth with its shelves of sound equipment glows, buzzes like cockpit, like miniature war room, like listening posts in science fiction. Meters of fine tuning like green pies closing. Needles that travel against arbitrary scales, past the reds and oranges of distortion toward baby blues of pitch-perfect harmony and balance. Round clocklike dials across dashboards of sound. Stereo cartridges like decks of cards, that look, sunk in their slots, like open tills, like queer, spit product. Cleverly notched steel spindles, turntables like reels of computer tape. And the gorgeous cargo of speakers like splendid crates, blank black domino shapes tight in their mahogany frames. The grooved and handsome ferruled knobs—AM, FM, AFC, vol. and bass, treble and balance, filter and phono, auxiliary tape. Contour control, "joy sticks." Jacks and fuse lights. Sliding levers, smoked-plastic dust covers. Headsets like the ears' furniture, their thick foam stuffing, their leathery vinyl skins. The broad wide-eyed faces of cassettes, the immense and careless weave of the 8-tracks. Digital AM–FM clock radios, their neon numerals the color of struck matches, the broken verticals and horizontals of the numbers like fractured bones, unkindled ghost digits just visible behind them like the floating, germ-like transparencies that drift across the surface of an eyeball. Other styles—card numbers that flip over like scores on TV game shows, or that rise into the radios like figures on odometers. There are pocket-size tape recorders, microphones built into them like snipers' scopes. And portable televisions like pieces of luggage. There are antennas like fishing rods, like whips, like window screens, like swatches of fence, like pen-and-pencil sets, like huge metal combs, like immense paper clips. There is specialized

stuff—marine radiotelephones; citizen's band transceivers; base stations, mobile; 8-channel FM scanning receivers with their movie
marquee light sequences. Tuned to crime, tuned to fire, tuned to
weather, tuned to all the ships at sea—earth, fire, air, and water
tuned. The notches of wavelength-like lines on rulers or the scale
on maps, all the calibrated atmosphere of frequency.

I have been in the Bowling Green shop just once. I am a personnel man finally, only an absentee landlord, a silent owner in the
sound trade. They rip me off, my managers, my hired help. They
aren't to be trusted. They skim. I know that. I've taken bartenders
and put them in charge of my franchises. I've turned vice-squad
detectives into bosses. Clerks in liquor stores, ticket sellers, head-
waiters, gas-station attendants—all those technicians in larceny.
My gray-collar guys of good judgment who know just where to
draw the line and just when to stop. What can it cost me in the
long run? Less than fringe benefits, less than Blue Cross, pension
plans. I tell them up front what I'll stand for. They appreciate that.
If they take advantage I send the auditors in or go myself. But
that's rare. The rule of thumb is, they work their asses off in order
to increase the profits from which they are allowed to steal. In the
long run I'm probably even, maybe a dollar or two ahead.

I came to the Radio Shack bash to buy. Chelton should have
come. He knows the stock better, the clientele. I'm his operative
really, just following orders.

It's just that I've got to do *some*thing.

We were all in our seats. They dimmed the lights in the Century
Ballroom. The great collar of equipment from the display booths
that lined three sides of the ballroom glowed like electric Crayolas.
It was really rather pretty. The franchisers applauded. Even I
started to applaud but it hurt my hand. Then someone yelled,
"Bravo, bravo," and this was taken up and soon everyone was clapping and cheering, giving a standing ovation to a lot of colored
dials. It was like applauding dessert, the waiters' parade of cherries
jubilee at a catered dinner, luminous baked Alaska at a golden wedding anniversary. Businessmen are *so* dumb.

Then—I don't know how they did this, some linked rheostat arrangement or something—they brought down the lights on the

equipment until the ballroom was pitch black. A white pin spot flared on some Fort Worth guy on the dais and we sat back down.

"Ladies and gentlemen," he said, "there's to be a demonstration."

The pin spot, round as a pancake, large as his face, reduced itself, burned briefly on the tip of his nose, and went out. The Century Ballroom was bereft of light, blackness so final it was void, a vacuum of light. We could have been locked in the subterranean on the backside of moons. I thought of the brownouts I'd fled, but this was darker, melanistic, the doused universe and the pitch of death.

And they applauded *this*, applauded darkness. *So* dumb. And I thought—the Wharton Old Boy—it's a miracle Dow Jones *has* an average, a miracle that there's trade at all. The dollar's a miracle, the dime a wonder, America astonishing, all organization a wondrous serendipity. Higher the handicapped and Excelsior to all. Applauded *darkness!*

Self-consciously—oh, the demands of level good will—I thought perhaps I should join them. Even in the darkness—who could have seen me?—I felt this pressure to join in, to add my two-cent increment of invisible loyalty, pressured like men at ball parks to stand with their fellows for the anthem, to move their lips over the words flashed on the scoreboard, and make a noise here and another there when the song descends to their key. But it hurt my hand to applaud and I kept still. And then, the *odd*est thing.

A man called, "Bravo, bravo." Then the chant was taken up, and through the sound of applause and cheers I could hear chairs scraping all about me as they were pushed back and the Radio Shack people stood. It was ludicrous. Cheer darkness! As well applaud lawns, crabgrass, hurrah the sky and clap for rain. The givens are given. I wouldn't move. I hadn't the excuse of my game hand but I wouldn't move, would not rise with my clamorous colleagues.

"Ladies and gentlemen," the Fort Worth man said, "there's to be a demonstration."

The lights came on in the Century Ballroom. The Fort Worth man was not on the dais. No one was standing. The chairs were just where I had remembered their being when we had sat down after applauding the new line of equipment. We looked at each other.

"What happened?" my neighbor asked.

"I don't know."

"What was all that clapping? Why did you get up when the lights went out?"

"I didn't. Why did you?"

"I never moved."

All around me people were asking the same questions of each other. It seemed that no one had applauded, no one had stood.

"Where'd what's-his-name, Fort Worth, go?"

"I don't know."

"There he is."

"Where?"

"By that console. *There.* Beside the dais."

The man from Fort Worth, his arms folded across his chest, stood smiling at us. He moved toward the microphone stand again.

"How did you like the demonstration? We played a little joke on you. We played a little joke on you and you've just heard the future."

"What's this all about, Sam?" This was called out by a man in my row.

Sam, the Fort Worth guy, nodded and smiled. He shaded his eyes, pretending to look where the question had come from. "We recorded your initial response and played it back for you."

"Was that some kind of quadraphonics?"

"Quadraphonics? Honey, it was decaphonics. It was quinquagintaphonics. It was centophonics. Myriaphonics. It was the whole-kit-and-caboodlaphonics! The system's perfected. It's on line now. Well, there's nothing to it from an engineering standpoint, or even from a recording standpoint. All they have to do is plant a mike wherever they want. The technology's been licked since stereo. We could do that all along, make as many tracks as we wanted. It's just multiplex. It was at the other end, the delivery system, where the trouble came in. Now we've got these miniaturized speakers that we can plant anywhere. Well, you just heard."

"Is it expensive?" I had the impression there were shills in the audience.

"Initially. Initially the customer buys the receiver. That's that console over there. That one's professional of course and costs about four grand, but we can give him something almost as good, at least for his home entertainment purposes, starting at about eleven hundred and fifty dollars and going up to about eighteen or nineteen hundred. About the same price as professional-quality stereo equipment."

"It's high, Sam. These are kids, newlyweds."

"They'll go crazy for it," Sam said. "You still haven't caught on, have you? Anybody here with the vision to see what we've done?"

"I have." Ben spoke. He rose and stood beside his chair.

"Pardner?" Sam said.

"I have. The vision. *I* have. It's the Barbie Doll principle gone sound. It's Mattel. *Mattelio ad absurdum in spadessum.* We kill them with accessory. They start with three speakers, four, and build toward infinity. Like model railroading—all the crap you could get. The station and stationmaster and a little signalman waving his tiny lantern with the teensy light inside. The gates and the bridges, the tunnels and tracks. The switches and couplers, the toy towns and trees. The Rockies and billboards and whistles that blew. The smoke. The freight cars and passenger. Cabooses. The observation car where the weensy President stood. The refrigerator cars cold to the touch. The flatcars with their lumber and perfume of evergreen. All the specialized carriers for oil, gas (non-flammable, non-toxic), natural resources. I have. I do."

"Yes," Sam said, "that's it. That's right."

"I have," Ben said. "I do."

"Sign that pardner up," Sam said, the man from Fort Worth. "Get an order blank back there, someone."

"Because," Ben said, "we live in a century of mood and until this afternoon only headphones gave the illusion of 'separation.' There *is* no separation. There are no concert halls in life. Nor do we see in 3-D. The chairs do not stand out. Only in stereopticons are the apples closer than the pears. We will Ptolemaicize men and have them move in their rooms as in a headset. I have. I do."

"Hey now," Sam said.

"And pour percussion in the porches of their ears. Their left ear and right. Tumble treble and crack the sax into the helix. A trumpet in every tragus, and violins in the semicircular canals. The flute in the fossa, the bass in the stapes. Quinquagintaphonics in the adolescent's bedroom, the whore's house, and doctor's office. I have. I do. Mattel their minutes, Lionel their lives. Accessory them."

"Hey," Sam said, "you doin' too much."

"Cole Porter," Ben said. "Hammerstein."

"Buddy?" Sam said. "Buddy, you hear me?"

"In both ears."

"Settle down, friend. We're talking the new line."

"That's what I'm talking," Ben said. His hand hurt him, his legs. Everything tingled. Only his ears. I am up to my ears, he thought.

"Come on, now," Sam said, "give us a break."

"Put another record on. I'm having a Rodgers and Hart attack. Hah!"

Macintyre and Frommer were beside him. Lloyd has come up. He spies Ned Tubman through his nystagmic eyes. Ned and all whirl like pinwheels.

He put a call through to Riverdale.

"Yes?" It was Cole, the one who suffered from plant diseases.

"Hello, Cole. How are you? It's Ben."

(Not "Hi, who's this?" but "Hello, Cole. How are you?" Even though they'd reached an age—Cole would be almost thirty-seven—when distinctions, were they to appear, would have begun to reveal themselves. But time itself thwarted, something in their Contac, time-released lived lives that stalled the oldest and ever so slightly aged the youngest prematurely, the seven-year point spread of their existence narrowed to an arithmetic mean so that they all seemed to be about thirty-three years old—in their prime his guarantors of the prime rate. But withal, the solidarity broken for him like a code, known like a secret, his best gift—poor Ben, poor sick, sad Ben—his connoisseurship for their voices and faces, his wine buff's palate for their Finsberg body and Finsberg being. A gift. God-given. Poor Ben. Poor sad, sick Ben. Then why, for

God's sake, did he prefer Lorenz to Irving, Irving to Oscar, Cole to Lorenz? Did he see nuances in twin and triplet character as well? *Character?* He? Him? Poor Ben? Poor Ben.)

"Ben. How are *you?* Gee, we've been trying to get in touch with you for about two weeks. We called Phoenix Ford, we tried your H. Salt Fish, your Arthur Treacher in Stockton, the Jacuzzi Whirlpool in Columbus. Everywhere. We thought you might be at the Mister Softee in Rapid City, but the lines are down and we couldn't get through."

"I'm in Colorado Springs."

"Colorado Springs? Are you looking over a new franchise, Ben?"

"Why were you trying to reach me?"

"It's Mom, Ben."

"What happened? Cole, is something wrong with Estelle?"

"She's dead, Ben. She died ten days ago."

"Estelle?"

"I guess that makes you head of the family."

"What are you talking about? What do you mean 'head of the family'?"

"Well, you're the oldest, Ben. We figure that makes you our godfather."

"I'm your godcousin, your godbabybrother. How can I be your godfather?"

"Relationships change, Godfather."

"Stop that. What happened to Estelle?"

"It was tragic, Ben. It was the comeback."

"What comeback? What are you talking about?"

"The comeback. After the sensational reception of *No, No, Nanette*, Mother—well everyone, really—saw the terrific potential in revivals. You know, nostalgia. Ruby Keeler's reviews ate her heart out, Ben. She was Patsy Kelly's pal but Kelly's raves really got to her, I think. Well, we still have our contacts on Broadway and Mother learned that they're planning to do a revival of *Irene*. She thought it could be her big chance. She hasn't been the same since Father died. You know that, Ben. The musical theater is in our blood."

Yes, Ben thought.

"Well, she found out where the auditions were to be held and she went down. She used her maiden name. She wasn't looking for favors and figured that after all these years the Finsberg name packed more clout than the name she used to dance under, so she deliberately used her old stage name. These producers are young. They aren't the old-timers."

"Yes?" Ben said.

"So what can I tell you, Ben? They asked her to tap dance to 'They Go Wild, Simply Wild over Me.' She dropped dead. What can I tell you?"

"She dropped dead?"

"She was out of condition, Ben. She'd prepared 'Alice Blue Gown.' She never expected the other."

"I'm sorry, Cole. I don't know what to say."

"So that's the story. What can I tell you?"

"Gosh," Ben said, "a heart attack."

"Yeah," Cole said dreamily, "that and stage fright. Comeback fever. It's getting them all, the old-timers. It's a terrible thing, Ben. These revivals are killing them all off. The ex-hoofers are dropping like flies. So how have *you* been?"

"Is the family together?"

"Until a few days ago. Most everyone's gone off by now. Gertrude and Gus-Ira went back today. There's just a few of us in Riverdale."

"Who's there now, Cole?"

"Oscar," Cole said, "Noël, and myself."

"What about the girls?"

"Patty, LaVerne, and Maxene," Cole said coolly.

"I'd like to speak to Patty, please, Cole."

"Sure," Cole said. "Sure you would." He could hear Cole call out. They must all have been in the drawing room. "It's himself. He wants to speak to *you*, Patty." There was a pause. "She'll take it upstairs—*Godfather*."

He understood Cole's feelings. He had slept with almost all the boys' sisters by this time. "How are you, Cole?" he asked gently.

"Oh," Cole said, "you know. The Japanese beetles have been pesky this summer, but aside from that I'm managing."

"That's good, Cole, I'm glad."

"Hi, Ben, it's Patty."

"Hello, Maxene. I'm sorry to hear about your mother."

"Darn it, Ben, we never could fool you."

"No."

"Hello, Ben."

"Hello, Patty."

"I'll get off now, Ben."

"Goodbye, Cole."

"Goodbye, Ben."

"Goodbye, Maxene."

"Have you got to see me, Ben? Are you at a hotel now?"

"Patty, I've got to see you. I'm at a hotel in Colorado Springs. The Broadmoor. Get a plane to Denver, then fly down from there."

"I'll come out tomorrow," Patty said. "I've been waiting for your call. I knew it would be you. I knew you would need me. That's why I stayed on."

"I know." He did. Patty, who could not hear loud noises, was the one he needed.

She wired her arrival time and he met her plane. "I'm sorry about Estelle. I sent a contribution in Mom's memory to the River-dale Temple Sisterhood." Patty nodded and opened her arms. They kissed. She flicked her tongue around inside his mouth, darting it like a mouse across the vault of his palate. "Woof," he said, releasing her. "Woof."

"The Black Studies Programs in the nation's high schools and universities," she said, "are racist in intent. They're designed to induce in young colored people a pride of such fantasy dimensions that an entire generation of blacks will voluntarily return to Africa."

"Where'd you get that?"

"I'm not the Insight Lady for nothing," she said.

He had loved all the girl twins, all the girl triplets. From the time he was twenty-four until now they had been his collective type. All that could happen to married men had happened to him. He had courted them, loved them well, had affairs, been unfaithful, kissed, made up, moved in, moved out. He had loved and won, loved and lost, pined, mooned, yearned. He had had understandings, stood up at their weddings, given the brides away, proposed the toasts. He had flown in for their operations, collared the surgeons in the corridor, spitting his tears in their faces, thrown down his distraught warnings, pleading always his passionate *sui generis* priorities. Over the years his love letters to them would have made thick volumes. And though they were identical physically, he had loved each in her turn—achronologically—and despite the monolith of their triplet and twin characters, for different but not quite definable reasons.

"I don't know," Ethel had once said to him when he was falling in love with Mary, "what you see in her."

"What," Mary had asked when he was beginning to see Helen, "has she got that I haven't got?"

And he could not have told her. Could not have told any of them. It was as if love were the most solipsistic of energies, spitting and writhing, convulsing on the ground like a live wire, uncoiling, striking at random.

"It's—what?—a feeling, an emotion," he told Kitty when he was starting to itch for balding Maxene, "like anger, something furious in feeling that will not listen to reason."

"All *us* cats are gray at night, surely," Lotte said when she learned he was seeing LaVerne. "Don't you *know* that?"

And it was so. If he knew anything it was their replicate bodies, their assembly-line lives, their gynecological heads and hearts, informed about their insides as a mechanic. Which, for one, made him a great lover, the official cartographer of Finsberg feeling, expert as a pro at the free-throw line, precise as a placekicker. And lent something cumulative to love, some strontium nineties in his ardor, the deposits compounding, compounding, till the word got round, the sisters deferring after the third or fourth, hoping probably to be last, as heart patients, say, might want their surgeons to have performed an operation a thousand times before it was to be performed on them.

"Oh, *God*," Gertrude screamed in orgasm, "the last *shall* be first!"

And for him cumulative, too. But if the sex was better each time for his practice, that did not mean it had ever been fumbling. No. Never. The kiss he had given Lotte beside the bus all those years before had had in it all the implications of his most recent fuck. And some increment of the social in his relations with the girls, of the historical. Because he had seen them through not only their own puberty but the century's, had heavy-petted them in the fifties, taken them, stoned on liquor, in lovers' lanes in the back of immense finned Cadillacs, like screwing in a giant fish, worrying with them through their periods, sometimes using rubbers, sometimes caught without—who knew when one would fall in love?— driving them in the late fifties to gynecologists in different boroughs and waiting for them in the car while they were fitted for diaphragms. And in the sixties going with them to the gynecologists' offices while their coils were inserted. Discoursing about the naughty liberation of the Pill and, when, in the late sixties, the warnings and scares began to appear, going with them right up to the shelves in pharmacies where they picked out their foams. Something of the mores of the times associated with each act. Could he, then, have fallen in love with history, with modern times, the age's solutions to its anxieties? Have had with each girl what other men had never had—the possibility of a second chance, a third, of doing it all over again, only differently, only better? Sexually evolving with them during the sexual revolution.

But sentiment, too. That refractive as well as cumulative. Associating with each sister the song, the device, the clothing and underclothing peculiar to her incumbency. A living nostalgia, differentiated as height marks inked on a kitchen wall. An archaeology of sex, love, and memory.

And Patty was the last. (She was *not* the Insight Lady for nothing.)

They drove up to the Broadmoor, a pink Monaco castle at the foot of the Rockies, and he showed her the hotel in a proprietary way, taking her through the nifty Regency public rooms with their beautiful sofas, the striped, silken upholstery like tasteful flags. He showed her huge tiaras of chandelier, soft plush carpets.

"Yes," she said, "carpets were our first floors, our first highways."

"I didn't know that."

"We call the rug in the hall a 'runner.' It's where the runners or messengers waited in the days of kings and emperors."

"I never made the connection."

"It's an insight. Chandeliers must have come in with the development of lens astronomy at the beginning of the seventeenth century. I should think it was an attempt to mimic rather than parody the order of the heavens, to bring the solar system indoors."

"Really?"

"Well, where, to simple people, would the universe seem to go during the daylight hours, Ben?"

"But chandeliers give light."

"Not during the daytime. The chandelier is a complex invention—a sculpture of the invisible stars by day, a pragmatic mechanism by night. But a much less daring device finally than carpeting."

"Why, Patty?"

"Because carpeting—think of Oriental rugs—was always primarily ornamental and decorative. It was a deliberate expression of what ground—our first flooring, remember, and incidentally we have to regard tile, too, as a type of carpeting—*ought* to be in a perfect world. Order, symmetry, design. And since rugs came in before lens telescopy, how could they *know?* Oh, carpeting's *much* more daring. A leap of will."

"Of will?"

"Men will the laws of nature."

"I'm glad you came, Patty."

"Oh, look," she said, "just look." They had stepped through the great French doors onto the broad cement patio behind the hotel where small wrought-iron tables and chairs had been set up. People chatted, sipped drinks, and watched the promenade of guests as they moved across the patio and onto the smooth, flower-bordered paths that circled the man-made lake. Cheyenne Mountain and Pikes Peak rose unobstructed behind the lake.

"It's very beautiful, isn't it?" Ben asked.

"It's so sad," Patty said.

"Sad?"

"Look," she said, "look at the arrangement of the chairs. Look at the round tables."

"So?"

"Ringside seats, Ben. It's a *play*. They've pettied the mountains, turned them into a kind of nightclub act. They've made them a spectacle. Our rooms," she said, "they're rooms with a view, I suppose."

"Yes," Ben said, "we have a suite in the new building."

"How European!"

Ben agreed, though he had never been to Europe. There was a Marienbad quality to the place, a sense of spa. It wasn't what she meant. She meant that the idea of rooms with views was European, that the practice of pegging rates to one's proximity to a mountain, or, as in the case of hotels and apartments lining Central Park, was, not so much a matter of commerce—surely hotels could fix the price of their rooms and suites so that they could make just as much money without charging extra for a view—as a throwback to an aristocratic principle that had, she supposed, its source in some notion of succession, a crown prince higher than a duke, a duke higher than a count.

"*Certainly*," she declared. "*Now* I see! It comes from the Court and the seating arrangements at table. The greater the revenues one could provide the royal treasuries, the closer one got to the king."

"Gee," Ben said.

"But it's all so *unnecessary*. With the advances of architecture all rooms could have views. Rectangles are the enemy of democracy, concavity is its best friend."

"I'm sick," Ben said.

"What a lovely tie, Ben."

"They told me I have multiple sclerosis. I got into my car and just started driving."

"Men's ties are a sort of male brassiere, of course. In the phallic sense of *straightening* the chest. I don't go much for the plumage theory. What's more interesting is that ties complete the circle of the throat, much as a priest's collar does. Shirts, open at the throat, are arrows to the genitals. Do you suppose there can be a correspondence between the tie and the hangman's noose? Idiom says 'necktie party,' but the operative word is 'party,' I should think, with its comic insistence on the collaboration between the celebrational formality and seriousness of death. Then there's the notion of the knot, a clear adumbration of the Adam's apple. But overriding all is the tie's tattoo symbolism."

"Overriding all, yes," Ben said.

"To suggest the throat's tattoo. Marvelous. And to do it in silk, wools, the softer cottons. Pleasure/pain. Velvet bondage. *God!*"

"Maybe we'd better go up."

"When they told you," she said, turning to him, "did you ask, 'Why me?'"

"No."

"Listen," she said, "this is important. Later, during your mad dash about the country, did you say it? Did you ever think it?"

"No," he said, "not once."

"Good for you, Ben," she said. "Let's go up. I want to make love."

"Why me?"

As she unpacked, hanging her pantsuits so they would not wrinkle, carefully arranging her blouses and dresses on the hangers as one might tug and fluff clothing on a dressmaker's form, making a chorus line of her shoes in the closet, setting out her lotions and creams on the counter, her combs and her brushes, like one setting out plants in a garden, putting her jewelry in the drawer like a shopkeeper seeding his cash register in the morning, Ben lay in the center of the king-size bed and watched her, another's chores tranquillizing to him, soothing, seductive. The FM played softly and the insights poured from her as she moved about the room.

" 'La la la' in songs is code for 'love.' Music is missionary. The church has its hymns, nations their anthems, every song is a serenade. Don't kid yourself. *Every* song. And I'm not talking sombreros now, or greasers beneath the baked brick or near the stucco. What, you never heard the expression 'They're playing our song'? Music is primal salesmanship, Ben. Its most basic terms—'notes' and 'scales'—can be traced back to banking and commerce. What's the commonest word in a lyric? 'Gold.' Consider musical comedy, Ben. The kind of song that made the Finsberg fortune. 'I Found a Million Dollar Baby in a Five-and-Ten-Cent Store'; 'There's No *Business* Like Show Business.' 'There's a bright *golden* haze on the meadow, there's a bright golden haze on the meadow.' (And a gold record, incidentally.) Or"—here she broke into song—" 'Longing to tell you but afraid and shy, I'd let my *golden* chances pass me by.' And 'by,' incidentally, is a play on words. 'I'll get *by* as long as I have you.' By—buy."

Bye-bye, Ben thought.

"And '*have*,' Ben, '*have*.' Good Lord, Ben, wake up. Think things through. 'Pennies from Heaven.' "

" 'He's just my Bill,' " Ben said.

"That's it, that's it. You're making fun, of course, but subliminally that's precisely what's going on in that song. Remember, *Showboat* wasn't written until America went off the gold standard and paper money came in. 'I bought you violets for your *furs*.' 'A kiss on the lips can be quite sentimental, but *diamonds* are a girl's best friend.' "

"You know a lot of songs," he said.

"Oh, Ben," she said, "I know *everything*."

They made love. Her cries during orgasm were insights.

"I wonder," she moaned, "why the group photograph has always been a convention? It must be because the group is aware that the next minute one of them could be dead. We are good. We *are*."

"Oh. Oh," Ben cried.

"Have you ever noticed," she squealed, "how bottles of salad dressing are all the same shape, tall necks and wide, bell-shaped t-t-torsos?"

"Oh, God," Ben shivered. "Oh, God."

"And how," she panted, "the la-labels are the-these little co-collars at the neck, and the-these sh-shield shapes on the front and back, and how there's al-always a r-recip*e?*"

"Oh oh," Ben raptured.

"That's," she groaned, "so they can all be sh-shelved to-together, so they may *com-com*-compete *oh oh* openly on the *oh oh* open market."

"Uhnn. Oooh. Ahnn," Ben whined.

"State capitols are legislative surrogates for the church architecture of Europe," she keened.

Afterward they smoked some marijuana Patty had brought with her from New York. They passed it back and forth wordlessly. Ben was grateful for the silence.

"You know," she said after a while, "you have this amazing insight into our bodies." She meant hers and her sisters'.

"Yes," he said, "by now I know exactly what you'll do if I do this or that."

"Why are you so stuck on us, Ben? Why are we so stuck on you?"

"You're the Insight Lady."

"The greatest neologism in the history of the English language is Tarzan's cry when he's swinging on vines—'Awawawawawaw!' What else could Burroughs have put in his mouth? *'Gee!'*? Believe me, it was a stroke of genius, Ben. You can demonstrate the reactionariness of reactionaries by showing how liberal they are about the distant. Policies that have them up in arms in their own country are a matter of indifference to them in underdeveloped nations. This is also true, incidentally, of people's attitudes toward death. The best sentence is made out of the best combination of tenses, not out of the best words. Likewise the great work is the great action. Plots are more important than language. Plot is the language of time. How pompous pomp in a new country! The aristocracy, the army, and the pecking order in General Motors are all alike. All organizations equal all other organizations. Parliament and Barnum and Bailey. A Harvard professor I once saw on the Today show showed me that genius seems to have thought about what it has only just now been asked and, speaking beautifully about a subject, is actually inventing what it seems merely to be remembering. Other people's lives are art. That's why there's a Broadway and a West End, why there's literature. Spartacus was an antipacifist preaching exactly what Martin Luther King

· 185 ·

preached, but in reverse. Thus, ends *are* justified by means, since all means, if they work, are ultimately equal, that is, *efficient*. It is only ends which are unequal. We would both agree that some ends are nobler than others. Since means are interchangeable then, it is only ends which ever need to be justified. Oh, Ben," she cried passionately, "I'm only this archaeologist of the daily. I read the quotidian is all. To me today's newspaper is already nostalgia. Don't look to *me* for the secret of your life!"

And no small talk even at dinner in one of the hotel's restaurants. The menu her muse:

"Oh, look," she said, "look at the *menu!*" They were in the Penrose Room at the top of the old building with its view of the Rockies beyond a solid wall of glass. "*Feel* it. The paper like a certificate of stock. Blue chip. If you look close you can see the tiny colored threads that run through it like a precious aspic of lint on money."

"I can look close but I can't feel it," Ben said.

"Look at the cursive font distinctive as signature, the prices like distinguished addresses."

"My hand."

"Oh, Ben," she said, "it's as if printing costs determine the range of one's appetite and fix it forever. Movable type and the destiny of hunger. When this menu was designed, it was designed once and for all. The chef and the man from graphics in consultation. Preordained, don't you see, by what would look good on the document, for that's what such a menu becomes—a document—legal and binding. Yes. A contract, if you please. 'What do you do best?' the graphics man must have asked. 'Decide now, because you can't change your mind later. The cost of this thing is like putting out a magazine.' And he would have to have told him. Don't you see what it means? Image and printing costs are responsible for the tradition of mediocrity in American restaurants."

"But if the chef is doing what he does best—" Ben said.

"And how long must he do it? Chained to a years' old assembly-line expertise, he must finally get bored, the quality *has* to suffer. How can he experiment? Where can he try out new recipes?"

"The food's supposed to be very good here," Ben said.

"Oh, Ben, don't be naïve. Idiom only is informed. 'Stop,' it tells us, 'where the truck drivers do.' Do you suppose a truck driver's palate is more knowledgeable than a rich man's?"

"But you said—"

"It's because they don't usually have printed menus in such places. A mimeographed sheet shoved behind a hard clear plastic, and tucked like a snapshot into corner mounts in a photo album. Yes. And the blue-plate special in blue. You've seen him, surely you of all people, Ben, with your seventy thousand miles a year, you've seen him, the owner of the diner or the cook at the truck stop up on the last stool at the counter an hour before closing with his stencil in the typewriter and his hunt and his peck, doing tomorrow's menu."

"Usually such places the food is lousy."

"The food, perhaps, the principle no. I don't know this for a fact but it's my guess that the Michelin people rarely list restaurants where the menus look like the Magna Carta."

"Try the Rocky Mountain Rainbow Trout," Ben said.

She was looking off in the distance. Ben followed her glance. Apparently she was studying a table of seven people near the western wall of glass.

"Never so much the family," she said, "as when sitting together in a restaurant, the group leavened by an outsider, the daughter's boyfriend or the son's pal from university, say. A grandfather there, a father to pick up the check, a younger son ten. It's the simultaneity of ease and showing off which makes the effect work."

"You're an expert on atmosphere," Ben said. "But if you want to know, it's the simultaneity of generations which does that."

"What is it?" she asked. "Is something wrong?"

"I wanted to tell someone," he said. "I wanted to tell someone what's in store for me, and all you do is give me Significance drill."

"You told me your symptoms. You gave me Gibberd's prognosis. It's very hopeful."

"I want my remission back," he said and burst into tears.

If she understood she chose to ignore it, unless the fact that she walked on his left—his right hand was the paresthetic one, his right arm the numbed one—both her arms wrapping his in the doggy stance of a woman without insights, like a gum chewer or a teenager window-shopping with her date. If he had looked into her face at such moments he would have seen it scrunched, beautifully cutened, her cheek high up on the sleeve of his sport coat and her eyes closed. If such cheerleader conditions were meant to make him feel the letters bloom on his jacket, her efforts were wasted. He felt mocked, a jackass old man fifteen years her senior. (Her Senior, yes.)

They walked around the lake while she continued to chin herself on his left arm.

"That's the ice rink," he said. "They train for the Olympics in there."

"I was just thinking," she said.

"What?"

"Do you remember the menu in the Penrose Room?"

"Oh, Christ, Patty."

"No, really. Do you?"

"Yes, sure, but—"

"The Gothic typeface."

"What about it?"

"I was thinking about the masthead on *The New York Times*."

"*The New York Times*."

"Well, that's Gothic. Many newspapers use it. That's because it looks like Hebrew. All newspapers are a sort of Scripture. Gothic type must have evolved from monks trying to duplicate the look of the sacred texts."

"I thought we might watch them," Ben said.

"What? Oh. All right."

Next to the auditorium was a sort of annex where the skaters limbered up or worked on figures which they could study themselves performing in mirrors along the entire length of one wall and the width of another. The room, rather like the practice room in a ballet studio, was the length of a bowling alley and perhaps seven lanes deep. Ben and Patty went up to the long glass spectator windows and looked in.

There were only three skaters working out in the practice room, which, with its thick ice flooring and the mirrors everywhere reflecting it, would have to be very cold, it seemed to Ben, unbearably cold. All three were girls. They wore leotards and their strong slim legs in the rich thermal nylon were the color of graham crackers or the crust on white bread. One girl began suddenly to spin, her momentum accelerated by her arms, which she drew slowly in toward the sides of her body until they were pressed so tight against her that she seemed literally to be supporting her twirling weight by the points of her elbows. The elbows should stop her, he thought. It seemed in defiance of some physical law that her body should continue its furious coil while her elbows held her so tightly. Ben could not tell whether her eyes were open or shut in the blur of her propulsion, but he guessed that they must be open or the mirrors would be pointless.

"My God," he murmured.

"Yes," Patty said.

The girl reduced her speed by extending her arms in a sort of Indian petition, then spun even more fiercely as she pulled them back in. Oddly, she looked like someone stylishly, melodramatically cramping. She looked an expertly demonstrated toy, a Yo-Yo perhaps, whipped about its cat's-cradle track of string. They followed her gyroscopic feints, her speedy yaws and peppy bucks and pitches. Then the girl stopped herself suddenly with the blade of one skate, sending up a showery splash of silver ice like vapor burning off at the base of a rocket.

"Oh oh," Patty said, and pointed to a newcomer on the ice, a girl who skated out pushing a strange device in front of her at present arms. It was exactly like a kid's compass, only it was as tall as, taller than the girl.

"She's going to make— Look," Patty said.

The girl stopped in the center of the practice room, fixed one spiked leg of the compass on the ice, widened the arc of the second leg, and proceeded to trace an immense and perfect figure 8.

"Could you have imagined?" Patty asked.

"That instrument?"

"Yes."

"No."

"Good Lord, Ben, I'd never have dreamed. Oh," she said, "oh, the world's closed systems, it's thousand thousand dialects and shoptalk. Thank you for showing me this."

"I didn't know about it myself."

"Let's go into the arena. Do you suppose they'll be practicing?"

There were at least twenty-five people on the ice. Ben and Patty stood near where the timekeeper would have sat at a hockey game.

"Look," she whispered, "some are wearing shoes. They're the coaches. They must be the coaches."

"I guess," Ben said.

"It's amazing."

The skaters moved, propelled by an invisible torque, their incredible strength disguised by the rich caramels of their hose, their fetching costumes like a kinky lingerie, each hard-muscled ass yellow-ruffled, white, the gorgeous paydirt of their tough crotches—"They must *shave* themselves!" Patty said—a state secret, cunningly guarded. On their high skates they were tall as goddesses, and Ben ferociously watched them, angrily studying their silent fury, his own heart pounding at their long quiet glides and sudden swoops, the transcendent self-possession of their punishing narcissism. He wanted to kill them, to climb high, high up into the arena, take Texas Tower potshots at them from beneath the broadcasting booth. He wanted them to collide, to explode against each other, and though they came close, must in their floating, driving imminence have sniffed the ice-shrouded odor of each other's personal gall, they always swerved at the last moment, almost driven off, bounced off the secret laws of right-of-way like people come up against force fields in science fiction. It was as if he were watching natural traffic patterns, a misleading random decreed by instinct.

He could not understand his anger, which went deeper than jealousy, closer to the bone than envy. There was despair in it, the accusation of a wasted life, of the wrong moral choices. He wanted to lacerate himself with it and edged away from his friend.

"Listen," she said. "Listen."

The coaches, only a couple of them men, had been shouting instructions to their skaters in a jargon that sounded to Ben like military code, secret password.

"Your threes, your threes and brackets."

"Go to a mohawk."

"That's it. Choctaw. Choctaw."

"Double lutz."

"Rockers. Rockers."

Now the coaches were silent and all one could hear, what Patty had asked him to listen to, was the steam-engine hiss of the skates, the *shhh shhh* of ice being torn at its surface by the speeding blades. It was the flat unconsummated sound of surf. Tea kettle and shore, train engine and the whistle of standing, sibilant jet.

"So?"

"It's the sound of water, Ben, in all its states at once."

"Why are they so dedicated? They're like Brides of Christ."

"They're wonderful."

"Yeah, yeah, they'll live forever. Not one of them smokes and they practice eleven hours a day and they'll dance on my grave. They're not out of fucking high school. What are they doing here? Who pays their way?"

"I wish I could skate," Patty said.

"You can't? That's good news. Let's go back. We'll drink coffee and smoke cigarettes and stay up all hours. It gives me the creeps this place. It makes me old and multiplies my sclerosis."

In the room Patty rolled two joints. She handed one to Ben and kept the other for herself. "Too much is wasted," she said, "when you pass it back and forth."

"Is that an insight?"

"It's an observation."

Ben had had grass before, of course. He had turned on with several of the people who ran his franchises. He had always found it pleasant. Now he discovered its analgesic properties. His hand—he knew it was an illusion—felt almost normal to him. He was not so conscious of the grainy quality of all surfaces. They lay in bed and Ben stroked Patty's naked back with his bad hand. "This is very nice," he said.

"Twice as many women as men are homosexuals," Patty murmured comfortably. "This is because from toilet training on they are required to touch themselves at both ends."

"Is that an observation?"

"It's an insight. Let's speak insights, Ben. I'll do one, then you do one. It's your turn."

"No. You could have had that one saved up. Give me a different one."

"Don't you trust me?"

"Me? I trust everybody."

"All right," she said, "*The Last Picture Show* turned our culture around and started the nostalgia business. That and that song— 'American Pie.' "

"That's a lousy insight."

"You do better."

"Okay. All your insights relate to music."

"They don't. What about the salad dressing? What about the menus and the thing about twice as many, what did I say, twice as many girl queers? They have nothing to do—to do with music."

"Those are exceptions. Many of your insights relate to music."

"That's because—"

"That's because Julius Finsberg had this theatrical costume business. Because he dressed all those musical comedies."

"That's right."

"That's right. There's a lyric in my godblood la la."

"All right. But it doesn't count unless you do one about the culture."

"The culture."

"The culture—salad dressings, menus, top of the pops."

"It wouldn't be fair," Ben said. "It wouldn't be a fair contest."

"Try. You can do it, Ben."

"I know I can do it. What, are you kidding? It wouldn't be fair to *you*. I'm Mr. Softee, I'm the chicken from the Colonel. Cock-a-doodle-do and the sky is falling. I'm the Fred Astaire man. I'm the Exxon dealer, we thought you'd like to know. It wouldn't be fair to *you*. To you it wouldn't be fair. I'm a— What was I saying? I was going to say something. Oh yeah. I'm a cultured man. I'm One Hour Martinizing and the Cinema I, Cinema II in the shopping center. I'm America's Innkeeper, I'm Robo-Wash. I'm Benny Flesh, K-O-A, and Econo-Car International. I'm H & R Block, but it's seasonal. The culture? *I'm* the culture! Ben Flesh, the Avon lady, Ben, the Burger King. Or maybe you meant something more academic? Sure. Okay. Howdoyoudo? I'mEvelynWoodofEvelyn-WoodReadingDynamics. Pleasedtomeetcha. Wannaread*Warand-Peace*onyourlunchbreak? The culture. Sweetie, I've got ice-vending machines in every Big Ten campus town in the Midwest. Want, want to know something? My hand don't work but I'm—hah hah, this'll kill you—Mister Magic Fingers. *Yes!*"

"How's business, Ben?"

"Insights, insights, let's see. Insights. Ho. Hah! Ho ho. Yes. It's coming to me. I think he's got it. Oh yes. Sure. Wonder Woman fights crime with her bracelets, right? Well, what is this if not a variation on the old theme that diamonds are a girl's best friend? The envelope that film comes back in—I'm Flesh of Fotomat—is really only a sort of origami of paper boxes made in the image of the suitcase. Think, Patty, think. The yellow outside envelope has a little punched-out paper handle. Then there's a wide white envelope inside—this is the suitcase proper—with little photographs printed on it. These are emblematic of the travel stickers one finds on steamer trunks. If you open it up you'll find a little slip, a pocket where the negatives go. Just like the puckered pockets on the raised lid of a suitcase. Just *like* it. Why? Why *this* shape? Because, because, my dear Patty, because a photograph is a holiday thing. More pictures are taken on summer vacations than at any other time of the year. There's a relationship between travel and photography. So, there's this subliminal suggestion on the photo lab's part that pictures and trips and the paraphernalia of trips—luggage, the suitcase—are all interrelated. We say 'take a picture,' we say 'take a trip.' The film 'comes back' from the drugstore. Eureka! Eureka City! What we're dealing with here—film, vacations, life's golden goddamn highlights—is memory, the illusion of eternity, the hint of resurrection. Memory 'comes back,' too. Pictures 'come back' and people 'come back' from their trips. That's why they pack those damn photographs in those damn envelopes like that. So that's, that's one insight."

"All right. Cereal boxes!"

"Cereal boxes, cereal boxes, let's see. Yes. A family food. Breakfast. The cereal box is designed to be breakfast's centerpiece, to stand there in the middle of the kitchen table. While Father reads the nutrition panel on one side of the box, Mom can look at the spoon premium on the other side. Meanwhile, the kid studies the cartoon on the back and learns about the toy. I haven't figured out the front yet. Yeah, I have. The front is the title, the name. Kellogg getting in its licks."

"Well—" Patty said.

"I know. I'm not too crazy about that one myself." They were both silent for a moment.

"Do my ass," she said. He did her ass.

"You know," he said, "what we're talking about here is shapes. You know what I think? I think the cereal box, the film envelope, the salad dressing, packs of cigarettes, the cartons they come in, all packages really, the mustard jar, the jelly, the bottle of ketchup and the carton of milk, everything, the pack of gum, the stick, the bag of potato chips, yeah, the bag of potato chips, the, what was I going to say? Yeah. The bag of potato chips, the box of strawberries, the ice-cream *cone*, the whatchamacallit, Fudgicle and Popsicle, the candy *bar*, yes, *yes*, the candy bar like a kid's ingot, the candy bar, I could go on forever. Tomatoes in their cardboard and cellophane boxes, the bottle of nail polish with the little brush attached to the cap, tins of shoe polish, right? Loaves of white bread?"

"What's the point? You've been talking for hours."

"Wait. Don't mix me up. What was that last one? Loaves of white bread. *Decks of cards.* Huh? Decks of cards. Wristwatches in their boxes. Three or four bananas with a strip of green tape around their middle and, uh, men's shirts with those little pins always in the same places and lollipops and the ridges on licorice and, my God, *automobiles, airplanes,* cuts of *meat*—Kansas City strip, New York, porterhouse, chuck roasts, chops, cutlets—I mean Jesus, Patty (*patties,* Patty!), the animals aren't *built* that way. Those are just arbitrary shapes. Why isn't gum like a wafer? Why is it always a *stick* of gum? Why a *bag* of potato chips? Why *wrist*watches? I mean, this is it, there's going to be a breakthrough here tonight."

"You're not doing my ass."

"I can't do your ass and concentrate on the breakthrough. All right. Did I say lipsticks? Lipsticks. Spaghetti boxes, boxes of soda straws, you know how there's always a little window in the box? You remember seeing that? I don't know if they still do that but they used to. *Postage* stamps! With their serrated edges. Well sure, I know, that's functional so you can tear them off the sheet without ripping them. But that's not the real reason, because you have the example of money, too. Why are there milled edges on dimes, quarters and half dollars but not on really small change like pennies and nickels? Why?"

"Why?"

"Traffic lights. Red. Amber. Green. The world *over*. Ethiopia and Iran. Ohio and Tasmania. *Canned goods*. The label goes all the way around. Top to bottom. Wall to wall. Why?"

"Why?"

"Uniforms—cops', soldiers', firemen's. The metal badge on the front of a bicycle. Bicycle pedals. Who said that bicycle pedals have to look the way they do? Shoes! Sixteen holes for the laces. The laces. *A pair of shoelaces*. Think how *they're* wrapped. The little armband of paper. Spools of thread and balls of yarn."

"Toilet paper."

"Toilet paper, right. Kleenex, Puffs. Paper napkins. Baby powder with those round holes punched in the top like a solar system. *Tubes* of toothpaste. Why not a jar of the stuff? Tubes of toothpaste but jars of cold cream. It could have been the other way around, you know. Yes, and money could be serrated just like postage stamps. As a matter of fact, it would be easier for banks to handle if it came that way. They could give you a sheet of money and you'd tear the bills off yourself. Jesus, Patty, do you see? Are you with me on this, Insight Lady?"

"What?"

"We read shapes. The culture is preliterate!"

"You think?"

"Sure. I think so. It's tactile, a blind man's culture. White canes and dark glasses. Or umbrellas wouldn't furl left to right in both hemispheres. There'd be more variety in dog leashes. In our belts and boots. It's never been taken for granted that anyone can *read!*"

"You think?"

· 195 ·

"Why books have dust jackets."

"Gee," the Insight Lady said.

"Why bulbs look like pears and how the world got its curly tail. Nobody. Nobody ever. Nobody with money invested ever took it for granted that a single mother's son of us could read. They think we're so *dumb*. We *are* so dumb. And they are, too. So we get these *symbols*. The mustard jar a symbol and the candy bar a symbol, too. We live with molds, castings, with paradigms and modalities. With recognizable shapes. With—oh, *God*—trademarks like the polestar. I could go it alone in an Estonian supermarket. We live in Plato's sky!"

"That's a hell of an insight," Patty said.

"It's a farsight."

"It's a faroutsight."

"Tactile."

"Good, Ben."

"Oh, God," he said. "Tactile, tactile," he said. "Men. Paradigms. Modalities."

"Yes."

"Women. The Finsbergs. The world like a chunk of Braille. Tactile."

"Yes."

*"I want my remission back!"*

And rented horses the following day and rode without a guide into the mountains. The animals, both a rich brown the color of their saddles, knew the trails. Ben had not been this excited since that day in the Bucket. He whistled John Denver songs until he caught himself doing it. In San Francisco once he had suddenly become aware that he'd been humming "I Left My Heart in San Francisco" and one time at the shore he heard himself sing snatches of "Ebbtide."

Patty was in the lead—neither was expert; Patty led because her horse had taken the initiative—and Ben, still stimulated from the night before, called after her. *"Horses! Their names. Horses' names. Cherry, Thunder."* These were the horses they rode. "Lightning. Flicka. They're sexual traits. Male and female."

"I'm sorry?" Patty said. "What was that? I don't follow. 'Lightning flicka,' you said. 'Their sexual traits. Male and female.' What-ever are you talking about? What does 'lightning flicka' mean?"

"Huh? Oh." She hadn't heard him when he'd shouted. She'd gotten only the last part. He explained his new insight in a low voice so she could hear, but it was difficult to keep his voice down when he was so excited.

"But pets, dogs and cats, often have joke names, usually the name of their owners' interests and obsessions. An English profes-sor might call his dog Hemingway, and once I knew a stockbroker with a dog named Florida Power and Light. It's a sort of inexpensive self-mockery. But boats, sailboats, small craft that sleep four to eight, rarely have funny names. That's because boats are a big in-vestment. There's money involved. The men name the boats and give them the code names of sweethearts, their dead sons, and an-cient dreams."

"LaVerne and Maxene," Patty said. "Ethel, Mary, Lotte, and Kitty. Helen. Gertrude."

"Yes," Ben said. "Gee." There was a sort of clearing off to the side of the trail. They were perhaps nine thousand feet up now. "Would it be all right if we got off for a while? My balls are killing me."

"You don't have a jockstrap?"

"I never use them." It was true. He never wore jockstraps and didn't really understand their purpose. Into this he had no insight. They dismounted. Ben stumbled. It was as if he had been strad-dling an elephant. "You suppose they'll wander off? I guess we could sit on that log and hold on to their reins."

"How's the hand?"

"Not bad. I'm glad I thought about the glove though." He had asked to borrow the wrangler's glove to wear on his right hand. It was odd. His hand was protected but not his balls.

The view was spectacular, immense. The trail had led through a pass in Cheyenne Mountain, and though the view was open and they could see for miles on almost every side, only the mountain it-self walling their vision, they felt themselves separated from the culture they had talked about, on which each thrived and endlessly explained. It was nowhere visible. Colorado Springs had disappeared. Not even firebreaks were to be seen, nor the cog railroad that climbed Pikes Peak, nor the mysterious strand of electric lights visible from the Broadmoor—never identified—that followed the contours of the mountain into the sky. Not even the trail itself, now they had left it and led their horses down the gentle six- or seven-foot slope to the clearing.

"Hansel," Patty said.

"Gretel."

They were in nature. Ben let go of Thunder's reins and stretched out on the ground, the soft scrub just downhill of the log he used for a pillow.

"Ought you do that? He might take it into his head to go back to the stables. Then Cherry would follow and we'd have to go back down the trail on foot."

"They won't," Ben said. "They'll go off to eat the mountain, but I don't think they'll leave us. You can let go."

"I don't know, Ben," Patty said.

"Trust me," Ben said. "Don't foreshadow. I'm going to die of multiple sclerosis and you of loud noises. We're safe. Lie down. Use the log." She lay down beside him. "Can you feel it?" he said.

"What?"

"Gravity. Nine thousand feet of gravity sucking at our bodies, drawing our blood. The lines of force like tide."

"Yes," she said.

"Mother Nature's blow job, Her Magic Fingers."

"Yes," Patty said.

"I feel wonderful," Ben said.

"I do, too."

"I feel wonderful. I feel magnificently stupid."

"Stupid? No, Ben, not you."

"Sure me. Oh boy. *Stupid*. It's good. It's fine. The incredible stupidity of a man in the sea, or on a mountain—well, I *am* on a mountain—or some place cold, freezing. Dumb as guys in mines or tumbling in the avalanche or breathing recycled air in submarines. Dumb as astronauts, as men in space, or clumsying the moon. You know what it is?"

"What?"

"It's throwing yourself on the planet's mercy, I think. Up here. Up here—a storm could come up. The lightning could whack us, we dassn't screw or our hearts would explode. Even like this, at rest, they pump away at the thin air as if it were a punching bag. The forests could catch fire. We could die, Patty. The horses could take off. We could stumble. Misjudge the time, let it get dark, let it get too cold. It's so dangerous," he said. "All of it. It's so dangerous. It's terrific. Shhh. Shhh. I'm out . . . I'm out of breath."

He was in nature. As far as he could see. Wherever he looked. In the path of the Ice Age, the scars and pockets gouged by the glaciers. He was in nature, his head as high as the timberline. He was in nature. At the scene of the planet's crimes and explosions, its rocks thrown up from the center of the earth like an anarchist's tossed bombs. In nature. His scent in the thin air like a signal to the bears, to the cougars. Out of his element, the franchiser disenfranchised. Miles from the culture, from the trademark and trade routes of his own long Marco Polo life.

And talked, when his breath was recovered, of wonders. Because that was all there was to do in nature, the only way he could protect himself, no place to hide in nature save in the wonderful. He meant the bizarre, he meant the awful, strangenesses so odd, so alien, they were religious. Vouchsafed to die of his disease, it was as if here, in nature, where everything was a disease, all growth a sickness, the mountains a sickness and the trees a sickness, too, with their symptomatic leaves and their pathological barks, the progress of his disease could leap exponentially, travel his bloodstream like the venom of poisonous snakes or the deathbites of killer spiders.

"I heard," he said quietly—was this praying? was this some crazy kind of prayer?—"I heard of a man who had a bedspread made out of wolves' muzzles. He kept them in a freezer in St. Louis until he had enough for his tailor to stitch together. I once," he said, "knew someone who would tell his troubles to strangers on elevators, just the way travelers on buses and trains unload when they know they'll never see the other party again. He talked very

if he never met her? —It has to. —Why? —Because he has to use everything he's got. Because otherwise . . . —What otherwise? —Never mind, don't get personal. —I was only asking. —I know, and I'd help you out if I could. It's what they all say, of course, but I really would. I'd tell you about his lousy life expectancy. I'd tell you about his sister. —What about his sister? —Well, this guy, this franchiser, had a sister, *has* a sister. —Yes? —She lives in Maine. Outside Waterville. Her husband works for Colby College as a professional fund raiser. —That's nice. That must be interesting work. —He has no franchises in Maine. They don't see each other much. The sister's barren and, he gathers, the guy, the franchiser, that it's sort of, well, made her, well, very unhappy. I know what you're going to say, that they could adopt, but for a long time they didn't really want kids and now that they do, when they did, it was too late. She's in her fifties. His sister is in her fifties. The agencies don't like to give women that age . . . The husband wasn't doing too good. It was during the Vietnam war. The kids were acting up, trashing buildings, rioting. People didn't want to give money to a school where kids behaved like that. —But they all behaved like that back then. —People don't like to give their money away. The husband wasn't doing too good, too well. Colby's kind of a small place. No government contracts. No state support. It depends upon alumni gifts. —Yes? —The husband wasn't doing too well. I don't remember now how he got into fund raising. Yes I do. He used to be a social worker. That's the ironic part. He used to be a social worker in Chicago, where the franchiser's sister lived. —This is an awfully long story. —Not so long. Hang in there. He'd been a social worker. With the agencies. ADC. HEW. HUD. All those letters. He had an in with the adoption agencies. He could have had all the kids he wanted. He could have picked them up in the Delivery Room. But they didn't want kids back then. At least the sister didn't. She was jealous, well, *envious*, of her brother. She thought he lived kind of an exciting life. He had all these franchises and he was always on the go. He didn't. I mean, it wasn't an exciting life, but that's what she thought. She wanted to live an exciting life, too. On a social worker's salary. They don't make much, you know. —I've heard that.

—So she worked, too. She saved. They went to Europe on their vacations. To Hawaii. After they'd been to Europe about a half dozen times, after they'd been to Hawaii, she got it in her mind that she really ought to go to school. That if she were educated, maybe then her life would be more exciting. She put herself through college. She was already in her thirties. She majored in—get this—Oriental Studies. Learned Japanese. Took an M.A. in Japanese. So she had this M.A. and would have gone on for the Ph.D. but their savings were all used up and anyway her adviser didn't think she was good enough for the doctorate. They gave her what they called a 'terminal M.A.' Funny name. —I still think it's a long story. —She was very disappointed and figured she was all washed up in the life-can-be-interesting department. This is when her husband heard about this fund-raising position in Maine. He'd been giving away money and food stamps and stuff all his professional life and he figured that if he was good enough to give it away, then he was good enough to collect it, too. So he asked his wife about it and she was anxious to get out of Chicago anyway because by now all the people she knew that she'd gone to graduate school with had either earned their Ph.D.'s or were writing their dissertations and she felt sort of funny about being around them. You know? —Sure. —But by this time it really was too late for them to adopt, even if she had had the energy. Which she didn't, hadn't. For she was worn down to the nub with all that trying to make her life interesting. —I see. —Yes. So he was very serious about the job and when the people at Colby thought there just might be a position for the franchiser's sister in the Comp. Lit. department, that really reinforced their decision to go. —Did she get the job? —The sister? Yes. She taught Japanese literature in translation. —Well then. —She was a lousy Japanese-literature-in-translation teacher. After three years they decided to drop her. She was pretty good in Japanese itself, but they didn't offer a course in that. Well, they had some friends in the college but mostly they were what her husband brought in, *his* colleagues, people in the Bursar's Office, in Admissions, not the faculty itself. That crowd. —Oh. —And just about when the guy was running out of ways to write up proposals and get grants from the government, Vietnam came along and the kids acted up and the alums had a good excuse to stop giving. To make a long story short . . . —You said it wasn't long. —I had to say that. It was a white lie. To make a long story short, it looked like the guy was going to lose his job. —Really? —Yeah. —Well, what about the franchiser? —Oh, him. Well, he waited until the last minute. —And? —He gave his brother-in-law $100,000 for Colby College so they would keep him on."

"Ben."

"—He wanted his sister's life to be interesting, too. He felt bad that she envied him."

"Oh, Ben."

"—That's another ironic part. She still envies him. She doesn't know shit about interesting lives."

"Oh, Ben."

"—He never told her about this woman he knew who made up contests for magazines."

"*Ben*," Patty said.

"There was this woman—the Contest Lady."

"Please, Ben."

"Maybe you know her."

"Please, Ben."

"After college she knocked around some, traveling, working a bit, taking lovers—like that."

"Why are you—"

"But Lotte wasn't satisfied. Things *bored* her. I never knew anyone so easily bored. Your sister must have been very religious, I think, to be so bored."

"Religious?"

"Well, she wanted everything to have a point. She had the highest expectations of anyone I've ever known. *Wondrous* high. Expectations higher than these mountains, higher than my sister's. Expectations to give you the nosebleed. 'Come,' I'd say, 'I'm your godlover, I like you, come home, I'll take you to the ball park and buy you a hot dog.' But the hot dog has not been packaged that would satisfy your sister. When she bought her cooperative in the East Seventies—Tower East—she bought on the top floor, the thirty-eighth."

"The thirty-sixth," Patty said.

"See? She thought it was to be the thirty-eighth. See how high her expectations? See? But there she was, forced to live two stories beneath her expectations. What was that guy's name she liked so much?"

"Bob Brown."

"Yes. Bob Brown. You know why she wouldn't marry him?"

"Because he lived in Oklahoma City. 'How can I marry a man who chooses to live in Oklahoma City?' That was her reason. That was what she told me stood between them."

"Do you know the only time she ever saw the apartment in daylight was when the agent showed it to her?"

"She slept till dark."

"She slept till dark. She could see how boring things were in the daytime. They stood out more plainly in daylight. Sharper definition. Greater resolution. She never once—*think* of this—she never once saw the view—the bridges, midtown Manhattan. Only by night. And then only until the drapes came. I don't think she opened them once they were up. She ate her meals at Elaine's. All she kept in her refrigerator was club soda, tonic water, and shriveled lemons. Elaine billed her. It cost her $8,000 a year for her dinners."

"She saw her friends there."

"Yes. Her friends. They'd sit around and play her contests. Those crazy contests she made up."

"They were funny. Did you ever do one?"

"I'm no good at that stuff. What were some of the good ones?"

"The inventions."

"Oh yeah. Right. The inventions."

"The Planet of the Apes."

"Right. The apes were very advanced but couldn't see the obvious. Wasn't that it? Something was always left out and an earthman had to set them straight."

"Blowing," Patty said.

Ben laughed. "Blowing. Blowing was terrific. These ape kids would go to the zoo or the park with their mothers and fathers and there'd be this ape selling colored balloons and the kids would make their parents buy them one and then they'd shlep the goddamn balloons along the ground on a string. Until the earthman said, 'They're beautiful balloons, why don't you blow them up?' And that was how blowing was invented."

Patty laughed. In the thin air she had difficulty catching her breath.

Ben held his stomach, his sides. "Oh, God," he said, "it is, it *is* dangerous. We could die laughing up here."

Patty couldn't stop. Slime spilled from her nose like blood from a wound. "And when he . . . he . . . hee hee hah hah . . . oh, Ben, sl-slap me or hah hah hah *some*-something."

"Their fountain pens," Ben said, roaring. "They had these fantastic fountain *nch nch* pens. Much more advanced than ours. Parker 22's! But whenever—whenever they wrote any*nchnchthing* they al-always rip r-r-ripped the pa-*pa*per."

"Till the earthman told them about *ink*. Oh, God, Ben," she said, exhausted.

Ben was completely lightheaded now. He was no longer convulsed because he had run out of air, out of breath. "They had radios," he said quietly. "Transistorized AM–FM stereos that never made a sound. Only some static if there was a bad storm. TV's with blank screens."

"I don't remember that one," Patty said.

"The earthman asked why they hadn't invented programs."

"Oh yes," Patty said. "I forgot that one."

"The Wild Idea contest."

"The Physics jokes."

"They were too complicated," Ben said. "But she was a hell of a Contest Lady, Insight Lady."

"Yes," Patty said.

"She was this fucking princess setting tasks, her ass to the guy who won her goddamn contests."

"Don't talk like that."

"How do you think she met Brown? He was out there in Oklahoma City, for Christ's sake, entering those stupid contests and picking off first prize or honorable mention every week. She finally called him, *summoned* him. And it wasn't because he lived in Oklahoma that she didn't marry him."

"It was."

"But because she got bored with making up contests. Because your sister got bored with laughter."

"What?"

"Because finally, if you want to know, just plain being *happy* didn't come up to her expectations."

Patty was crying. "Why did she have to kill herself? Oh, God, I miss her," she sobbed.

"Those grotesque childhood diseases. The bad fairy's chicken's pox. The delayed measle and the mopey mump like a pea under her hundred mattresses. (Because she was, too, a princess and did, too, live in a fairy tale.) The colic of a kid's sky-high fevers and all deferred disease. Her tardy terrible times. Lotte's laggard, dallying, dilatory death. Let's get off the mountain."

"Oh, Ben."

His bad hand felt as if it were housed in a sandpaper glove. "Because boredom is the ultimate childhood disease, and your sister had too damn many more rainy days than she could handle. Tell me, tell me, how high are *your* expectations? Are they bigger than a bread basket?"

"No."

"Mine neither. How about boredom? Are you bored?"

"I'm excited."

"Yes? Good. Long life to you."

"Ben—"

He pushed himself up to his knees. He was breathless and his balance was bad and Patty had to help him and it was a good thing the horses had not left but were standing just the other side of the trail when, Patty helping him up the slight incline, they got back to it, and lucky that Patty was there to help him work his fingers into the proper sheaths of the glove, for he could feel nothing in his right hand and was unaware, who was aware of the significance of his encounters with princesses from fairy tales, that he had jammed his index and forefinger together with all his strength into a single sheath of the wrangler's borrowed glove, unaware of this till Patty, Insight Lady that she was, saw the wide salami casing of his jammed hand and helped him with it, splaying his paresthetic fingers that burned if they touched something that was merely warm and turned icy if they touched that which was only cool and could not distinguish textures or else confused them, mistaking the blunt for the sharp, the rough for the smooth, but could feel well enough, when it came right down to it, pain but never pleasure, unaware that he had made this mistake who understood not merely the significance of his old lover's, Lotte's, death but the continued presence of the horses as well, that, riderless, freed, one might have expected to return to the stables of the Broadmoor—why certainly! clearly! because we are dudes and they know it and are dude-trained, broken to dude habits, knowing by heart of course the dude-resting and dude-dismounting places on this dude mountain, horses like good dancing partners who by this time could follow anyone, even franchise dudes like me and Insight Lady dudes like her, but not doing us any favors either and not even just doing their job but lessoned in this, made to go right fucking back up the mountain unhayed and unwatered with the wrangler if they return empty-saddled to a class dude place like the Broadmoor!— and lucky, too, that she was there to help him back on his horse, well, *a* horse, for God knew—not an Interstate, civilized trademark dude like him—whether it was Thunder or Cherry whose back he rode or she rode, and they pulled the reins just as the wrangler had told them to if they wanted to turn the horses and the horses, who were also in nature, too, recall, turned easy as pie and they went back down the trail together, half dude and half horse, just like something else from the fairy tales.

They spent part of their last day together at the Broadmoor with Patty analyzing the handwriting in the logos of some of Ben's franchises. They found their samples in the advertisements of the Colorado Springs Yellow Pages. She told him that the *F* in the "Fred Astaire Dance Studios" was very interesting.

"See," she said, "how at the lowest point of the downstroke there begin to be right and left tending upward spirals. The *F* is practically a caduceus. God, Ben, it *is* a caduceus. In classical mythology this was the staff carried by Mercury. Mercury the messenger, fleet and nimble-footed in the sky. What *is* dance if not the defiance of gravity? Oh, I say, Ben, see the *A*, the hiatus at the top

of the oval, the long *l* loop that doesn't touch the base line. These
are 'irresistible eyes.' This writer exerts a compelling influence on
people. He wins their affection and confidence."

"That's Fred."

Dairy Queen wasn't in cursive, or Radio Shack, or Colonel
Sanders' Kentucky Fried Chicken or Econo-Car, or most of the
other of his franchises that had branches in Colorado Springs. But
he'd had a Ford dealership once and Patty had a lot to say about
the *r* in Ford, though it was poorly printed and didn't show up
clearly on the page.

He asked her to analyze Holiday Inn, said it might be useful to
know about the competition when he opened his Travel Inn.

"When one leg of the *H* has a firm downstroke and the other is
generally the same length but has a generously deflated concave
loop, these are 'horns,' and the writer can become very obstinate
and will almost always insist on his own way of doing things re-
gardless of opposition or consequences. See how the *H* is crossed?
Graphologists call this 'airplane wings' and think it indicates a tendency to press people for information which will be of advantage to
the writer. When the wings cross both downstrokes, these are 'riding crops one upon the other' and the writer—"

"Do you believe this crap?"

"I get many prospectuses from corporations offering their
stocks," she said. "The numbers mean nothing to me. I've a head
for figures but figures change. I look only at the signatures of the
corporation's officers. I am a rich woman."

Ben nodded and they went to bed together one last time. It was,
from Ben's point of view and almost certainly from hers, the most
satisfactory screwing they had yet done. As usual, at climax, the
insights came pouring out of her, a mile a minute and on every
subject under the sun. Ben tried to follow, for she was very interesting and made a lot of sense, but his own groans and whimpers in-
terfered, blocking out much of what she had to say, until all that he
could hear at last were his own cries of pleasure, the baritones of
his fulfillment and tenors of his dude ecstasy and, listening to
these, to his own forceful shouts of completion and triumph, it was
as if he tried to distinguish between speakers on two contending

frequencies on the radio—they were now *truly* in nature—and as he concentrated, squeezing all meaning from Patty's lucid, fastidious orgasm, the better to hear his own barks and cackles and yaps of relish, he heard his noises coalesce, thicken into speech, the vowels and consonants of violence contained, intelligently rearranging themselves into an order and form that may have been there from the beginning.

"*I*," he roared—from "ahh"—"want," he demanded—from "oh," "nh"—"my remission"—from "mnmnh," from "shhh"—"*back!*" From shudders caught in his throat like chicken bones. "I want my remission back," he said quietly.

He rolled off her and onto his back, his penis wetting her thigh, marking it with its contact and scent as animals mark other animals.

They turned on their sides away from each other, joined curiously at the ass, making an *X*. These were "railroad crossings" and the writer wants his remission back.

"Yes?" the Insight Lady said. "You want your remission back? Yes? Ben, you know ever since you first told me that, I've wanted to say certain things to you. I think I have an insight that might help you. It seems to me, Ben, with all this talk of remission, that you want to live like a man with his bladder empty, to travel light and even weaponless, but be protected anyway. It's interesting, for example, that you have always had all that power equipment in your automobiles. Power steering, and power brakes, Ben, power windows. A power aerial that rises from a hole in the front fender. Oh yes," she said, "you want to live even emptier-handed than the rest of us."

"My hand?" he shouted angrily. "My *hand? Graphologist!* What *about* my hand? Did you ever once analyze *that?*" he yelled. "What the fuck do you think it would show?" he screamed. *"The sand, the fucking sand!* It's a Sahara. Riffs ride their horses in it and shoot at the Foreign Legion. It's a sandbox. Kids piss in it and make mud pies. My hand? This? The writer is in agony and only wishes, only *prays* he were fucking *contagious!*" he cried. "Silly bitchbody with your jerk-off insights and your pukey mind!" he thundered at her.

Patty turned to him. She touched his shoulder, pulling on it, turning him toward her. She leaned forward and kissed him sweetly on the lips and smiled.

"Oh, Ben," she said, "it's been a wonderful week. You're a good listener," she told him. "I wish my husband were. Well. I guess I'd better get dressed now. It's only two hours till my plane. I love you, sweetheart. I love you, Ben."

For of course she hadn't heard him, hadn't heard even the least of his loud noises.

". . . a disgrace," the guy from Fort Worth said. "Fun is fun and boys will be boys and it's all very well to live it up at a convention, but to come in drunk and disrupt a meeting like that, the full plenary session with a new line on the line, that is quite another story altogether and really it would be best for everyone concerned, best for Mr. Flesh, best for the people in the Bowling Green area, best, frankly, for Radio Shack, if Flesh would just quietly relinquish his franchise, sell it back to the mother corporation, which would of course buy back his stock as well, all at a reasonable price. We assure you, sir, that you will not lose by the transaction. If anything, it's Radio Shack which will suffer the most immediate financial setback. So, while we cannot force you, while we cannot—"

"How much?"

"What?"

"How much? What's your best offer?"

"Well, we'd have to send someone down there to take an inventory. We'd have to have an audit. We'd want to—"

"Sold."

"Well, I don't know what to say. I hadn't thought you'd be so—"

"On one condition."

"Condition? Now look here, mister, you don't have to sell to us, but we don't have to sell to you either. We can cut off your purchasing privileges, you'd have to find some other supplier. So don't you start waving any 'on one condition's' around."

"That if he wants it you've got to resell the franchise to Ned Tubman of Erlanger, Kentucky."

"There's a franchise in Erlanger. Isn't Tubman . . ."

"Tubman, yes. He owns the Radio Shack in Erlanger."

"Why would you care . . . Listen, if you're thinking of making some sort of dummy corporation, selling to us and using Tubman as a front . . ."

"Tubman, yes. Tubman must have first refusal. I'm not in it. Tubman has always wanted to see Bowling Green, Kentucky."

"He wants to see Bowling Green, Kentucky?"

"Like other people want to see Paris or the Great Wall of China."

"He's never seen it?"

"No, but he's heard so much about it. He's studied up. He's got picture postcards, but it's not the same. He goes back to his Radio Shack after hours. You know those special aerials you rig up to make the stuff sound good?"

"Yes?"

"He pulls in the Bowling Green stations. He listens to the home games on the best equipment. He catches the local news."

"I see."

"You see shit, but if you want my franchise, you've got to offer it to Tubman. I'm not in it. I'll get out, I'll step aside. Gracefully. But Tubman gets first crack."

"Why is this so important to you? Are you kin?"

"We met at the convention and exchanged a few words."

"Then what the hell difference does it make to you who we sell to?"

"Tubman."

"Why Tubman?"

"His name."

"What the hell are you talking about, Mr. Flesh? I don't *smell* booze, but—"

"TUBMAN! Doesn't that mean anything to you?"

"No."

"It's a *sheriff's* name!"

"A sheriff's name," the man from Fort Worth said.

"Can't you see it? I mean, I can close my eyes and see it on a hoarding. NED TUBMAN FOR SHERIFF. Big red letters on a white background. Standing out in the weather on the General Outdoor

Advertising. He isn't cut out for it. He's cut out for the cut-rate radio business. If he doesn't get to Bowling Green, I promise you he'll follow the destiny of his name. He'll run in the Democratic primary. With that name he can't lose. He'll wipe out the Republican: WILLIAM R. RANDOLPH FOR SHERIFF. Ned's no pol. They'll eat him alive at City Hall. They'll give him a heart attack. Or he'll be blown up in his car by the Erlanger syndicate people."

"You are one crazy son of a bitch."

"Me? Nah."

"You sure got a hell of an imagination."

"No no. Really. What I have—what I have is total recall for my country. What I have is my American overview, the stars-and-stripes vision. I'm this mnemonic patriot of place. Look at a map of the U.S. See its jigsaw pieces? I know where everything goes. I could take it apart and put it together in the dark. Like a soldier breaking down his rifle and reassembling it. That's what I have. And if I tell you you can save Ned Tubman from the destiny of his name, you must believe me. You want the franchise back? Fine, it's yours. But my conditions are my conditions." He reached out and patted the Fort Worth man on the sleeve of his silverish suit. "We'll work something out. My lawyers will be in touch with your lawyers."

# 4

Because he was in remission, he thought, hanging a right at the Kansas Turnpike just south of Wichita (Swank Motion Picture rentals) and swinging on down I-35 toward Oklahoma City.

"Because I have my remission back," he told his hitchhiker, "and manic rage, anger, petulance, exuberance, exul- and exaltation are its warning signals, the half dozen warning signals of remission. As well, incidentally, as of its opposite, exacerbation. Because I have my remission back and I got up with the lark this morning. But, big deal, I am in remission. Big deal, it's a long time between drinks. Big deal, I can shuffle a deck of cards again and pick the boogers from my nose. Big deal. Because the truth is, we live mostly in remission. Death and pain being the conditions of our pardon. What, that surprises you? But of course. Childhood a remission, sleep, weekends and holidays, and all deep breaths and exhalations. Peacetime, armistice, truce—the world's every seven fat years and *muthikindunishtiks*, its bull markets and honeymoons. Its Presidents' first hundred days. Why sure thing, certainly, remission is as much a part of the pattern—well, there's no pattern, of course—as the disease. Hell, it's a part of the disease. It's a *symptom* of the disease, for goodness' sake."

His rider was a man his own age he had picked up at the service plaza in Wichita. Dressed in a gray double-breasted suit with heavily padded shoulders and trousers that had been tucked into big brown workman's boots, he had been standing near Ben's Cadillac when he came back from breakfast. He had set his suitcase down between himself and the Cadillac, a dated, buff-colored valise with vertical maroon stripes at the corners vaguely like the markings on streamlined passenger trains, everything the cheap sturdy closely pebbled texture of buckram, like the bindings of reference books in libraries. Flesh noticed the old-fashioned, brassy clasps, amber as studs in upholstery. Oddly, the man's suit, his early-fifties fedora with its wide brim and pinched, brain-damaged crown, and the suitcase—everything but the boots—seemed not new or even well kept up so much as unused, like an old unsold car from a showroom. He understood at once that he was looking at *old* clothes, at an *old* suitcase, that he was in the presence of mint condition, and that the man was a convict. An ex-convict who, to judge from his styles, had spent at least twenty years in prison, which meant, he supposed, that either the fellow was a recidivist whose last sentence had been so stiff because of his previous record, or a murderer. He did not look like a criminal, had not, that is, anything of the concealed furtive about him, motives up his sleeve like magicians' props. He was, if Flesh had ever seen one, a man quits with the world and, what's more—where did he get these ideas? how had vision come to perch on his eyes like pince-nez?—his hitchhiker would not have looked like this yesterday or even this morning, or whenever it was he had last still had time to serve. Five minutes before his release, five seconds, he would have given the state what it still had the power to exact—his respect and submission. He was with, Flesh knew, a totally scrupulous man. A man of measure, taken pains, meticulous as the blindman's-buff Justice lady herself with her scales and pans, honest as the day is long, and a bit of a jerk. The ideal franchise manager.

"Which means, finally, that there's something in it for you."

"For me? God's spoons, sir, what could you possibly—"

"It's all right," Flesh said, "I can dig it, old-timer. I've got your number. You're free now. You're a free man. Right now, this minute, maybe the freest man in America. For whatever it was you did, there was no parole for it. The judge said, 'Twenty years,' and you gave them sixty minutes on the hour, a hundred cents on the dollar. That's why you can cross state lines today, why you have no parole officer to report to, why, in fact, you probably have no job waiting. You're quits with them."

"God's overbite, mister—" The man's strange oaths were delivered in a level, inflectionless voice, but for all their curious Elizabethan ring, Flesh was aware that his epithets were like blank checks, that at any moment—this was the danger of picking up hitchhikers, of leveling with men who had done twenty years—they could be hiked, kited with wind and murder and rage, but Ben's remission was on him and he was no more capable of holding his tongue than of choosing his next symptom.

"No no, it's all right. Let me take a wild stab—no offense, fella—and suggest to you that the reason you stood by my car—you never asked which way I was headed, that service plaza serviced both east and west—was that you wanted a ride in a Cadillac, wanted to see what it felt like, test its shocks and leathers against the springs and metal bench in the pickup that took you out to the work farm in the morning and picked you up in the evening to shlep you to the slammer."

"God's service for twelve!" the man said delightedly. "You're a fortuneteller!"

"Who, me? No no, not even a keen observer most of the time. It's only the juices of remission give me my power today. But that's not in it. I want to make you an offer, I want to give you a job."

"God's nostrils, what would I do for references?"

"Did I ask for references? Did I say anything about references? What do you think, life is a term paper? I want *you*, not your references. I'm opening this Travel Inn in a bit, and I could use a good reliable man to run it. I'll pay you fifteen thousand a year and you can take your meals in the restaurant and have a double that opens out onto the swimming pool."

But in the end it was the convict who wanted Flesh's references, the convict who was frightened off by Flesh's own blank-check talk. By that and some quality he must have detected in him that was out of whack with his own notion of what was fitting. He made a speech, still uninflated and controlled. "Reality wants us," the convict said. "What you offer me is very kind, what with your suspicions of me and all, and as to those I'll say you aye or nay, neither one, for what I did if I did something and who I am if I am someone is none of your business. God's gym shoes, sir, it isn't that sort of world that you should get carried away, and even this, what's happening right now, I mean me riding in this grand automobile, why that, too, is a sin against reality. I asked for the ride and you give it, *gave* it—I'm correcting myself because I know better and bad grammar is another sin against reality—and so that part's my fault and I'll have to watch myself and make my amends some way or other, but the point is that we come into this world and sooner or later an obligation is created and we have to be real. Real with each other and real with ourselves."

"I'm real," Flesh said.

"Maybe, maybe not. That's not my business or for me to say. From what I understand, you got this sickness and now it's given you some kind of breathing spell. —Well, sickness is real enough in its way, I guess, but it isn't as real as health, and if I was you and I got the breathing spell you got—"

"You've your own breathing spell, Mister Convict."

"—the breathing spell you've got, I wouldn't go around crowing about how wonderful it all is."

"No?"

"No, sir. I'd find my reality."

"Who are you to talk, with your vintage luggage and your twenty-year-old suit?"

"That suitcase is what a suitcase is supposed to look like, and the suit is what men of my time wore. I'm not talking about clothes anyway. Why you traveling highways? Where you off to? Where you been? You got a wife? You got a son or sweet daughter at the University of Michigan?"

"Is that reality?"

"God's glands, it is. You know what I'm hoping?" Flesh didn't answer. "You know what I'm hoping? I'm hoping you got sample cases in the trunk of your car, yes, and casters on their bottoms to grease your gravity and road maps and Triptiks in the glove compartment and receipts from the oil companies because once you thought you might want to check your mileage, how much oil you burn. I hope you know to fire a sheet of newspaper and hold it up to warm the chimney so the fire draws. That your dampers are open in their season to be open and closed in their season to be closed."

"I have plenty of road maps."

"That you live in the middle of the middle class the bull's-eye life. And that restaurants are for special occasions, birthdays, anniversaries, and once or twice a year just for the hell of it because you're feeling good, because your ship came in or your uncle from California. I hope you have an insurance broker named Harry who sends you to a doctor who jiggles the results, systolic and diastolic, a dozen points up or down like a difficult window, and that your stocks aggravate you, that hindsight or foresight could have made you a rich man."

"I *am* a rich man."

"It ain't the same. I wish you honorable lusts and one or two close calls with one of your wife's bridge pals or a buyer, perhaps, when you're both a little tight. And guilt like a whopping down payment you can't manage so you draw back at the last minute and jerk off on the toilet seat that night like everybody else. I wish you the hypochondriacal concerns. May you find a lump you can't figure at three o'clock in the morning and may a cough make you suspicious. Examine your stools like a stamp collector for two weeks running and give to a charity when it all blows over. Take an interest in the Super Bowl. Think about lamps, a davenport, finishing the basement, and settle for reupholstering what you've already got."

"Reupholstering."

"But spring for new carpeting every ten years. Talk arithmetic to yourself when you do your bills. Go on a diet and stick to it. Jog for a while and give it up. Cut down on smoking, *really* cut down. And may you have a nightmare you don't understand or a dream that makes you cry and hear two jokes that crack you up but aren't so funny when you tell them."

"It sounds very exciting."

"God's rec room, who said anything about exciting? Exciting you already got. I'm talking about real, I'm talking about normal and the law of averages."

"The law of averages," Flesh said.

"All right, the Ten Commandments then. You can let me off up ahead." They were still about seventy miles from Oklahoma City.

"There's nothing up ahead."

"That's all right. That's where I'm going. Thanks for the ride. Anywhere's fine."

Was he going to try something?

"God's germs, man, stop the car, will you?"

Flesh took his foot off the accelerator to slow the car while he thought.

"God's buttons, get a reality. I'm not going to hit you over the head." He showed his hands. "Empty, see? You ain't going to be cut. Just let me out, all right?"

Ben pulled over to the side and waited nervously while the fellow removed his suitcase from the back. He closed Ben's doors and Flesh watched him carefully, expecting, once he realized he was safe, the man to cross to the other side of the highway. Instead, the convict simply moved a few feet down the road and put his thumb up. Flesh, annoyed, shifted to neutral and nudged the car in his direction, alternately depressing the power brake and releasing it, so that Ben, inside the big automobile, had the impression the Cadillac was actually limping up to the man.

"Hey," Ben said, pressing open the electric window next to which his rider had been sitting. "You're ruining my remission, do you know that?"

Their conversation was conducted with the fellow's thumb still raised. It was, Ben Flesh suddenly realized—who had seen tens of thousands of hitchhikers in his day, his Flying Dutchman life bringing him up to, abreast, and beyond them (when, as most times, he chose not to stop)—the oddest gesture of petition there could be—a rakish prayer, more shrug than request, indifference in it, democracy. "Three years of suffering and you're ruining my remission."

"Get a reality," the man said, only the corner of his mouth on Ben, his eyes on the road for cars. Ben watched him.

"Another shot in the dark—no offense—you'll never get a ride with my car sitting here. You spoke of references. Surely to anybody passing by it must look as if I've just dumped you, given you bad references hitchhikerwise."

"God's rash, fellow, give over. Leave me be. All right, I made a mistake going with you. Well, I've served my time. Spring me, we're square."

"Let me just steal—no offense—a minute of your time—no offense."

"Well then?"

"What's wrong? Why do I put you off so? We're perfect strangers."

"We ain't strangers," the man said.

"I never saw you till this morning."

"We're not strangers. I been shut up with fellows like you decades. Crook, all crimes are crimes of passion. Adventure lays in the bloodstream like platelets. We're not strangers. Get a normality. Live on the plains. Take a warm milk at bedtime. Be bored and find happiness. Grays and muds are the decorator colors of the good life. Don't you know anything? Speed kills and there's cholesterol in excitement. Cool it, cool it. The ordinary is all we can handle. Now beat it. Goodbye."

"Listen—"

"God's unlisted number, God's toenails and appetizers! I told you, mister, get out of my way." Flesh raised the electric window and drove off.

A few miles down the road he spotted another hitchhiker. His heart was still pounding from what the convict had said and he felt under some compulsion to stop for this new stranger, a fellow—he'd slowed to study him while he was still a couple of hundred feet away from the man—in his late twenties, Ben judged, without parcels or luggage and dressed not for the road—a mile or so back Ben had spotted an abandoned late-model Pinto on the shoulder of the highway, its doors closed and hood raised—but like a man with car trouble.

"Get in," he said. "Run out of gas?"

"Yes," the young man said, "or something with the engine. The last sign I saw said there are service stations at the next exit. I figure that would still be about ten miles or so up ahead."

"I'll take you."

"Thanks, I appreciate it."

"No trouble," Ben said.

And then the nice young man in the good clothes—it was closer to twenty miles than to ten—began to address Ben in public-service announcements.

"Only you can prevent forest fires," he said.

"I beg your pardon?"

"I was just thinking," the young man said, "only you can prevent forest fires."

"Me?"

"Well. You and me. You know—us."

"Uh huh."

"Another thing. We should keep the drunk driver off the highway."

"Yes," Ben said.

"And hire the handicapped."

Ben nodded and pressed down on the accelerator.

"More accidents occur in the home than anywhere else."

"Yes, I heard that."

He took a tube of Rolaids out of his pocket and extended it toward Ben.

"No thanks."

"No?" The young man took one from the roll and put it into his mouth. "I keep this and all medicines out of the reach of children," he said, chewing.

"That's good," Ben said. He drove even faster.

"Unh unh," the young man said. "Slow down and live."

It was odd. It was what the other one had been trying to tell him, too.

"Yep, discrimination in housing is not only wrong, it's illegal. Save the children," the man said. "Get your pap test, and remember," he said, "if you're an alien you have to register your address by January 16. Forms are available in any post office."

When Ben reached the exit he took him to the first service station.

Sure, he thought, back on the highway, the manageable ordinary, yes. And where was it to be found?

Under the unicorn fast asleep.

He had said big deal his remission was back, big deal he could shuffle a deck of cards, but in his motel room in Oklahoma City he used and savored his suddenly recovered powers.

He trawled his right hand over the brocade spread, digging his fingers pleasantly into its rough plains, bristled as underbrush or stubble. He knew that his nerves were lying to him, that his brain had scrambled his sense of touch, that his fingertips moved over only temporarily coded textures, but there was a lump in his throat, and he was happy. This was the only reality he needed, had ever needed, to receive sensation in its more pleasant disguises, quenching after three years his nerves' long thirst for the smooth, the soft. Happy is he, he thought, for whom gunny is as silk, burlap as cashmere, wool as percale, instead of—his experience of the past years—the other way around. He would have browsed textbooks of textiles like large tomes of wallpaper samples, would willingly have caressed all dry goods, all bolts, rolls, lengths, and swatches. He wanted jute between his fingers, sackcloth, linen, cambric, mohair. He longed to touch toweling, vicuña, worsted and jersey, tweed, homespun, duffel and mull. Serge, he thought, flannel. Muslin and calico. Chintz. He would have set his fingertips against the grain of sharkskin and dimity, gingham and voile, handled poplin and madras, satin and taffeta, the chiffons and the velvets. Corduroy, tulle, organdy, lace. Grosgrain, chenille. He was a sucker for seersucker, would have felt felt.

Oh oh, he thought, son of his tailor pop and godson of many-costumed Finsberg, how queer a fit my punishment has been. How unsuitable. How wickedly fate has taken my measure. For three years and more, health's yokel, its clock-sock boob, fetching stares from the natives, those fashion plates, all the customized robust. Men and women with muscle tone, good color, sound tactile good sense, their protein levels in the Swiss banks of being. What I have missed! How deprived! And of all the fabrics the one most missed was woman's, and next to that, perhaps even before it, the natural feel of his own now middle-aged skin.

He took himself in hand. Entered the shower. (He would not use soap, had no need for the protective glaze of lather.) Adjusted the temperature of the water with the thermostat of his body, his skin like a good thermometer, registering for the first time in years hot as hot, cold as cold, lukewarm as ecstasy. And focused the showerhead like a portrait photographer, shooting with needlepoint, fine spray, the splat of raindrop and heavy weathers of cloudburst. His body calling a spade a spade, even with his eyes closed discriminating, calling out the f-stops of velocity and feeling, feeling—God, had *that* gone too? had *that* abandoned him?—a strange sensation now, something new under the sun, no, something rerecognized—feeling *wetness*, distinguishing dampness, all the marvelous degrees from dry to soaked, the splendid spectrum of humidity.

And when he left the shower stall—he had no need for the traction of bathmats, his balance, which had been slipping away now for months, had returned—he dived into the thick motel bath towels no longer rough to his skin as sandpaper or ground glass or cat-o'-nine-tails. He rubbed himself down, however, with a pulled-punch vigor, making the stinging noises of hygiene—bah*rruh*, prrrt, shashashashasha—but holding back at last, fearful lest he accidentally press some raw nerve which would, like a linchpin tumbler falling into place in a lock, cause his brain to renege on his remission and return his body to its zipper condition. So he dried his scalp gently, even as he made his curious warpath movements, and ventriloquized the whoops and yaps of a remembered zealousness. And combed his hair wet.

And froze, alarmed and despairing because there was suddenly a queer, faintly burning, salt-in-wound sensation in the outside corners of his eyes. Oh, Christ, he thought. "Oh, God," he said, "time's up. I have counted my chickens. Death is not mocked." And touched the tender spots where the gates of his disease were still open, where his M.S. had stood stupidly in the draft. And the tips of his forefingers came away wet. "Why, they're *tears*," he said in the profoundest wonder he had ever known. They're tears and I *felt* them, my skin as honed as that! Feel them, *feel* them, delicate and baroque as the tracings of snails or the feathery strands of spiders. "Thank you," he said. "Thanks. Thank you." And lay naked on the bed, his skin taking the full force of the impression of the spread, imagining he could feel the warm reds and cool blues and neutral browns of its pattern beneath him, while the tears—he would not touch them, would not stanch them—flowed and flowed and finally stopped. And he could feel, enjoy, their evaporative lift. And even the molecular heft of the salt they left behind.

Then he touched with the fingers of both hands every square inch of his body. And the insides of his ears. And explored his nostrils. And poked about in his mouth to feel his teeth on his fingers, his cavities, to touch his tongue and dip it into the well behind his jaw. And reached into his asshole, going deep as a doctor.

His body was still there.

He called the front desk and asked that a bellman be sent to his room.

"Listen," he told the man, "I'm going to give you ten dollars. I want you to send a woman. Cheap, expensive, I don't care. I don't care what color she is or what she looks like or anything about her age. I just want—"

"You want to be chucked out of here, that's what you want."

"No, no, you don't understand—"

"Mister, it's eleven-thirty in the morning. Oklahoma City isn't New York."

"Oh, I see," Ben said, "the call girls haven't started yet. I misunderstood. Oh, I see. Oh, that's different." He was addressing the bellman like a pimp but in his heart he felt as rehabilitated as Scrooge on Christmas morning. In another minute he would give him money to fetch a goose.

"Put your clothes on," the bellman said.

"What? Oh." He was still naked. Christ, had he traded his sanity for his remission? He couldn't hope to explain. "Will you take the money anyway? I'm not—I didn't know—look, I know what you're thinking, what you'd *have* to be thinking, but it isn't— It's— Where's my Bible?" he asked desperately.

The bellman sneered and Ben, when the man had gone, laughed his ass off, the same one he could touch again with his fingers and feel when he wiped himself.

Which didn't butter any parsnips. He should have been at his Cinema I and Cinema II in the Draper Lake Shopping Mall, but he wasn't leaving the motel till he got laid. He called his manager and said he was still in Wichita but was about to leave and would make it down by that evening.

He dressed and went into the dining room and had his lunch. The waitress was a young and pretty girl, and under the napkin on his lap he had an immense hard-on. He chewed his food nervously and stammered when he asked the girl for water. He made her stand by while he added up his check and his brain raced with schemes to engage her personally. He ordered desserts he did not want, commented on the weather, what people did before there was air conditioning, how interesting it must be to work in a motel, meet all those people, American people, who lived—he recalled his rider's phrase—in the middle of the middle class. "You learn," he said wildly, "about their different tastes. I mean, coming from all over as they do, they bring, they, uh, bring their customs with them, their peculiar, well, er, *folk* dishes. That would be, uh, be a, a fair statement, wouldn't it?"

"Very fair," she said. "In the morning the kids want Sugar Frosted Flakes and the grownups eat bacon and eggs."

"Yes. Well . . ."

"Was there anything else? One of the girls is out today and I have her station, too."

"Anything else? No no. It was, er, delicious. My compliments to the chef."

"I'll tell her."

"Yes. Well . . . Good luck, good luck to you. Only you can prevent forest fires," he added lamely. He felt like an idiot and tipped her two dollars for a three-dollar lunch. His salvation now, his only hope not to seem like a fool in her eyes, was to seem insane. Madness had a certain integrity which stupidity lacked.

He started back to his room. It was absolutely necessary that he have a woman, yet, in a strange way, his desire had little to do with lust. Even his hard-on had been more a fact of his remission than of lasciviousness. He had told his brain what to do and it, in its new health, flexing all its recovered muscles, had done it. "See," his brain said, "watch this. It's like riding a bicycle."

A maid was making up the room across from his. He let himself in with his key and cleared the motel soap off the bathroom shelves and hid it in his suitcase. He scooped up the towels he had used and shoved them into the shower stall.

"Miss," he said, standing in the doorway of his room, "oh, miss?"

"Yes yeah?" She looked to be a woman in her late forties or early fifties, but it was difficult to tell. She may have been an Indian. She was extremely short, very fat.

"I don't seem to have been left any soap."

"No yeah? Take from cart what you need."

"Oh." He had had the idea she would bring it to him. He made a great to-do about selecting the soaps, strolling about the big canvas wagon as if it were a sweet table or a notions counter, looking into the cartons of matchbooks and the sheaves of treated shoe-shine cloths like bundles of fresh dollars in a teller's drawer. He examined the cutlery of ballpoint pens and poked about among the waxy motel postcards and stationery. "Well," he said, when the Indian woman came out with a roll of dirty bed linen, "there's certainly a lot of things you have to remember to give out. All these pens and cloths and"—he looked directly into the woman's face—"*sanitary napkin disposal bags.*"

"Mnh."

"Oh hey," he said, "look at that, will you? The sheets." From where he was standing he could not see the sheets. "All crumpled and *soiled* . . . A lot goes on in a motel room, I bet."

"What yeah?"

"I say, a lot goes on in a motel room that you and I wouldn't know about. Or that *I* wouldn't. You must see it all though. I mean, if you could only talk I bet you could tell some stories." She had walked back into the room and started to make up the bed. Ben followed. "Could you use some help? I don't claim to be much of a hand at *making* beds, but—uh, a little lady like you, I mean, well, if both of us . . ." She moved very quickly, so short she barely had to stoop to tuck in the sheets. Ben watched as, inverting the pillowcase and aligning one end of the pillow with it while holding the four edges, two of pillow and two of pillowcase, she flipped the pillow into its case. "That's good," Ben said. "I'm going to watch you closely on the next one. That's a real time-saver." She

seemed unaware that he was in the room. "That's really something," he said when she had done it again with a second pillow.
"That's one of the tricks of the trade, I guess, what you pick up
over the years. Yep yeah?" She had covered the bed with its
spread. Ben took a deep breath. "I can't get over how fast . . . I'll
bet you could muss up a bed *and make it again with the same sheets*
without the housekeeper ever . . . Let me ask you something up
front. Do you know what the hell I'm talking about?"

"No yeah."

"All right. We'll put it this way: You must get all kinds in a
place like this. You must even get kinds like me."

"Yes yeah? You yeah?"

"Lonely."

That was not it, of course. He was not lonely. He was coated
with the need to use himself. Ben Flesh, the restored Bourbon, the
found Louis, the exile returned and looking for ways, literally, to
feel and make himself felt. He did not so much want to screw—he
had screwed in the last three years; he had not run out of godcousins; there was the "Looks-Like Lady," the "Way to Make a
Million Dollars Lady," there were others, some even who were not
his godcousins—as to touch another human being, to hold someone, to feel their two lives, his, the other's, like sparks arcing between two rods, to catch a pulse—this morning, lying on the bed
after his shower, he had taken his own pulse, able to feel for the
first time in years in the tips of his fingers the rhythm of his
blood—his hands like heat-seeking devices, holding the life signs
and interior parameters of another human, to feel her tremble, to
hold her and feel her sweat, to know her body temperature and
search out beneath her skin the muscles and bones, to feel hair and
know it from flesh and flesh from cosmetics and with his eyes
closed trace the calluses on her fingers and distinguish the fine
down on her arms. His disease had deadened others as well as himself, had turned whole populations to wood and stone and given
them the dead, neutral texture of plastic. It needn't even be a
woman. A child would do. He would have pinched cheeks and
held their small heads, or dandled babies on his lap, and the
squirmier the better. Oh yes. And been arrested. The curious fact

of his civilization was that all intimacies save the ultimate were out of the question. You could fuck but not touch. He wanted nothing more now than to stand beside this small woman and close with her, feel her breath on his hand, or even, just to shake hands with her. But it was impossible, finally, to ask. She would have to know his life. From the beginning to this moment. Then, the most curious thing of all, she would yield, lending him her humanity as eagerly as if he had been her child. They would lie beside each other and he could touch her wherever he wished. She would run her finger across his palm. He would let down her hair. Everything would be permitted, nothing withheld. But it was impossible. There were no words save those of proposition and he could humiliate neither himself nor her any longer. "Thank you," he said, "for the soap. You're very kind."

And a few minutes later—he was on the way to Cinema I and II, the hell with what his manager might think—he saw something which made him stop his car. He looked about desperately for a place to park, a vacant meter. Someone was pulling out a dozen yards down the street. He moved quickly to protect the parking space. He had no change for the meter and only about five minutes of parking time remained on it. To hell with it, let them give him a ticket, let them tow.

He walked inside.

"You're next, mister."

"The works," Flesh said, and climbed into the barber chair.

"Shine?" a black man asked.

"Yes, yes, please," Flesh said. He whispered to the barber.

"Dorothy," the barber said, "the gentleman wants a manicure."

"Get the cuticles," Ben said, "don't forget the cuticles."

The girl brought her tray and stool up to Ben's chair. "The cuticles are part of the treatment," she said.

"Yes," Ben said, "of course." She held his right hand powerfully and began to file his nails. "Yes," he said, "that's good. That's very good. And a soak?"

"It's all part of the treatment," she said.

"Part of the treatment, yes," he said, and surrendered his hand to the warm soapy water and his face to the hot towel and his feet to the vigorous movements of the black man's hands, the wonderful tickling sensation when he ran the polish-dipped toothbrush around the base of Ben's shoes. And to the tears under the towel that came from his connection to these three people, and even to the sobs, the huge heavy heavings of his cured chest that they would see under even the great loose barber's sheet that covered him.

The Franchiser goes to his movie.

My movie is wonderfully splendid. The white stone building looks something like a naval officer's hat. I know only approximately what a parabola is, but my movie is paraboloid, I think. It isn't rectangular, it isn't flat; the rear wall—where the screens are, the cyclorama, I believe—is higher than the front or side walls. A naval officer's hat, a pilot's, something pinched and rakish, like, given distance, low furniture. The entrance is boulder and Thermopane, the boulders tan as Hush Puppies, broken ovals and oblongs of stone, snugged in their mortar mounting like facets. In daylight the tall, thick Thermopane is faintly green, pale as martini or bath water. Outside, along an angled, projecting corridor of bouldered wall are the movie's locked framed glass cases—I have a key to these displays, I carry it on my Prince Gardner, top-grain cowhide key holder—where my movie's beautiful posters are sealed beneath the permanent rubric: Now Playing. (And the posters *are* beautiful, so much better than the stagy, glossy stills of the old days with their look, even if the picture was actually in Technicolor, of having been tinted, cosmetized, rouge on the actors' cheeks, eye shadow visible as birthmark above their eyes, stills like tableaux in a wax museum, like the mortician's finagling. The posters are much better. Art work. Line drawings. Spare and promising. Logotypes even the shut-in—the big weekend ads in the Friday and Sunday papers—has by heart. As much a part of the film's image as its theme music. No, but I saw the poster.)

Inside the lobby—more later—to the side, the movie's twin ticket booths like tellers' cages, the stainless chrome panels like a double sink, which spit out my movie's lovely oversize tickets, wide as 35-millimeter film, yellow with a narrow blue edge like a soundtrack, and capable—depending who springs, how large the party—of producing a string of tickets long as a yardstick, longer.

The movie's glass candy cases as big around as a boy's bedroom. With their gorgeous tiers of cellophane-wrapped, cardboard candy boxes with their miniatures—their individually sheathed Heaths and Peter Paul's Mounds and Almond Joys and Milky Ways and Mars. Milk Duds and jujubes like boxes of marbles. No *bars* any more. Oh, the immense dark Hershey's of course, yellow Butterfingers long as a ruler (seventy-five cents some of them, practically nothing under forty-five cents). And popcorn in cylinders large as Quaker Oats boxes, with dollops of my movie's drawn butter and high drifts of buff popcorn in the greased glass case like a spell of cockeyed weather. (We have done away with the hot dogs, slow rolling in grilled place like logs in a river.) And my movie's juices, its carefully sized grape drinks and orange, its Pepsi and Fresca and Seven-Up. My movie's immense carats of crushed ice, its napkin dispensers and straws.

Beautiful Naugahyde benches clear of the Thermopane and near twin easels of Coming Soon with their startling—it's a first-run house—new posters, novel, like a king's proclamation, banns, latest policy, fresh law, new rules. My patrons sidling up to these, studying them while they wait for the show to break.

The movie's thick carpets, a bright, gentle meld and tie-dye of color giving ground to color like the progress of landscape, laws of geography. My movie's toilets, its Women's rooms and Men's, with its urinals white as pillowcase, its stalls of decorator colors not found in nature, and its tiny discrete colored tiles like squares on a board game, its modern, functional sinks with their cockpit fixtures, their wonderful dials for hot water, cold, the pushbutton for soap pink as bubble gum. Paper-towel dispensers built into the walls like pewter mailboxes. My movie's toilets' textured walls with my movie's toilets' motifs, its indirect lighting and its hidden, gentling sound system that plays the themes from big hits at the box office.

Have I mentioned my movie's sign? An immense white rectangle of tabula rasa, split down the middle by a length of black metal—CINEMA I, CINEMA II—and looking like a domino in a negative. The simple statement of the titles—*The Longest Yard, The Gambler*—in sharp black letters like the font of scare headlines, brooding and important as assassination or a declaration of war. The name of one actor up there, or none at all. This is my single whimsy: From time to time I call my manager. "What's playing?" I ask. He knows I mean, "What's coming soon?" "*Godfather Part II*," he'll tell me. "I'll get back to you," I'll say. I do my homework. "We'll go with Robert De Niro." "It's Al Pacino," he tells me. "They're doing a major piece in *Time*. Al Pacino is hot." "Robert De Niro." "We'll catch shit from the distributor. It's in the contract. We've *got* to put Pacino up there. It would only confuse people." "They know by now. They know how I operate. They'll love it." It's the truth. My sign has read "*That's Entertainment*, Ann Miller"; "*Airport*, Helen Hayes." And people *do* enjoy it. If they even notice. They think they're in on some inside joke. And the film buffs—the Draper Lake Mall is close to Norman, where the University of Oklahoma campus is located—somehow have the idea that seeing a big commercial blockbuster—the only pictures I ever show—at Cinema I, Cinema II somehow endorses the film, makes it *Cahiers du Cinéma* material, themselves—what's the word?—cineasts. But the truth is, I do not intend it as a joke, or even as a means of drawing people to my theater. (Though it may have that effect, I think. In the early fifties certain independent exhibitors took the chains to court on the grounds that their exclusive right to show particular films was in restraint of trade. People can go almost anywhere to see my movies. I saw in the paper that *The Longest Yard* and *The Gambler* are playing in at least five different first-run houses in the greater Oklahoma City metropolitan area.) It is an act of willfulness on my part, a blow against my franchise being. To see if I can take such blows. That go against the homogeneous grain of my undifferentiated heart. I cannot. But this is how I worry my loose tooth, push against my character, isometrize habit and inclination and the interchangeable parts of my American taste. I am really more comfortable that the sign reads "*The Longest Yard*, Burt Reynolds; *The Gambler*, James Caan." I am glad that the girls behind my candy cases look like ex-babysitters, my ushers like high-school seniors who lack force, who will go on to junior colleges or take their courses at the extension centers of the state university. I am glad I show blockbusters, all the "PG's" and "R's" of our collectivized soul and Esperanto'd judgment.

I enjoy my customers. (My Travel Inn isn't open yet, but I look forward. It will be the capstone of my career, I expect.) I enjoy watching them, being among them. Better than the Fred Astaire folks, the DQ and McDonald's trade, One Hour Martinizing, the Jacuzzi Whirlpool bunch—arthritics—my Radio Shack and Chicken from the Colonel clientele. I prefer them to the patrons of any of the franchises I've owned. It's the grandest part of my Grand Tour. This is the public I love. Oh, not the weekly matinee crowd so much, the Golden-Agers and widows and kids cutting school. The night-shift bunch and all those of the off-center life who come to my movies to nurse their wounds, or to sit quietly in my dark. (I have heard them weeping at my comedies.) But this is a Friday night, the seven o'clock show. In the lobby I mingle with the cream of my American public. Who have driven the Interstates to come here, the wide four-lane bypasses, the big new highways, median'd, cloverleafed, the great numbered exit signs every two and a half miles, every mile and half and quarter mile, the off-ramps that segue to on-ramps, such and such North, so and so South, over the great concretized, bulldozed no-man's-lands of the new America. Shuttling at fifty-five miles an hour, sixty, better, past, through, the almost invisible suburbs, under the overpasses with the fine, clean names—Birch Road, and River, Town and Country Lane, Five Mile Road, Country Club Causeway (Port Wonderful, Heaven on Earth Way, Earthly Paradise Park, Good Life Gardens: this is not satire, only the realism of our visionary democracy)—going by so fast that the cyclone fences are a blur, the back yards and barbecues, the aboveground and in-ground pools seen as through a scrim, the cheesecloth vision flattering as mirrors in the suburban Saks Fifth and branch Neimans that perch the landscape, the low high schools like architects' sketches. The prize-winning glass churches. Driving to the movies in their splendid, multi-thousand-dollar machines, and snappy, perky compacts—these would be the younger people—like bright sculptures or cars like tennis shoes. Where have all the headlights gone? What, has night been done away with? Where are the windshield wipers? What, it ain't gonna rain no more, no more? See the aerials of the car radios laminated in the windshield glass, the ruled rear-window defrosters like blank sheet music, unfilled-in scales.

Two and a half dollars they pay, three, handing over their tens and their twenties with more nonchalance than people inserting tokens into subway turnstiles. A beautiful people, a confident, lovely paired public, casually well groomed and boisterously gracious, the clothes of the men bright as tattoos, of the women color-coordinated as the appointments in bathrooms. Later they will go to the International House of Pancakes and work their way down the sweet stacks and through the exotic combinations, experimental, choosy as chemists among the alembics of syrups. Polishing it all off, cleaning their plates. What could be better, more innocent? Their hunger piqued, whetted, honed, keened by the emotions in the film they've just seen, hunger an emotion itself now, at nine-thirty, at midnight. The cathartic omelet, the denouement of waffles and sausage and coffee.

"Do you want to go over the stats, Ben?" Cliff Lockwire, my manager, asks. "It's remarkable. The economy's supposed to be in a slump, but it hasn't affected attendance much. Not that I can see. The other exhibitors tell the same story."

"The play's the thing."

"Yeah. Hah. Want to see the stats?"

"Later."

"I wanted to ask you about an idea for kiddies' matinees on Saturday mornings and school holidays. I hate a dark theater."

"Later, Lockwire. It's show time. I'm going to look around."

"You want to see a picture? I've got some calls to make. You want to see a picture? *The Longest Yard*. Terrific. *The Gambler*, good but too sophisticated, you know? I was a little disappointed. I thought it would do better than it has. I bought it for two weeks with a third-week option, but I don't think I'll pick it up. But if you want to see a picture—"

"I just want to look around."

"The place is clean as a whistle, Ben. This crew is terrific. Your shoes don't stick to the floor. We Scotchgard the seats once a month. They're as good as the day we opened. Farts bounce off them. The image is bright, the sound is excellent."

"Who am I, the Inspector General? I'm a mingler, I mingle. Make your calls. I just wanted to look at the auditorium. I'm absolutely all business. I want to get a sense. I think in the dark."

"In the dark?"

"You didn't know that? Oh yes. Go, go to your office. I'll think in the dark and get a sense and be back to you in half an hour."

Who thinks in the dark? The blind? I enter my movie's auditorium.

The houselights are still up. I take a seat, change it, change a third time. The crowd is a good one, but no sellout. Here and there the seats are empty, the auditorium like an incomplete crossword, the vacant seats like dark squares on a puzzle, five down and three across like a roomful of *L*'s of the absent. There is music, sourceless, anonymous, background, standards flattened to international Palm Court arrangements, the ticky ticky of the snares and cymbals vaguely Latin, all percussion's cushioned bumpy paradiddle, the roof-garden strings urban alfresco, the hotel horns of high-society bands, debs coming out, thousands to charity. I like it. It is the music in elevators and department stores and doctors' waiting rooms. It is the music of all shopping-centered air-conditioned space, an anthem of the universal. In Norway it's in people's ears like wax. Hip hip hurrah for the brotherhood of man. They're playing our song, Finsberg's brassy showstoppers tamed, declined to lame fox-trot, the threatless noise of motivational research like the soothing pasteurized pastels of walls in women's prisons. (My movie's walls are colorless. I mean, I do not know their color. They are neutral, I'd guess, as primed canvas behind a landscape. Right now concealed spots blue the auditorium like east twilight, golden the curtains like a glass of beer.) All about me I hear a snug delicious chatter like peppertalk around an infield. I cannot quite catch what's being said, but I know that it is optimistic, spoofing, vaguely—they've come in pairs, in pairs of pairs, the engaged, the double dating, the married—flirtatious, mock aggressive. It's the sound of prosperous good humor. (The prime interest rate is through the roof and counting, rising like tropical fever into the treacherous red end of the dial face, but here, in my movie, the talk is manic, the will chipper, bright as the checks and plaids of their styles. Why is it I think the men are dressed in Bermuda shorts? They aren't, yet they have about them this Miami and island aura, a heraldry of the golf course and day trip, this cruise nimbus.)

"What do you like, chocolate-covered cherries? I'll bring chocolate-covered cherries. I'll bring caramels and lollipops. I'll bring licorice and jujubes. I'm the tooth-decay fairy and what I say goes."

"I won't eat it."

"Take it home to the kids in a doggy bag, Ginny. A souvenir from Uncle Pete like saltwater taffy from the boardwalk. Anybody else? Last orders. Time, gentlemen. Anybody else? All right, that's it then." People up and down the row are laughing.

"He's very nice," I tell Ginny.

"Pete's sweet," she says.

"Pete's a sweet tooth," her husband says.

"No," I say, "he's a good man in a good mood."

Pete's wife and his two friends look at me. I am an intruder, but an older man, well-dressed, clean. Alone on the aisle, perhaps someone recently widowed. They let me in under their mood as if it were an umbrella.

"The best," Ginny's husband says.

"What business are you folks in?" (Where do I get my nerve? From my remission.) It is a strange question, but what can *I* do to them, a clean, older, well-dressed, wifeless man? They will answer, but before they can I reach into the pocket of my suitcoat and take out four passes. (My fingers can do this. Blind they can find the flap of the pocket, lift it, go in with all five fingers extended, no pinky unconsciously snagged on the lip of the pocket, discriminate between my car keys and the paper passes, count out four from the dozen I have taken from Lockwire, and bring them out.) "Here," I say, "I happen to have the franchise for this theater. I'd like you to take these passes and use them at your convenience."

"Say," Pete's wife says, "are they really passes?"

"Sure," I say. I give them to her. "Pass them on. Pass on the passes."

She looks at them. "They're real."

"What did you think, counterfeit? You'll see they're not good on Friday or Saturday nights, but otherwise there are no restrictions."

"Well thanks."

"I'm a good man in a good mood."

"Well thanks."

"What business? What line of work?"

"I'm a supervisor with Southwestern Bell," Pete's friend says. "Name's Eckerd." He looks down at the passes. "Mr. Lockwire?"

"Oh no. No no. Mr. Lockwire's my manager. I'm Benjamin Flesh. I'm not normally in the Oklahoma City area. I'm here on business about the theater. I'm here on show business."

"Oh," Eckerd says. "I didn't think you sounded like an Okie. Got an Eastern accent, sort of."

"We're all Americans."

"Well, that's so," Eckerd says. "This is my wife Ginny, and that's Angie Solberto. Pete, Angie's husband, has Solberto's Pharmacy in the Draper Lake Mall."

"That so? Solberto's? I parked nearby. That's very nice." We shake hands. (Hands!) "Yes," I say, "all Americans. There are over fifty thousand people throughout our land who will see this picture tonight. Who are going to watch Burt Reynolds as he whips his team of convicts into shape. In New York, a different time zone, they're already seeing it. The game's already started. In California they're still picking up their babysitters, but fifty thousand of us and tomorrow another fifty thousand. And over the course of the week say another seventy-five thousand, and in a month maybe close to a million people. That's what holds us together, you know." Pete had come back and we were formally introduced. He'd heard of me. Owning Solberto's, he knew Lockwire and he'd heard of me.

The music stopped in the middle of a phrase and an image came on the screen while the lights were still up. I rose. "Enjoy the picture, folks. It was nice talking to you. Mr. and Mrs. Eckerd, Mr. and Mrs. Solberto."

"Aren't you going to—"

"Oh dear me, no, I've seen it. Wonderful meeting you. You seem very nice. Like you know what you're doing."

"Hey, shh," someone said behind me.

"Yes, sorry. Yes of course. Quite right. Enjoy the picture. I'm sorry, sir. It's just the trailers, only the coming attractions. A lot of late-model cars being destroyed. I saw that one, too. Well, again—it's been a genuine pleasure. We're all Americans. We all love Burt. He reaches something in each of us, and though he's the star, we needn't take a backseat. Not for a minute. How competent people are! How their authority bespeaks some grounding in natural law itself, God's glorious injunction to be. My godfather was wrong, I think. Life not only is not flashy, a kick in the head of the rules of probability, it's normal, fixed as thermostat."

"Hey, buddy—"

"Come on, mister, up or down, in or out. We paid good money."

"Efficiency and integrity around like the gases and elements. How we do our homework, every mother's son of us. Enjoy the picture."

"Come on, will you?"

"Yes, yes, I'm going." I backed up the aisle. On the screen—*Freebie and the Bean*—cars were screeching around corners and slamming through plate-glass windows, flipping over guard rails, and landing on cars below like bombs dropped from planes. "We're all Americans. Look, look. Do you spot the motifs? This couldn't have happened before the Yom Kippur war and the energy crisis. We've become disenchanted with our automobiles. This too will pass."

"Fella, if you don't shut up—" a man said. Lockwire was beside me and I beside myself.

"Enjoy the picture. You know? I think Burt Reynolds once lived in Oklahoma. I think I read that somewhere."

"Hey, Ben," Lockwire said, "what is it? Come on."

"Lockwire," I whispered, "did someone report me to the manager?"

I retreated with him up the aisles, my face to the screen and quiet now, as he gently held me. "Take it easy, Ben," he said. "Take it easy."

"Yes. I will," I said softly. We were standing at the back near the doors. "Wait. Just a minute. Wait. I just want to see this part."

On the screen it said, "Cinema I Feature Presentation," and then there was the big animated image of a sort of gear, like the sprocket flywheel of a wristwatch, or like a kid's mandalic picture of sunshine. It turned around and around, ticking to weird electronic whistles and beats. "Yes. This is the part." It was supposed to represent a projector spinning off film like line from a fishing reel. It was the logotype of Cinema I, Cinema II, and all over America in the eastern time zone and the central, mountain, and Pacific ones, people were watching it, as if Greenwich Mean Time itself were unwinding, unwinding. But it was the gears, the gears with their deep notches and treacherous terrible teeth that held me, that translated the zippered nerves which were just then coming unstuck again, the remission remissed, in my hands and fingertips, in the stripped caps of my knees and the scraped tines of my ears, loose as rust, as nuts and bolts in the blood.

It was to be his last remission, and he was to remember it like a love affair, like some guarded, precious intimacy, parsing it like a daydream, an idyll, the day he broke the bank at Monte Carlo. (And would dream about it, too, the dreams realistic but with a certain cast of sepia-tone nostalgia, like dreams of dead parents, bittersweet with love and recrimination.)

Lockwire had thought he'd gone crazy of course, and in a way he had, though not crazy so much as heroically excited—M.S. is a stress disease—his febrile talk like the aura of migraine, the incoherics of inspiration. But in a minute he was all business: More than ever. His plans and off-the-cuff schemes a desperate attempt to make a connection to his health, fear's black coffee.

This is what he said:

"I want smoking permitted back of the first ten rows. There's to be no public announcement. You'll continue to run the 'Fire Regulations Prohibit Smoking in Any Part of This Theater' footage, but don't do anything about enforcement. In the beginning you can have one or two of the ushers light up. This will serve as a signal. When the inspector registers a complaint, offer him a self-perpetuating free pass. If he doesn't go for it, call the Fire Commissioner. Discuss it with him. Mention one thousand dollars. If he gives you static, go back three spaces, play it their way.

"Candy: I want vending machines put in. No gum, of course. Gum fucks up a theater. Just good, relatively inexpensive stuff. Name brands. You can keep the soft-drink and popcorn apparatus where it is, but replace the candy with paperback versions of the books the movies are based on. With records of the score if it's a good one. *The Sting*, for example, *Love Story*. As a matter of fact, stock up on all the good movie music. Get an inventory together. And movie mags: *Silver Screen*, *Photoplay*. Posters are very big. Get in some Robert Redfords, Marlon Brandos, W. C. Fieldses, that sort of thing. Why should the headshops get all the play? Let's get off our asses, Lockwire. I want to make Cinema I, Cinema II a goddamned Grauman's Chinese, a regular little Merchandise Mart of the spin-off. Use those shops in museums where they sell post-cards, art books, and twenty-five-buck reproductions of famous statuary as your model, those goofy imported handmade toys. We'll make the candy girl—that redhead—our curator. Take her uniform away. Get her a smock and a patch that goes on the shoulder that says 'Volunteer,' or 'Friends of Cinema I, Cinema II.' Something like that."

"But . . ."

"I'm way ahead of you. You're thinking about the movies, what happens if we try to turn the place into an art house. We don't. We run the same stuff. Blockbusters. Every movie a picture. You even *hear* Al Pacino, Hoffman, Gene Hackman, Paul Newman, Red-ford, you grab. They make a James Bond sequel you raise your finger, jerk your earlobe. And after the Academy Awards don't fart around with reruns, ads in the paper 'Nominated for Seven Academy Awards.' Forget that crowd. Go on to the next blockbuster. Roll it! You got TV?"

"TV?"

"TV. Television. You got TV?"

"Well, certainly. Of course. Who doesn't have T—"

"In your office?"

"In my office? No. Not in my office."

"Get a little Sony. Watch Merv. Watch Johnny. Watch Mike. Get up early in the morning. Watch Barbara, watch Gene. They told us about *The Exorcist*. They told us about *Last Tango*. They told us about *Harry and Tonto*. What, you think it's only the energy czars go on those programs? Stop, look, and listen, Lockwire. If you hear about it twice, it's a blockbuster. Three times and it's S.R.O. They have a lot to tell us."

"To tell us."

"To tell *them*. Us. Them. They have the franchise on the public taste. I don't know how they do it. Magicians. But they *know*. They know and know. An exhibitor can learn more from those five guys than from forty junkets to the screening rooms of Los Angeles and New York. I'll give you a tip. Don't ever for one minute trust your own taste. Don't trust mine. Where do you think I'd be today if I trusted my taste? Trust theirs—Barb's and Johnny's, Gene's and Mike's. Trust Merv's. Those fellows are geniuses!"

"We've been doing pretty well. I'll show you the figures."

"You don't have to. The figures are beautiful. I could *qvell* from the figures. You'd show me figures I'd go 'hubba hubba,' I'd follow them blocks and buy them a beer. We're talking business—turnover, overhead, buy cheap, sell high.

"I want free passes in every thousandth popcorn box. If they say the secret word at the box office, give them double their money back. Invent, inaugurate, introduce, make up. Let there be 'Special Daylight Savings Time Matinee'; package deals—they pay two-fifty for the show at Cinema I, you take off seventy-five cents for a ticket to Cinema II. *Cards*. Print up reaction cards. They fill in the blanks, you give them a fifty-cent rebate. Four stars, three, two, one, a half. Let them feel like critics. You do different categories: lighting, best performance by an animal, an Indian, a bad guy, an orphan over nine. Stuff about costumes, crap about sex.

"Look, Lockwire, hound them, please. Stick a line in our advertising that we run only those films that have no radiation hazards."

"But no films—"

"Then where's the lie? What's the harm? Break their bad TV habits. Hound them, please. Did you know that more people collapse while jogging than while watching a flick, that there are fewer deaths per hundred thousand in motion-picture houses than in airplanes, football stadia, bathtubs, beds, restaurants, or living rooms?"

"Are there?"

"Who knows, but that's where to hit them, in their life span. That's where they live. Where we all live. If you would know me, learn my blood pressure, count my cholesterol, and taste my lipids. If you would look into my heart, read my cardiogram. Check my protein level every five thousand miles. A man's character is his health, Lockwire, and I feel crummy, Egypt, crummy."

He had been pacing up and down in Lockwire's small office, excited, thinking to slow the force of his new symptoms by ignoring them, by concentrating on business, making the staggered kidney-shaped journey about Lockwire's desk, passing by the small, discreet safe, by the telephone-answering device that gave out recorded information about what films were currently being shown, their stars and ratings and show times. He looked at the telephone, glanced at Lockwire.

"Put it on."

"Pardon?"

"Put it on. Let me hear."

"It's just a recorded announcement. It saves time, the girls don't have time to—"

"Put it on."

Lockwire fiddled with some buttons, played the tape. His voice said, "Thank you for calling Cinema I, Cinema II. Our feature presentation this week at Cinema I is *The Longest Yard* starring Burt Reynolds and Eddie Albert. *The Longest Yard* is rated R. No one under seventeen will be admitted unless accompanied by an adult. Performances of *The Longest Yard* will be at 1:00, 3:00, 5:10, 7:30, and 9:45. The feature at Cinema II is *The Gambler*, starring James Caan. Rated R, no one under seventeen may be admitted to *The Gambler* unless accompanied by an adult. Times are 1:15, 3:30, 5:50, 8:00, and 10:00. Cinema I, Cinema II is located in the Draper Lake Shopping Mall. Take Exit 11 off Interstate 35 or Exit 22 if you're coming from U.S. 40. For additional information, please phone 736–2350. Thank you."

"Again," Ben said. "Again, please." He listened to Lockwire's recording a second time. "That's what I mean," he said. "Lacks zip. Where's the pep?"

"Zip? Pep? It's an information service, it's supposed to be clear.

People want to know what's playing, when it goes on. They have to know if they can bring their kids."

Flesh nodded. "You think if we sent him a cassette we could get Burt Reynolds to read the copy? 'Hi, this is Dinah's great good friend, Burt Reynolds. Thanks for calling Cinema I, Cinema II. The feature this week, etc., etc.' Then he finishes with 'Ladies and gentlemen— James *Caan!*' 'Thanks, Burt. Burt Reynolds, ladies and gentlemen, a terrific guy and a dynamite H-bomb flick. At Cinema II today, I'm doing *The Gambler*, which I really think you'd enjoy. I read seventy-eight scripts, some of which I thought might actually work for me, but when they showed me *The Gambler* I knew this was it. I mean like, wow, this is the sort of part an actor could wait ten years to do. And while I guess I shouldn't be blowing my own horn, I think I'm as proud of myself and my co-workers as it's possible to be. You can catch *The Gambler* at 1:15, 3:30, 5:50, 8:00, and 10:00. Take Exit 11 off good old Interstate 35 or Exit 22 if you're coming from good old U.S. 40. Fight cancer with a checkup and a check.' "

Lockwire stared at him.

"Yeah," Ben said, "what do you bet they'll do it? You know how to reach these people. Find out and get back to me. It wouldn't hurt to throw in a couple of Rona Barrett items either. Get back to me. I want to see lines. I want to see Oklahoma City policemen doing traffic control like it was the High Holidays and people are coming out of *shul.*"

Lockwire shook his head in wonder.

"Yeah," Ben Flesh said, "that's right. Get back to me." And *still* the Jacuzzi Whirlpool was in the franchiser's skin, Magic Fingers in his businessman's tissue, all his body pinned and needled. Oh oh oh, his milled being, all his flesh grooved as the stem that winds your watch.

Back at the motel there was a message for him. He called the desk.

"Yes, Mr. Flesh, just a minute, please. I took it down myself. I put it—yes, here it is. 'Please tell Mr. Ben Flesh that if it's at all possible he should catch a flight out of Oklahoma City and come to New York. He is needed in Riverdale.' "

# IV

I t would have been wrong to call. The message was clear enough. He was needed in Riverdale, they said. To call, even to ask what was wrong, could be read as extenuation, a sort of plea bargaining. It had been their arrangement—his, the twins' and triplets'—to serve, forever to come through, simply to be there when the chips were down, the mutual designated hitters of each other's lives, the gut priorities of love. Yet did he love them? Had they loved him? How well? Was it not rather into a life-long category of mascot that they had enlisted him? (This thought out while still on the flight to LaGuardia, so, as far as he could determine, no damage done, those instincts still alive in him, for all the haywiring of his nerves, to set aside the at hand, the this, then this, then that sequences of his life, by which he meant, of course, his plans.) Yet emergency had its advantages, too. It took, like so many weeks in the sun, years off. There was, it was impossible to mistake it, a kind of bittersweet glamour in the big-time, big-stuff catastrophes of interruptions and drastically changed plans. He thought of scenes in pubs in certain films of the forties—Finsberg's years—of men and women in nightclubs, in rich men's mansions, their lawns and ballrooms done up in prom prospect, their dreamy society dance bands driving out the world, covering it with moony fox-trot and the claims of love. Then someone makes an announcement, the host himself, perhaps, that honest, understanding squire of a man. "It's war, ladies and gentlemen." Or glances at a scrap of paper the butler has handed him, nods, thanks his servant, signals his orchestra leader—it is almost prearranged, this transoceanic seriousness

· 243 ·

that shouts from his eyes like an agreement—and the music stops, though comically the drummer, looking down, still continues to work his traps and top hat and snares and the fiddlers bow their instruments and the saxophones croon till, hearing the silences around them, they look up, surprised as people on whom jokes have been played, and a few last dregs of music, even after they have stopped, clatter like dropped marbles, an orchestra tuning up in reverse, and, in the silence, the man finally speaks, almost apologetically. "The Japanese have bombed Pearl Harbor." "The barbarians are at the gates." "The British are coming." "The Visigoths have entered Marseilles." And the dancing partners push off from each other as if it were a step in the dance. "I have to get back to my unit. I'm sorry." And a hundred young officers the same. And inside all this seriousness and farewell, within this altered mood while life zeroes in on the tragic, a joy, too. A joy and pride in deflection, in *being* deflected. Decamped. Debouched. No time really for the last embrace, kiss, which is, one feels, *suffered*, the young bloods reduced somehow to nephews again, their girlfriends avatar'd to well-meaning aunts. Yes. Years off. Years. So if he didn't call, if he went automatically to his Finsberg unit, maybe it was no feather in his cap after all. He was returning to Riverdale a younger man than he had left, and perhaps it was not so much that he loved the Finsbergs as that he hated his life.

Well, he did. He thought he did. What had happened to him. (His unbecoming, he meant, pulled back through geologic time to neanderthal condition. Perhaps his jaws would clamp and he would be unable to walk upright or use tools. Cold, cold, the descent of Ben, his pre-Leakey, pithecanthropic fate.) And yes, was pleased, was certain that whatever was waiting for him in Riverdale—he hadn't called; "if it's at all possible," the message said; he hadn't called, was that why? was "if it's at all possible" the loophole of extenuation that could have kept him in Oklahoma City had he called and discovered what? that no one was worse off than himself?—it would be better than what he left behind. For all he had left behind—the lion's share of his clothing, of course, his valises, the motel room he continued to pay for even though he would not be occupying it, his precious car, the latest of the late-model Cadillacs—was his itinerary. Which was what he had in lieu of a life. His ridiculous itinerary like an old treasure map, his itinerary, no master plan or blueprint but only his itinerary like a mnemonic string round his finger. Only that. His itinerary. He could have wept.

When the plane landed in St. Louis for a fifteen-minute stopover, he briefly considered deplaning, calling New York, for if it wasn't necessary that he come, then his coming was all the more an admission of his, Flesh's, need to come. If he was ready to admit that, then he was ready to admit it all. That his life hadn't worked. How awful. How terrible.

He had flown first class, and while they were still on the ground he asked the stewardess for a drink. It was against federal regulations, she said. He could not be served till they were in the sky. "Sorry."

"I understand. It's all right. I will be served in the sky," he said.

And was drunk—martinis—when he landed at LaGuardia. (Only two cocktails were permitted a passenger—more federal regulations—but he worked out a deal with a man across the aisle who didn't drink.) And whiled away the two hours not with the headset or the magazines but by looking out the window, studying an America he was too far above to see. Studying the American heavens over Oklahoma, over Missouri, over Illinois, over Indiana, over Ohio, over Pennsylvania, seeing (or not seeing) from one angle what he knew so well from another, and feeling—wasn't it odd?—its ultimate homogeneity, a homogeneity squared, the final monolithism of his country, the last and loftiest franchise, the air, the sky, all distinctions, whichever remained intact, whichever he had been unable to demolish in his capacity as franchiser, as absent, as blasted away as the tactile capacities of his poor motherfuck fingers and his lousy son of a bitch hands.

"Cole?" Ben said.

"It's Lorenz, Ben," Lorenz said.

"Hi, Ben."

"Hello, Gus-Ira."

"I'm Moss," Moss said.

"What's happened?" One of the godcousins shrugged. "Jerome?" Ben said.

"Maxene," Maxene said.

"I don't get it," Ben said. "What's happened?"

"Folks change, Ben."

"Is that you, Noël?"

"Yes," Noël said.

"Jesus," Ben said. It wasn't anything he could actually put his finger on—but what was, eh?—but in the two or three years since he had last seen them all together they had changed. Though they were unmistakably brothers and sisters, even unmistakably twins and triplets, and even just possibly still unmistakably identical twins and triplets rather than simply fraternal, something had altered, the coarsening of a feature here, the flattening of another there; and now that they no longer looked absolutely alike he had, for the first time since he had known them, difficulty telling them apart. When he had mistaken Lorenz for Cole, Moss for Gus-Ira, and Maxene for Jerome, a few of the sibs had begun to make those nervous overtures of the nostrils and edges of the mouth prefatory to crying. (Christ, he thought, their identicals are in remission.)

"Hey," Ben said, "hey."

"It's just that I'm pregnant," Gertrude said. "That's all. If it weren't for the fact that I'm pregnant, I'd still look the same. When Ethel was pregnant with Anthony-Leslie she changed, too. Then afterward she, she—" Gertrude's jaw trembled.

"Hey," Ben said.

"I was never the same afterward," Ethel said.

"It's got nothing to do with pregnancy, Gertrude. It's got nothing to do with pregnancy, Ethel. I never got knocked up, but it's the same story. With me it was teeth. I had a couple of bad teeth that had to be pulled. The dentist made a bridge. I couldn't get used to wearing it. My mouth— I don't know— My mouth changed. It settled. Like a house."

"Your mouth looks fine," Ben said. He wasn't certain whom he was addressing.

"Yeah? Does it? Yeah? I go into a men's room and they think I'm the cocksucker."

It had to be Oscar. He had seen Irving in St. Louis and "the cocksucker" was what they called the mincing, epicene Sigmund-Rudolf, whose disease it was to act like a fairy but be none. It had to be Oscar. It was like being a participant in a brain teaser, set down live in some puzzle condition. Three men of equal intelligence stand in a straight line one behind the other. They may not look around. A fourth man comes by. He has five hats, three white and two black. He puts a hat on each man and says he will give a hundred dollars to the man who can first say what color hat he's wearing. The first man in the line tells him the color of the hat on his head and wins the hundred dollars. What color is his hat and what is his reasoning? Cole, Lorenz, Gus-Ira, Moss, Jerome, and Noël had been accounted for. The person had said "men's room." Ben had seen Irving just weeks ago in St. Louis. Sigmund-Rudolf was called "the cocksucker." It had to be Oscar. So now he lived on the high pure level of the logical. Ben Flesh like the featureless and perfect character in a conundrum. It had to be Oscar.

"It's true," Kitty said. "Something happens."

"Kitty?"

"Uh huh."

"Hello, Kitty."

"It's true. Hello. Something happens. You prime it out. In your thirties. You go off like milk."

"Well, I think you all look just fine," Ben said. It was so. They would be what now? The youngest thirty-four, the oldest forty. Why, he was only forty-eight himself—though he thought of himself as older—and they had somehow become his contemporaries. Yet it was so that they looked fine, their paunches and heft only signals of the good uses to which life had put them. Evidence. The smoking guns of their existence. And if this made them less magical, it made them, for him, only a little less magical. (Then he *did* love them.) To them apparently a miss was as good as a mile, however.

"Well," Gus-Ira said, "at least we all feel lousy. We've discussed it. Identical lousy."

"Nonsense," Ben said, wanting them, he discovered, as much like the old them as they wanted it themselves. "You've still your Finsberg esprit de corps."

"We've gone back to jungle," Mary said. "Nature has reclaimed us and green crap pushes up through the cracks in our sidewalk."

"I came eighteen hundred miles," Ben said. He was asking for an explanation.

"Another thing," Jerome said.

"The clothes," Helen said.

"We don't even have" Jerome said

"our figures," Maxene said.

"I don't think Ben wants to—" Lorenz said.

"A size here, a size there," LaVerne said.

"It makes a difference"

"in the styles."

"That's when we first noticed," Kitty said.

"Because," Helen said, "oh, not that we always dressed alike, but *when* we did—"

"When we were kids and still all living together," Mary said.

"Yes, then," Helen said, "but afterward, too. On special occasions."

"Yes. Well," Noël said.

"Because there is something in color," Patty said, "because there is something in color related to size, implicit in pattern demanding its shape. How would a curly tail look on a rabbit, do you suppose? Or the stripes of a tiger on the fur of an ape?"

"Hey," Ben said.

"We grew—" LaVerne giggled, *"apart."*

"Stop it," Oscar said.

"Right," said Moss.

"You don't fool us, sisters," Gus-Ira said.

"Bastards," Cole said.

"Yes, well, what do you expect?" LaVerne asked.

"Lotte broke the fucking *set*," Noël said angrily. "That's what you're thinking."

"Ah," Ben said.

"So cut out the sizes crap," Sigmund-Rudolf said. "Cool it about the Dress Code."

"They want one of us to die," Noël said. "They think that would change things, even the score in the Magic Kingdom."

"Don't be silly," Gertrude said. "That's not what we mean. It isn't."

"It isn't," the girls said.

"We grew *apart*," LaVerne said again.

"Only Ben. Only you're the same, Ben," Ethel said.

"I'm not," he said. "I'm not the same."

"You are," Oscar said.

"I'm sick," Ben said.

"Sitting down," Noël said, "it's an invisible disease."

Ben looked at Noël sharply. "You *are* silly," he said. "Gertrude's right, it isn't what they mean." He was speaking to all of them.

"Nobody wants anybody dead," Mary said. "That's ridiculous."

"How do you live, Ben?" Gus-Ira asked. He supposed it was Gus-Ira. He was straining to keep them separate.

"You know how I live."

"No. How do you live? Where do you go?"

"You know how I live. You know where I go."

"We've grown apart," LaVerne said.

"This one's in Texas, that one's in Maine," Cole said. "And once a year, twice, you check in, drop a card, touch base. We get a call, meet for dinner, have a few."

"It was better," Sigmund-Rudolf said, "when you were still getting it from the sisters."

"I never minded that," Oscar said. "That wasn't important."

"No," Helen said.

"I came eighteen hundred miles," Ben said.

"How *do* you live? Where *do* you go?"

"I live along my itinerary," Ben said.

"Joey," Kitty sang softly, "Joey, Joey."

"Yes," Ben Flesh said, "sure. My life like a Triptik from the AAA. Here today and gone tomorrow. What is all this? Why are you behaving so? You know about me. I love you, for God's sake. What is all this?"

"The showdown. Only the showdown."

"The little stuff, Ben. Tell us the little stuff."

"Outdoorsman," Jerome said, "give us the inside dope."

"Only what your life is like. Do you take a paper? What do you do about laundry? Is there Sarasota in you? Some winter quarters of your heart, hey?"

"I take *all* the papers," Ben said quietly. "I buy magazines from the newsstand. I watch the local eyewitness news at ten. Everywhere they have blue flu I know about it. Where garbage isn't collected. There's something for you, if you want to know. There's no garbage in my life. Except what collects in the car. The torn road map and the Fudgicle wrapper, the silver from chewing gum. But by and large I'm garbageless. I miss it, you know? The maid comes in and makes up the room. The Cokes come from machines in the hall and the dirty dishes go back to Room Service. Mail's a problem. I use the phone. I don't vote. Not even an absentee ballot. I could never meet anybody's residency requirements. The franchiser disenfranchised. I file my taxes, of course. I use my accountant's business address as my domicile. This? Is this what you mean? What you want? I have neurologists in twenty states, internists in a dozen, dentists in four. (One of my suitcases is just medical records.) There's same-day service, so laundry's no problem. Dry cleaning isn't. But my bowels don't know what time it is and buying clothes can be tough if there have to be alterations. Where do they deliver, what happens if the fit's no good? Nah, there ain't no winter quarters. Am I getting warm?"

"Riverdale," one of them said.

"What?"

"Riverdale. You could have used Riverdale. As your domicile."

"As easily Riverdale as your accountant's business address."

"I was never asked. Nobody asked me."

"Oh, Ben," Patty said.

"Well, it's not the point really," Lorenz said.

"What's the point, Lorenz?" Ben asked.

"Did we have to *ask* you? Is *that* where you were standing? On ceremonies like a station of your itinerary?" Mary said.

The girls fussed over him. One took his hand. Another hugged him, a third kissed his cheek. But Ben was more interested in what the brothers were doing. There seemed just then to be a conspiracy of tolerance among them, the soft ticking glances of a deferred cruelty. These looks darted from each to each like a basketball passed around a circle. Maybe it was what one of them had said it was, the showdown. It seemed a theatrical term, but it was a theatrical family. He nodded to the girls, acknowledged their concern for his feelings, but moved carefully away from them and toward the brothers.

Ben and the family were in the big living room. There were theatrical posters behind framed, glare-proof glass, the musical comedies and dramas that Julius had dressed. "I did come eighteen hundred miles," Ben said. Then it occurred to him how far they must have come. As LaVerne had said, they'd grown apart, as Cole, this one's in Texas, that one's in Maine. The Finsbergs had long ago taken their show on the road. There were second companies, third, eighth, and eleventh all over the country by now. Only two of the women and three of the men still lived in New York. Helen had moved to London last year. They must have traveled a greater distance than the circumference of the earth to get here. Thousands had been spent on air fares. "What's the occasion?" he asked.

"The occasion?"

"Why are we here?"

"Didn't you know?" Ethel said.

"It's the unveiling."

"The unveiling."

"Of Estelle's stone."

"And Lotte's."

"But they died years ago, at least Lotte— Isn't the unveiling usually on the first anniversary of the—"

"Yes," Helen said. "But there was that business of the suicide."

"The girls were very angry," Gus-Ira said.

"Angry?"

"The boys, too," Mary said. "You were furious, Sigmund-Rudolf."

"Angry? Furious?"

"Water under the bridge," Sigmund-Rudolf said.

"Angry? Furious?"

"He doesn't understand," Patty said.

"Of course not. How could he?"

"No."

"No," Ben said. "I don't think I do."

"We were *identical*, Ben," Noël said.

"Identical," said Maxene. "Human MIRV's blooming from a single shaft."

"As like as grapes on a cluster."

"Identical."

"Who gave the lie to snowflakes."

"To fingerprints."

"To keys on pianos."

"If one of us boys had died, only another of us could have made the identification."

"We would ask, 'Are you here, Gus-Ira?' 'Are *you* here, Cole?' "

"Calling the roll."

"Subtracting from nine."

"That's how we'd work it."

"I could have identified you," Ben said.

"Identical."

"Homogenized as milk."

"Of course we were angry."

"Certainly we were furious."

"Because"

"when Lotte took"

"her life"

"it was like saying"

"we"

"all would."

"We shoved her in the plot."

"And left her grave unmarked."

"We were so *mad*."

"Then when Mama died and we returned for the funeral"

"we saw that we'd changed,"

"grown apart."

"It was silly to stay angry. We were different now anyway. What Lotte did,"

"there was no guarantee"

"that we'd do"

"too."

"And besides"

"we hadn't,"

"had we?"

"So we counted Lotte's death"

"starting from then"

"and waited a year"

"and counted Mama's death starting from"

"the anniversary"

"of Lotte's."

"And waited a year."

"A double stone ceremony."

"Because that was only fitting."

"Because Mama herself always did everything"

"by twos or threes."

"I didn't know any of this," Ben said.

"Well, there you are," Oscar said.

"Sure," said Jerome.

"How could you?" one of the boys and one of the girls asked.

"I was your godcousin," Ben said. "I was closer to you than I am to my own sister."

"Good old Ben," one of the girls and one of the boys said. They looked at him.

Of course, he thought, if they had grown apart from each other, then how much further must they have grown apart from him? It was like his eighteen hundred miles compared to their trip around the world. So that's what it was, a question of family. That's why the girls had let him sleep with them, why it made no difference finally to the boys. He recalled Julius's last words to him. He *wasn't* one of them.

"So, Ben," Jerome said, "how's business?"

"What?"

"Business. How's business? What do you make of the economy?"

"The economy?"

"We'd like to hear your side of things, get your viewpoint."

"We would, Ben," Sigmund-Rudolf said. And, oddly, those who weren't already sitting hurried to take seats. Only Ben was standing.

"Give us the lowdown."

"The view from the field."

"We want to hear just what you think. Would you mind?"

"Well, I—"

"Just how bad do you think it really is?"

"How much worse—"

"Hush. Let Ben tell it."

"Go ahead, Ben."

"Yes, Ben. Go ahead. Tell us. How's business?"

And he told them.

What did he tell them? What could he tell them? That after all these years, after his years at Wharton and his time on the road, after all the deals he had done, the profits turned like revolving doors, and his negotiations with banks, writing and reading letters of intent, contracts, after paying due bills and collecting debts, after picking his people and selecting his locations, and learning his several dozen trades and making what had come to be, starting from scratch, from the G.I. Bill and the serendipitous fillip of his godfather's fortunate deathbed shove, his money, that—well, that he knew nothing of business, that he was no businessman but only another consumer, like them, he supposed, like anyone. A franchiser. A fellow who had chewed such and such a hamburger—McDonald's, Burger King, A & W, Big Boy—at such and such a lunchtime, who licked such and such an ice cream—Howard Johnson's, Baskin-Robbins, Carvel, Mister Softee—during such and such a heat spell or when this or that drive for something sweet had struck him, gratuitous as pain or melancholy, who sought out this or that gasoline station—Shell, Texaco, Sunoco, Gulf—when the gas gauge on one or another of his Cadillacs had been more or less on Empty (as his stomach had been more or less on Empty, as his sweet tooth), who lay down in such and so a motel—Best Western, Holiday Inn, Ramada, Travelodge—when his body had been empty of energy and his spirit of all will save the will to rest,

· 254 ·

squinting through the dusk and darkness at the sign shining above the Interstates. Who came to sell, almost always, what he had already first used, tried, bought himself—not excepting the Jacuzzi Whirlpool, not excepting the stereo tape deck in his automobile, not excepting the One Hour Martinizing that cleaned his lonely laundry, not excepting the Robo-Wash that bruised the dirt from his car—and all of it testimonial to nothing finally but his needs, to need itself. So they were asking the wrong fellow. He was no businessman. They were asking the wrong fellow. He was not in trade. Or if he was, then it was only because he did business as some people painted pictures—by the numbers. It was already there, all of it, all of them. "The greeting card," he said, "was invented for me. There's no franchise," he pointed out, "called Flesh's."

"Skip it, Godcousin," Cole said. "How's business? When's the economy going to turn around? What about the prime rate? What's with the energy crisis?"

"Oh," Ben Flesh said, "the economy, the prime rate, the energy crisis."

"Are you businessman enough to tell us something about that stuff at least?"

"That stuff, yes. But not because I'm businessman enough. The economy is spooked. There's a curse on free enterprise. The prime rate grows big as shoe sizes in large men's closets. Ten, ten and a half. Eleven."

"You don't see it coming down?"

"Like a belt buckled by someone troubled by his weight. On a diet. Off it. This hole one month"—he touched his belt—"this one"—he moved his finger toward the buckle—"the next. It makes no difference. I don't understand the prime rate. But it makes no difference. *I* don't think so."

"You were left the prime rate."

And that, he saw, was what frightened them. "Yes."

"That was your inheritance."

"Yes. I know. Yes. I don't understand about it. It's only a decision. Thinking makes it so. It doesn't mean much. Hard money, soft. I don't know. It's only an attitude. Don't you think so?" He was very tired. If they were going to the unveiling he wished they'd go. He too. That would be something to see. Lotte's stone. Estelle's. He had to ask them something.

"When I die," he said.

"What?"

Hadn't they heard him? He had probably spoken too softly. "I say," he said, "when I *die*— I know we haven't talked about this— To tell you the truth, I haven't even thought about it— When I die, could I be buried with the Finsbergs? In your plot? I have no place to go. I mean," he said, "it'd be a hell of a thing if I had to be stowed in my accountant's office. —You know? I'd like it, I'd like it stipulated that I could lie with you people."

"Gee, Ben," Lorenz said, "that's a hell of a thing to say. I mean, why do you want to talk like that? Die, lie with us? I mean, what kind of crap is that supposed to be? You'll dance on our graves."

"Like Fred Astaire," Ben said.

"Come on, what's this horseshit?" Oscar said.

"I have no place to *go*," Ben wailed. "I understood your questions about business. I know my name isn't Finsberg. I know you're troubled by the prime rates, what your dad did. His putting you under an obligation to me. You don't have to worry about that. —I'd buy the plot. —I'd pay whatever . . . You guys are in my will. My sister is. I'm closer to you. My parents are under the ground in Chicago. I've known you longer. I could make it a condition of my will. I wouldn't do that. Why do I say a thing like that? You'll get the money anyway. I swear to you. I just thought—"

"Don't be so damned morbid," Gus-Ira said irritably. "What's this talk about dying? What's this horseshit about burials?"

"I want you to promise," Ben said. "What about it?"

"Once you're dead what difference does it make?" Noël said. "I don't see what difference it makes. I mean, *I* don't care. They can burn me for all I care. Maybe I'll give my body to science. What are you worried about? Once you're—"

"*What about it?*" Ben demanded.

"Well, it's just that this isn't the time," Moss said quietly.

"For Christ's sake," Patty said, "the Finsberg plot's big as a fucking football field. Lie with me."

"Patty," LaVerne said.

"He lies with me," Patty said. "That's a good idea. I want that," Patty said. "Lie with me. Ben lies with me. You got that? *You got that, you sons of bitches?*" she screamed at her brothers. She took Ben's hand. He said something she couldn't make out. "What? What's that?"

"I said," he said, "I want to talk business. I'm no businessman, but I know all there is to know. I want you to know, too. I'm talking to *you*, Noël. I'm talking to Cole and Gus-Ira and Oscar and Sigmund-Rudolf and Moss and Lorenz. You, Jerome, I'm talking to *you*. Because I see what it is here. Lotte's dead— Estelle. I see what it is here. The men have the votes."

"The votes," Sigmund-Rudolf said, "oh, *please.*"

"The men have the *votes*," Ben said. "I'm answerable to the corporation. All right. You want to know about business? You want to be filled in, I'll fill you in. The economy. All right. The energy crisis . . . There isn't enough."

"Come on, Ben," Lorenz said.

"I'm talking energy," Ben said. "There isn't enough. There isn't enough in the world to run the world. There *never* was. How could there be? The world is a miracle, history's and the universe's long shot. It runs uphill. It's a miracle. Drive up and down in it as I do. Look close at it. See its moving parts, its cranes and car parks and theater districts. It can't be. It could never have happened. It's a miracle. I see it but I don't believe it. The housing projects, for God's sake, the trolley tracks and side streets, all the equipment on runways, all the crap on docks. Refineries, containers for oil, water tanks on their high tees like immense golf balls. The complicated ports with their forklift trucks and winches. All the hawsers, tackle, sheets, and guys. All the braided, complex cable. All the gantry, all the plinth. The jacks and struts all the. The planet's rigging like knots in shoes. The joists and girders, trivets, chocks. Oh, oh, the unleavened world. Groan and groan against the gravity in stuff. *How's business?* How's dead weight? Archimedes, thou shouldst be living at this hour! How do we handle the barbell earth? With levers and pulleys and derricks and hoists. With bucket brigades of Egyptian Jews tossing up pyramids stone by stone. How's *business?* They're not hiring in Stonehenge, they're laying them off in the Easter Isles. How's industry? Very heavy.

"Where shall we get the churches, how shall we have the money for the schools and the symphonies and stadia, for the sweet water and railroads, all the civilized up-front vigorish that attracts industry and pulls the big money?

"It ain't in me. I couldn't have made the world. I couldn't have imagined it. My God, I can barely live in it.

"Though it may be a franchiser, I think, who'll save us. Kiss off the neighborhood grocers and corner druggists and little shoemakers. A franchiser. Yes. Speaking some Esperanto of simple need, answering appetite with convenience foods. Some Howard Johnson yet to be.

"But I don't know. There isn't enough energy to drive my body. How can there be enough to run Akron?"

"Oh, Ben."

"But I may lie with you? You heard her, Cole; you're a witness, Lorenz. I may tuck in with Patty. I have her word."

"You have her word," one of them said.

"What's all this shit about dying?" Ben said. "For God's sake, cheer up, we're going to an unveiling."

They did not withdraw their pledge, their father's pledge, to guarantee the prime rate. Though he had to pledge not to test them—in truth, he had rarely done so, except at the beginning—and when he left Riverdale nothing had really changed. Though he knew he had been given warning, was on notice, posted ground, thin ice. The boys had the votes.

# 2

He resumed his tour, his businessman's Grand Rounds. From Oklahoma City he went to Amarillo, Texas, from Amarillo to Gallup, New Mexico, and then to Albuquerque. He did Salt Lake City and Elko, Nevada (where he made a two-hundred-mile dogleg to Boise to trade in his car for a '75), and pushed on, Cadillac West, to Sacramento, California. Up through Oregon he traveled—Eugene, Portland—and climbing Washington—Seattle, Bellingham. Resting there, breathless, slouching along the broken coastline's broken jaw like the underedge of a key. It was now high summer.

Never, having told the Finsbergs that he was no businessman, was he one more consummately. At a time when the country was dragging the river for its economy, when inflation and stagflation and depression were general, he calmly carried on his shuttle finance.

Nor am I talking merely about money now. For if I told the Finsbergs that I was no businessman, at least one of the things I meant was that it was money I had never properly understood. By which I mean coveted in sums large enough to make a difference. By which I mean rich. By which I mean so many things: seeking the tax shelters like lost caves, Northwest Passage, the hidden, swift currents, all those fiscal Gulf Streams that warm the cold places and make fools of the latitudes, topsy-turvying climate with the palm trees of Dublin and Vancouver's moderated winters. Swiss banking my currency, anonymating it behind the peculiar laws of foreign government. Hedging against inflation with diamonds, gold, pictures, land. Seeking hobby farms or going where the subsidies were, the depletion allowances, all loophole's vested, venerable kickbacks. Though I am not disparaging, have never disparaged, the value of money and understand full well, understand with the best of them—the richest and poorest—that peculiar sensation of loss and even insult concomitant with—not picking up checks; that's never bothered me; no, nor getting stuck with the bad end of an unequal division, paying for wine I didn't drink, splitting down the middle the cost of appetizers or desserts I never ordered, the lion's share of the food going to the couple I am with (I am alone) but paying anyway, dollar for dollar, as if what is being paid for is a wedding gift one goes in on with a pal or a present for a secretary in the office, say, who's going to Europe for the first time; and not even *purchase*, springing for an admired but overpriced jacket or shirt, yet feeling anyway because I *do* admire it, that I have gotten the best of it somehow, have only given money and gotten goods, fabric—the *leakage* of money: the terrible disruption of sensibility if, in a taxi, in the dark I have mistaken a ten for a five or a five for a single. Or breaking a fifty or even a twenty, disturbing the high, powerful round numbers of currency, and feeling actually wounded, or at least unpleasantly moved, irritated, insulted, as I say, suffering inordinately, as if from a paper cut or a chip of live cigarette dropped on my skin. Mourning like God my lost black-sheep bucks. Getting nothing for something's what's terrible. Misplacing change or not being able to account for twelve dollars which I knew I had. Oh awful, awful. Ruined, wiped out. A hole in my substance.

But just that I never dreamed of being wealthy, never expected it, never did what would have to be done to be it. And I'm not poor-mouthing the big dough, money so important it ceases to *be* money, becomes—what?—capital, some avatar of asset and credit and reserve and parity, all the complicated solvency of diversification and portfolio. Let them fiddle the tariffs at their pleasure, for the fiduciary is only another foreign language to me, and I leave to others the ins and outs of tare and cess and octroi. All that I ever wanted was enough cash. Death duties never bothered me, only death. (And even at that, even with all my opportunities, all my missed chances, *still* I have had to do with the stuff. More than most. A guy with his money "tied up." Think, think: a fellow with tied-up money. Knotted dough, bread braided as *challah*. Ben Flesh like those strapped Croesi. Well, not in *their* league, of course, not even in the towns which hold their ball parks, but nevertheless, except for living expenses—high on the highway—with the rest of that fraternity, what I have all in the frozen assets of the frozen custard: the rent and payrolls and equipment and insurance, the petty cash, all the incidentals.)

But because in the last leg of my journey, on notice as I was, warned as I was, politely ultimatum'd, cautioned by the boys and only tenuously *laissez-faire'd* by the girls, who did not have the votes now anyway, Lotte's suicide having shifted the balance of power and adulterated their fabulous consanguinity in some, to me, fathomless way—and how struck, *hurt* I had been to see them differentiated at last, to see *their* diversificatio, the awful introduction of nuance into their Finsberg portfolio—I knew that for the first time since the war, when I had put in those long-distance calls to my dead, killed parents—who died, as I lived, on the highway—that I was alone. That something had been withdrawn in Riverdale, taken from me, the godcousinship which had been my ace-in-the-hole, my letter of credit to the world, the carte blanche smeared, *shmutzed*, and that I had only one peeled wire of connection left, Patty's IOU. That I could lie beside her in death like a puppy at the foot of a kid's bed.

So what else was there to do? What choices *did* I have? Why, only to put on my decorous act of business-is-business propriety. To try to live as they had tried to teach me to live at Wharton. To try, as if I were cramming for an exam, to recall those principles of business administration, finance, and double-entry sobriety which are only finally solid solvency's serious style.

For the fact is that in all those years he had merely gotten what he wanted—enough cash. That he had spread himself too thin, that there had been too many split ends. Mister Softee in the frozen north, a Robo-Wash in a neighborhood where half the cars were destined to be repossessed, a Radio Shack in a Kentucky town where reception was lousy and there was only one FM multiplex station, a Baskin-Robbins in a section of Kansas City too far from any neighborhood for there to be kids, a dance studio in a part of town where people wouldn't even *walk* at night, a dry cleaner in a wash-and-wear world. As if he could live forever, outlast the phases, eras, and epochs of faddish geography and sociology. Like a player of Monopoly who built his hotels on Baltic and Mediterranean and Ventnor Avenues, say, all those low-rent districts of the spirit, whose strategy it was to go to jail as often as he could, to stay there as long as he could, and to win by attrition. Some strategy. Who did not turn out to have the body for strategies of attrition, for whom attrition was a reflexive disease. Who, going such distances, could not go the distance. Some strategy. And all it ever got him was all he ever wanted: enough cash, lolly, dough, brass, spondulicks—the ready. And if he bought and sold so much, if he was so active, perhaps, too, there was something else he wanted, something nobler and more spiritual even than enough cash: something no less than empire itself—to be the man who made America look like America, who made America famous. What had he called it for the murderously divided twins and triplets? Oh yes. The "Esperanto of simple need." Convenience necessity and the universalized appetite. And if the outskirts of Chicago resembled Connecticut or Tulsa Cleveland and Cleveland Omaha and the north the west and the west the south and east, why *he'd* had a finger in it, more than a finger—some finger!—a hand. Some hand. There wasn't a television in all the thousands of motel rooms in which he'd slept which wouldn't show him in the course of a single evening at least two sponsored minutes of the homogenized, coast-to-coast America he'd helped design, costuming the states, getting Kansas up like Pennsylvania, Georgia like New York. Why he *was* a Finsberg! A Julius and his own father Flesh, too, loose and at large in his beautiful musical comedy democracy!

Yes. *Loose. At large!* Those were the operative words now. So what else *was* there to do? What choices did I have? None but to dredge up Wharton, recalling the patter like a foreign language.

"Yes, sir?"

"I'd like a word with Friendly Bob Adams, please, Miss. My name is Ben Flesh."

"Ben," friendly Bob, spotting him, said, "I expected you last week. When you didn't come I tried to—"

"I'm sorry. I should have gotten you on the blower. I had to fly back to New York on some rather urgent business. I hope this isn't an inconvenient—"

"No, no, of course not," Adams said, smiling and taking his hand warmly. "Harriet, this is Mr. Flesh. Harriet's our new receptionist, Ben."

"How do you do, Harriet?" Harriet smiled. "She looks a crackerjack girl, Friendly. What happened to—it was Jean, wasn't it?"

"She turned sourpuss, Ben. She wouldn't let a smile be her umbrella. I had to get rid of her."

"Of course. Nice to see you, Harriet. Miss—"

"Lapaloosa."

"Look at the teeth on her, Ben. When she grins."

"Very good to have you with us, Miss Lapaloosa. Oh, say, Adams, since I *am* running late, it might be a good idea if we skipped lunch this time. I'd like to take some things up with you."

"Of course, Ben. Why don't we go back to my office?"

"Splendid," Ben said. Then, in his manager's office, he let him have it.

"Cash flow," he said, "hard times."

"Demand has never been—"

"Hard times. *Hard.* The price of money to us. Ten cents on the dollar. The truth-in-lending laws. Price tags on our dollars like notarized statements from the appraiser."

"But demand, Ben, the phone never stops ringing. *They* don't care, Ben, they *don't.* You think someone down on his luck comparison shops? We do the arithmetic for them, we show them the vigorish like a cop reading them their civil rights, and they *still* don't care. 'Where do I sign?' they want to know. 'How soon do I get the money?'"

"And this doesn't make you *suspicious?* Wipe that smile off your face, Friendly. This doesn't make you *suspicious?* You've got a good heart, you weren't cut out to be a shylock. Schmuck, of *course* they don't care. They know about bankruptcy. Sylvia Porter tells them in the papers."

"But the credit checks, Ben, we run credit checks, we know exactly—"

"Yesterday's newspapers, kid, history. Yesterday's news, last year's prospecti. The times have changed on them, their mood has, their disposition. A depression comes, the first thing that goes, after the meat on the table, after the fruit in the bowl, the first thing that goes is optimism, the belief they can pay back what they owe."

"We can garnishee—"

"What? *What* can we garnishee? Their unemployment checks? Their workman's compensation? What can we garnishee? Their allowance from the union? What, *what* can we garnishee? The widow's mite? The plastic collateral? What can we garnishee? We going to play tug-of-war with the dealer to repossess the car? We take their furniture? Their color TV? And do what? We got a warehouse? We got storage facilities? Tracts of land in the desert for all the mothball fleet of a bankrupt's detritus? *Credit checks!* On what? Old times? The good old days? It doesn't make you suspicious white-collar guys come to you for dough? College graduates? The class of '58? *That* doesn't bother you? Your ear ain't to the ground? Take your credit checks in the men's toilet. Hear what they're saying in *those* circles. Sneak up behind them where they eat their lunch, taking their sandwiches from a paper bag, their milk from mayonnaise jars, because these are the people never owned a lunch pail, a pencil box of food, who wouldn't recognize a thermos unless it was beside a Scotch cooler on a checkered cloth spread out on the lawn for a picnic. Fuck your credit checks, cancel them they bounce. Overhear the rumors they overhear—the layoffs, the open-ended furloughs coming just after the Christmas upswing, the plants closing down in this industry and that, and only a skeleton crew to bank the furnaces, only the night-watchman industry booming because we live in the time of the looters, of the plate-glass smashers, in the age of the plucked toaster from the storefront window and somebody else snitches the white bread. This is the credit you're running down? No no. They won't pay. They can't. And they don't care."

"But so far . . ."

"Sure so far, certainly so far. So far is no distance at all. I'm shutting us down, I'm getting us out. Even now I am negotiating with banks and savings and loans and even with shylocks to buy up our paper at a discount." Friendly Bob Adams had stopped smiling. It was the first time Flesh had seen him unhappy. It was very strange. His expansiveness gone, he seemed not so much sad as winded. Ben gave him a chance to catch his breath. Adams shook his head slowly. He moved from behind his desk and past the safe where they kept the money and to the window, where he looked out onto the street.

"You'll find something," Flesh said. "I tell you what. If nothing turns up you can always come back to me. I'll find a place for you in a different franchise. I'm not getting out of everything. I'm simply taking stock, inventorying my situation, trimming my sails. Don't worry. You'll be all right. I swear to you."

"It isn't that," Adams said.

"It isn't what?"

"It isn't that. I wasn't thinking about myself. I can make it."

"Sure you can," Ben said.

"It isn't me."

"You'll be fine."

"Sure," he said. He looked stricken.

"What is it?"

"Miss Lapaloosa," he said. "You know me, Ben," he said, "my make-up. I'm sunshine soldier, summer patriot."

"Yes?"

"Jean was different. When she turned sourpuss I had to let her go. She depressed me. She tried my friendliness."

"You want me to fire Miss Lapaloosa? Is that it?"

"You saw," he said. "That smile. That was from the heart, Ben."

I put my hand on his shoulder. "I'll do it," I said.

"Would you?"

"No problem."

"That's swell, Ben. That's a load off my chest."

"She's as good as out on her ass this minute."

"You're all right, Ben," Friendly Bob Adams said.

And giving them the benefit of his best judgment at Railroad Salvage.

"It's all wrong," he said, walking with his manager up and down the big hangar-like room, past the bins of canned goods, the stands of steamer trunks and open drawers of hardware—nails, tacks, screws, bits of pipe, washers, bolts, and nuts—like boxes of font, the appliances, mixed, blenders next to portable radios, side by side with steam irons, waffle irons above pressure cookers, toasters and hot plates and bathroom scales laid out on shelves like prizes in a carnival booth. Past the toys, the bins of practical jokes—fake dog poop, joy buzzers, dismembered suppurating fingers, whoopee cushions—like a warehouse of toy pain and joke shit. Through wall-less, shuffled rooms of cheap furniture, kitchen tables set up beside bedroom sets and next to raised toilet seats, vanities, double basins, sinks heavily fixtured as consoles in control towers next to porch furniture, lawn—swings, hammocks, chaise longues, big barbecues like immense cake dishes—beside living rooms that melded into each other, stocky Mediterranean alongside Mapley Colonial and near art-deco Barcaloungers, stack tables, glass and aluminum pieces, a dozen different kinds of lamps. Polyglot as the site of a tornado. "It's all wrong, it won't do."

"Business hasn't been bad, Mr. Flesh. Sure, the economy's in a bind right now. Things are a little tight, but our figures are only marginally behind last year's. Down maybe 7 or 8 percent, but there'll be an upturn. The President says, his advisers think—"

"It won't do. Bring a hammer. Get a nail."

"A hammer? A nail?"

"Have you got a piece of glass somewhere? From costume jewelry. Fetch a zircon."

"But I—"

"Do it," Flesh said.

His manager whispered something to a stock boy who was passing by. When the boy returned Flesh took the hammer from him, beckoned them both to follow. The kid caddied Ben's zircon, his nail.

They returned to the bins of canned goods. Ben set a can of peas down on the cement floor and, stooping, carefully slammed at the top of the can. "See?" he said, holding it up, "now it *looks* damaged. Hand me the nail. See," he said, "you make a little scratch on the label. Don't tear it all off, just a little scratch." He straightened up. "Here and there. I don't mean everything. But here and there. Use the zircon to scar the glass tabletops, the legs of coffee tables. Get tools that etch your driver's license into metal. Burn long numbers on the back of TV sets. They'll think stolen goods. Be careful. Don't cut yourself. I don't want anybody hurt." He looked at them. "Goodwill Industries is killing us, they're busting our brains. All right, I'm not really frightened of Mr. Goodwill Industries. Mr. Goodwill Industries is in for a kick in the ass, too. People aren't so quick in these times to clear out their junk. They'll make do. They won't rifle their wardrobes or wring out their basements. Mr. Goodwill Industries is living on borrowed time. His sources are drying up. That's when we make our move.

"For people need junk," he said. "There's a hunger for the secondhand, the used, the abused. I don't understand this need—me, give me a shiny motel by the side of the road and be a friend to man. But others, our others, the people who come here, there is a flotsam tropism in such people. The jetsam set. A longing deep as lust for the overboard, the castoff, what's found in the plane wreck, what's seared in the riot or ruined in the hold. The dead man's new suit, the suicide's coat, her shoes and her slip. People want such things. They have a sweet tooth for remnant, for rubbish, remainder. All the derelict and marooned, the ditched and scavenged. Debris, dregs, lees. Dregs addicts. All the multitudinous slag of the ordinary. Is it economy that puts this thirst in them? I don't know but I don't think so. I think acquisition, some squirrel vestige in the instincts, something miserly and niggardly, basic but not base, the things of the world as heirloom. The *world* as heirloom, handed down and continuing. History's hugged dower. A sort of pin money in the shit in the attic.

"Bang the canned goods. Put little holes in the shirttails. Dent the toasters, nick the toys. We're Railroad Salvage, all aboard. We're Railroad Salvage. Give them train wreck, give them capsize, give them totaled, head-on and what's spilled to the road from the jackknifed rig.

"Is this good business?" It was as if he were appealing to the Finsbergs rather than to his help. "Is this sound business practice? Efficient management? Solid policy?"

As everywhere he went these days he was thinking of Finsbergs, addressing Finsbergs when he addressed his managers, their auras with him like cartoon consciences.

"I want," he told his people at Fotomat, "to see the pictures."

"The pictures?"

"The pictures, the photographs, yes."

"That's invasion of privacy, it's like opening someone's mail."

"We're professionals. We're developers here. It's a customer service. Quality control. An audit. Show me," he said, when they had shut down for the evening and he was assured no customers would come to claim their snapshots—it was a small *butke* of a building, a Checkpoint Charlie, a Mandelbaum Gate thing, a booth in the open center of a shopping mall— "Bring me a viewer for the slides, a magnifying glass for the contact prints."

"Mr. Flesh—"

"It's an audit, I tell you."

It was. Of American life. The human condition as it relaxed, as it sat for its portraits at birthday celebrations and family reunions, at weddings and picnics and summer vacations—it was just past the season of summer vacations—at special celebratory dinners and homecomings—soldiers, sailors with their duffels up on their shoulders, perched there like the parrots of adventure.

"Look, look," he said, providing the commentary, lecturing them like a man with home movies. "See, here's the snowman in the yard, the children in leggings, in mittens on strings. See? Look how the girl has grown. How much higher her shoulders seem against the fence in the background, how the hedge has flowered. Oh, God, it's the same roll. Three seasons on the same roll. Their aboveground pool stands closed like a piece of giant canned goods—see, see the tarp—yet in this one it's open. The neighbor kid splashes. Oh oh. Three seasons. One roll of film. My. My oh my. Three. And only one roll shot.

"Look, look here. Black and white. And—what's this name?— Daigle. Daigle's pictures are black and white, too. And Libby's. And Rosenthal's. Wheat's are, Colameco's. Black. Black and white. Tch tch."

"Black and white's a faster film, Mr. Flesh."

"Of course it is. Yes. But—oh, oh," he groaned, "these are out-doors. Out*doors* and black and white!"

"Some photographers prefer it. It's better at stopping action."

"These are *people*," Flesh cried. "These are *people*, not photo-graphers. And what, you need a fast film for this? Can't you see? It's their *house*. They're selling their house. What's the address here? Let's see the envelope. Two sixty-one Crownsville. Where's that? What sort of neighborhood? Changing I'll bet. Sure, that must be it. See? Here in this picture, the kids in the street, two of them black. The neighborhood's changing, the film's black and white. All over the same story. Oh the inroads and encroachments. Posing their houses for realtors' books. This block is busted. You can kiss it goodbye."

"I don't—"

"*They have Polaroids.* The blacks. *They have Polaroids!* It's only natural, what do you think? They're impatient. They've had to wait. They have Polaroids. They want results. They hold the film in their hand and watch the faces bloom like flowers. It reminds them of Madam Palmyra's crystal ball. We're ruined, ruined."

"Mr. Flesh, do you think you could hold the photographs by the edges? If the customer sees—"

"We're ruined," Ben said, "we'd best cut our losses. See? See the strain on these people's faces? Uh oh. I don't like it. I don't like the looks of this."

"The looks of what, sir?"

"The monuments. Something about the monuments. Here, hold the viewer. Look at the Herman Schieke family. The Schiekes at Yellowstone, Old Faithful going off behind them like a liquid fire-work. At the rim of the Grand Canyon. Here, look, some Schieke kid standing on a petrified log in the Petrified Forest. And, here, this one, Herman himself probably, the photograph angled so Schieke's face appears beside the Presidents' at Mount Rushmore."

"That's a darned good picture," his manager said.

"Good? *Good?* You don't understand? We're living in the last days. Schieke thinks so. He's making a record. These pictures, the others, the ones in Europe, they all say the same. They say, 'We were there. Us. Here's the proof.' *Because they never expect to go*

· 269 ·

*again!* It's a last fling. Open your eyes. It's a last fling in the last days. Because a man of confidence doesn't mar a Colosseum with his worn-out children—why, the whole family's there; worse, worse and worse; they've asked some stranger to take the picture—unless he believes he'll never return. In London the same. In Paris, in Greece. Terrible, terrible, a terrible thing these terrible times. It's lucky I saw these. We know what to do."

"What to do?"

"Shh, go, go home to your families, I'll close up, I have work. I'd rather be by myself just now. Go. You can pick up the keys at my motel in the morning."

"But . . ."

"It's best that you go. I'll be honest with you. I don't like it. I'm *forced* to sell. I'll give you wonderful references. Maybe I can get the new man to take you on. Have you saved money? Maybe you can go in with someone and buy me out. I want only what I paid. Go home, think about this. Sleep on it. Discuss with your wife."

Then, alone, by a Tensor lamp on a desk in the qualified dark, he sat, rummaging the photographs like a numismatist, prying detail from his customers' lives. That they had dogs, cats, gerbils, plants. Tapping, for the first time it could have been—he'd lied to his manager, he didn't intend to sell; this wasn't good business; he was as bad a franchiser as ever, as indifferent to his prospects as ever, as distant as ever from motives of money and as close to his single interest, the backstage Finsberg propinquity to staged life, his need to costume his country, to give it its visible props, its mansard roofs and golden arches and false belfries, all its ubiquitous, familiar neon signatures and logos, all its *things*, all its *crap*, the true American graffiti, that perfect queer calligraphy of American signature, what gave it meaning and made it fun—into a ring of the domestic. Father's chair, the television/stereo/tape recorder hidden in its monstrous cabinet like a Murphy bed in the wall, some teenager's set of drums in the family room, the boy's name like lush spangled fruit on one face of the bass, palms on the taut skin, dice, champagne glasses, the painted liquid jaundiced as specimen and the bubbles rising like smoke signal, tilting up and back like a stupa of suds. He saw crosses on walls, pictures of long-tressed Christs, here and there a menorah in a breakfront overwhelming the minia-tures—he passed his magnifying glass over these—around it. Mah-Jongg sets, decks of cards, poker chips, chess boards, magazines, *Reader's Digest* condensations like grammar-school dictionaries. Where the rug was worn, where the paint was peeling. The land-scapes above the sofas—he could tell which ones had been done by the wives—and the framed glass portrait photography on the man-tels. What newspapers they took, what the news was months ago. Tapping into a ring of the domestic. Seeing behind the prin-cipals—it could have been Asia it was so strange to him—boxes of soap flakes, pails, brushes in the cabinets beneath the kitchen sink, the iron elbow joints of plumbing. Seeing kids' bedrooms, the pie slices of pennants, ship models, model airplanes. A daughter's col-lapsed doll looking breathless, unconscious against the baseboard. Seeing—there would be company—heaped coats, wraps upon a bed in the master bedroom. Formal poses—children sitting in pri-mogenitive succession on a sofa. A wife fixing her hair, a husband shaving. (The medicine cabinet, ointments saved years, the last chipped pills of ancient prescriptions, yellowing aspirin, tooth-brushes caked with paste.) And it forcibly struck him. Why, I *have* lived my life like an outdoorsman. Itchfoot the Peddler, Westward the Itinerant, Footloose Flesh, Ben Bum, the Horizon kid. Not to have been—this was true, excepting childhood, excepting the Fins-bergs and Riverdale—inside, indoors, even as a guest; never to have bought, never to have rented, never to have lived in an apart-ment, to have signed a lease, lived a lodger. How does it happen, I wonder, that I have never killed anyone, that I am not a wanted man?

"I think," he told his H & R Block man, "that I shall have to shut down this office."

"It's the off-season, Mr. Flesh, that's why it seems so slack. From January to May you can't hear yourself think. The phones never stop ringing. Most of our off-season work is audits, people called in to bring their records down to IRS, go over their returns. The spot check, you know? I've got twenty appointments of that nature this month alone."

"I'm sorry," Ben said.

"Mr. Flesh, there's a saying, 'The only thing you can be sure of is death and taxes.' This is a sound business, Mr. Flesh."

"I'm sorry."

"If you'll just look at the commissions, even in these off-months—"

"Where's the return in returns?" he asked. "Look," he said, "I know you do a good job. But that was yesteryear. You own your own home? Rent?

"We rent, but—"

"You don't get around like I do. I'm Wharton, I know things. My ear's to the ground like the white line on the highway. They're closing the loopholes, they're graduating the taxes, *gaudeamus igitur*. Texas Instruments has us by the short hairs. With the pocket computers any kid can figure his old man's taxes. They teach this shit in school now. Like good citizenship. Like Driver Training. Anyway, what's the matter, you never heard of the Taxpayers' Revolution? Shh, listen, they're dumping tea in the harbor."

"But without a warning, with no notice—"

"Finish your case load. Take twice your commission. Triple. We're closing shop, we're going out of business, everything must go."

"But—"

"I told Evelyn Wood the same. What, you think you're a special case? I told Evelyn Wood, I told her, 'Eve, there's trouble in Canada, in the forests. The weather's bad, the stands of trees are lying down. There's no wood in the woods, Wood. The pulp business is mushy. Where's the paper to come from for the speed readers to read? They're reading so fast now they're reading us out of business. Publishing's in hot water. Magazines are folding, newspapers. (What, you never heard of folded newspapers?) If we want to keep up with the times we have to slow down, go back to the old ways. We have to teach them to move their lips.' "

"Mr. Flesh—"

"A month, I give you a month's notice."

Which *was* good business. And now he was conscious always of Finsbergs on the other end of his line. He performed for them. His best foot forward. Living as if within the crosshairs of their sharpshooter observation and understanding. Every move a picture. His deals dealt for them more than for himself. Like a kid behaving for Santa Claus.

At night he dreamed of them, changed now, grown apart, the shifting sand-dune arrangement of their bone structure—all gone now their '50's and '60's tract-house mode—their features left out overnight in a human weather, hair colors changing, styles, growing piecemeal paunches, gestures, asses, the girls moving toward some vague Estelledom while the men grew more like Julius and less like each other. An expanding-universe theory of Finsbergs. The Big Finsberg Bang. In his dream he was like some archaeologist at the Finsberg digs, reconstructing their old mass individualism, only with difficulty putting them together, a painstaking labor. Not something for someone with *his* hands. All the king's horsing them. And getting somehow the idea that if he could only shape his franchises in some more coherent way—this occurred to him: that if he could pace the routes from New York to Chicago, from St. Louis to Denver, Omaha to Los Angeles, Fort Worth to Dallas, Boston to Washington, planting the land mines of his franchising in such a way as to coincide with a traveler's circadian rhythms, his scientifically averaged-out need to pee, eat, rest, distract himself with souvenirs from Stuckey's and Nickerson Farms or get off the main route for a bit and go to town—all would be well, he would clean up, regain the respect of the boys, the love of the girls, and that respect and love for him would somehow force them back into their old odd single magical manifestations. But it was too hard, a job for a younger man, a healthier. All wouldn't be well, the Finsberg features would never again collect at the true north of their old selves. There was no way.

All he could do was tack, trim. Sacrifice Evelyn Wood Reading Dynamics and H & R Block for Dunkin' Donuts. Trading them off like baseball cards. If a depression came, Dunkin' Donuts would prosper. He felt that. He knew that. That was good business. With what he got for the franchises he dumped, he reinvested heavily in doughnuts and coffee.

Then the price of cream shot sky-high and sugar went through the fucking roof.

# 3

It was early 1975. The banks had begun to chip away at the prime rate, every two or three weeks bringing down the boiling point of money, its high tropical fevers, a quarter percentage point here, a half percentage point there. The temp tumbling like a crisis in old-time films. The price-of-money fix was in. The gnomes of Zurich and the Fed had put the brakes on. Gold, legal to own, went begging. Stocks recovered ground in their long Viet/guerrilla/Hundred Years War.

By his recent good husbandry, Ben Flesh had divested himself of many of his investments, adjusting his strange portfolio, his eggs in fewer baskets now than they had been for years. Money in the bank. The Finsbergs protected. A high wall of the respectable around them while his health failed daily, his own energy crisis unresolved, his body still demyelinating a mile a minute. Like a thaw revealing litter, garbages, horror.

He spoke with two or three Finsbergs daily, pressing them with his new goduncle love, the phone a genuine expense. (He subscribed to a WATS line, got special rates, dialing his coded numbers even at the public phones in gas stations and drugstores.)

Not wanting to nuisance them, as aware as any tentative, cautious, unsure-of-his-ground lover of the thinness of his welcome. So coming at them from another side, not deferent, not submissive. No Lear, no Stella Dallas. Not Père Goriot. Not asking for their healths, giving his.

"My testicles are acting up," he told Gus-Ira. "They feel weighted. A very peculiar sensory symptom. Annoying. I don't know how to describe it. It's as if I had loaded dice for balls. Or like those, you know, Mexican jumping beans."

"That sounds uncomfortable."

"Oh yeah. It is. I take a few steps and I feel the locks tumbling in my parts. I come and I feel magnets colliding. I piss and the ball bearings get out of line."

"Terrible. I heard that Moss—"

"But it's still chiefly sensory, I think. Oh my balance isn't that terrific. I trip but I don't always go down. I can touch my finger to my thumb. But what's the good of kidding? I'll be on steroids in a year—two at the outside. All I'm really holding out for is the opening of my Travel Inn. I'd like to get that under my belt. If it isn't one thing it's another. Now the damned electricians are out on strike. But there's talk of settlement. It could be open by this summer if they get down to business. Almost everything's ready, the furniture will be coming in, the TV's. It's just the electricians holding us up. It's going to be terrific, Gus-Ira. My biggest thing yet. I want you and the family as my guests for the opening. Hold July open."

"That sounds swell, Ben. We'll certainly try to make it."

"That's a promise now."

"Sure. We'll try."

"What's this about Moss?"

"Moss?"

"You said you heard that Moss something something."

"Oh. Maxene was telling me that he may have his driver's license revoked."

"Yes?"

"The insurance company is talking about canceling his policy. There've been some claims against him."

"Boy, the nerve of those guys. You pay your premiums—and those are some premiums. Believe me, I know. You pay your premiums, dent a few fenders, and they want to close you down. Sore losers. I can't get life insurance because of the M.S."

"Well—"

"The underwriters. Letters from a half dozen of the best neurologists in the country. I've seen the letters. Beautiful. Like good references. Like advise and consent on a shoo-in Secretary of State. The companies turn me down."

"Really?"

"They turn me down. Or want ridiculous premiums. I wanted to take out a million dollars. You know the premium those putz-knuckles are asking?"

"A million bucks? Why would you want to take out a million-dollar insurance policy?"

"My God, Gus, *you* have to ask something like that? For the kids, for *you* guys, but it's out of the question. They want a hundred twenty-five grand a year to cover me. Fucking whore-hearts. My neuros tell them it's sensory . . . Hell, their *own* neuros tell them it's sensory and they're still betting I won't live eight years."

"A hundred twenty-five thousand. That's wacky."

"Goofy."

"Incredible."

"Well, what the hell, I'll be on steroids in a year, my face out of shape as a whore's pillow. Lopsided as hobgoblin. Still, I could last years strapped to the wheelchair. But I guess I see their point. The payments. How would I keep up the payments?"

"Gee, Ben, when you talk like that—" Kitty said.

"Don't you worry, baby, just don't you worry. You guys are provided for. Have I ever cost you a nickel?"

"I hate to hear—"

"Have I cost you a nickel? Was there ever a time I didn't pay back? Did I ever once have to come to you and say, 'Boys, girls, I can't handle the payments, go to bat for me.'?"

"Come on, Ben."

"Not once. Not one time. Dad put you under an obligation and *I'm* obligated."

"Please."

"No. I'm obliged. All right," he told Mary, "it ain't the Ottoman Empire, but Monaco maybe, San Marino perhaps, whatever they call those postage-stamp republics they have over there. Something like that my tidy enterprises. For you, for Lorenz, for Helen, the others."

"Speaking of Helen," she said as if she wanted to change the subject.

"No no. Don't be embarrassed by my love. Please, Mary. Take it or leave it, but don't be embarrassed. And how do you like this? My old guy rhetoric, my stage-door style? Call me Pop and give me high marks for loyalty."

"Loyalty? Loyalty to what, Ben?"

"To what? To you. To *you*, Irving. To you like a toast. To *you*. Listen, I've taken plenty of loyalty lessons over the years. I'm a Finsberg patriot, hip hip hooray. Maybe loyaler," he said to Cole, "than you guys have been. Oh, not to me. I don't complain. All I got to complain are my toes tingling in my shoes like I'm walking barefoot in sandstorms. All I got to complain are my fingernails tickle. That my electricians don't settle—but I heard the Fed mediators are in on it now. There may be a break soon. I think August at the outside for the opening of my Inn. You can come, right? My guests. There's never been a Flesh/Finsberg Franchise Gala. What, you think I'd ask you to a Baskin-Robbins opening? You should fly in and look at the flavors before they melt? Though, you know," he told Gertrude, "it might have been worth it. The *colors* of those ice creams! Chocolate like new shoes, Cherry like bright fingernail polish. We do a Maple Ripple it looks like fine-grained wood, a Peach like light coming through a lampshade. You should see that stuff—the ice-cream paints bright as posters, fifty Day-Glo colors. You scoop the stuff up you feel like Jackson Pollock. There have been times—listen to me—there have been times it's busy, I'm tired from a trip, my symptoms are crawling in my ears like ants, and I go back of the counter to help out. I roll up my sleeves and I get cheerful. *Cheer*ful. I whistle while I work. No kidding," he told Patty, "I take one look at the ice-cream acrylics and I'm happy as Looney Tunes. I almost forget my teeth have goose bumps."

"Goose bumps?"

"This M.S. is no respecter of feelings. It blitzkriegs the nerves, gives your hair a headache. You think there are splinters in your eyes and the roof of your mouth has sunburn. But what the hell, the electricians are close to settling, the union representatives are seriously considering the latest proposals, they may bring them to the rank and file for a vote. Then—who knows?—five, six weeks' work and you can call it a Travel Inn. You'll be there, of course. I'm expecting all the kids. It'll be like old times."

"With Jerome the way he is—"

"Jerome? Jerome's fine. Shipshape. I already invited Jerome. I spoke to Jerome last week."

"He hadn't gone in for the tests last week."

"What tests? He didn't say anything about tests. He never mentioned tests. What's going on with Jerome?"

"That's what they're trying to determine, Ben. I don't understand it. Supposedly we'll know in a few days."

He called Jerome but there was no answer.

He called Helen.

"Christ," she said thickly, "who the hell is this?"

"It's Ben. Did I wake you? Gosh, I'm sorry. It's only just past midnight here. I didn't think you'd be asleep yet. You're what, nine o'clock in Los Angeles?"

"I sound like the time and temperature lady to you, jackoff?"

"Hey, Helen, it's Ben. It's Ben, darling."

" 'Hey, Helen, it's Ben,' " she mocked. "Jeepers, douchebag, you're some fucking bore. I spoke to you a month ago. You told me your knuckles had temperature. What's up now, you getting electric shock in your snot?"

"It's about Jerome, sweetheart."

"Screw Jerome."

"Helen, have you been drinking? You know how you get when you're drinking."

"Mind your business. What do you think this is? You some kind of wise guy? Nuts to you. Wanna fight? Get off the planet."

He'd been calling them, feeding them his symptoms, the heavy weather, all the isobars and thunderheads of his multiplying sclerosis. (It was crazy, but it was as if the days when his paresthetic hands had troubled him, when his skin crawled in anything but natural fibers, when the nerves in his feet sent out shoots of electric quiver, had been a golden age, the halcyon good old days of manageable discomfort.) Now his body shipped a queer illicit cargo of intolerable contraband sensation. Things no torturer could make up. His body a host to amok feeling—and all still below the level of pain, things *not* pain, as if pain, as he remembered it, was only a matter of the degree of things honed and sharp, tender through sore to pinched, some verb wheel of friction and thorned flesh, only the surgical cutlery of bruise, nip, sting, stitch, ache, and cramp. Pain, he thought, he could take. Or could have afforded the addiction that would have purchased relief. These other things, these new proliferating sour dispensations were something else and lived, thrived—he knew, he'd tried them—beneath all the powerful analgesics—Demerol, codeine, laudanum, morphine. And had held back from his godcousins the really big stuff, the monstrous that he dared not put in words, dared not try them with. Held back all that was unimaginable: sounds that tickled his eardrums; his tongue rubbed raw in his saltwater saliva; the steady, constant Antarctic cold of his hands and feet and eyelids—he could not endure air conditioning and wore thick furred gloves in even the hottest weather—the impression he had that his body was actually striped like a zebra's, the dark strips of skin and flesh, or what he imagined were the dark strips—he could see that he was not *really* striped—heavier somehow than the light, harder to negotiate in gravity; the sensation he had that he was wet deep inside his body, wet where he could not get to it—like someone with an unreachable itch—where he could not dry it with towels or rub it with toilet paper, though he tried. Though he wiped and wiped himself, he felt always as if he sat in some medium of diarrhea, minced, oozy, slippery shit. Also, his olfactory system was faultily wired so that he hallucinated tastes and smells, confused them crazily with their sources till finally, experimentally breaking the code, he ordered desserts and cakes at dinner if he felt like seafood, seafood if his body craved meat, meat if he had a taste for something sweet. Had not told them any of this who kept on now—he couldn't say why, couldn't account for why he did not kill himself, or had not died—by dint of a will and a set of motives he knew to be as illusory and unfounded as his impression that his body was striped.

"I have arrived," he told Oscar, "at a stage of my life where I must manufacture reasons to keep going," but not explaining this further, certainly not giving any indications that his love for them might be one of those reasons. But perhaps he did not believe this himself.

Was worried. Concerned. Not hurt (*everything* beneath pain). Even though he knew they knew where to find him, where he hung out to keep his eye on the landscapers and supervise the movers who daily brought the suites of motel furniture, where he oversaw the construction of the swimming pool and sauna and signed for the television sets he had bought over a year before from Nate Lace at the Nittney-Lyon, and kept a weather eye out for any nuance of movement in the impasse with the electricians, and conducted the business of all his remaining baker's-dozen franchises throughout the country, become a sort of Nate Lace himself now, holed up, at once waiting and doing business. And *still* they didn't call. Even though they knew of his illness (though not its degree, he having spared them that, spared them, even as he spoke to them, when he, that is, called them, the terrible symptoms of speech itself: that talking, making sounds, seemed to chafe the soft insides of his cheeks, raising blisters). Not even forgiving them. What was there to forgive? They'd told him. They'd grown apart.

"Loyaler," as he told Irving, "than you guys have been, not even to me, I'm not in it, but to each other. Growing apart. What was it, you didn't watch your diets? You let yourselves go? Genes, genes like that, like you had, are holy. A responsibility. Once-in-a-lifetime genes. To be protected. What's the matter? You're Finsbergs. Don't you know anything about endangered species?"

"But why complain to me?" Irving said. "Jesus, Ben, I'm the one who held on. Don't blame me," racially prejudiced Irving said, "for the mongrelization of this family. Sure, I married a darkie, but damn it, Ben, I'm the only Finsberg who *hasn't* changed. I look the same. A year older but still charting the Finsberg course, still with the old twin and triplet telemetry and trajectory. It was them. I'm right on target for what would have been the manifest destiny of Finsberg evolution. Gee, Ben, *I* didn't grow apart."

"I know," Flesh said, "I know, Irving. You're a good boy, a nice man, but how could I say such things to the others? To the ones who *did* let themselves go? Who *did* grow apart? Forgive me, pal, I'm just letting off steam."

And the more worried, the more concerned—Jerome's tests—the less there was to forgive anyone. Perhaps they didn't want to upset him, felt they needed to protect him, as he protected them from his darkest symptoms. So he didn't call. He stopped calling. Waiting for good news, waiting for the strike to be settled, waiting for something nice to tell them for a change.

It was settled in April. Ben nodded to the man who told him and went immediately to the telephone.

He called Gus-Ira. When the ringing stopped and he heard the connection completed, he began talking at once. "We're cooking, the rank and file ratified and the boys will be . . ." There was a voice against his own voice. "Gee, I was so excited," he said, "I didn't even say hello. It's me, Gus-Ira, it's Ben. Say, I just . . ."

". . . and that's just for starters," Kitty's voice said, "you haven't heard the . . ."

"Kitty, is that you? Hi, it's Ben. There must be some freak connection. How are you, Kitty dear, how are you, Gus-Ira?"

". . . thing is he doesn't stop. I think someone should call him off, tell him that (a) number one . . ."

"Kitty? Gus-Ira?" Ben broke in.

". . . our own troubles, and (b) number two . . ."

"Hello? Hello?"

". . . water is thicker than godblood."

"Can't you hear me? This is a freak connection. Hello?"

". . . and Patty's grandstanding that time: 'He can lie beside me.' All right, I know she said it to get him off our backs, but statements like that only encourage him. These damned phone calls. I tell you, he's a sick man. *I* tell you? *He* tells you. How much longer do you think he can continue to function? I mean it. He expects to stay in Riverdale and have the family care for him. Do you realize what that would *mean?* The man's a bore with his love and loyalty. And not just Riverdale. You won't escape. It'll be Ben Flesh, the traveling invalid, Ben Flesh . . ."

"Hello?"

". . . shlepping his roadshow symptoms around the Finsberg bases like King Lear. A month or so in Riverdale. Then we parcel-post him to Noël in San Antonio. Dying on the circuit, only instead of doing his Grand Rounds on his own time and at his silly franchises it'll be at our places, *we'll* be his franchises, and don't kid yourself, it'll end up being at our expense, too. The man has no head for figures."

"No," Ben said involuntarily, "I have a head for figures. Hello?"

"Well, *I* won't have him," Kitty's voice said. "And I've spoken to Lorenz and Gertrude and Cole. I've spoken to Moss, Maxene, Oscar, Irving, and poor Jerome."

"*Poor* Jerome? Why 'poor' Jerome? What's wrong? Kitty? Gus-Ira? Hello?"

". . . feel the same. So I'm calling to tell you, Gus-Ira, *I* won't have him, no one will. And my thinking is, there ought to be a solid front on this thing. We've got to get it together, we've got to be prepared. Ben will take any advantage. Okay, when we were kids it was different, he even filled a need, I suppose, but now we've got our own families. I won't have him, Noël won't, none of the girls, none of the boys I've spoken to. So the next time he calls, try to give him some inkling. No one wants to be actually rude to the old man, no one wa—"

Her voice broke off in the middle of the word. It was as if there had been a sudden power failure, or, rather, as if the lights in one part of the house, the living room, say, had suddenly gone out while the lights in the dining room continued to burn, for Flesh could still hear the crepitation of connection. Perhaps she was catching her breath, he thought, perhaps she was biting her tongue. Water is thicker than godblood? Than *godblood?*

"No," Ben Flesh said into the phone, "you've got me wrong, Kitty. A man organizes his life around necessities, principles. Only some people, me, for example, are born without goals. There are a handful of us without obsession. In all the world. Only a handful. I live without obsession, without drive, a personal insanity even, why, that's terrible. The loneliest thing imaginable. Yet I've had to live that way, live this, this—sane life, deprived of all the warrants of personality. To team up with the available. Living this franchised life under the logo of others. And do it, these past years, under impossible burdens of discomfort. Have some feelings, Kitty, have a little pity, Gus-Ira. What, you think I like these random patterns? I'm irregular as the badly toilet-trained. The strange, the personal have been spared me. Nothing happens but disease. *Nothing* . . ."

"Hello," Gus-Ira said jovially, "this is Gus-Ira Finsberg. I'm sorry that I'm not in to take your call. This is a recording. If you'll wait for the little electronic beep and leave your name, number, and message, my Phone-Mate 270 will record you for two minutes and I'll get back to you just as soon as I return." There was a pause. Ben heard the beep.

"It's me, Gus," he said, "it's Ben. Your Phone-Mate 270 is fucked up. Probably you put the reels in backward. You were never mechanically inclined, Gus-Ira. Even as a little boy. Goodbye."

Gus-Ira called.

"Ben," he said gloomily, "oh, Ben."

"It's all right," Ben said, "don't feel bad. Kitty's a bed wetter. I consider the source. Don't fret, Gus," he said. "Only tell me, level, do *you* feel that way? Kitty's—"

"Kitty's dead, Ben," Gus-Ira said.

"What?"

"She died. She's dead."

"When? How? What are you . . ."

"She bought it, Ben. She chafed to death."

"She . . . ?"

"All those years of wetting herself. $C_5H_4N_4O_3$."

"Is this a code? Gus-Ira? Is this a freak connection?"

"$C_5H_4N_4O_3$. It's uric acid. The basic component of gout, of kidney stones. The salts of piss, Ben. She'd been thrashing them into her thighs for a lifetime. In effect, she'd driven kidney stones into her capillaries and flesh. They blocked the blood. Uremia, too. Uremic poisoning. Her body choked on her pee. She chafed to death."

"She died of pee-pee?"

"That's about it, Ben."

"Of sissy? Of number one?"

"Yes," Gus-Ira said, "tragic."

"Death by *tinkle?*"

"We were shocked."

"I don't know what to . . ."

"We never thought. We were shocked."

"Gus-Ira, I'm so sorry. If there's anything . . ."

"We knew it would happen, we just never thought—it just never occurred to us that— She used to read in bed. We'd tell her, we'd plead with her, 'Kitty darling, get yourself grounded. Suppose you dozed off, suppose you're lashing about and your bedlamp falls over. If the wire is worn, if there's a hairline crack in the insulation . . .' "

"In the insulation?"

"She could have been electrocuted in her urine, Ben."

"Jesus."

"So we always anticipated, we just never thought she'd chafe herself to death. You never know."

"I don't," Ben Flesh said, "I can't— Listen, is Kitty in Riverdale?"

"They're shipping her body to LaGuardia. I'm flying in today. I've been out of town. I'm out of town now. They had to call me in Cleveland. When I heard, I asked if anyone had gotten in touch with you. Helen didn't know. There's a lot of confusion. When something like this happens . . . I figured I'd take a chance. I hate having to break news like this, but you had to know."

"Yes," Ben said, "thanks, thank you for calling. I'll, I'll get up to Riverdale. I'll see you this evening."

They said goodbye.

So he hadn't heard. He'd been out of town and hadn't heard Kitty's bitter message about him on the Phone-Mate. He felt Gus-Ira was an ally and was immediately ashamed that he could feel such cheap relief when poor Kitty lay dead. Poor Kitty. What he'd said was now true and he *did* consider the source. She had been chafed; even as she'd complained of Ben to Gus-Ira, she had spoken out of her chafed, worn, cricket irritability, a woman rubbed a lifetime the wrong way. Poor Kitty. And then he thought of something else she'd said on Gus-Ira's device. "Poor Jerome," she'd said. He'd forgotten about the tests. He called Jerome and got Wilma, his godcousin's wife, a girl he'd met only once. The woman was crying. He felt bad that he had not been closer to his godcousins' families. "I'm sorry," Ben said when he had explained who he was, "I just heard about it. I appreciate how torn up you must be. How's Jerome taking it, Wilma?"

"Who is this?" she shrieked. "Who *is* this son of a bitch?"

"It's Ben," he said. "I told you. We met once when I was coming through Fort Worth. I took you and Jerome to dinner."

"Who the hell do you think you are?" she demanded fiercely. "The man's dead and you ask how he's *taking* it? What kind of a son of a bitch . . . ?"

"Dead? *Who's* dead? Kitty's dead. *Who's* dead?"

"Jerome's dead. My husband. Oh, God," she wailed. "Poor Jerome."

"Jerome? Oh, Wilma," he said. "Oh, Wilma. I didn't . . . I meant about Kitty. Jerome's dead, too? *Jerome?* When? What happened? Oh dear. How? What happened?"

He had died that morning. Wilma had been with him. It was the tests. The Fort Worth doctors were not satisfied with the explanation about Jerome's lifelong chronic constipation. They suspected cancer of the bowel, the colon. They didn't buy the theory that his body simply didn't produce enough fecal matter. They thought a virus or some kind of tapeworm must be attacking, devouring his godcousin's shit. The tests were enemas which produced nothing but the soapy water they had just shot up his behind. High colonics. Oil enemas. They fed him roughage and gave him massive doses of the most powerful laxatives. They put him on a sort of potty and made him stay there until he went. It was like being toilet-trained, Wilma said. His legs went to sleep, his arms and hands. He begged to be put back to bed, but they insisted they had to find out was causing his constipation. They named a dozen diseases that could kill him if they weren't able to analyze, not the normal, beautiful stools he faithfully produced every two weeks, but the incipient shards they were now convinced were incubating morbidity in his gut. They had to find out what was destroying these. They could not reach it, take samples, with even the longest of their instruments. Cutting into the intestine was too dangerous. The roughage, the potent laxatives were the only way, the last resort. He had to stay on his giant potty until he did his duty. Wilma was with him. He squeezed and squeezed. Poor Jerome. He tried to cooperate. He forced himself, he labored. (It was *like* labor, like giving birth.) The tests killed him. The laxatives were too potent. He shat out his empty intestines, his long red bowel of blood. Death by caca. Death by crap.

And so one was dead of bed wetting. And one of constipation. Number one, Ben thought. Number two.

He wanted Jerome's body sent to New York. Wilma couldn't think. He made the arrangements with Fort Worth himself. He would handle everything—death's take-charge guy.

He gave funerals away as others might bring a coffee cake to the mourners, or a Jell-O mold. "It's the least I can do," he said and gave away funerals as perhaps his godfather Julius might once have papered the house for an ailing show. Left and right he gave them away. So many were dying.

Moss rented a car at the airport to drive up to Riverdale. He and it were totaled when he smashed broadside at forty-five miles an hour into the side of an oil truck made out of a particular metal alloy his perfect, beautiful eyes could not see.

Helen, in her grief, drank heavily. The Finsbergs hid all the liquor and she left the house in a black mood looking for a tavern. She hailed a taxi. They tried to follow, but lost her in traffic. The police called from the morgue. She had found a place on Eighth Avenue, a hangout for whores, pimps, and degenerates. She drank more heavily than ever—a hell of a binge—and in her foul mood picked a fight with a very butch bull dyke. The dyke tried to defend herself as best she could, but Helen, made vicious by drink, was hitting her with everything she had. The poor bull dyke was terrified and broke a beer stein on the bar and cut Helen's throat with it before Helen could choke the life out of her.

"It was self-defense," the police said. "Everybody in the bar will swear to that. We don't think you have a case."

"We know," Noël said, sobbing heavily. "Sometimes she got like that. She was a mean drunk."

"Couldn't handle the stuff, eh?" the cop said sympathetically. "That's too bad."

"Oh oh," Noël said and, in his grief, plunged his long nails into his hair, scratching fiercely at his cradle cap.

The doctor said it must have been the bacteria he picked up in the morgue that caused the blood poisoning he rubbed into his head like shampoo and killed him.

The Finsbergs were inconsolable. In their sorrow they closed their decimated ranks and turned once more to Ben.

"We don't" Lorenz said,

"understand," said Ethel.

"We were always" Sigmund-Rudolf said,

"musical comedy sort of"

"people," said Patty, LaVerne, and Maxene.

Ben nodded.

It had all happened so quickly—five deaths within thirty-six hours—that even Ben could not absorb it. He asked the people at Riverside Chapel to stall, to prepare the bodies for burial, of course, but to keep them in a sort of holding pattern before they were interred. He did not tell the twins and triplets that he was waiting for all the returns to come in, an official body count.

"Mr. Flesh," said Weinman, the Director at Riverside, "what can I say at a time like this? You and the family have my deepest sympathy."

"Thank you," Ben said.

They were in the coffin room, a sort of display area for caskets not unlike an automobile showroom. The coffins, open toward one end, looked oddly like kayaks. Ben wanted identical caskets for the twins and triplets—cherry walnut, the best.

"We don't have them," Weinman said. "Something like this, so unusual, we just don't have that many in stock. There's the floor sample and the two in the basement, and that's it. I suppose I could call Musicant in Lodi, New Jersey, he might have one, but he's the only other funeral home in this part of the country that handles this particular item."

"We need five," Ben said, "maybe more. The floor sample, the two in the basement is three."

"I'll call Gutterman-Musicant, but if they won't give me a wholesale price, well, I'm afraid you'll have to absorb the cost, plus, of course, our legitimate profit."

A young man was walking among the caskets. He was red-eyed, unshaved. He looked as if he had a cold. One of Riverside's salesmen walked along silently beside him. The man stopped beside a dark walnut coffin. "This one?" he asked, his voice breaking.

The salesman, who wore a bright plaid-patterned suit, glanced at the coffin, at the young man in blue jeans. "The price is at the foot."

"Thirty-five hundred dollars? So much?"

"It's walnut. There are no nails. As I explained, the price is inclusive. You get the preparation of the body, you get the use of our chapel. The cheap coffins are down this way." The salesman moved off.

"This one is beautiful. It's like a, like a bed. Like a berth the porter makes up on a sleeper. It's beautiful. My mother loved beautiful things. Me you can burn up, but my mother—thirty-five hundred dollars." He looked toward the salesman, who was standing beside a stained pine box. The young man went toward him.

"Take the walnut," Ben Flesh said thickly.

The boy turned around. He looked at Ben. "It's thirty-five hundred dollars," he said.

"I own the franchise," he said. "Sons don't have taste like yours today. We're discontinuing the model. I just told my funeral director, Mr. Weinman."

"Look, I don't want to bargain," the boy said.

"Who's bargaining? It's a sin to give a discount on a coffin. It's against our religion. I just told you. Take it. It's free."

"I can't . . ."

"You can't?" Ben roared. "You *can't?* You can't, get out. Your mother loved beautiful things and you can't? It looks like a bed made up on a sleeper, and you can't? You *can't?* You can't give Mom a ride in the dirt? You *can't?*" He turned to the salesman. "Burn it. *Burn* it! He don't want it, burn it. I told you yesterday we were discontinuing. He don't want it for nothing, everything all inclusive, the preparations, the chapel, the flowers, the death certificate in triplicate, the notice in the *Times*, the hearse and limo, burn the goddamned thing."

"The flowers," the salesman said, "the notice in the *Times*, the cars are— All that's—"

"All inclusive," Flesh said, "all inclusive is all inclusive, all death's party favors. *Burn it,*" he shouted.

"No," the boy said, "if you're going to burn it . . . I mean, if you're really going to burn it—"

"All right, then," Flesh said. "Fix him up."

"Hey, listen," the boy said, "thank you. I mean, well, thank you. I . . ."

"Look, please, we're doing inventory here." He turned to the salesman. "Take him. Write up the papers."

The young man came up to Flesh and extended his hand. "Hey . . ." he said.

Ben took his hand but couldn't feel it. "Listen, what can I say at a time like this?" Flesh said. "You and the family have my deepest sympathy." Weinman looked at him. "Look," Flesh told him, "about the cherry walnut—it makes no difference. Just so they're identical. They grew apart, but they died together. Identical boxes. That's a must." He turned to go, then looked back at Weinman. "You make them look real, you understand? *Real.* It takes make-up, all right use make-up. They know the smell. These are boys and girls grew up backstage. Make-up wouldn't dishonor them. They wouldn't faint from pancake powder. All their lives they lived behind the costumes of their faces. But *real.* No waxworks. You'll do your best, yes, Weinman?"

There were no more deaths. All the returns were in. At the graveside he thought about this. Three of the girls were dead. (He included poor, bored Lotte, who had childhood diseases as an adult, and who, in her suicide, had died of her peculiar symptoms, too—tantrum.) Three of the boys. The two houses were in equilibrium again. The checks and balances. No one had the votes now, and he was safe. And ashamed of his safety.

In their grief—their noses and eyes swollen with tears and floating behind faces puffed with sorrow like people pouting into balloons (for they had identical emotions as well as identical taste buds, identical hearts, tempers, sympathies, sensibilities)—they were as alike as ever, differing more from their dead sibs than from each other. Weinman's people had done a good job. The look of waxworks had been unavoidable, but cosmetics suited them, death's rouges and greasepaints, its eyeliners and facials—all its landscape gardening, all its prom night adjustments. They might have been Finsberg chorus girls and boys seen close. Fleshed out in their morticianed skin, identical as skulls.

The rabbi, the same man, now grown old, who had officiated at Julius's funeral twenty-five years before, and then at Lotte's and at Estelle's, said the prayers.

Then Ben stepped forward.

"One died of tantrum, her grownup's colic, and one of pissed beds, and another angrily tight. One of constipation and one of freak eyesight and one massaged poison into his cradle cap." He thought he knew what they were thinking. How they wept as much from contemplation as from loss. How Gertrude thought of her gravid bones and LaVerne of her organs strapped like holsters to her rib cage, how Oscar brooded over his terminal compulsive speeding and Sigmund-Rudolf about his epicenity. How Mary wondered what to make of her inability to menstruate and Ethel of her heart in its casket of tit. Each mourning for each and for his own doom. As he was moved by his multiple sclerosis, his own flawed scaffolding of nerves. Everyone carried his mortality like a birthmark and was a good host to his death. You could not "catch" anything and were from the beginning yourself already caught. As if Lorenz or Cole, Patty, Mary, or himself carried from birth the very diseases they would die of. Everything was congenital. Handsomeness to suicide. "There are," he said, "no ludicrous ways to die. There are no ludicrous deaths," and, weeping, they all held each other as they made their way from the graveside like refugees, like people blinded by tear gas, and stumbling difficult country.

He mourned the full time. A few had to leave early but he stayed on in the house in Riverdale. His position in the family restored now, they believed he would outlive them. (It had given them a new respect for him, their own sudden sense of having been condemned altering their opinion, his promise that there were no ludicrous deaths oddly reassuring to them.)

Stayed on for a week to sit an improvised, crazy *shivah*, in which Ben played the old '78's, original cast recordings from their father's hit shows: *Oklahoma! Lady in the Dark, Showboat, Brigadoon*, and

*Bloomer Girl. Allegro. Call Me Mister. Carousel. Finian's Rainbow.* All of them.

Listening, concentrating, as if at a concert, as if stoned. Not "You'll Never Walk Alone" or any of the songs of solace that Ben, or any of them, might have expected, not "Ol' Man River," or any of the you-can't-lick-us indomitable stuff, not even the showstoppers—"Soliloquy," "My Ship"—but the chorus things, the entire cast, all the cowboys and their girls singing "Oklahoma!," the veterans singing "Call Me Mister," the elf and townspeople singing "On That Great Come and Get It Day," the fishermen and their families doing "June Is Bustin' Out All Over." It was, that is, the community numbers that reinforced them, the songs that obliterated differences, among men and women, among principals and walk-ons, not the love songs, not even the hopeful, optimistic songs of the leads who, down and out, in the depths of their luck, suddenly blurt their crazy confidence. Again and again it was the townsfolk working as a chorus, three dozen voices singing as one, that got to them, appealing to some principle of twin- and triplet-ship in them, decimated as their ranks now were. The odd bravery of numbers and commonality, a sort of patriotism to one's kind. And Ben, more unlike them than ever, now he looked so old and felt so rotten, as cheered and charmed as any of the Finsbergs could have been.

And talking, talking non-stop, neither a stream of anecdote nor reminiscence nor allusion to their dead brothers and sisters, nor even to themselves, but a matrix of reference wholly out of context to their lives, telling them, for example, of the managers of his franchises, people they hadn't met, didn't know, had never heard of, people, he realized, he himself rarely thought of except during the five or so days a year he spent with each of them during his Grand Rounds.

"I go," he said, "with the Dobbs House heart, with the counterman's White Castle imagination, his gypsy's steam-table life. Hillbillies, guys with nutsy tattoos on the insides of their forearms. People called Frankie, Eddy, Jimmy—the long *e* of the lower classes. Men with two wives and scars on their pusses, with clocked socks and black shoes. One guy, the manager of my Western Auto, was totally bald, and instead of a wig he sprung for a head of tattooed hair. From fifteen feet you couldn't tell it from the real thing. It had a tattooed part, I remember, and when sideburns came in back in the sixties he had *them* added on; only the color, the dye, wasn't an exact match and it looked a little goofy.

"But that's where I pick them. My middle-management people from the barrel's bottom. Bus depots my employment agencies, the waiting room of the Cedar Rapids railroad station. If you can't find reliable people there, you can't find them anywhere. You didn't know that? Oh, sure. Certainly. An eye out always for guys who pump quarters into jukeboxes and bang the pinball. I cover the waterfront, I hire the handicapped.

"Yes, and your dropout always your best bet, battered children from broken homes and alcoholism in the bloodlines like a thoroughbred's juices. Bringing on line entire generations of those who live with expectations lowered like the barometric pressure, who neither read the fortune cookie nor spell out even their own horoscopes in the funny papers. Can you *imagine* such indifference? Not despair, not even resignation finally, just conditioning so complete you'd think bad luck was a congenital defect or a post-hypnotic suggestion. Yes, and the statistical incidence of failure Euclidean, pandemic. These are the people I work with, who work for me, these are my partners, the world's put-upon, its A.W.O.L.'d and Article 15'd and Captain's Masted, its chain-ganged and undesirably discharged, all God's plea-bargained, all His sharecropper'd migratory-worked losers, His scummy, heavily tail-finned Chevrolet'd laid-off. Last hired, first fired. This is company picnic we're talking, softball, bratwurst, chug-a-lug'd beer. The common-law husbands of all high-beehived, blond-dyed, wiry waitresses and check-out girls.

"And I as fairy godfather to them as Julius to me. Having to talk them into it. Having to talk them into even talking to me, talk them into listening to my propositions, who think at first I'm just some queer—and that itself working to my advantage, because they think I'll buy them beers and they'll pretend to go along with me, thinking: Afterward, when he makes his move, I'll hit him on the head, roll him in the alley—looking for action, rough trade, God knows what. And using even that, their low opinion of me—always kept to themselves, always suppressed and even, in an odd way, *polite*, not ever, you understand, condescending, simply because I'm well dressed and well spoken and outrank them good-luckwise, which they mistakenly take for a sort of talisman or voucher, *Good Housekeeping*'s Seal of Approval, the earnest money of my faggot-or-no-faggot superior humanity—confronting them with it, hitting the nail smack bang dab on the head like the palmist or astrologer they don't go to, not because they're not superstitious—they're superstitious: Catholic saints on their fundamentalist Protestant dashboards, rabbits' feet, dice adding up to seven whichever way they're turned—but because they don't believe they have a fate, and behind that, the bottom line of that, not really believing that they even have a life—such patient people, such humble ones—laying it all out for them, their plans to rob me, to knock my head even as they maintain a genuine respect for me, for the clothes I wear, so that afterward what they'll remember of the knockabout won't be the body contact but the feel of my wool suit and silk shirt and rep tie and felt hat and the soft leather of my shoes. Second-guessing their plans and conspiracies, an armchair quarterback of my own muggings and beatings. And all that just to get their *attention!*

"And only then, when I have it, hitting them with what even they can see is just good business, no scheme, no wild-ass proposition, no sky-high pipedream, but a plan. Plain as the cauliflower on their ear, true as a calendar.

"That who was there better in this world to bet on than guys who have nothing? References? I don't want references. If anything the reverse. Records let them show me. Strange, unexplained lacunae in their *curriculum vitae*. Bad write-ups from Truancy, Credit, Alimony Court. Then convincing them that they can do the job, a lead-pipe cinch for persons like themselves who had, some of them, actually *used* lead pipes, or anyway pickaxes, handles, the tough truncheons of the strikebreakers, the ditch digger's hardware, who'd horsed the unskilled laborer's load, and done the thousand shit details, all the infinite cruddy combinations. 'Putz,' I've said, 'you've hauled hod and worked by smells in the dark the wing nuts of grease traps. What, you're afraid of a pencil?' 'I never got past the fifth grade,' they'd say. 'Terrific,' I tell them, 'then you know your multiplication tables. Long division you can do. Calculus there's no call for in the Shell-station trade.' 'But I ain't no mechanic,' they object. 'Who? You? No mechanic? A guy who jumps wires and picks locks? You're fucking Mandrake. Look, look at the hands on you. Layers of dirt under the nails like shavings from the archaeologist's digs. Enough grease and oil in the troughs of your knuckles to burn signal fires for a day and a night. *You?* No mechanic? You got a feel for leverage like Archimedes. Don't crap me, pal. Don't wear my patience. You're a bum, you know character. You can hire trained mechanics from the Matchbook Schools of Repair. I'm making you Boss, you can sit back and interview guys who take jet engines apart.' 'But why me? I'm a nobody. Why would you give *me* this chance?' 'Because you're a nobody. I raise your expectations like a hard-on. Where else can I buy the loyalty and devotion I'm looking for if not from a nobody like you?'

"And this way with all of them—the fast-food franchises, the goods and services, the Roto-Rooter and Burger King. This my edge as much as the prime rate: that if you want somebody who'll work like a dog you get a dog. And no one in the business with better employee relations, no one with as good an efficiency record. Because we're talking *business*, you see, small shopkeep and the bourgeois heart. Certainly. Yes."

"Yes," Gus-Ira said.

"Yes," he said. "It's late. I'm wearing you out. I've worn myself out. We'll talk more in the morning."

But Gertrude died. Even with some of the Finsbergs gone, dead, or returned to their homes in other parts of the country, the Riverdale house was still quite full: the twins' and triplets' wives and husbands and their small children crowding the huge home. Ben offered to stay in a motel, but the others wouldn't hear of it. They doubled up, rented cots from Abbey Rents. Ben himself sleeping with his godcousins' small sons and daughters in Julius's and Estelle's old room, the big bedroom lined with Porta-cribs and rented cots and looking oddly like some specially outfitted casualty ward.

One of the wives said she'd heard Gertrude say she felt sort of grotty and that she thought she'd take a shower, but the bathrooms were occupied, all but the maid's, which had a deep tub but no shower. They found her in the morning. She had drowned. From her position—her belly to the bottom of the tub—and from a discrete kneecap-shaped dent in the Cashmere Bouquet, they determined that she had evidently dropped the soap and was searching for it on her hands and knees in the cloudy water. Apparently she'd struck the bar with her knee, slipped, and gone under. With her heavy marrowless bones she'd been unable to raise herself.

"She couldn't swim of course," Cole said.

"Well, she had wonderful form, but she couldn't float," Ethel said.

"She never took baths," Irving said.

"Doctor's orders," Lorenz said.

"Just sponged herself off in the shower," said LaVerne.

"Why couldn't she wait till a shower was free?"

"She was always impatient."

"She was a damned fool," Cole said. "You know, you have an affliction like that, a frame like the Petrified Forest, you take a bath you're just asking for it."

"She died," Ethel said, "a gangster's death."

"A gangster's death? Oh no, darling, she was just a little careless is all. Don't say she died a gangster's death," Ben said.

"A gangster's death, yes," Ethel said, "like some hoodlum in a cement kimono, a lead coffin, steel galoshes. Oh no," she sobbed, "it's awful, it's so grotesque."

"There are no ludicrous deaths," Ben said.

"There are," she cried. "Oh, Ben, there are. We die them."

"Don't jinx us," Irving said. "Why do you talk like that? Are you trying to jinx us? I think we should bury Gertrude and get the hell out of here before anything else happens. It's been some week."

They looked at racially prejudiced Irving. They seemed to agree with him. Even Ben agreed. Gertrude was cremated and it took three men to carry her ashes.

"Slag," the funeral director said. "I never saw anything like it. The woman was slag."

They left New York after the funeral. Ben went back to his Travel Inn site. Where there was a message from Lorenz.

Bad weather in St. Louis had caused Irving's flight to be diverted

to Chicago. Bad weather in Chicago had caused it to be diverted to
Detroit. The weather in Detroit was beautiful but Irving, out of
sorts from his tiring journey, died there in a race riot of his own
devising.

Ethel had a simple, or limited, mastectomy. They got all the
cancer but accidentally cut off her heart.

Cole complained of headache one morning and was dead that
afternoon. The autopsy revealed that his brain was crawling with
termites.

Sigmund-Rudolf called.

"I don't want to hear it," Ben said.

"Listen to me, Ben, it's—"

"I don't want to hear it."

". . . important."

"I don't want to hear it. No," Ben said, "I'm hanging up. I don't
want to hear it."

"Ben, listen, will you?" Sigmund-Rudolf said.

"I don't want—"

"There are only a few of us left."

". . . to hear it! I'm not listening to this!"

"There are only a few of us left and the prime rate is going up
and down like a Yo-Yo. Father couldn't have anticipated when he
wrote his will that so many of us would die."

"I won't hear this," Ben said. "I don't want to hear about one
more death. I won't listen. I don't want to hear it."

"Nobody's dead, Ben. I mean nobody else. Gus-Ira, Lorenz,
Oscar. Myself. LaVerne, Patty, and Mary. Maxene. We're still
alive, Ben. Nothing's happened to us."

"Nobody else has died?"

"No. I'm trying to tell you."

"Gus-Ira and Lorenz? Oscar? Patty? LaVerne and Mary? Maxene? You? You're all well?"

"We're fine. I'm trying to tell you."

"That's all right then."

"Sure. It's just that Father couldn't have known. When he stipulated that we'd guarantee your loans— There were eighteen of us.
Ten are gone. Listen, Ben, you're welcome to live in Riverdale.

Everyone's agreed on that. God knows, none of the rest of us wants the place, but that other stuff, the prime interest thing, we can't go along with that anymore. We'd be spreading ourselves too thin. You're on your own, Ben. I mean, I know you've never stuck us for a penny, but with so many gone, with conditions the way they are, the risk is too great. We can't hold your paper, Ben. You understand, don't you? Don't you, Ben?"

"I don't want to hear it!"

# 4

In Ringgold, Georgia, the prime rate was 7½ percent. Elsewhere it was 8 percent, 8¼, 7¼, 9. Ben had never seen anything like it, the economy heavily fronted, arbitrarily banded, whorled with high pressure and low, laid out like yesterday's weather on the meteorological map in today's paper. All climate's swayback boundaries like wavy strokes of chocolate on scrunched layer cake, the jigsaw arrangements of contested territory. Freak, unseasonable economy.

He needed additional funds. The strike, cost overruns, forced him to take out a second loan. He wanted more, but all Modell Sanford would let him have was an extra $125,000. He offered his ice-cream interests, his Dairy Queen and Baskin-Robbins and Mister Softee, as collateral. (They were already into him for his Western Auto and his Taco Bell. Indeed, almost all his franchises were pledged, hostage to the success of the motel.)

Sanford had asked to see the list again, his portfolio of franchises.

"The One Hour Martinizing," the banker said, "the One Hour Martinizing *and* the ice-cream parlors, and we'll shake hands, part friends, and have us a deal."

"Not the dry cleaners," Ben had said.

"Well, heck," Modell Sanford said, "I don't see why you'd stick at that. I don't figure you have you more than twenty, twenty-five thousand tied up in that place."

"Sentimental. The One Hour Martinizing is of sentimental value to me."

"Yeah, but lookee, friend, you're about fifty thousand shy."

"But you'd have the motel," Ben said. Modell was dubious. "All ight," Ben said, "here's what we'll do. Keep the ice creams, forget about the dry cleaners, and I'll put up my Cinema I, Cinema II."

Modell Sanford looked at him.

"Mr. Ben, that's funky. Them theaters is worth 'bout a quarter million. They your biggest asset. You a serious businessman. Why'd you want to make a deal like that?"

"Because I'm very confident. I feel very confident about the Travel Inn venture. Look, Mr. Sanford, it's my risk. You can run an audit on the theaters. I'll pay for it myself. If everything isn't exactly as I've represented it, throw me out. Take all my flavors and the two picture houses and the motel, too."

"Don't have to run no audit. Just have to make one phone call to my credit people in Oklahoma City. All right, Mr. Flesh, you come on in tomorrow morning and I'll give you my decision."

The decision was yes, of course. And since the banker didn't wish to take advantage of him, Ben was permitted to withdraw his Dairy Queen stand. But before he drew up the papers, Modell Sanford reintroduced the One Hour Martinizing. For some reason he fixated on the dry-cleaning plant in Missouri, perhaps because he sensed that Ben was telling the truth about its importance to him. Flesh was incensed. He said that if Sanford still wanted the One Hour Martinizing he would take back all his ice-cream businesses, *plus* his Cinema I, Cinema II. He refused to budge. "I'll borrow money in Chattanooga," he said.

"Interest rate's a point higher in Chattanooga."

"Fine," Ben said.

"Oh, come on now," Modell Sanford had said, "what you want go grandstanding me, what you want get so hot for? This motel is gone be good for you and good for Ringgold, Georgia. Tell you what, you promise to make sure all your help is Ringgold folks and I'll drop the One Hour Martinizing."

"Where we stand?" Ben asked. "I forget."

The banker explained where they stood and they shook hands and signed the papers.

By the time the Inn was ready, he had had to take out a third loan. His godcousins, as Sigmund-Rudolf had warned, withdrew their support. Ben would not contest their decision in court, but by now his investment in the Inn was so great that all his franchises, the One Hour Martinizing included, were hostage to it, his businesses held for ransom.

Lorenz's temperature dropped from its constant 102.4 degrees to 98.6. He hung on for three weeks and froze to death.

Though the surviving Finsbergs were all invited to the opening, none could come.

"But I don't care about the prime rate thing," Ben told them on the telephone. "I don't even blame you. We're still godcousins. Please," he said. "Please come. Let's be together."

Patty promised to try to make it, but even she did not show up. Ben meant it, understood, and forgave their reluctance to co-sign for him—the motel would cost about a million dollars—but was hurt when not a single Finsberg would accept his invitation.

The truth was, they would not go out. They were afraid to die.

Ringgold, Georgia, population 1,381, is a mile east of Interstate 75, less than ten miles south of Chattanooga, Tennessee, where Interstate 24 crosses 75. It is 539 miles north of Orlando, Florida, and Disney World.

Ben Flesh had chosen it for the site of his most important venture with a good deal of exactitude and care. Indeed, almost five years before, even before Disney World had officially opened in October 1971, or Interstate 75 and 24 were completed, Flesh had consulted the Automobile Association. He had wanted to know near which large city a family of four, starting out from the Chicago, Cleveland, Indianapolis, St. Louis, Cincinnati, and Columbus metropolitan areas and hoping to make it to Disney World in two days, might be likely to stop for the night. Chattanooga, Tennessee, seemed, according to all the parameters that could be known at the time, the most probable location. Though it would be a long, difficult drive from Chicago or Cleveland, it was merely a pleasant day's ride from Indianapolis, St. Louis, and Columbus, and an absolutely leisurely one from Cincinnati. There were, however, either built, or projected, or already under construction, four Travel Inns in Chattanooga. A fifth would have been redundant. Flesh looked at his maps again.

Of course, he'd thought, the state line. Chattanooga sat exactly on Tennessee's straight, ruled southern border like a house on a blueprint. The state line, America's and distance's gravitational pull, and Georgia, beneath it, even northern Georgia, the South, the *deep* South like a trench in the ocean. The South for those vacationing Midwesterners anyway, their one-night stand and grits for breakfast in Dixie, an edge to the trip, for somehow one knew, even if one had never been there, that Florida was not the *South*. Florida was the deep East, and Tennessee was not southern either but merely defunct hillbilly, some queer smudge of country and industry. Georgia was the South, Georgia was where they would stay, the father driving, breasting—if not for the romance, then for the accomplishment—one more state line, one more milestone, like a runner busting a tape.

He felt that way himself; traveled as he was, he felt that way himself, a mystique about state lines, a sense one had that there was something not just foreign but perhaps even illicit, perhaps actually illegal, about the devices offered there. They were, for a few miles this side and a few miles that, free ports of a kind, where ordinary ordinance and day-to-day due process could be fudged—law's and territory's olly olly okshen free, an odd three-mile limit where fireworks were openly sold, gas discounted, and liquor and cigarettes offered at reduced prices, where kids could drive cars at fifteen, and couples got married without waiting for blood tests, where you could bet on horses or purchase lottery tickets and the pinball machines paid off in cash, where whorehouses thrived and gambling in roadhouses. West Memphis, Arkansas; West Yellowstone, Montana; Covington, Kentucky; Crown Point, Indiana; Calumet City, Illinois—American Ginzas. Wide open, but somehow cutting both ways and watch out for the speed traps. And everything up front, Wisconsin pushing its cheeses at you once you left Illinois, Florida its oranges, Georgia its pecans, Louisiana its pralines.

So it would be on the Georgia side of Chattanooga, yet close enough to pull in the Tennessee television stations. It was astonishing, once one stopped to think about it, that *all* the motel were not in Ringgold, Georgia. To Flesh, who had worked it out who, once the Interstates were complete and Disney World had opened, had actually hired drivers, starting out in Indianapolis and Columbus and St. Louis, to tail families driving south—he paid reservation clerks in various motels around the park for names and anticipated arrival times—it seemed inevitable. How delighted he'd been when report after report came back: *Chattanooga*, they stay in Chattanooga.

But that was before the Yom Kippur war, that was before the oil embargo, that was before the energy crisis, that was before the 55-mile-an-hour speed limit had been imposed nationwide. That was before, finally, the two-day drive from St. Louis or Chicago or Indianapolis or Columbus to Disney World had become a three-day drive. Come on, he thought, come *onnn*, Cincinnati!

Oh, he thought, farseeing Flesh, prophetic Ben, oh, oh, the Ezekielized connections, the, to him, visible network of causality. Dial the phone in Texas, it rings in Paris. (And yet, and yet, if it turned out I was mistaken, why, I was honestly mistaken, nobly mistaken, for this is the way things are done in the world. He thought of polls, straw votes, telephone samplings, trial balloons, sneak previews with their audience-reaction cards, consumer research, feasibility studies, all enterprise's three-spoon tests. Of handicapping the world, of infinite possibility like hats in the ring, of flags run up flagpoles to see who salutes, of all ever-diminishing options which reduced themselves at last to a sort of Hobson's choice, the inevitable if-this-then-that sequences of science and syllogism. Nobly mistaken. For if I paid off room clerks in Orlando, if I had Impalas tailed and station wagons, and studied the progress of the Interstates, or, more, connived—and I did—to discover where they would be, where the exits would be placed, learning the distances between gas stations, between rest areas, toilet facilities, the Gas/Food/Lodging synapses of American physiology, reconnoitering the as yet no-man's-land and enemy lines and possible beachheads of the tourist buck—the images military because the discipline was—if, that is, the bulk of my accomplishment was mere dog-soldier spadework, why then at least the cause for it was anchored in inspiration. Disney World, I thought, when I first heard it proposed, when the name was itself a trial balloon, my God, it will draw Americans like flies to sweets, entire families— for surely, I recognized, no one, no *one* would go to such a place alone; this was something collective; there was something exponentially tandem in the very prospect of such a journey, and one could almost forget about single rooms or even tables for two; this would be big, *big*—and I shall have to get roll-away beds, Porta-cribs, playground equipment, candy machines, comic-book stands, refrigeration units for bottles, formulas. Noble. In a way, heroic, even epic.

Of course noble. Of course heroic. Of course epic. For I was in the big time now. Up there, at least in spirit, with Aeneas, Brigham Young, Penn and Pike and Penrose, with Roger Williams, Theseus, Dido, Brutus, and Peter the Great and Alexander, Czar of all the Alexandrias. With Moses and Paul and Del Webb and Bugsy Siegel. With Disney himself, the Disney of Anaheim no less than the Disney of Florida. Up there, at least in spirit, at least on their wavelengths, with all those Founders, legendary and historic, with a sense of timing and prophecy on them, perfect pitch for the potential incipient in what lesser men might have looked on as hills, desert, swampland, stony ground. There in spirit and brotherhood with whoever it was who first said, "Let there be Chicago, let it be here." That long line of visionaries who defoliated jungle simply by giving it their attention, who, looking at mountains, saw fortresses; at valleys, the laws of gravity pulling sweet water. Who second and third guessed the shabby givens of place and impediment, Johnny Appleseeds of commerce and government and a dozen God's countries, swell places to raise kids or nice to visit.

Having, that is, what *they* had—criteria, standards, the surveyor imagination, the blueprint heart.)

Ringgold, Georgia, with its labor force of busboys, waiters, maids, auditors, desk clerks, and the rest, its honest day's drive from major cities of the north and midwest, its blunt smack dab existence almost exactly between the points of origin and destination, was, would have been, and would be again, if there was lasting peace in the Middle East, if OPEC came round and detente worked, the perfect place for Flesh to pitch his now million-dollar tent. And how far off was he, anyway? Less than two hundred miles. (Atlanta would be the logical stopping point on the second night of the now three-day drive to Disney World.) What's two hundred miles? In a universe that was probably infinite, what *was* two hundred miles? Not a stone's throw, not a good spit, less than a lousy molecule of space. What's two hundred miles? Bank-fuckruptcy, that's all.

And even that anticipated by bright Ben, by farseeing Flesh. After, admittedly, he had already committed, after the land had been purchased, bulldozed, and the foundations were laid and the buildings almost up. So it wasn't really too late. Things could be done. He could, for example, together with the Motel Owners' Association of Greater Chattanooga and the Ringgold Chamber of Commerce, arrange to bribe all the state troopers of Tennessee, Kentucky, Missouri, Illinois, Ohio, and Indiana not to stop speeders, or the high-ups in the highway departments of those states not to post speed limits. Sure, sure he could. Or, shifting emphasis, capture the Lookout Mountain trade, the Rock City clientele, the Incline Railroad and Confederama crowd. The See Seven States set. Oh yes. But he meant it. For once he had gotten the gist, picked up the seismological vibes of his earthquake times, even, that is, before the Finsbergs had begun to die—his invitations to them to join him there as his guests had been, well, love, of course, but in part, at least, his way of papering the house—and while he marked time waiting for the electricians to return, he had begun to write copy for his brochures, brochures which appealed directly to those visitors to Chattanooga's tourist attractions: "Now that you've seen seven states, why not sleep in one of them tonight? Spend your evening in America's newest Travel Inn—Travel Inn, Ringgold, Ga." "Enjoy Lookout Mountain? Now Lookout for Travel Inn, Ringgold, Georgia—the world's newest!" To passengers on the Incline Railroad: "Inclined to recline in luxurious accommodations? Call Ringgold, Ga.'s Travel Inn's Famous Courtesy Car toll free. Spend the night in America's Newest Travel Inn." "You've seen Confederama. Enjoy an evening in the Gateway to the Old South—Ringgold, Georgia's Travel Inn. Old-fashioned Southern Hospitality in Old Dixie's newest Travel Inn."

And took the copy, together with photographs and an architect's sketches, to printers in Chattanooga. And his best slogans to a firm in Atlanta which printed bumper stickers. (These he would give to employees in the souvenir shops of Rock City and Confederama and Lookout Mountain and all those other places, paying them to slap them on out-of-state cars in the parking lot while their owners were out seeing the sights.)

Except that he was oddly—inasmuch as he did not yet understand why he should feel this way—disturbed that he should do this (not because of the licking he expected he might have to take, not because of the reverses—he'd had reverses—not even because he could not stand up to adversity), feeling what he took to be a sort of commercial queasiness at such methods. Then he understood, the meaning as clear as *prima facie* dream. That—that he had come out of the closet, stepped out from under, and taken leave of, his anonymity. No longer Mister Softee, no longer Fred Astaire, no longer Colonel Sanders's lieutenant or just another subject of the Dairy Queen, but Ben his-own-self Flesh, out in the open, standing up to be counted. Travel Inn or no Travel Inn, dis-, as it were, enfranchised. Cut off and grown apart as the suddenly changed features of the twins and triplets. Which, too, he had now begun to understand. As he was beginning to understand their oddball deaths. (Maxene died. She, whose hair had begun to thin while she was still a girl, and who had had to wear wigs woven from her brothers' and sisters' barbered locks, had become completely bald. She lost her cilia, her eyebrows and lashes, lost her pubic hair, the tiny hairs in her behind, all the downy hair along her legs and arms that defended the pores, the protective bristles in her nostrils that could no longer screen and trap the tiny particles and bacterial motes that, now she was only skin, invaded her system and killed her. The news came to him on a postcard from Patty: "Dear Ben, Maxene bought it. She lost all her hair and died, one could say, of terminal baldness. Maybe the wigs we gave her to wear from our clippings were some sort of hairy homeopathy. You think? With so many of us gone, there just wasn't enough hair to make her wigs anymore and she died. The boys have the votes now. Love. P.")

As he was beginning to understand everything. Everything. Seeing, in the shadow of Lookout Mountain, all connections and relations, all causes linked to their effects like some governing syntax of necessity and fate.

It was clear, for example, that with two-day trips become three-day trips and three-day trips four and five, and so on, the country had been stretched, an increment of distance thrust between any two points. He foresaw a lowering of public standards, taste's tightened belt, the construction of cheap cut-rate motels like the tourist cabins of the thirties, meager, frill-less. (The frill is gone.) What was happening was almost glandular. The scale of things was changing, space compounding itself like the introduction of a new dimension. He should have had a Wayco parking garage, he'd be sitting pretty. Without any additional outlay of cash he could, in two or three years, when most of Detroit's cars would be smaller, actually have increased the capacity of his garage by at least a third. It was the expanding universe here, America's molecules drifting away from each other like a blown balloon, like heat rising, the mysterious physical laws gone public. That was how to think now. (Though perhaps Wharton had known, suspected something when they had tried to drum into his head terms like "volume" and "mass.")

Take food, for example. Because of the increasing cost of energy, the day was coming when there would be sliced loaves of prepackaged toast. Industrial toast. People would be eating meat the day they bought it. Which would mean more shopping. Which would mean more walking. Which would mean more shoes. Which would mean more resoling, more replacement of heels. Or *sturdier* shoes, women walking around like practical nurses. Which would mean other ways to flaunt their femininity, which would mean tighter blouses, tighter skirts, more cosmetics, brighter colors, newer dyes.

It was all set out. The new dispensation. But not for him. Not for Ben. He was an old-timer. If he lived he would live crippled in the new world, would tch tch and my my at its strange new ways. Modern times county-courthousing him, old-timering his personality, shoving shucks in his vocabulary, thrusting by gollys into his mouth, whooshes, goldarns, I'll be's, all the phony awe and mock disgust. For he knew no other way, only the old vaudeville routines of the stagy quaint. Why, this *was* a problem. Gee whiz, shucks by golly whoosh goldarn. I'll be. I'll be.

I'll be old.

This alone had not occurred to him.

I'll be old. And I won't know how.

And it was frightening to him as it had been when as a small boy he knew that one day he would be grown up and he hadn't a clue how he would handle that either, convinced he was the only child in the world who would not know how to be an adult. Yes, and he'd been right. What sort of an adult *had* he been? A halting, stumbling one (and don't forget his disease, his M.S., which was perhaps merely the physical configuration of his personality) who made up adult life as he went along. Was he married? Did he have children? Family? Only a dead godfather and an ignored sister, only godcousins—*that* strange fairy-tale crew. Who were now only a remnant, fragmented, scattered, marginal as Shakers.

His godcousins like a chorus line or the chosen sides of childhood. How could there ever have been eighteen of them? How could they have been identical? How could they have guaranteed his loans, unconditional as magic wishes? How could he have taken all the girls for lovers and all the boys for pals? How could they have had those fantastical diseases, illness like signature, like customized curse? How could they have died off of mean drunkenness, bed wetting, monkey-wrench bones, baldness, termites, prejudice, constipation, cradle cap, and all the rest? Was all that imagined? No. None of it. He'd told them there were no ludicrous deaths. He'd been right. There was only ludicrous life, screwball existence, goofy being.

Well, he thought, I'd best get on with it, and phoned the bank manager and went into town and recruited his staff. The wives of farmers would be his maids, their teenage daughters and sons his waitresses and busboys, the poor whites of Ringgold his bellboys and clerks and maintenance people. A pick-up combo culled from the unit school's marching band his Entertainment Nitely. The mother of the man who ran the Gulf station his chef and the girls and men laid off at the nearby carpet factories his kitchen help.

# 5

RINGGOLD, GA. INNKEEPER:
BENJAMIN FLESH P.O. BOX 18 (30702)
404-727-4312 INN-DEX: 225

I-75 @ Ringgold/Chickamauga Exit. Dwntn 1
mi. Lookout Mtn 6 mi. Chickamauga Nat'l Mil
Pk 4 mi. Color TV. Pool open May–Sept. Dixieland Room Restaurant. Live Entertainment.
Babysitters. Kennels.
2 Stories. 150 Rooms. Suites. Meeting Rooms to
100.
1 Person, 1 Bed, $12 to $16. 2 Persons, $19 to
$22. Extra Person, $3. Full American Plan Available @ $14 Additional per Person. Tax 3%.

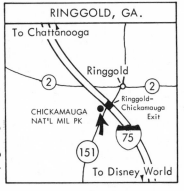

He opened for business July 22, 1975, four months after his original target date.

He was, he realized, nowhere. It was not a place. Not geographi-
cally viable. It had been, he supposed, before the Interstate had
cast down its pale double lanes of coming and going with their
white margins and their long stuck Morse of broken dashes—*I*'s,
*t*'s, *m*'s, and *s*'s—down the center of the highway like great cement
stitches—forest, foothills, frontier. A trace, perhaps, for deer,
bear, or that Indians passed through to be somewhere else. But it
was not a place. As most of earth was not a place. It took its significance from its proximity to Ringgold, to Chattanooga, to Chickamauga (which itself had become a place 112 years before and then

only for a few days, for only as long as it took the Confederate and Union soldiers to kill each other, and was then returned, after the battle, to nowhere again). But even after the road had been laid, it was something, somewhere, seen only in passing, not even observed—for it was not spectacular, pleasant country enough but never spectacular—so much as registered peripherally, there only in the marginalia of the eyes. So it was not a place until he made it one, until he had spent money to clear, chop, bulldoze, raze, as if place lay sunken beneath stone, trees, brush, the natural cloud cover of ordinary unbeautiful earth.

And now, in the fullness of his expended fortune and of a time that went back to a time before his disease had declared itself—so ambitious had he been in those days, Ben, the empire builder, the from-sea-to-shining-sea kid connecting the dots, Howard Johnson to Burger King, Burger King to IHOP, IHOP to Midas Muffler—he had made it—what? A sort of place. A feeder or way station of place—Chattanooga, Atlanta, Disney World. A sort of place as Collinsville, Illinois, was a sort of place outside St. Louis. (As the Sunoco service station which went up only after Ben had built his motel was.) As all suburbs were only a sort of place throughout the world. Throughout the solar system. (As the moon was only a sort of place because of its relation to earth.) Everywhere place sucking sort of place into its orbit.

And this, on the day he opened, is the sort of place it was:

First of all, nothing spectacular. In keeping with the sort of place it was before the furrows of Interstate had been turned.

From the outside a bracket of double-storied buildings like immense rows of mailboxes in a lobby. Brushstrokes of gold stucco the color of drying sand veneered the pile of cinder blocks that framed each unit—a wide wall of intersecting Thermopane set in aluminum splints the color of warships.

The corridors were just wider than the passageways in steamers and a long runner of carpet deep and rich as flowerpot supported a design like the thick geometry on a bandanna.

The rooms endlessly repeated themselves behind each door on either side of each corridor on each floor of each building. Eleven rooms long at the top and bottom of the bracket (times two times two), sixteen rooms long on one floor of the long center building (times two) fifteen (times two: here were the pair of suites) on the other.

Two beige headboards like the carved, distressed lengths of a child's casket were mounted like trophy at the level of one's belt on the wall and presided above an illusion of bed—box springs, mattress, thick metal frames set into large inverted "nails" like the panties on lamb chops—that was sustained by bright caramel paneled, olive bedspreads studded with a long, unbroken ganglion of print stem and leaf and flower, a Möbius strip of fabric vegetation repeated on the thick lined drapes (the lining vaguely the texture of good shower curtains). There were two captain's chairs upholstered in a tough Naugahyde the shade and texture of the cushion on a physician's chair in a consulting room. The cushions, like the mounted headboards, were inseparably joined to the chairs, as almost everything in the room was locked or bolted to something else. (A wooden wall mounting like a forearm and fist—the wood, like all the wood in the room, the color of the skins of Idaho potatoes—clenched a lamp. The mirror, the notches of its frame like those in harmonicas, was locked flush with the thin wallboard. The room's two paintings—one tenuously abstract, bold, black-stroked bark, a jagged vertical timber against a clouded, milky silver; the other strongly representational, a tobacco-colored barn that seemed to float on a field of 24-carat wheat, scratchy black trees like the tank traps on Normandy beaches, a sky blue as water in a swimming pool, Van Gogh's huge black birds like widely spreading W's—were screwed steadfastly into the wall above each headboard. A lamp on thick linked chain looped like immense fob from two fixtures in the ceiling. The television set was locked in its clawed metal tee and seemed tied to the wall itself by a broad-gauge rubber cable.) The only other furniture was a wide nightstand between the two beds; a table next to the drapes whose octagonal top bloomed from phlebitic newel; a long low dresser with two deep drawers and a composition top—the same that surfaced the nightstand and table—which looked exactly like the leather corners on a desk blotter. There was a chair on casters. There was a two-headed lamp on the nightstand. There were electric sockets like surprised hobgoblin. There was a plastic wastebasket the color of chewing gum. There was a telephone exactly the shade of ham in a sandwich, with a red message bulb blossoming from it like a tumor. There was a thermostat with a knob for High, Medium, and Low; there was a wake-up buzzer, a grill for the heating and air conditioning, a carpet the color of coffee grounds, a Bible opened to Psalms 105 and 106. There was a rough ceiling the texture of sandpaper magnified a hundred times. There was a white plastic ice bucket and four plastic glasses in a plastic tower. And a dashboard of bathroom fixture, bottle opener sunk like a coin-return slot into a wide projecting vanity, its contact paper a ruled cirrus of grain not found in nature. A shiny toilet-paper dispenser with an extra roll in the chamber. Butterscotch slabs of tile like so many pieces of toast above the bathtub and a foolscap of successively smaller towels and cloths folded like flag in a vertical rack. A spotlight of heatlamp. A grill like a speaker set in the wall. Outside the bathroom was an open recessed closet with chrome-plated pipes and slotted key rings of hanger. The metal door with its locks and chain link of bolt, its reversible multilingual DO NOT DISTURB sign hanging from the doorknob by the narrows of a perfect punched-out pear. And the framed glass fine-print innkeeper statutes of the state of Georgia, two long columns like the tiny font in accounts and dispatches from the front in old newspapers—one big Welcome and a hundred codicils of warning. The Room.

In the small lobby with its registration desk the carpet is patternless, a blend of deep russets and failing greens pale as money. A crown of chandelier above the furniture. A palimpsest of dark low Mediterranean table, notched, carved as old chest, wood nailed across woodlike artisan'd slabs of condemnation. Two lamp tables beside the couch, higher but with the same vague apothecary effect, the tables studded with rounds of brass the size of shotgun shells, the lamps that stand it a sequence of diminished and expanded wooden pots and dowels. (It is a Hindu confection of a universe—the world on an elephant, the elephant on a tortoise, the tortoise on a lotus, the lotus on the sea.) The long faint and patient curve of the brown velvet couch between the lamp tables no greater than the natural slouch and slump of a man's shoulders. There are four red lounge chairs of a slightly purplish cast like the cherries in chocolate-covered cherries. Velour, they seem to refract light, but it is only the oil slick of conflicting weave, weave set against weave like a turbulence of fabric. Where the buttons are set in the chairs' soft backs, cracks radiate like geologic flaw. At the other end of the lobby—the furniture makes walls, creating an illusion of parlor— are four deep vinyl chairs exactly the shade of ripe tomato and glossy as shined shoes.

Rising above the southern wall made by two of the strange velour lounge chairs a large display board is fastened to the wall. The ledge at the bottom, like the ledges in banks where one makes out deposit and withdrawal slips, holds brochures like a miniature newsstand (points of local interest, Disney World literature, and, under glass, seven typed index cards with the addresses and times of worship of Ringgold's churches: Seventh Day Adventist, Pentecostal, Southern Baptist, First Christian Church, Church of Christ, Church of Jesus Christ the Son of God, Church of God the Father of Jesus Christ). Above the ledge is a jagged globe of the world like a flattened, fragmented eggshell—Africa west of the United States, Australia between South America and Madagascar. The map is shaded, shows the off-white of sea level, the pale green of plains, the deep greens of hill country, the rusts of high ground. To the left of this a wheel radiates six 100-mile concentric circles of map that spin about Ringgold, Georgia, the center of the world.

He is more comfortable in the public rooms, the dark lounge with its mural Chickamauga and carriage lamps and the plain lumber of the bar like the gray timber of outhouse. Feels there the anticipation preceding a party, or, no, the sense rather of readiness, preparedness, some soldier security in the ordnance of bottles—the Scotches and bourbons and blends and gins, the handsomely formed bottles of liqueurs with their lollipop liquids, the brandies like the richly colored calligraphy on beautiful invitations (and thinks, too, of ink in old ledgers, letters, checkbooks), the vermouths and wines. The labels on the bottles are like currency. Even the glasses with their upright cords and sheaves of swizzle stick. Even the bowls of peanuts and pretzel. The bar itself a fortification, the gunmetal IBM cash register like some weapon of ultimacy, the cocktail napkins like gauze, like bandage, the infantry of glasses. The uniformity is reassuring. (The competent barman in his gold jacket, a very veteran of a fellow with all the sergeant major's crisp demeanor.) The clean ashtrays, eighteen inches apart, with their closed blue Travel Inn matchbooks. Everything. The handles of the draft beer like detonators. The refrigerator units for cans and bottles. The ice machine. The cocktail shakers. The round measured jiggers on each bottle. Everything. Even the black cushioned ledge eight inches wide that travels the edge of the bar like a soft coping. Everything. The pleasant scent of the booze, a masculine cologne smelling oddly of air-conditioned afternoons in a cinema. Yes. All is readiness, all the equipment of business and seduction and solace. (Flesh is no drinking man, but even he can appreciate the peculiar decorum here, the clean, surgical rituals of such place. More than anything else there is *that* quality in the lounge, an aura of spiffy, readied operating theater. He supposes banks have this sort of potentiality before they open for business in the morning, that planes do before they board passengers for the day's first flight.) Whatever, it is pleasant to take the air here, to see the spotless precision of the stools, correct as chorus line, disciplined as dress parade. (It is the way, too, his motel rooms look before anyone occupies them.) To take the air, deep-breathing the rich oxygen of contending liquors.

And likes, too, the restaurant—the Dixieland Room—the tables with their dinner-party aspect, the white overhanging tablecloths pleated as skirt and the bright blot of the deep blue napkins pitched as tent, discreet as wimple beside the place settings, the perfectly aligned silverware. He is pleased by the clean plates, the cups overturned on their saucers, and admires the tall mahogany salt-and-pepper shakers, the tiny envelopes of sugar in bowls at the center of the table by the netted red glass of candleholders. He likes the ring-a-rosy of captain's chairs that circle the large round tables, enjoys the solid confrontation of chairs about the tables set for four and two, notices with something like surprise the knock-kneed angle of the chair legs. And sits to a sort of practice lunch, reads, the butter set before him, stamped BUTTER, the letters so smudged they look like Hebrew characters.

He walks the grids of the new plaid carpet.

He looks about him at the strange, dark, implemented walls. (No effort has been made to fit the restaurant's decor to its name. The plans had been drawn up long before, before the two-day trip became a three-day trip.) They bristle with weapon, with ancient farm equipment, with plow and ax and hoe, with things he cannot name, all earth's agricultural backscratchers, all its iron-age instrument, its homely spade, pick, harrow, sickle, and pitchfork, all its cultivant tool, its cusps and its blades like the housekeys of ground and rock and dirt.

Yes. He is pleased. He is proprietary. More than with anything he has yet franchised. He owns all this. Owns the spare, no-nonsense meeting rooms with their accordion walls. Owns the long banquet tables and metal card chairs that wait for the Kiwanis of Ringgold, for Ringgold's Jaycees and Vets of Foreign Wars, for its ecumenical prayer breakfasts. Owns the swimming pool with its thousands of gallons of water pale green as lettuce, the blue-and-white rope floating through the blue-and-white buoys. Owns the turquoise-trimmed diving board, the surface of the board studded with friction, the shiny ladders that grow from the deck like great staples. All the contour pool furniture, the lounges of sunbath and the lanyard weave chairs, the beach umbrellas that rise through holes in the round all-weather tables on notched broad-gauged spindles and blossom above their scalloped fringe into a dome of bright pattern like wallpaper in kitchens. Owns the big Ford shuttle bus. Owns the playground equipment. Owns the 170 or so telephones. (He was, he realized, nowhere. If by nothing else he knew this by the hollow ratchety sound of the dial tone, the shrill feedback of voices like echo in tunnels. A phone company in exile. Mary was dead, the one who couldn't menstruate. Mary was dead. She had complained of a tummyache, and when, after a week, it had not gone away, she entered the hospital for tests. She died on the operating table during the exploratory. They found a compost of ova, compacted, rubescent, hard as ball bearings, a red necklace of petrified gametes like a lethal caviar.) Owns—partly owns, rents the space for—the vending machine big as a breakfront—the Convenience Center. Behind the forty windows of the big console are collapsed bathing rings, water pistols, joke books, puzzles, nose clips like chewed bubble gum, swim caps, beach balls, lighter fluid, packets of Confederate money, decks of cards, nail clippers, Chap Stick, panty hose, toothbrushes, Modess tampons, Tums, hair spray and hand lotion, sewing kits, aspirin and Alka-Seltzer, Pepsodent and rubber combs, Vitalis, deodorants, shaving cream, razors and blades, Aqua Velva and a mystery by Peter M. Curtin.

Owns the Travel Inn Grand Sign like a big blue flag trimmed in a curving fringe of bright 150-watt bulbs. A thick metal shaft, or "flagstaff," supports the sign, its long looped neon like glowing rope. A huge T burns at the top of the pole on a squat wick and is caught in a web of flaring bolts of fluorescence. It is the ultimate trademark, so huge it is potted in its own landscaping, a long mortared planter five bricks high.

He owns it all. Yet in a certain sense, though it's his, it's his by charter. A dispensation, some paid-for grace-and-favor arrangement like Maryland, say, before the Revolutionary War.

Richmond is a hard taskmaster. There is a ninety-three-acre Travel Inn University in eastern Virginia where his manager has been required to attend classes in motel management. Two weeks before the opening a team had been sent down to Ringgold to conduct field-training sessions for his employees. There have been dress rehearsals, dry runs.

Beds have been rumpled and remade. The kitchen has prepared each item on its menu. Waitresses have served dinner to the maids and bellmen and other surrogate guests. The dishwasher has returned his steak saying it is too medium. His chief maintenance man is called in to change a guest's tire. His manager goes to his chef with a complaint from his bartender that her children are disturbing the people in the next room by playing the TV too loud. He thinks they may be jumping on the beds. He is as diplomatic as it is possible to be. The chef promises to see to it that the children behave. The manager is very understanding. The day desk clerk requests a babysitter for his small boy and hires the manager. A busboy complains of chest pains at three in the morning. The team from Richmond looks on approvingly. Flesh looks on approvingly. Inspired, he grabs a night auditor from the cashier's office and tells her that he is worried about his puppy in the Inn's kennels. He explains that the puppy, so recently taken from its mother, must be held while it feeds. The bookkeeper reassures him, says she will see to it that the request is relayed to his dining-room hostess. Ben asks a maid for the best route to Bar Harbor, Maine. Pretending drunkenness, he asks his bartender for one more for the road. The bartender suggests coffee. Ben becomes belligerent, makes a racial slur against white people. The bartender coaxes him into passivity, gently reminds him it's time to settle accounts, and hands him his check to sign. Ben writes a hundred and fifty dollar tip across the bottom of his bar bill. The bartender crosses off the last two zeros, puts a decimal between the one and the five, and helps him to his room. A waiter from room service hands the news dealer, who places the Chattanooga and Atlanta papers in the Honor Box, a Master Charge card which the man checks against the numbers on the latest list of inoperative accounts that Master Charge sends out. Ben's accordion player from the marching band asks the cashier to help carry the lifeguard's wheelchair with the lifeguard in it up the stairs to the second-floor room they have taken. One of the men from Richmond drowns in the swimming pool. The telephone operator lugs him to the shallow end. They are all having a wonderful time.

"I'm," a black housemaid tells the desk clerk, "Horace Tenderhall, General Sales Manager of the Volume Shoe Corporation of St. Louis, Missouri. I arranged with your people months ago that my people would hold our semiannual Southeastern Sales Conference here in Ringgold in preparation for the opening of the new fall line, and what do I find when I get here but that the meeting room where the meeting is to take place is all set up for a banquet with the Daughters of the Eastern Star? Now I have no intention of making a foofaraw, but I put down a $550 deposit and here my people are arriving on every other airplane that flies into Chattanooga and there isn't any place to put them. Now whut you gone do 'bout dat?"

The driver of the courtesy car goes through a guard rail at the top of Lookout Mountain. Three people are killed and four are critically injured. Ben's manager immediately contacts the four other

Inns in the Chattanooga area on the Inn-Dex machine and, pressing their courtesy cars into service as ambulances, dispatches them to the scene of the tragedy. In this way they are able to save three of the critically injured guests.

The team from Richmond beams. Ben and the staff and the Richmond people shake hands all around and Ben throws a switch and the lights of the Travel Inn Grand Sign come on and the team is driven back to the Chattanooga airport in the courtesy car and the one thousand two hundred eleventh Travel Inn in the continental United States is officially open for business.

And three hours later no one has come.

The staff, which has nothing to do, drifts back into the lobby. His chef takes a place on the sofa. (The tables are set for dinner, the salads are crisping on a bed of ice, the side of beef warming on the steam table.) A few of the maids step out onto the driveway with the head housekeeper to watch the traffic on I-75. Ben joins them, has an idea, signals the maids and housekeeper back inside, addresses them and the rest of his help still seated in the lobby.

"Go out back," he says, "where your cars are parked. Drive them around to the front. Park them where they can be seen. Two of you drive right up to the office, leave your cars in the driveway. Afterward," he tells the housekeeper and her people, "open the drapes in every second or third room that faces the highway. Turn on the lights."

Still no one comes.

"Well, it's just only four o'clock," John Shoe, his manager, says.

"They should be here by now," Ben says. "*Someone* should be here."

"Richmond is supposed to get us some guests. They've been alerted. I know that. They've instructed the toll-free number to divert some of the Chattanooga business our way."

"I didn't know that," Ben says. "Why didn't they say something?"

"Maybe it's supposed to be a surprise," his manager says.

The housekeeper has come back with the maids. The people have returned to the lobby after reparking their cars. Ben feels simultaneously in Lord of the Manor and Head Butler relation to them. His staff. His crew. His people. Ben's men. "Suppose no one comes?"

"That's not possible," his desk clerk says.

"But suppose. Suppose no one comes? There's no guarantee. I'm in over my head here." It seems to him an astonishing admission. A strange way to talk to his employees. And something occurs to him. The notion of employees. In his life, except for the time he was in the army, he has always had employees. People dependent upon him for their living. He has always been Boss. It is a remarkable thing. Why, he thinks, I have been powerful. It's always been my word that goes. I am higher than my father, who, before he was a boss, had been only a partner. How strange, he thinks, how strange to be a boss. How peculiar to tell others what to do, how mysterious that they do it. And how odd that so frightened a fellow, a man running scared, should command payrolls, control lives. Who had elected him to such office? Where did he get off? How many had worked for him over the years? Hundreds? At least hundreds. What could have possessed so many to do what he told them? A man who had not even come up from the ranks? Who had never lifted a finger? A mere beneficiary of someone else's bad conscience? How many more must there be like him? he wondered. Baskin-Robbins hotshots who had no calling for ice cream? His life had reduced itself to what the dozen and a half people who stood before him in Ringgold, Georgia, could do for him. To what the men and women, total strangers, whizzing by on I-75 could. The 220 million or so Americans who hadn't the vaguest notion who he was. (A franchiser, hiding behind others' expertise, paying them for their names.) If they failed him he would fail. The banks would get him. He was struck by the enormity of things and had to tell them.

"Listen," he said, "you don't know. A lot's at stake here. My God," he said, "we've got a dining room, place settings, service for eight hundred. Think," he said, "the linen alone. A hundred fifty rooms. Three hundred double beds. That's six hundred pillows, six hundred pillowcases. The towels. Think of the towels and washcloths and bathmats. A thousand maybe. What are we into here? I'm a bachelor, I've got a thousand towels, three hundred sheets for three hundred double beds."

"More," his housekeeper said.

"What?"

"More. For every sheet and pillowcase and towel there's another for when they get dirty."

"Jesus," Ben said, "I didn't even think about that. Twelve hundred pillowcases. Jesus. Two thousand towels." He thought of all the other Travel Inns, of all the rooms in all the Travel Inns. He took a Travel Inn Directory from the registration desk and opened it at random. It opened on pages 120 and 121—Michigan, Grand Rapids to Kalamazoo. There were seventeen motels with 2,136 rooms. He multiplied this by the 204 pages that listed Travel Inns in the United States. There were 435,744 rooms. "That doesn't count Canada," he said. "That doesn't count Japan. It doesn't count Mexico or Zaïre or Indonesia. That doesn't count Johannesburg or Paris or Skanes in Tunisia or Tamuning in Guam.

"Almost half a million rooms," he said. "Service three and a half million. That doesn't count Ramada, it doesn't count Best Western. It doesn't count Quality. That doesn't count Hilton, Travelodge, Hospitality Inn. It doesn't count Rodeway or the Sheraton motels or Howard Johnson's or the Ben Franklin chain. It doesn't count Holiday Inn. It doesn't count Regal 8 Inns, Stouffer, the Six's, Day's Inn, Hyatt, Master Hosts, Royal Inns, Red Carpet, Monarch, Inn America, Marriott. It doesn't count all I can't think of or those I don't know. It doesn't count the independents. It doesn't count hotels. And it doesn't count tourist cabins in national parks or places where the Interstates ain't.

"What are we up to? Twenty million rooms? Twenty-*five*? What are we up to? What are we *talking* here? Service for 250 million? A ghost room for every family in America? And almost every one of them air-conditioned, TV'd or color TV'd, swimming-pooled, cocktail-lounged, restauranted, coffee-shopped.

"How will they find us? How will they know? What's to be done? Yes, and occupancy rates never lower or competition stiffer. Go! Reroute traffic. Paint detour signs. Paint FALLING ROCK, paint SLIPPERY WHEN WET, paint DANGEROUS CURVE. Paint CAUTION, MEN

WORKING NEXT THOUSAND MILES. Paint BRIDGE OUT AHEAD. *How will they find us? What's to be done?*"

He wrung his hands. "See?" he said. "I wring my hands. I am wracked. I chafe. I fret. I gall. I smart and writhe. I have throes and am discomfited. All the classic positions of ballet pain."

"Mr. Flesh," his housekeeper, Mrs. Befilicio, says.

"Yes? What? You know a way? Something's occurred to you? Say. Mrs. Befilicio? Anyone. Everyone." He speaks over her shoulder to Mr. Shoe. "A suggestion box. Have Mr. Wellbanks put a suggestion box together for the employees." Mr. Wellbanks is the chief maintenance man. "Mr. Wellbanks, can you handle that?" He turns to his employees. "There's bonus in it for you. How will they know us? What's to be done? How will they find us? Yes, Mrs. Befilicio, yes, excuse me."

"It's just that . . ."

"What? What is it just? It's just what? Just what is it?"

"Well, sir, it's just that it's past four-thirty and the maids go off duty."

He stares at the housekeeper. "They'll take their cars? Remove their cars from the driveway?"

"Well, yes, sir, that's probably what we'll have to do. Yes, sir."

"Yes," Ben says, "of course. We'll see you in the morning."

And at six the two desk clerks go off duty. His cashier leaves. Mr. Wellbanks does. John Shoe says he'll stay on awhile.

Two people come in but it is only Miss McEnalem and Mr. Kingseed, his night auditor and night clerk.

Then his first guests arrive.

The couple are in their thirties. The woman, who holds the car keys, speaks for them. The waitresses, the hostess, the man from room service, the chef and her assistants hang about to watch them register. John Shoe glances peremptorily at his personnel and lightly claps his hands together, dismissing them.

"Have you a reservation, Mrs. Glosse?" the night clerk asks.

"No. Do we need one?"

"How long do you plan to be staying with us?"

"Just overnight."

"Oh," the night clerk says, "in that case I think we can fix you up then. Room 1107." He gives the Glosses their room key and tells them how to get there. The instructions, as Ben has always found them to be, though he has slept most of his life in motels, are extremely complicated.

"Excuse me," Ben says, "I happen to be in the room next to yours. I was just going there. I'm the blue Cadillac. You can follow me." They walk along with him as he goes toward his car. "You're lucky," Ben says, "that room happens to be poolside. The water's terrific. I took a dip before dinner. Dinner was great. The prime ribs are sensational. They do a wonderful Scotch sour. I'm going to watch television tonight. There are some swell shows on. It's color TV. The reception is marvelous. I may doze off though, the beds are so comfortable." He drives around to the rear of the long central building, stops and waits for them to make the turn. When they are abreast of him, he lowers his electric window. "Yours would be the fifth room in from the end of the building." They nod and drive on to where Ben is pointing. Flesh slips his car in just next to theirs in the otherwise vacant parking area. "It's convenient, isn't it? The parking."

"Real convenient," Mr. Glosse says.

"Well, you folks get comfortable," he tells them. "Maybe I'll see you in the lounge later on. They've got a super combo. Really excellent. Young, but real pros. The kid with acne on drums is something else."

The Glosses stare at him. "There's free ice," he says lamely. "In the corridor. Very cold." Ben lets himself into his room and turns on the television set. He waits a few minutes, leaves by the door that opens onto the corridor, and returns to the lobby.

"Did anyone check in while I was gone?"

"Yes, as a matter of fact," John Shoe says. "Some people named Storrs. A couple with kids."

"Teenagers? Babies?"

"No. About ten, I guess. A girl ten, a boy about seven."

He bites his lips. Teenagers would have been $3 extra apiece. A baby would have meant another dollar for a crib.

Ben sat with his manager in the small office behind the wall of room keys. He could hear everything that happened at the front desk, could hear the switchboard operator as she took wake-up calls. It was not yet midnight.

Ultimately twenty-seven rooms were let. Five to individuals, nine to couples, four to families with two children, five to families with one child. Four doubles went to sisters or to friends traveling together. There were seventy-two guests in the motel. The last room had been rented at twenty minutes to ten. It was an 18 percent occupancy rate. They broke even at 60 percent.

"Why don't you get some sleep? Anyone traveling this time of night would just keep on going, I expect."

"We'll be killed," Ben said.

"No," his manager said. "They told me at school that unless you overlook a place like Niagara Falls, or you're in one of the big towns, and only then if it's some skyscraper setup that gets a lot of advance publicity and makes a mark on the skyline, you can't expect to do much business the first month or so. At service locations like ours it could be three or four months before an inn takes hold."

"Eighteen percent?"

"Eighteen is low."

"They'll kill us."

"We've got fifteen reservations for tomorrow night, Mr. Flesh. That doesn't include what comes in off the highway. Like today, for example. Only eleven rooms were reserved. We picked sixteen up off the street. Two rooms are staying over. We do just as good off the highway as we did today, that's thirty-three rooms occupied. And you've got to expect we'll get another ten reservations at least. That's forty-three rooms."

"Twenty-eight percent," Ben said. They would kill him. It was so. This was the busy season, when people went on their vacations. It was different with his other franchises. Convenience foods, for example. Appetite was a constant. Appetite was seasonal, too, of course. It had its rush hours, its breakfasts and lunch hours and dinners. But it also had its steady increment of whim, the sudden gush of appetite, the cravings of highs and pregnancy, its coffee breaks and gratuitous lurching thirsts, its random sugar-toothedness, all the desiderata of gratification and reward. How had he so miscalculated? They would kill him. The 18 percent would climb to 28 percent, the 28 to 35, to 40, the 40 to 50 or 52.

And level off. Things could be done, he knew, measures taken. The break-even point could be lowered, perhaps even met. There could be cutbacks among the staff, maids could be let go, some of the waitresses and kitchen help, one or two bookkeepers made redundant. People could double up on jobs. His debt could be slowly amortized by the piecemeal selling off of his other franchises. There were plenty of things that could be done. They would kill him. He would be killed.

"Why don't you?"

"What?"

"Why don't you get some sleep?" Shoe asks kindly.

"No no. You. Kingseed's out front. He can take care. It's interesting. Go home. I'd prefer it. It's interesting to me. To be on this end of the motel. I figure I sleep 250, maybe 300 nights a year in them. But lobby life— This I know nothing about. Go get your rest. Tomorrow's another day. I read that somewhere. This way, the both of us up, it's too much like a deathwatch. Go on. Kingseed doesn't need either of us. It's just that I feel more comfortable minding it through its first night. Go on. Why should your wife be alone?"

Ben insisted and Shoe left.

"I think I'll walk around a bit," he told Herb Kingseed after a while, and went through the lobby past the closed lounge and closed restaurant to the long central building where all the guests had been given rooms. He walked along the corridor and came to 1109, his room. Through the door he could hear the television set still playing. He opened the door, went in, and turned the set off. He was about to go out again when he heard voices behind the thin wallboard.

"Suck me, suck me," Mr. Glosse says.

"What's this?" Ben says softly.

Mr. Glosse groans. "I'm coming, I'm coming," he cries. "I'm coming in your mouth. I'm shooting my dick off inside your face."

"What's this?"

"No no," he pleads, "swallow it, swallow it. Don't spit it out, what's wrong with you? All right. It's all over your lips. Kiss me, kiss me now."

· 324 ·

"What's this?" Ben says. "What's this?" He listens but can make out no other words.

He returns to the hall. Now he is conscious of the sounds that come from behind each door. He hears Mr. Kith, a single in 1134. He is talking to Elke Sommer. She is a guest on Carson's program. He'd seen her when he went into his room to turn his set off. "Take that, Elke. Take that, you German bitch. How do you like my cock in your hair?" What's this? Is he beating off against Nate Lace's television set? Flesh puts his ear to the door and hears what sounds like meat being slapped against glass. He hears growls and the falsetto whimper of masturbate orgasm. What's this? What's this?

And blazes a trail down all the long corridor, stopping at each occupied room. He is able to remember exactly who is where. He listens at 1153. The Renjouberts' room. A couple in their forties with a son about fourteen or fifteen.

"Shh," Mrs. Renjoubert says softly. "Hush, darling. Be very quiet. Oh, that's good. That's very good. But be quiet. Oh, that's lovely, sweetheart. Rub the other. Oh, oh. Shh. Hush, you'll wake Daddy."

*What's this? What's this?*

It is twelve forty-five when he goes to the Inn-Dex machine and sends his first message. He has the Travel Inn Directory open like a phone book beside him. He depresses the Enter button, sees the top light go on, and knows he is on the air. He punches the Inn-Dex code number and painfully taps out his message:

MAYDAY. MAYDAY. RINGGOLD, GA. TRAVEL INN CALLING VINELAND, N.J. IT'S LOVE NIGHT. IT'S LOVE NIGHT. AND HERE'S WHAT'S HAPPENING.

He tells Vineland about the Glosses, about Tim Kith in 1134, about the Renjouberts. He describes the goings on between the Buggle sisters in 2218. Finally it is too uncomfortable for him to type. His paresthetic fingers vibrate like flesh tuning forks and he asks Kingseed to take over for him. "Tell Vineland," he tells Kingseed, "that Elly and Nestor Pewterball make love in the shower."

· 325 ·

"But, Mr. Flesh—"

"Send the message," he commands.

"What do I say?"

"Dear Vineland, New Jersey, Travel Inn," he dictates. "Elly and Nestor Pewterball of St. Paul, Minnesota, who checked in at the Ringgold, Georgia, Travel Inn at approximately 7:15 p.m. driving a—just a minute." He goes to the records, slips out the Pewterballs' charge sheet and registration form. "—driving a 1971 Olds Vista Cruiser, Minnesota plates J75-1414-R2, dinner charges $12.47 with tip, representing—let's see, can you make this out, Kingseed? Does that say 'Crossroads Furniture'? It does, doesn't it?—representing Crossroads Furniture and paying by BankAmericard—am I going too fast?"

"Was that $12.47 with tip?"

"Right." He repeats himself slowly, waits till Kingseed catches up. Talking so slowly he is aware of a certain thickness in his speech, the words slightly distorted, as if the sides of his tongue were curling, rolled up like a newspaper tossed on a porch. With effort he is able to flatten it again. "Mrs. Pewterball is a tall, slender, gray-haired woman, almost as tall as Nestor, who is perhaps six foot. Though I couldn't hear all they said due to the interference of the shower, adjusted, I should say, to something like fine spray, full force, I was able to make out a good deal, Elly's ringing yelps, Nestor's laughter, Elly's desire to have her genitals soaped, Nestor's predilection for lathered buttocks. I take it that they were standing face to face. I take it that they used washclothes. I only hope they remembered to close the shower curtain and put it inside the tub. I only hope there was a bathmat on the floor.

"When they were finished they dried themselves off. From what sounded like the crinkle of tissue paper, I would say that Nestor was probably wearing new pajamas. This impression was reinforced by a compliment I heard Elly pass on to her husband, perhaps not a compliment so much as an affirmation of her own judgment and taste. 'See' she said, 'those checks aren't at all loud. They're quite elegant, really. I like a pajama top you don't have to button. With everything wash-and-wear, the buttonholes get all out of shape, Ness.' She calls him Ness. I'm not at all certain that Elly wears anything to bed. At least I couldn't hear her poking

· 326 ·

about in their suitcase and it seemed to me from the angle and pitch of her voice that she may have been the first in bed. I distinctly made out a sort of grunt when she removed the bedspread. This was before I heard the crinkle of tissue paper. What follows is rather personal and more than a little touching.

"When they were both in bed—and they slept in different beds, incidentally, for I heard Ness pull back *his* bedspread—and had turned off the lights—I could see the little strip of light go out where the door just barely misses meeting the carpet—and I was just about to go down the corridor to see what was with Marie Kripisco in 2240, I suddenly heard Mrs. Pewterball's voice.

" 'Ness?' she said. 'Ness? Are you awake, darling, are you still up, dear?'

" 'Yes,' he said, 'what is it, Elly?'

" 'I'm frightened,' she said.

" 'Oh, El,' he said, 'I promise it will be all right.'

" 'But *Florida*, Ness.'

" 'It's three years yet before I retire, El.'

" 'Yes.'

" 'The St. Paul winters.'

" 'I know.'

" 'All that snow.'

" 'I *know*.'

" 'We'll make friends, El. There'll be people there. Why, goodness, 95 percent of the people *in* those condominiums are from up north. People like us. And we're just looking. Though I'll tell you, El, prices are going up all the time. If we find something we really like, I think we ought to snap it up, make a down payment. That way, too, darling, we could take our vacations in the winter and rent it out when we're not using it. And don't forget, there's a Crossroads branch now in North Miami Beach. With my discount we could furnish the whole place for under two thousand dollars. Golly, El, if we *did* rent it out, our tenants would be making the down payment for us.'

" 'It isn't that, Ness. *I* get just as cold in the winter, *I* know we'll make new friends, I even agree about the economics of the thing. It isn't that.'

" 'Then what?'

· 327 ·

" 'The water, Ness. The water's so *hard* down there. Do you know how much effort it takes to work up a good lather? People our age? Sweetheart, have you any idea what the heck that's going to do to our love life?' "

He contacts Huntsville, Alabama, contacts Lumberton, North Carolina, contacts Fort Myers, Florida. He tells on the Glosses, tells on Mrs. Renjoubert, on Kith and the Buggle girls and the Pewterballs, and relates the normative one-on-one passions of the Marshes and Mangochitnas. He has Kingseed patrol the corridors of the motel and sends the news to Wilmington, Delaware, that Ron and Minnie Cates, talking in their sleep, each call out the name of different lovers. "Oh, Hubert," Minnie pleads. "Sylvia, Sylvia," Ron Cates cries out.

"Wilmington, Wilmington," he has Kingseed ask their Inn-Dex, "what's this? I recall," he has him spell out on Travel Inn's worldwide reservation system, "coming across scumbags in forests, panties in wilderness, love's detritus on posted land, everywhere the flotsam and jetsam of concupiscence scattered as beer can, common as litter. What's this, what's this? Everyone everywhere is evidence, datum. The proof is all about us. We're the proof. Everyone at the Super Bowl a fact of fuck. Every schoolboy, each senator, and every officer in every army, all the partners in law firms, and anyone on a mailing list or listed in a phone book or cramming for the written part of his driver's exam. Each civil servant and every Pope and all the leads in plays and films and all the walk-ons and everybody in the audience. Everyone with anything to sell and anyone with money to buy it and all the faces on the cash exchanged for it, and every old man and all the dead. And also every representation, every sketched face in the funny papers, and every piece of clothing on every rack in every store in the world. And even furniture. Every chair or table or lamp to read by and all the beds. Every sideboard where the dishes are put away and every dish as well as every machine ever made, the toaster and the nuclear submarine, and every musical instrument and every rubber comb and each piece of chewing gum and all the pot roast. As though the world were merely a place to hold it all, as if gravity and Rumania and history were only parts of some great sexual closet. The world as Lovers' Lane, drive-in, back seat, front porch, park bench, and blanket on the beach. Am I right about this, Wilmington, Delaware? How's your love life? Over."

And an answer came, Ben reading it like stock-market quotation as it ticked out on the Inn-Dex:

YES. YOU ARE. A CONVENTION'S IN TOWN. WE'VE SEEN EIGHT HOOKERS GET INTO THE ELEVATORS SO FAR. EARLIER THIS EVENING WE HAD A CALL FROM TOM KLEINMAN IN 317 OBJECTING TO THE NOISE THAT THE HONEYMOONERS, EARL AND DELORES SIMMONS, WERE MAKING IN THE NEXT ROOM. MR. KLEINMAN SAID HIS BOY, TOM, JR., ELEVEN, COULD HEAR EVERYTHING THAT WAS GOING ON BETWEEN THOSE TWO. HE ASKED THAT EITHER WE CALL THE SIMMONSES AND TELL THEM TO HOLD IT DOWN, OR PUT HIM AND TOM, JR., IN A DIFFERENT ROOM. WE COULDN'T DO THE LATTER BECAUSE WE'RE FULL UP—THE CONVENTION. AND WE WERE RELUCTANT TO DO THE FORMER BECAUSE, WELL, YOU KNOW HOW IT IS, YOU CAN'T CALL GUESTS UP AND TELL THEM NOT TO FORNICATE. IT IS THEIR HONEYMOON, AFTER ALL. WHAT MR. PITTMAN, OUR INNKEEPER, FINALLY DID WAS TO CALL EARL SIMMONS UP AND TELL HIM HE'D HAD A COMPLAINT HE WAS PLAYING HIS TELEVISION TOO LOUD. YOU HAVE TO BE DIPLOMATIC. BUT YOU PUT YOUR FINGER ON IT, RINGGOLD, THE WORLD IS A VERY SEXY PLACE.

They Inn-Dex'd Chicago, contacted Denver, rang up L.A. Everywhere it was the same story. Not even the time differential made any difference finally, Ringgold's nighttime, California's evening, love's mood obliterating time and space and all zones erogenous.

They put out all-points bulletins, calling Fort Wayne, Indiana, Springfield, Missouri, Lancaster, Pennsylvania, Burlington, Vermont, Wichita, and Great Falls, Montana and Albuquerque, Phoenix, and towns up and down the Pacific coast. It *was* the same. Sperm was in the air like humidity. Heavy breathing was, and squeals like imprint sounds in nature. Love's high-pressure systems and lows, its fronts and squall lines and small-craft warnings only a sort of generic weather at last. Everything reduced finally to the skin's friction, the fusion of agents and objects and all the moleculars of love.

Flesh couldn't stand it. He had hoped to be torn off the air, to have been comeuppanced, jammed like the Voice of America, warned by Richmond itself perhaps. What he had not wanted was endorsement, all hunches confirmed. He should like to have been told by Houston that, no, folks round there seemed tuckered out, content, after a long day's drive from Lubbock or a rough flight from Cleveland, to shower, in clean p.j.'s take their dinners on trays from room service, watch the telly, read the local papers, doze off.

"What's this, what's this?" he asked Kingseed. "Look, look," he said, taking up the long printout. "Oh my. Oh. Oh my oh my."

"Why are you upset?"

"Why? Because love happens," he said. "It really happens. It actually takes place. It occurs. Why am I upset? Because love is sweeping the country and lyrics are the ground of being, singing the literature of the ordinary, and romance is real as heartburn. Because guys score and stare at the women next to them and trace their fingers gently over their sweetheart's eyebrow breaking like a wave. Twelve million are epileptics."

"Sir?"

"Twelve million are epileptics. A million and twenty-one thousand three hundred and eighty died of cardiovascular diseases. Three hundred and nineteen thousand of cancer. A hundred eleven thousand were killed in accidents. Pneumonia and influenza knocked off seventy thousand. Diabetes thirty-eight thousand, four hundred and seventy. Bronchitis and emphysema and asthma thirty-three thousand. Twenty-nine thousand died of cirrhosis of the liver and seventeen thousand of birth defects. Kidney diseases got twenty thousand and *hernias* close to eight, for Christ's sake. TB killed sixty-six hundred and there were twenty thousand homicides. And one died of heaviness and one of bed wetting and one of prejudice and another of cradle cap and one of constipation and one

of a blindness to metal and another of orneriness and one of household pests and one of left tittedness and one of female hard-boiled
eggs and another froze to death when his temperature hit 98.6."

"Where do you get this? What is this stuff?"

"Two million," he said.

"Pardon?"

"Two million a year die. It's a ball-park figure."

"Only two million? I would have thought more."

"Be patient. I told you. Twelve million have epilepsy."

"I don't see—"

"If thirty-eight thousand four hundred seventy died of diabetes,
how many more have it and are still alive? Ten times that number,
twenty? I should think twenty. Conservatively twenty. Be patient."

"But—"

"And if twenty have diabetes for each one that dies of it, and
diabetes is only the fifth biggest killer, how many people do you
suppose live with bad hearts, with cancer growing in them like
food turning in the refrigerator? Be patient. How many have Par-
kinson's disease, how many VD?"

"Every other?"

"We're standing water, fucking roosts," Flesh said. "Plague
builds its nests in us."

"Gee," Kingseed said, "put that way, it's kind of depressing."

"Kind of," Flesh said. "There's scarlet fever and muscular
dystrophy and Hodgkin's disease and a special strain of kid leuke-
mia. There's the heartbreak of psoriasis."

"The doctor told me my pressure's a little high."

"There you go," Flesh said.

"Gee."

"And *still* they smooch."

"What? Oh. Yeah."

"They come calling, call coming, go courting, hold hands, sip
soda through a straw, French kiss with their throats sore and their
noses running."

"My gosh."

"*My* gosh."

Flesh stares blankly at the silent IBM typewriter and suddenly it begins to clatter out a message:

INN-DEX 225. INN-DEX 225. *¢&%#$@)*¢&%%#@!*& THE INN-DEX IS NOT A TOY! YOURS, INN-DEX 000, RICH-MOND.

Then the top button, like Hold on a telephone, fills with a square of solid yellow light. "We're off the air," Ben says. "Love Night's over. Richmond pulled our plug."

"Will we get in trouble?"

Ben shrugs. He comes out from behind the registration desk and sits down in one of the velour chairs. He yawns.

It is Kingseed's snores which finally awaken him. His clerk is sleeping with his face on the desk. It's three-thirty. The man will have a stiff neck when he gets up.

Ben stretches. He can have slept no more than an hour and a half, yet is fully rested. He could go to his room now, but he doubts if he could sleep. Still, Kingseed's heavy snores are unpleasant to hear, though he has no wish to wake the man, no wish either to disturb the night auditor working on her accounts in the small office behind the wall of keys and letter slots. He rises, intending to go to his room, when his eye is caught by the map on the big display board opposite the registration desk. The concentric hundred-mile circles make the states behind them a sort of target, twelve hundred miles of American head seen through a sniper-scope. He goes up to the map, to dartboard America, bull's-eyed, Ptolemaic'd Ringgold. He examines it speculatively. And suddenly sees it not as a wheel of distances but of options. It's as if he hadn't seen it properly before. Though there are dozens of road maps in the glove compartment of his car, he has rarely referred to them. Not for a long while. Not since the Interstates had made it possible to travel the country in great straight lines. Why, there are signs for Memphis and Tulsa and Chicago in St. Louis now. Signs for Boston and Washington, D.C., in the Bronx. Seen this way, in swaths of hundred-mile circles like shades in rainbows, he perceives loops of relationship. He is equidistant from the Atlantic

Ocean and the Gulf of Mexico and Pine Bluff, Arkansas, and Centralia, Illinois. He could as easily be in Columbus, Ohio, as in Petersburg, Virginia. New Orleans rings him, Covington, Kentucky, does. He is surrounded by place, by tiers of geography like bands of amphitheater. He is the center. If he were to leave now, striking out in any direction, northwest to Nashville, south to Panama City, Florida, it would make no difference. He could stand before maps like this one in other Travel Inns. Anywhere he went would be the center. He would pull the center with him, the world rearranging itself about him like a woman smoothing her skirt, touching her hair.

It was the start of his ecstasy attack.

# V

He turns the ignition key. Hey, he's down a few gallons. He sees that one side of the island of pumps nearest him is clear, but keeps his Caddy idling in neutral until he knows what the fellow in the Pontiac Grand Am just pulling in off the street means to do. It, too, is an out-of-state car—Minnesota. The land of sky-blue waters.

Ben smiles and waves expansively at the Grand Am to go ahead of him. The bells ring as Minnesota drives over the rubber line that signals the attendant. Jack comes back out and goes up to the driver's side of the Pontiac, clears the gas pump, and carries the heavy hose toward the gas tank. Ben presses down the electric window on his side and leans his head out. "Can you get to her, Jack, or should I back off some?" he calls.

Jack looks at him quizzically. "No," he says, "there's room."

"There's room? You sure? It wouldn't be any trouble for me to back it up a bit."

"No," he says, "that's all right."

"Okay," Ben says, "think I'll just stretch my legs a bit while I'm waiting." He gets out of his car with difficulty. Jack has begun to wipe the windshield and Ben goes up to him. "She's a scorcher, ain't she?"

"Radio said 92 at noon," the young man says.

"Ninety-two degrees! At noon? Is *that* a fact? She could bust 100 then."

"I guess," Jack says.

"Say, look there, will you?" Ben Flesh points to an elderly

woman on the sidewalk who is holding a parasol above her head. "You don't see that up north much," he says. "It's a good way of preventing sunstroke. I wonder why more people don't carry sun umbrellas in weather like this. It's kind of pretty, too, don't you think?"

"Pretty?"

"Well, old-fashioned. Reassuring. Pretty, yes. *I* think so. Many folks carry sunshades around here?"

"Mostly the older women, I guess."

"Well, that's wonderful," Ben says. "It's very charming and genteel. That sort of thing makes heat itself charming."

Jack asks the driver if he wants him to check under the hood and the man nods. He pulls out the oil stick and wipes it with a rag.

"Gee whiz," Ben says, "will you look at all the machinery down there?"

"You're down just over a half," Jack tells the driver. "Shall I put in a quart?"

"Please," the driver says, "and could you check the water level in my battery?"

"That's a good idea," Ben tells the man. "It probably evaporates on a day like this. That young man told me it was already 92 at noon today."

"It feels it. It must be almost 100 now," the man from Minnesota says.

"You probably aren't far off," Ben says. He looks at the man. "But you know," he says, "the hottest I've ever been was once when I was up in your part of the country."

"Minnesota?"

"Well, South Dakota. Rapid City. This was a few years ago. 1971."

"Yeah," his friend says. "I think I remember. It was hot that summer."

"*Hot?* It was in violation of the Geneva Conventions, it was so hot. It was *brutal*. And the air conditioning wasn't of any use."

"No?"

"Heck no. There were power failures. I was in the hospital at

the time. This was when I had my multiple sclerosis diagnosed—
I'm a multiple sclerotic—and though the hospital had its own gen-
erators, it wasn't enough to drive the air conditioning and—"

"She took sixteen gallons, sir. A dollar five for the quart of oil
makes it $10.96."

"You take Master Charge?"

"Sure." Ben's friend slips the card out of his wallet and hands it
to Jack.

"Sixty-one and nine tenths for a gallon of Regular," the man
says. "Sixty-two cents."

"It was really something. They put me in a ward with a young
British lieutenant named Tanner. He was on detached duty from
the Royal Air Force. He pronounced it 'Raf.' That's the first time I
ever heard it pronounced that way. God, the poor guy was in bad
shape. He had a rare tropical disease called Lassa fever. It's fatal.
Ever hear of it?"

"No," his pal says.

"Well, neither had I. As a matter of fact, he was only the ninth
person in the world to come down with it. He actually sweated
blood. That's not a figure of speech, either. The man perspired
blood. It was a symptom of the disease, though I don't suppose the
heat helped any. I would wipe it up for him. I'd use Kleenex or
toilet paper. Well, you know how it is, guys get close in a situation
like that. *We* really did anyway. We were the only people in the
ward. I don't think it would be too much of an exaggeration to say
that he was the best friend I ever had."

Jack has returned from the office with his clipboard. He goes
around behind the Grand Am to take down the Minnesotan's license number. "We were *thick*, my friend. He kidded the pants off
me about how worried I was about my disease. I had the Mister
Softee franchise up there, and every time I'd whimper about my
bad luck he'd say, I remember, he'd say, 'Be hard, Mister Softee.'
And you *know?* I was that scared I needed to be talked to like that
back then. Oh gosh. We had some time of it." Jack has brought the
charge slip for the man to sign. Ben has to move his head, standing
behind Jack's back, talking to him over the young man's shoulder.

"There wasn't much power to give the loonies their electric shock, so the poor guys were up all night screaming their heads off. We could hear them. It was awful."

"Thank you," Jack says. "There's your card, sir. Come back and see us."

The man nods and starts his car.

"Wait up," Ben says. "I wanted to tell you something. Oh yeah. So, as I say, it was during those long hot nights when neither of us could sleep and the crazies were screaming like the damned and Tanner and I just, well, we just told each other everything. I've probably never been that close to anyone. I know he helped me. I hope I helped him.

"So. Anyway, to make a long story short, there wasn't much they could do for my M.S. in the hospital and they discharged me.

"Well, sir, Tanner didn't say much. I figured he must have figured, here *I* was going off, and there *he* was, strapped to a goddamn wheelchair and condemned to die. Friends or no, he must have thought, well, that I was deserting him. So . . . What can I tell you? I went back to where he was behind the screen to shake hands and say goodbye and to wish him luck and, well, he was—he was *dead*."

The Minnesotan shakes his head. Ben understands. What else can he do? Ben acknowledges his friend's sympathy with a nod of his own and backs away from the Grand Am to let it drive off. "Well," he says cheerfully, turning to Jack, "I guess you can pump me full of Premium."

"You'll have to pull the car up, the hose won't reach."

"Oh, sure," Ben says and, stumbling, gets back into his car to bring it abreast of the young man.

It's while the tank is being filled that he remembers his promise to Tanner. Oh, Christ, he thinks, and his eyes moisten. Then he remembers something else.

There's only a quarter in the shallow little dish on his dashboard where he keeps change. It would be too unpleasant to have to reach into his pocket to see if he has a dime. "Say, Jack," he says to the attendant, "trade you this quarter for a dime." He fumbles the coin into his left palm by brushing it with the side of his right hand. "What do you say, is it a deal?"

Jack gives him two dimes and a nickel for the quarter. He doesn't want to hurt Jack's feelings by insisting he keep the fifteen cents. Also, he remembers he's already tipped him ten dollars to tell him what city this is. Ben smiles at him and thinks of him fondly. He's not just another greedy kid. That's good, Ben thinks. Moral fiber like that. The country's in safe hands. "Thanks," Ben says. "Is there a phone in the office?"

"Just to your left as you go in the door."

"Thanks a million," Ben says.

He has some difficulty lining the dime up with the slot, but finally he's able to do it. He dials the operator.

"Operator," he says when she answers, "could you please get me Rapid City, South Dakota, Information. I have some trouble with my fingers or I'd dial it myself. Thank you, dear. Oh, and Operator? Would you hang on, please? This will be a credit-card call. Thank you."

"What city, please?" the operator in South Dakota says.

"Rapid City."

"Yes, sir, go ahead."

He gives the operator the name he had remembered in the car.

"Eight seven three, two zero nine six," the South Dakota operator says.

"Did you get that, Operator?"

"Yes, sir."

He gives the operator his credit-card information and in a moment he can hear the phone ringing all the way up the country in South Dakota. Ben smiles at Jack, who has come into the office, and he holds up a finger to indicate that he'll just be a moment. The young man steps out to take care of a car that has just driven up to the pumps.

"Hello?"

"Yes," Ben says, "hello there. Could I speak to Dick Mullen, please?"

"*Dick* Mullen?"

"Richard Mullen. Yes, please."

"Who is this?"

"My name's Ben Flesh. I was in the hospital with him that time he was so sick. I just wanted to know how he's getting along."

"My husband's dead," the woman said. She started to cry.

"Oh hey," Ben said, "oh hey, listen, I'm sorry. Listen, I didn't mean—I'm awfully sorry. Look, is there anything I can do? Anything at all? I mean, if I can help out moneywise, I'd be more than happy . . . Life's been good to me in that department. It wouldn't be any hardship."

Mrs. Mullen was weeping uncontrollably. Ben waited for her sobbing to subside, finally overrode it. "You must think I'm some kind of nut," he said, "but I mean it about the money. Your son was very kind to me one time when *I* needed help—and, well, I just had nothing but good feelings for Dick. I mean, everybody did."

"You knew Richard?"

"Well," Ben said, "it's just that we were in Rapid City General together."

"I don't understand," Mrs. Mullen said. "He was in Intensive Care. He died just after . . . How could you have . . ."

"Well, you know the Mister Softee on Rushmore? That's *my* place. I . . . Look, I mean it about helping out," Ben said, but all he could hear were the woman's sobs and finally he had to replace the phone. Someone else was waiting to use it anyway.

So he paid Jack and left the gas station and drove off to check into a Holiday Inn.

All in all he felt pretty good. Not physically of course. Physically he'd never been worse. His hair was bothering him. Indeed, he hadn't combed it for days because it felt as if current were running through it when he held a comb to it. His other facial symptoms were bad. Bright light made his eyes tear and he could not look at the sky. His lips were heavy and felt as if tiny chips of buckshot were sliding about inside them. Also, he felt a sort of girdle effect about his forehead. The sclerosis was amok. He had the odd sensation that there were paper cuts in his lungs and kidneys, and the queerest feeling that his thighs were filled with a sort of stuffing, like sensitized furniture. Though he had been the one to offer that the day was a scorcher, he actually felt cold. (He'd heard the same weather report Jack had. That's how he knew it was hot.) He drove with the air conditioner off and his windows shut in order to trap what heat he could, and still his steering wheel was icy to the touch. He felt weakness in all his limbs and a kind of cushion of chilled air flowing beneath his skin.

Still, things weren't so bad. He felt pretty good. Look at the way Mrs. Mullen had cried about her husband. Four years dead and she could still be moved merely by the sound of a stranger pronouncing his name. And how kind Jack had been. Not wanting to take the fifteen cents. Two dimes and a nickel for his quarter. Giving fair measure. People were good. His friend from Minnesota. The way he'd bought that oil when he was only down just over half a quart. He probably wanted to help the kid out. People were good. Life was exciting.

Think of all that had happened to *him*. His disease. It was a major disease, very big league. There was even a campaign on television now. And his parents had been killed in a highway crash; *that* was dramatic. And he'd served in the war, though he hadn't seen action. Not *that* action. But there were other things. He couldn't list them all. He'd been to Wharton, maybe the top school in the country in the business field. All the things he'd done. He'd stood in a bucket and given a speech. He'd smoked marijuana, broken a law. He'd owned probably two dozen Cadillacs and driven two million miles. He'd had a godfather. That was something. How many had godfathers? Or stood by at deathbed scenes? Or were left the prime interest rate? The twins and triplets. The boy Finsbergs and girl. The Insight Lady and Contest Lady and the Looks Like Lady who could look at anyone and instantly come up with someone that that person looked like. The You Could Make a Million Dollars Lady. All the others.

And musical comedy in his blood. What a heritage! Songs. Standards. Hits. Top of the charts. Whistled. Hummed. Carried on the common American breath. Coming down the street on a transistor held to a kid's head like an earmuff of sound. Carried on the electrical American breaths of stereo, quad, the million swollen amplifications, speakers suspended like mistletoe in the archways of record shops or ringle-dingled in electric campaniles everywhere the air was. Melodies familiar as appetite and as pressed upon others as their habits. What a heritage! Ben Flesh himself like a note on sheet music, the clefs of his neon logos in the American sky. All the businesses he'd had. The road companies of Colonel Sanders, Baskin-Robbins, Howard Johnson's, Travel Inn, *all* his franchises. Why, he belonged everywhere, anywhere! In California like the sound of juice, Florida like the color of sunlight, Washington and Montana like the brisk smell of thin height, and Missouri like the neutral decent feel of the law of averages.

Nope, he couldn't complain. And ah, he thought. And looked forward to checking into the motel. Where he'd wait for dusk, have dinner in his room, open the thick-lined drapes, and watch out for his signs as they came on in nighttime Birmingham, all the blink-bulb neon and electric extravaganzas that stood out sharp against the sky and proved that every night Broadway opens everywhere.

Ah, he thought euphorically, knowing that his happiness was real, chemical, of course, symptomatic, but there, there under his disease, under the chemicals.

He was broken, they would kill him. The Finsbergs were an endangered species and his Travel Inn a disaster. They would kill him. Within weeks he would be strapped to a wheelchair. And ah, he thought, euphorically, ecstatically, this privileged man who could have been a vegetable or mineral instead of an animal, and a lower animal instead of a higher, who could have been a pencil or a dot on a die, who could have been a stitch in a glove or change in someone's pocket, or a lost dollar nobody found, who could have been stillborn or less sentient than sand, or the chemical flash of somebody else's fear, ahh. *Ahh!*